The minute I saw the letter, I knew it was hers. There was no mistaking it: the salutation, the tiny and precise handwriting, the date, the content itself, all confirmed its ancient status and authorship...

"Syrie James successfully creates a world of Jane Austen."
—*Austenprose*

"Syrie James is a fine storyteller, with a sensitive ear for the Austenian voice."
—*Jane Austen's Regency World*

"A novel within a novel honoring what we love most about Austen: her engaging stories, her rapier wit, and her swoon-worthy romance . . . Pitch-perfect, brilliantly crafted."

—Austenprose

PRAISE FOR THE NOVELS OF SYRIE JAMES

The Lost Memoirs of Jane Austen

"This fascinating novel will make readers swear there was such a man as Mr. Ashford and that there is such a memoir . . . Tantalizing, tender, and true to the Austen mythos, James's book is highly recommended." —*Library Journal* (starred review)

"James creates a life story for Austen that illuminates how her themes and plots may have developed . . . The reader blindly pulls for the heroine and her dreams of love, hoping against history that Austen might yet enjoy the satisfactions of romance."

—*The Los Angeles Times*

"Austen and Mr. Ashford seem a perfect match in matters of head and heart . . . Though she hews closely to the historic record, [James] creates . . . will-they-or-won't-they suspense that culminates with a proposal and an 'intensely' kissed Austen. It's a pleasant addition to the ever-expanding Austen-revisited genre."

—*Publishers Weekly*

The Secret Diaries of Charlotte Brontë

"For fans of biographical tales and romance, Syrie's story of Charlotte offers it all: longing and yearning, struggle and success, the searing pain of immeasurable loss, and the happiness of a love that came unbidden and unsought. I did not want this story to end."

—*Jane Austen's World*

"James adapts Brontë's voice, telling Brontë's story as though it came straight from the great writer . . . James offers a satisfying—if partly imagined—history of the real-life experiences that inspired Brontë's classic novels." —*BookPage*

Dracula, My Love

"James gives readers an intriguing alternate theory as to the events that occurred in Stoker's classic horror tale while at the same time delivering a spooky yet thoroughly romantic love story."

—*Chicago Tribune*

"Syrie James weaves a tale of quite a different Dracula: a mouth-wateringly handsome, powerful, cultured, and passionate one . . . We will never think of Dracula in the same way ever again. I . . . Loved . . . It!" —*American Book Center*

Nocturne

"Lyrical, lush, and intensely romantic, this infinitely touching, bittersweet story . . . will weave its way into readers' hearts, with its complex characters and compelling emotions sure to linger long after the last page has been turned." —*Library Journal*

"A gloriously romantic story! Near-death experiences, a charming and enigmatic stranger, concealed dark secrets, forbidden love . . . An exquisite feast of passion, turmoil, adventure, and intrigue."

—*Austenesque Reviews*

Forbidden

"A YA novel that hits all the right notes . . . If you enjoy angels, 'forbidden' romance, and dashing heroes, then this should be added to your TBR." —*USA Today*

"Hands down the most fascinating book I have read in quite a while . . . You will find yourself wrapped up in their world, indulging in every kiss, and holding your breath with every twist."

—*Luxury Reading*

THE MISSING MANUSCRIPT OF JANE AUSTEN

SYRIE JAMES

THE BERKLEY PUBLISHING GROUP
Published by the Penguin Group
Penguin Group (USA) Inc.
375 Hudson Street, New York, New York 10014, USA
Penguin Group (Canada), 90 Eglinton Avenue East, Suite 700, Toronto, Ontario M4P 2Y3, Canada (a division of Pearson Penguin Canada Inc.) • Penguin Books Ltd., 80 Strand, London WC2R 0RL, England • Penguin Ireland, 25 St. Stephen's Green, Dublin 2, Ireland (a division of Penguin Books Ltd.) • Penguin Group (Australia), 707 Collins Street, Melbourne, Victoria 3008, Australia (a division of Pearson Australia Group Pty. Ltd.) • Penguin Books India Pvt. Ltd., 11 Community Centre, Panchsheel Park, New Delhi—110 017 India • Penguin Group (NZ), 67 Apollo Drive, Rosedale, Auckland 0632, New Zealand (a division of Pearson New Zealand Ltd.) • Penguin Books, Rosebank Office Park, 181 Jan Smuts Avenue, Parktown North 2193, South Africa • Penguin China, B7 Jaiming Center, 27 East Third Ring Road North, Chaoyang District, Beijing 100020, China

Penguin Books Ltd., Registered Offices: 80 Strand, London WC2R 0RL, England

This book is an original publication of The Berkley Publishing Group.

Cover design by Lesley Worrell.
Interior text design by Kristin del Rosario.

PUBLISHING HISTORY
Berkley trade paperback edition / January 2013

Library of Congress Cataloging-in-Publication Data

James, Syrie.
The missing manuscript of Jane Austen / Syrie James.—Berkley trade paperback ed.
p. cm.
ISBN 978-0-425-25336-6
1. Austen, Jane, 1775–1817—Manuscripts—Fiction. 2. Fiction—Authorship—Fiction. 3. Treasure troves—Fiction. 4. Mystery fiction. 5. Love stories. I. Title.
PS3610.A457M57 2013
813'.6—dc23 2012036733

PRINTED IN THE UNITED STATES OF AMERICA

10 9 8 7 6 5 4 3 2 1

For Yakun and Yvonne, who have brought such love and light to my life. You are lovely, graceful, gifted, dedicated, loving, and exceptional women, and I am so honored and grateful to be your "other mother."

And for all the Jane Austen fans across the globe, who share my reverence and passion for Jane, and always wished there was a seventh novel. This book is for you. I humbly pray that I did her justice.

How It Began

The minute I saw the letter, I knew it was hers. There was no mistaking it: the salutation, the tiny, precise handwriting, the date, the content itself, all confirmed its ancient status and authorship.

I came upon it entirely by accident. It lay buried between the pages of a very old book of eighteenth-century British poetry that I'd found at a used bookstore in Oxford—an impulsive purchase I'd made to add to my library back home and to keep me company during a few days of sightseeing in England.

It was to be a quick trip—less than a week. When I'd learned that my boyfriend, Dr. Stephen Theodore, was attending a medical conference in London, I hadn't been able to resist tagging along. Although I knew he'd be tied up almost the entire time, it was a great excuse to do some touring on my own. My first stop was Oxford, the site of my unfinished education. I still felt pangs about having to abandon my doctoral studies in English literature, and returning to the "city of dreaming spires" filled me with nostalgia. I'd spent a lovely June afternoon and evening exploring my favorite old haunts—wishing, every step of the way, that I could have shared them with Stephen—but we kept in constant touch via e-mail, phone, and text.

I'd found the book in a dusty pile on a shop's back table, unappreciated and ignored. I could see why. It wasn't the prettiest of volumes. It was still in its original, temporary binding—the pages hastily sewn together inside a cheap, cardboardlike cover, with the title printed on a tiny paper label pasted on the spine. The publication date was missing, but I judged the book to be at least two hundred years old.

I didn't have a chance to really study my new treasure until the morning after I'd bought it. I awoke to grey and stormy skies, and after a leisurely English breakfast at my B&B, I decided to wait out the rain with a cup of tea in my cozy little room. I sank down into a comfortable chair by the window, turned on the old-fashioned lamp, and carefully opened the aging volume.

The pages at the beginning were brown and soiled at the edges, but as I went further in they became clean and white, with only a light brown speckling in the margins. I slowly thumbed through the volume, smiling at the familiar, much-loved poems set in antique type. The edges of the pages were ragged where the original owner had used a knife to cut open the folds. Near the end of the book, I noticed that a few pages hadn't been cut, but were still joined at the edge, creating a kind of pocket. I borrowed a letter opener from the B&B proprietor and gently sliced open the remaining pages. To my surprise, tucked in between the leaves of the last pocket, I discovered a single sheet of paper neatly folded into envelope shape and size.

I opened it. It was an unfinished letter. The paper was of substantial weight and bore a watermark and the distinctive ribbing from the paper molds of yesteryear. The ink was black-brown. The date and elegant cursive hand proclaimed that it had been written by quill. I read the greeting, and my heart jumped. With disbelieving eyes, I read it through.

Tuesday 3 September 1816

My dearest Cassandra,

Thank you for your Letter, which was truly welcome. I am much obliged to you for writing so soon after your arrival, and for sharing the particulars of your Lodgings, which I suspect provided far more entertainment for the reader, than for the writer.—Although your Bedroom sounds comfortable enough, I am sorry you had no fire, and am appalled that Mrs. Potter thinks to charge three Guineas a week for such a place! Cheltenham is clearly to be preferred in May! Your Pelisse is no doubt very happy it made the journey, for it will be much worn. I hope Mary gains more benefit from the waters than I did. Do let me know how she gets on. We are well here. The illness which I suffered at the time of your going has very kindly taken its leave, without so much as a good-bye, and I am happy to say that my back has given me very little pain the past few days. I am nursing myself into as beautiful a state as I can, so as to better enjoy Edward's visit. He is a great pleasure to me. He is writing a Novel.—We have all heard it, and it is very good and clever. I believe it could be a first-rate work, if only he can bring himself to finish it.

Listening to Edward's composition has put me in something of a melancholy state and given rise to Feelings I had thought long got over, and of which I may give vent only to you. I promise to indulge for no more than five minutes.—It brings to mind that early Manuscript of my own, which went missing at

Greenbriar in Devonshire. Even at a distance of fourteen years, I cannot help but think of it with a pang of fondness, sorrow, and regret, as one would a lost child.—Do you recall my theory as to how it came to be lost? I still maintain that it was all vanity, nonsense, and wounded pride. I should never have read it out to you that night during our stay but kept it safe with all the others—although we did have a good laugh! (What banner years for me—two Proposals!) It is tragic that I had only the one Copy.—And yet perhaps it was simply fate, and it was never meant to be seen. You did *persuade me to tell no one about it while I was writing it, and you were right; it might indeed have troubled that most valued member of our family. Every time I thought of trying to write it out again, something happened to prevent it—all our travels—so difficult, you will recall, to work at Sydney Place—and then papa died, and it was quite impossible. To recall it now from memory would prove to be a task beyond my power. I have been inspired, however. Yesterday, I sat down and poked fun at my poor, lost creation with a piece of foolishness I call Plan Of A Novel. It is in part what I remember of that Story, embellished with hints from Fanny and others who have been kind enough to suggest what I* ought *to write next. I hope it will make you laugh.—Which reminds me. To-night, we are to drink tea with*

It ended there—a fragment, unfinished, and unsigned.

Hands trembling, I read the letter a second time, and a third. There was only one person who could have written that letter; one person, and she happened to be one of the most famous and beloved authors of all time: Jane Austen. That she was *my* personal favorite author—that I had studied her life and work in detail, and that she had inspired the topic of my never-completed dissertation—only added to my astonishment and excitement.

If this was authentic—and I felt in my bones that it was—then I had come upon something extremely rare and valuable. Jane's sister Cassandra, shortly before her death, had burned most of her correspondence with Jane, or expunged those parts she preferred to keep private, before giving them as mementos to her nieces and nephews. Some 161 letters survived and had been published—and I was certain *this* was not among them. This was something *new*.

I fired up my laptop to verify my theory and logged on to the Net. In no time, I found a website that posted all of Jane Austen's preserved letters. I was thrilled to confirm that the images of her handwriting did indeed match that in the letter I'd found. I jumped to the letters from 1816, near the end of Jane's life. There *was* a portion of a letter dated 4 September 1816, written to Cassandra when she was in Cheltenham—but the first two pages were missing, as well as the top of page three. Cassandra had deliberately disposed of those parts.

My pulse quickened. The fragment I held in my hands seemed to be an early draft of that letter's missing first half. Jane must have been interrupted in the act of composing the letter and hidden it within the pages of this book, not wishing anyone but Cassandra to be aware of its contents. Maybe Jane forgot where she put it, and the next day began the letter afresh. She was ill at the time. She died ten months later. The book of poetry must have been passed on to Cassandra, and at some point was sold or lost. No one had ever discovered the secret it contained.

I was so excited, I could hardly breathe. If I was right—if this was indeed the real thing, an unknown Jane Austen letter—it would make headlines. But even more thrilling than the letter itself was the mention of a missing manuscript. As far as the publishing world knew, Jane Austen had written only six full-length novels and miscellaneous shorter works, which had all been read, scrutinized, and canonized to within an inch of their lives. A newly discovered work by Austen would set off a global wave of Janeite frenzy!

I paced the room, uncertain what I should do with this precious find. Alert the media? Call a museum? No, I decided; they'd think I was a crackpot. I couldn't tell anyone about this until the letter was authenticated. But to whom should I go?

The answer came to me in a flash: Dr. Mary I. Jesse. She'd been my advisor, my mentor, and my teacher during my graduate studies in English Literature at Oxford, and I revered her. When I had to leave the university four years earlier to help take care of my mother, Dr. Jesse had been very supportive. "I know you'll come back and finish someday," she'd said. But I never did.

Dr. Jesse was considered one of the preeminent Austen experts of the day. She'd written countless scholarly papers on Austen as well as a celebrated biography, was a past president of the Jane Austen Literary Foundation, and had taught Austen for more than four decades. She'd retired and left Oxford about the same time that I did, to edit and authenticate a trunk of rare manuscripts discovered in the attic at Chawton House Library. We'd fallen out of touch since.

I knew I had to find her.

I pulled out my cell phone. I had an old e-mail address from my grad-school days, and I sent Mary a quick note, telling her I was in Oxford, and I'd love to see her. The e-mail bounced back with a "delivery failed permanently" message, informing me that the account I was trying to reach did not exist. I checked every online social-media forum I could think of, but Dr. Mary Jesse wasn't anywhere. Her phone number was unlisted.

For a few minutes, I was stymied. I'm not generally the bold, spur-of-the-moment type—but I couldn't sit still. I grabbed my raincoat and umbrella and walked the long, familiar blocks in the freezing rain to the St. Cross Building on Manor Road. The Faculty Office of the English Language and Literature Department was thankfully open, and even better, my friend Michelle—who'd nurtured me for two years while I worked on my doctorate—was sitting behind the desk.

"Hello there," I said, catching my breath as I dropped my dripping umbrella by the door.

Michelle looked up from her computer and greeted me with a huge smile. "Samantha! How wonderful to see you. And looking as beautiful as ever!"

We hugged and chatted like magpies, catching up on four years' worth of news in four minutes. I briefly recapped what I'd been up to: still single at thirty-one but dating a very nice man, and happily working as a Special Collections Librarian at a small university in Southern California.

"So you're not here to reenroll?" Michelle asked, disappointed.

"No—sorry. I'm here on holiday. My boyfriend's attending a cardiology conference in London."

"The boyfriend's a doctor? Ooh. Lovely."

"He is, rather." I smiled and moved straight to the point of my visit: I needed to get hold of Dr. Mary Jesse.

"Dr. Jesse? She moved somewhere up near Chipping Norton, I think. From what I hear, she lives a very quiet, private life now. She wouldn't leave us a phone number or e-mail, we just forward any thing that comes to her home address."

My spirits plummeted. No phone number? No e-mail? Really? I impressed upon Michelle how important it was that I reach Mary and that I didn't have much time; I was only in

England for a few days. With a fond smile and a shake of her head, she gave me Mary's mailing address, reminding me not to share it with anyone. I profusely thanked her.

After a warm good-bye and promises to stay in touch, I stopped in the shelter of an ancient passageway and looked up Mary's address on my phone. She lived in Hook Norton. There was no time to write to her—who knew when I'd hear back? According to MapQuest, Hook Norton was about twenty-five miles northwest of Oxford, on the A44.

I glanced at my watch. It was 1:30 P.M. and a Friday. It would probably take a little over an hour to get there, traffic permitting. I hesitated, reminding myself that Mary apparently relished her privacy these days, and it wasn't polite to drop in on people unannounced—but I quickly shook off those concerns. Mary was as obsessed with All Things Austen as I was—more, in fact. If she was home, she'd be ecstatic about this discovery, and she could not only authenticate it but tell me what to do with it.

I practically ran all the way back to the B&B. I made two photocopies of the precious letter, then slid the original back between the pages of the old book, rewrapped the book to keep it clean and dry, and stowed it in my purse.

Too excited to keep the news to myself, I decided to call Stephen. Dr. Stephen Theodore was the smart, handsome, forty-one-year-old cardiac interventionalist who had treated my mother for her heart condition. We had met four years earlier, shortly after I'd returned to Los Angeles from Oxford. Although *I* was an emotional wreck at the time, desperately worried about my mom, I saw at once that she was in good hands.

My relationship with Dr. Theodore had been strictly professional at first, but as the months went by, we both became aware of a mutual, growing attraction. He asked me out. I discovered that although Stephen hadn't read a book for pleasure since his teens, he appreciated that *I* loved them. Whereas I enjoyed cooking, he avoided kitchen duties like the plague—but we found commonality in other things. We liked the same types of music, food, and wine. His work schedule was very demanding, but we squeezed in pockets of time now and then to meet for dinner or at the gym, or for an occasional Sunday morning bike ride on the path along the beach. It wasn't long before I ended up in his bed.

Stephen was supportive about what he teasingly called my "Jane Austen Obsession." He watched several of my favorite Austen film adaptations with me. In return for accompanying him to various medical receptions (not my favorite thing), he—dubiously—had agreed to take a couple of English Country Dance lessons, and he'd actually rented a costume and accompanied me to a Regency ball, where we'd danced the night away, just like Elizabeth Bennet and Mr. Darcy. "This is more fun than I'd expected," my brilliant doctor had said with real surprise—and I'd floated on air the entire evening.

We enjoyed each other's company. We were a comfortable fit. And he took excellent care of my mother.

Sadly, however, my mom's heart failure continued to progress. She had died the year before of a sudden arrhythmia—her internal defibrillator wasn't able to restore her normal heart rhythm. I was suddenly parentless, an orphan, overwhelmed with grief, paperwork, and financial stress. Stephen was there for me when I needed him. In the three years that we'd been together, we'd made no commitment to each other, still living our separate lives—but he was important to me, and I believed I was important to him.

I could hardly wait to tell him about my discovery.

Stephen had said he'd be in back-to-back medical meetings

and seminars all day at the London conference, but I took a chance and called him. By some miracle, he answered.

"Sam?" There was the din of conversation in the background.

"Stephen! I'm so glad I caught you."

"Me, too. Just a minute, I'm having trouble hearing you." There was a pause. The background noise diminished, and he spoke again. "Are you having a good time?"

"I am. How's the meeting going?"

"Great so far. We had a good turnout at my program during the IME symposium. The poster sessions have been okay although a bit heavy on the genetics. And at the Satellite Symposium, they introduced some very interesting new research regarding dyslipidemia and effective parameters for measuring residual risk—it's going to be challenging to implement these findings with my patients."

"I think I understood about 45 percent of that," I said with a laugh.

"That's more than I did," he quipped in return.

"Stephen: do you have a minute? I have something incredible to tell you."

"What's that?"

"I bought a book yesterday at a used-book store—a two-hundred-year-old book of poetry—"

"Nice. Is it for Chamberlain U's library?"

"No, it's for me—for my collection. But that's not what's exciting. There was a letter hidden inside."

"A letter? What do you mean?"

"It's a handwritten letter, dated 1816. It wasn't signed, but I think—I'm almost positive—that it was written by Jane Austen."

"Jane Austen? Are you kidding?"

"I'm serious. Stephen: I can hardly believe this. I think I've discovered an original Jane Austen letter!"

"That's awesome. If anyone would know if it's the real thing, it's you, babe. What are you going to do with it?"

"I have to try get it authenticated." I told him about the little side trip I was taking.

"Sounds like a great adventure."

"It could be," I replied with enthusiasm.

"Well, good luck." He apologized, explaining that his next session was about to start, and we signed off.

I headed out to my rental car. It was still raining. I'd hired plenty of cars during my years in graduate school, so I was accustomed to driving on the wrong side of the road. The traffic on the A44 heading northwest out of Oxford was horrific, but once the elegant spires and towers of the city were far behind me, it opened up. Fifty-five minutes later, I left the tree-lined main road and took the local road into Hook Norton, a small village with a nice old church. The rain paused momentarily, but the sky was still bleak and grey. Following the directions on the GPS, I headed down a narrow lane to the edge of the village and found the house—a quaint, yellow brick cottage, half-covered in ivy. There was a small, late-model car in the drive.

I pulled up out front, strode up the path, and knocked. An unsmiling young woman in jeans and a dark sweatshirt answered the door.

"May I help you?" she asked in a clipped, British accent.

"I'm here to see Dr. Mary Jesse. Is she in?"

"Mary is very busy. She doesn't see anyone," the woman said abruptly.

I was thrilled—Mary was home!—and I was not about to be dissuaded. "I've come a long way," I insisted, reasoning that this was true if you figured in my point of origin. "I'm from Los Angeles. I'm a former student of—"

"I'm sorry, but as I said, Mary doesn't see anyone. You may leave your card, if you like."

"I don't have a card with me," I replied, straining for patience, "but if you would just tell Dr. Jesse that I'm here. My name is Samantha McDonough. She was my advisor at Oxford, and I have something important to tell her."

"I suggest you write and tell her your business. Include your phone number. If she's interested in speaking with you, she'll call."

"But—"

"I'm sorry. That's all I can say. Good-bye." The woman shut the door in my face.

I stood there, my mouth agape, utterly astonished. The Dr. Mary Jesse *I* remembered had been kind and welcoming. We'd had deep, meaningful conversations during my grad-school days, and she'd often invited me and other students to her Oxford apartment for tea. She would never have placed a guard dog at her door to turn people away! Instinctively, I felt that something was wrong. But what? I considered buying a card in the village, writing Mary a note, and leaving it in her mailbox—but I was reluctant to put the details of my secret find on paper, and afraid that Dragon Lady would either toss it, or worse yet, blab to someone about it.

With a sigh, I got back in the car and returned to Oxford, extremely disappointed. After a quiet dinner at a local pub, I decided to write Mary a brief note after all. I said I'd found a very old document that I knew would interest her, and I'd appreciate her help in authenticating it. I told her I was leaving the country on Tuesday, and included my cell-phone number. I figured the exercise was in vain. It was Friday evening by the time

I posted it. It probably wouldn't reach her until Monday, and my flight left the very next afternoon. When I returned to my B&B, I contemplated whether I should try to find another Austen expert—surely there must be several people at Oxford qualified to authenticate the letter for me—but I realized it would have to wait. The weekend had already begun.

Desperate to commiserate with someone, I tried calling Stephen, but he didn't pick up. I texted him instead, letting him know that I'd returned safely from my excursion.

I thought about going to bed, but I wasn't tired. I'd only been in England a couple of days, and my body didn't know what time zone it was in. Anyway, I knew I'd never be able to sleep. All I could think about was that letter. I took out the photocopy and read it again. Every single thing pointed to its authenticity. It was truly an incredible find—but I was particularly excited about this reference within:

It brings to mind that early Manuscript of my own, which went missing at Greenbriar in Devonshire. Even at a distance of fourteen years, I cannot help but think of it with a pang of fondness, sorrow, and regret, as one would a lost child.

Was it really possible that Jane Austen had written another manuscript—perhaps even a full-length novel—that the world did not know about? If so, was there a chance that it still existed?

I spent the next couple of hours dissecting every word in the second half of the letter, looking for clues, trying to determine the meaning behind them.

If the manuscript Jane Austen referred to had been lost fourteen years earlier, that meant it went missing in 1802, when she was twenty-six years old. I knew Austen was living in Bath with her parents and her sister at the time, having moved there in 1801 when her father retired from his position as rector of Steventon, a small parish in Hampshire. It had always been supposed that Jane Austen did very little writing during the years she moved to Bath, either because she was depressed or because she didn't have settled-enough conditions in which to work. But what if that wasn't true?

I remembered reading somewhere that Jane used to take some or all of her manuscripts with her in a box when she traveled, for safekeeping. She must have had *this* manuscript with her in Devonshire, because in her letter she said she was reading it to Cassandra, and it made them laugh.

But where was Greenbriar? Was it a town? No. A little recon on the Net confirmed that there were no towns called Greenbriar in the county of Devon. Could it be the name of a country house? Further probing established that there was indeed a manor home called Greenbriar in southeast Devon. According to an online article, it was a secluded country house built in 1785.

"And it's still there!" I exulted aloud. According to the Web entry, the house had been in the same family for generations. It was currently owned by Reginald Whitaker, a solicitor, now retired. There was a picture of him, taken at a garden party held at Greenbriar a few years ago. You couldn't see much of the house itself, but Reginald Whitaker was a tall, handsome, silver-haired man who appeared to be in his late sixties.

Could it be that Jane and her family visited that very house in 1802, and while there, one of her manuscripts somehow went astray? I had dozens of Austen biographies at home that could have verified her probable whereabouts at the time but nothing at hand. I couldn't find any thing on the Web to help me. I sat back, frustrated, when it suddenly occurred to me that I had the perfect resource at my fingertips, just a phone call away: my friend Laurel Ann.

Laurel Ann had been my first roommate in college, the one arbitrarily assigned to me by the dorm. We'd instantly bonded over our love of books, romantic movies, boys with blue eyes, mint chip ice cream, and Jane Austen. We'd been best friends ever since. She now managed one of the few remaining independent bookstores in Los Angeles, where her self-professed goal was to "sell Austen to the masses."

It was 11:00 P.M., which meant it was three o'clock in the afternoon in Los Angeles. Laurel Ann would be at work at the bookstore. I dialed her number. To my delight, she picked up.

"Hey!" she said, in her typically cheerful tone. "Where are you, and how jealous should I be?"

"Oxford, and green with envy. I'm in flannel P.J.'s at a B&B all by myself, and it's pouring down rain."

"Oh, poor you. Back *again* in the country I adore but can only dream about. A man who looks like Frodo just spent $150 on erotica books and asked for my phone number. I considered giving him yours just to spite you."

I laughed. "Do you have a minute to do a little research for me?"

"What kind of research?"

"Before I tell you, you should probably go into your office and shut the door. What I have to say is about Jane Austen, and it's pretty amazing. You might start jumping up and down, or possibly screaming, and that might scare the customers."

That got Laurel Ann's attention. Once she'd affirmed her privacy, I told her as succinctly as I could about my discovery that morning, and everything that had happened subsequently. Then I read her Jane Austen's letter. As I'd predicted, she could hardly contain her enthusiasm.

"My God, Sam, this is incredible! The letter *has to be* hers!"

Laurel Ann promised to find the information I needed in the store's biography section and to call me right back. While I waited, I paced the floor like an anxious, expectant father in an old movie. I grabbed my cell phone with anticipation on the first ring.

"Okay," Laurel Ann said on the other end of the line, "this mansion house, Greenbriar, is in Devonshire, right? Well, I looked up the time period in question, and you're going to love this, Sam. In the Deirdre Le Faye biography, it says there's a three-year gap in Jane Austen's surviving correspondence from May 1801 through September 1804, but from 'hints and glimpses found in other sources,' it's been determined that the Austens *did* visit the seaside resort town of Sidmouth in the summer of 1801, and probably went to Dawlish and Teignmouth in the summer of 1802—all of which are in Devonshire!"

I had a map of Devonshire open on my laptop screen, and I gave a happy gasp. "Greenbriar isn't far from Sidmouth!" If I'd been excited before, I was beside myself now. "She must have gone there!"

"And while there, she somehow lost a manuscript. To think there might be another Austen novel out there—I can hardly believe it!"

"But how can a manuscript go missing? What on earth happened to it?"

"Who knows? But the key to the mystery is obviously Greenbriar. Jane had the manuscript with her because she read it to Cassandra."

"Maybe there's some kind of evidence at that house—old family records or something, with proof that Jane Austen was a visitor, and a clue to the missing manuscript."

"Yes! You have to look into this, Sam. You just have to."

"But how? I only have four more days in England. If I write to Reginald Whitaker, I'll never hear back in time."

"So call him in the morning. Tell him what you found and go down there."

"What if I can't find his phone number, or can't get hold of him?"

"Go anyway!"

I laughed. "You do realize this whole thing is mad and impulsive."

"Some of the most thrilling things in life are done on impulse. If you hadn't dared me to drop in on the owner of this bookstore eight years ago, I would have never gotten this job. You always tell me I take forever to make up my mind about things, and am so afraid of making a wrong decision that I never take any action at all. It's time to grow some balls, Sam, and take your own advice."

"You're right. Okay, I'll do it." I thanked Laurel Ann for her help and encouragement and signed off, promising to keep her apprised of whatever happened.

Finding Whitaker's contact information was a lot easier than Mary Jesse's had been. He wasn't on any social networking sites, either, but I already knew where he lived, and after logging in to ukphonebook.com, I had his phone number inside of two minutes.

By the time I got ready for bed and crawled beneath the down comforter, it was after midnight. I didn't expect sleep to come easy that night, but jet lag suddenly set in with a vengeance, and I nodded off instantly, waking with a start at seven thirty. I leapt out of bed and immediately called Reginald Whitaker, hoping to set up an appointment—but nobody answered. There wasn't an answering machine or service; the phone just kept ringing. I showered, dressed, had breakfast, and tried calling him again. Still no luck.

Well, I thought with a sigh, there was no turning back now. Laurel Ann would kill me if I lost my nerve. And I knew that if I didn't go after this now, I'd never forgive myself. I had to drive down to Greenbriar and hope I could find Reginald Whitaker.

The Search

AT 1:30 P.M., I WAS TURNING OFF THE M5 IN DEVON. I was lucky with the weather. It was a beautiful day. All around me were vast emerald fields dotted with sheep and trees. During the car ride, I had chatted with Stephen by phone, explaining the purpose of my trip to Devon and the letter's reference to a missing manuscript. Although distracted, he'd been supportive, and reminded me to drive safely before ending the call to attend another one of his meetings.

I stopped at a picturesque country inn nestled on the bank of the River Exe, which boasted stunning gardens, river views, comfortable beds, a first-rate head chef, an excellent wine list, and ales from local breweries. I booked a room for the night, left my bag, had a sandwich in the pub, and got back in my car.

Greenbriar was purportedly near Witherford, about four kilometers away. I consulted my map, found the local road, and drove through the lush, green countryside until I reached the quaint village, which proclaimed itself to be "the prettiest village on Exmoor." There was a tiny main street, an ancient Norman church, and a number of thatched cottages. I had to pause for a gaggle of white geese waddling in a line across the road. Because Greenbriar didn't have a street address, the car's GPS couldn't get a lock on it, so I stopped at a small shop to ask for directions. The bored teenage boy behind the counter took out one of his earbuds to answer my question. His directions were blunt but obliging.

After some trial and error, I finally spotted the narrow lane he'd described, leading away from the road into a copse of trees. It took me over an even narrower bridge crossing a bubbling river, and just as it turned and crested a small rise, I caught my first glimpse of my destination. Below me, a wide meadow was intersected by a long, curving, tree-lined avenue that culminated at a gravel drive in front of an elegant, Palladian-style mansion.

Greenbriar.

It took my breath away. I stopped and got out of the car to drink in the view. The Georgian house was built of red brick, with a sloping dark roof topped by multiple chimneys, and two rows of perfectly symmetrical white casement windows. A wide, central staircase led up to an elegant portico. Surrounding the house was an oasis of green meadow, framed by scattered trees. It was secluded, peaceful, and serene, the perfect stillness broken only by the sound of buzzing insects and the rushing river that ran alongside one of the meadow's flanks.

To think that all this was still privately owned! I was suddenly envious of Reginald Whitaker and his entire line of ancestors and descendants. I got back behind the wheel and drove down the avenue. As I approached, I began to realize that the house had looked better from a distance. What had appeared to be a lush meadow, up close turned out to be an immense, overgrown lawn. The roof didn't look to be in ideal shape, and all the casement windows were badly in need of fresh paint. Still, it was a grand old house, an architectural and historical marvel in a location so beautiful it seemed almost too good to be true.

I rounded the last curve of the gravel drive, past an outbuilding that had been converted into a garage, and parked my car a few dozen feet from the entrance to the house. There were no other vehicles in sight, but on one side of the wide staircase leading up to the portico, I spotted a man working in one of the flowerbeds, which was choked knee-high with weeds.

He continued with his labor, yanking out weeds by the armful and dumping them in a wheelbarrow, glancing up only briefly as I walked over. I guessed him to be in his late thirties. He was tall and good-looking, with short, straight blond hair, and was dressed in jeans and a T-shirt that emphasized his lean, athletic physique. His eyes were a disconcertingly deep shade of blue, and I was so taken by them that I couldn't help but stare.

"Are you lost?" he said. His accent was exquisitely British, very refined.

"No—I don't think so." During the car ride down, I'd rehearsed what I wanted to say to the aging Reginald Whitaker when I got here, but this clearly was not he. Was he a workman? A gardener? If so, he had a funny way of pulling weeds. There wasn't a shovel in sight. And from his expression and body language, he seemed to be really pissed off about something.

"You're American." It was an observation, not a question.

"Yes. You'll never get the weeds out that way, you know."

"I beg your pardon?" He paused and looked at me.

"If you want to get rid of those weeds, you can't pull them out by the stems. You have to dig them out at the root. Otherwise, they'll be back in a week."

"Shite." He wiped his brow with the back of his hand, and said irritably, "Can I help you with something?"

"I'm looking for Reginald Whitaker. Do you know if he's home?"

"I'm sorry, he's not."

"Do you know where I can find him?"

"He passed away two weeks ago."

"Oh—oh." That knocked me for a loop.

I was struggling with what to say next, when he yanked off his gardening gloves, climbed out of the weed bed, and strode over to me. He stopped a few feet away, smelling deliciously of aftershave and sweat—an effect that was entirely destroyed by the scowl on his face.

"I'm Anthony Whitaker. Reggie was my father."

"Oh," I said again. "My name's Samantha McDonough. I'm sorry for your loss." I held out my hand for him to shake.

He didn't acknowledge my hand or my comment, just said abruptly, "What did you need to see my father about?"

"It's . . . kind of a long story." I shoved my hand in my pocket.

"Try giving it to me in one sentence."

Could he be more rude? I forced myself to remain polite. "I needed to talk to him about the house."

"About Greenbriar?"

"Yes."

He appeared confused. "Are you an estate agent?"

"No. I'm . . . a history buff, and in my research, I came across something that may relate to this house."

"Ah—you're a *tourist*." His frown deepened. "Well, it's a really old house, so it has a lot of history, but none of it's very interesting—and I'm afraid I don't have time to discuss it. I'm meeting with an estate agent in twenty minutes."

"You're selling the house?" I was aghast.

"I am."

"How can you sell it? It's beautiful!"

"It's a wreck. The roof leaks, the pipes are bad, the windows are rotting away, it's remortgaged and costs a bomb to maintain—and my father left the whole crumbling ruin to me. Now if you'll excuse me, I have a lot of things to do." He turned away.

"Wait! Mr. Whitaker: I drove all the way down from Oxford about this. It's really important." It was time to play my trump card. "I've come across evidence leading me to believe that Jane Austen might have visited Greenbriar, and actually stayed here."

He paused and glanced back at me. "Jane Austen? *The* Jane Austen?" He shook his head, letting out a wry laugh. "I'm sorry to disappoint you, Miss—"

"McDonough. Samantha."

"Trust me when I say that Jane Austen never graced the halls of Greenbriar."

"How do you know?"

"Because if she *had*, the whole world would know about it. Everything that woman ever touched, and every place she ever set foot, has had a cottage industry spring up around it. If Jane Austen had visited Greenbriar for even half an hour, the house would be on the route of every bus tour from London and Hampshire. My family would have made a fortune off it."

"But—"

"If you'll excuse me, I really do have to go. Enjoy your holiday."

With that, he strode back to the house and disappeared inside.

I stared after him, silently fuming. What a jerk! He couldn't have taken five more minutes to listen to me? Angry and defeated, I marched to my car and drove away.

As I recrossed the river and made my way through the idyllic countryside, however—although still deeply disappointed—my resentment slowly began to give way to embarrassment. What had I been thinking—dashing down here so impetuously and dropping in unannounced on a total stranger? Apparently, I'd come at the worst possible moment. The man had just lost his father. He was grieving, upset, and saddled with an overwhelming responsibility. All he could think about was getting that huge, (beautiful), old house off his hands. No wonder he didn't want to listen to the ramblings of some random, Austen-loving tourist.

I was so upset with myself that I drove straight back to the inn, where I spent half an hour wandering the grounds and gazing out at the river in an attempt to calm down. Under the circumstances, I understood why Anthony Whitaker hadn't given me the time of day. It was a shame, though, that I hadn't had a chance to mention the rare letter I'd discovered, or Jane Austen's reference to Greenbriar and a missing manuscript. Would it have made any difference if I had? It was hard to say—but as I thought about it, I felt a sudden, renewed rush of hope. Maybe, just *maybe* this wasn't over yet. Anthony Whitaker couldn't sell Greenbriar overnight. A few days or weeks from now, he might be in a better frame of mind to consider what I had to tell him.

I'd write him a letter, I decided, and share my theories about the lost manuscript. If he was open to it, I could always fly back to England to meet with him. In the meantime, I still had Jane Austen's letter, and that was a treasure all by itself.

My mood improved, I vowed to make the most of my trip down here. I'd never been to Devon. It was beautiful, and knowing that Jane Austen had enjoyed visiting its coastal villages at least twice made the area even more appealing. I'd intended to sightsee for a couple of days in any case after Oxford but hadn't made any definite plans; so Devon it would be.

I made a reservation for dinner at the restaurant, freshened up, and was unpacking the few things in my suitcase when the phone in my room rang. I answered, startled. Who would call me on the hotel phone? It was the man at the front desk. He said that a gentleman was asking for me: a Mr. Anthony Whitaker of Greenbriar. Did I wish to see him?

Truly astonished, I went downstairs.

Anthony Whitaker was standing in the lobby, looking freshly showered, wearing pressed slacks, a dress shirt, a sports jacket, and a contrite look on his face. Not knowing what to say, I let him begin.

"Hi. It's Samantha, right?"

I nodded.

"I've come to apologize. I was rude earlier. I felt bad after you left. I've been under a lot of pressure lately. All I can say is, I was having a very difficult day, and I took it out on you. I'm sorry."

Well, that was nice. "I'd like to apologize, as well," I responded. "I came at a very bad time. I had no idea your father had passed away. I truly am very sorry."

"Thank you."

"How did you find me? I never said where I was staying."

"You told me your name. There are only a few inns in the area. I'm glad you decided to spend the night nearby."

I nodded again. There was an awkward pause. He smiled,

and the genuine warmth in his eyes was so disarming, it caused an unexpected fluttering in my stomach. "I'd like to make up for my poor behavior," he went on. "Can I buy you dinner?"

I was about to tell him that wasn't really necessary, when I realized I'd been given an incredible gift: a second chance to talk to him here and now, and plead my case. He was here. He was being so civil and charming. How could I refuse?

A few minutes later, we were seated in the restaurant at a window table with a view of the river, and dinner and wine on the way.

"Samantha: you said you're from America. What part?"

"Los Angeles. Where do you live?"

"London. I hadn't been here for years until two weeks ago, when I arranged my father's funeral. I'm back again just for the weekend, to clean up the place a little before the sale. And as you saw, gardening isn't my strong suit."

"I'm no gardening expert, either," I admitted, "which is why I've had a lot of experience pulling weeds."

He laughed and relaxed in his chair. Our salads and wine arrived.

"I read that Greenbriar's been in your family for over two centuries," I said, in between bites.

"Lawrence Whitaker built the house in 1785. I'm his direct descendant, the last of the line, it seems."

"It's a shame you have to sell it."

"I agree. It used to be a much larger property. The surrounding acreage has been sold off bit by bit over the years to pay for its upkeep. My father didn't have the money to take care of it properly, and neither do I—the taxes alone will kill me."

"That's a difficult position to be in."

"It is." He sipped his wine. "So. Let's talk about why you're here. This afternoon, I believe you said you're a history buff?"

"Yes." I hesitated. "I guess I should start by explaining that I studied at Oxford four years ago, in the doctoral program of English Literature—"

"Oh? So it's *Dr.* Samantha McDonough?"

My cheeks warmed. "No. I have a master's degree in English Lit, and I got about halfway through with my dissertation, but . . . family circumstances intervened, and I couldn't finish it."

"I'm sorry."

"So am I. But—anyway, I'm now a Special Collections Librarian at a private university. And entirely by chance, I came across something the other day that seems to link Jane Austen with Greenbriar. It's actually very exciting."

"Well, I apologize for cutting you off earlier with an attitude of appalling skepticism. I promise you have my full attention now."

I smiled and looked around the room, wanting to keep my revelation away from other ears. Fortunately, the restaurant was still half-empty, and none of the other patrons were paying any attention to us. I leaned forward, and keeping my voice low, I told Anthony all about the old book I'd found, the untrimmed pages, and what I'd discovered inside. He listened with growing interest.

From my purse, I withdrew the photocopies of Jane Austen's letter and handed them to him. He glanced over the pages, his eyebrows lifting in surprise. "Has this been authenticated?"

"Not yet—I intend to do that, of course—but I have a great deal of experience with documents of this kind, and I've studied Jane Austen for years. I researched this last night, and everything checks out. I'm positive this letter is hers."

"What a great discovery!" He seemed impressed.

"It is. This letter can possibly shed new light on Austen's life as well as her work. But wait until you read what it *says*—it's truly fantastic. The second half is the part relevant to you."

He read the letter. When he got to the last section, his blue eyes widened. Then he began asking questions. Weren't there other places called Greenbriar in Devonshire? What made me so sure it was *his* house? Finally, he said, "If the visit happened, why isn't it in the history books?"

"There are huge gaps in our knowledge as to Jane Austen's whereabouts during her lifetime—particularly during the period in question. But we have reason to believe that she and her parents and her sister *did* spend the summers of 1801 and 1802 in Devonshire. Which makes it entirely possible that they came to Greenbriar. Based on that letter, it seems likely that they stayed for at least one night at the house in 1802, probably longer."

"No one in my family has ever mentioned a relationship with the Austens. If one of my ancestors had hosted them at Greenbriar, don't you think, after Jane became famous, he would have told someone about it?"

"Maybe not. Jane Austen didn't become famous until many decades after she died."

"Could Austen really have written an entire manuscript that went missing?"

"It's possible. I don't know if it's a full-length book or what. It could be a shorter work, or even an unfinished one. But she clearly lost *something*—and she lost it at Greenbriar."

He handed me back the letter, seemingly astounded. "This is beyond belief. To even think that it might be possible . . . Jane Austen!"

By now, our main courses had arrived. I savored my lamb chops, which were delicious. Anthony dug into his meal, deep in thought for a long moment. Then he darted me a slightly self-conscious glance. "May I be honest about something?"

"Please."

"I know the world adores her. But I've only read one Jane Austen novel in my life. Will you forgive me if I say that I didn't like it?"

"Which book did you read?"

"I don't remember the title. I only read it because it was forced on me in school. It was about a spoiled brat who lived in a tiny village full of dull people, who never did anything or went anywhere. As I recall, she spent the whole book trying to match up people who didn't belong together."

My lips twitched with the effort to hide my smile. "*Emma.* How old were you when you read it?"

"Maybe fifteen or sixteen."

"Your reaction is totally understandable. Unless presented in the right way, *Emma* might not be all that accessible to a teenage boy. In fact, it's a truly extraordinary book. If you read it again now, you might feel differently."

He shrugged. "I doubt it. I'm more of a mystery novel fan myself. For the classics, I enjoy Dumas, Defoe, and Dickens . . . Tolstoy, Tolkien, and Twain."

"I see you've named only male authors."

"Have I? That was not by design."

"There are lots of brilliant female authors—and the best of them is Austen."

"Many millions of people seem to agree with you. But honestly—and forgive me again, I don't in any way mean to denigrate what you do, or to disparage Austen's legacy—but I'm baffled as to how she became such a phenomenon. She wrote, what, four or five novels?"

"Six."

"Six romantic novels. And everyone treats her with this uncanny reverence, as if she were Shakespeare. What is it about her? What am I missing?"

I patiently replied:

"Austen's works have endured because she had a superb narrative technique and a gift for creating characters who feel as real as life itself. She didn't just write about romance. She covered subjects and social and emotional struggles that are still very relevant today. She could pull at your heartstrings, but she could also make you laugh and cry. At the end of her books, if you're paying attention, you come away feeling a little wiser about yourself and about what's important in life."

"Interesting. I've never heard it put quite that way before." He smiled at me across the table. "I admit, I'm intrigued—and not just because she might have paid a visit to my family house." We ate in silence for a while, then he added: "So what are you thinking? That if you can prove Jane Austen was at Greenbriar, however briefly, it's the first clue to this missing manuscript?"

"Yes."

"You'd want to have a look around the house, I suppose?"

Excitement spread through me. "Yes. I thought: maybe there's a guest registry or something stashed there, that dates back to 1802."

"I don't remember my mum and dad ever mentioning anything about a guest registry." He frowned. "If such a thing exists, I'd wager it'll be in the library. Why don't you stop by tomorrow morning, about nine o'clock, and we'll have a look."

"*We?*" My pulse quickened. "Fantastic! Thank you! So you'll help me?"

"Why not? I told you, I like mysteries. And God knows, it'll be more fun than weeding."

We both laughed.

Over dessert and coffee, we talked of other things. Anthony told me he'd graduated from Oxford a few years before I was there. He had been divorced for twelve years, and was still single. He'd married right out of college, but he and his wife had been too young, and had wanted different things. His mother had passed away about five years before. They'd been close. He'd been estranged from his father for decades, which I thought was sad. My own dad died when I was in high school, and I admitted that I missed both of my parents every day.

I told him about Stephen. "My mother used to look at me with a little smile and say, 'You should marry that doctor.'"

"Are you going to?" he asked, and seemed very interested in my reply.

I suddenly felt a little awkward. "I don't know. Maybe. I've thought about it."

When I asked what he did for a living, Anthony told me he was a vice president at a venture capital firm.

"I coordinate the financing to help start-up companies get up and running, and help established corporations get the money they need to expand," he explained.

"Do you enjoy it?"

"Very much. I like to say that I get people the money they need to follow their dreams. How about you? I'm going to take a wild guess and say that you . . . love books?"

I laughed. "I've been in love with books ever since I was a little girl and read *Charlotte's Web* and *The Secret Garden*. Later, I graduated to Austen, Dickens, and the Brontës, with Austen my hands-down favorite. I wanted to live inside an Austen novel!

When I was a freshman in college, I took an intro to literature class and realized that you could read good books, write about them, and talk about them, and actually get a degree in that. I was sold! My goal at the time was to be a college English teacher. And I did teach for two years at the community-college level, but it was a nightmare."

"Why?"

"I could never get enough classes at one location to make it a full-time job. I had to commute between three different schools, and one of them was sixty miles away. There's a glut of MA's on the market, and so many teachers are stuck in that position, there's a name for them: Freeway Flyers. It's mind-numbingly exhausting, and the pay is atrocious. When I took into account how much time I was spending in the car, prepping for classes, teaching, and reading students' papers, I was earning less than minimum wage."

"Good God."

"I did enjoy the *teaching* part, though—very much. I loved working with students and sharing my love of literature. So I decided I wanted to teach at the university level, which meant going back to school and getting my doctorate."

"Which you pursued at Oxford."

"Yes. Studying here in England—land of Austen—was like a dream come true for me. But then my mom got sick. I had to drop everything, go home, and take care of her. I needed a job, fast, to help pay my mom's medical bills. I had worked in the Special Collections department of my university library for years as an undergrad, and I spent a lot of time in the Bodleian Library while I was at Oxford. When I came back, there was an opening for a Library Assistant at Chamberlain University, and they took me in. When the Special Collections Librarian retired, I started filling in for her. It was supposed to be a temporary arrangement, but then the budget got cut. They couldn't afford two positions, and they couldn't hire anyone new, so they offered me the job permanently."

"Was that a difficult switch to make—from teacher to librarian?"

"It was—at first. But I really enjoy it now."

"Have you thought about going back to Oxford?"

"No. That ship has sailed. It's a sticky subject among some of my colleagues that I don't have a degree in Library Science—so I've been taking some online courses to earn my MLS."

He nodded. There was a warm, appreciative twinkle in his blue eyes as he looked at me, and I couldn't help feeling a tingle of attraction toward him. Immediately, I closed down that particular corner of my brain. I was already involved with a man I cared about very much. I had no business thinking about Anthony Whitaker that way. Quickly, I glanced at my watch, commenting on how late it was. We were both surprised to discover that we'd been talking for nearly three hours. I offered to split the bill, but Anthony wouldn't hear of it.

As I walked with him to the inn's front lobby to say good night, he said, "I'll see you in the morning?"

"You bet."

"I should probably warn you: my father was living in only one small part of the house. The rest is not very presentable. But the library was his pride and joy, so thankfully he kept it heated and clean."

"I look forward to seeing it."

He paused, then added cautiously, "You do realize it's been more than two hundred years since this hypothetical 'visit' by Austen took place, right?"

"Right."

"And even if we can prove she was there—if there ever *was* a manuscript, it's probably long gone. So the likelihood of us actually finding anything at all is basically slim to none."

"I know." I grinned. "But we have to try, don't we?"

The Discovery

When I got back to my room, I called Laurel Ann and told her everything that had happened. She was agog.

"You're going to hang out with him at his fabulous Georgian mansion?" In a teasing but affectionate tone, she added, "I was jealous before, but now I think I hate you."

I was just climbing into bed when my phone rang. Happily, it was Stephen. I gave him a complete update.

"Sounds great. But just remember, Sam, you're on vacation. You're not supposed to be working. You're supposed to be having a good time."

"I *am* having a good time," I assured him. "I haven't been this excited about anything in years." Realizing how that sounded, I added, "I mean, come on, it's a Jane Austen treasure hunt!"

"Who's this guy again—the one who owns the house?"

"Anthony Whitaker. He's a venture capitalist."

"Okay." There was an odd tone in his voice. "Well, I wish

you luck." Stephen reminded me that his conference was over on Monday at one o'clock and that we'd planned to spend the afternoon and evening together before flying home the following day.

"I'll be back Monday afternoon. Don't worry."

I awoke early the next morning, breakfasted at the inn, and arrived at Greenbriar at nine sharp. It was a grey, misty morning and there was a slight chill in the air, so I dressed in jeans and a lightweight blue pullover. When Anthony answered the massive front door, to our mutual amusement, he was clad in a similar ensemble.

"I'm glad you got the memo about the dress code," he said with a grin.

I laughed and followed him into the house.

"Welcome to the humble Whitaker abode," he added.

If I'd thought the outside was imposing, the inside was even more spectacular. He'd warned that the place wasn't presentable—it was falling apart, he said—but it didn't look that bad to me. Yes, the walls needed paint, the oak floors were scuffed and worn, and the carpets, drapes, and furniture were dusty and a bit threadbare—but the rooms were massive in scale, and retained many of their period features and charm. As we passed through the entrance hall and into the drawing room, I marveled at the high, plasterwork ceilings, carved-marble fireplace, mahogany doors with gilded handles, and wide, arched doorways. Elaborately framed portraits of Whitaker ancestors graced walls that were a foot deep.

"Wow," I said.

"It *is* big. Would you like tea or coffee, Samantha?"

"No thank you, I'm fine. Just eager to get started."

"This way, then."

Our footsteps echoed on the hardwood floor as we proceeded down a long passage. "From what I can tell, my father only lived on this side of the house. He kept a couple of bedrooms habitable upstairs, and seems to have spent the rest of his time in the kitchen, or here in the library."

We entered, and I gasped in wonder. It was immense—a library worthy of the finest ancestral homes in England—and it seemed to be the best-preserved room in the house. It was outfitted with ancient, comfortable-looking couches and chairs and an antique desk, and was lined with bookcases filled with thousands upon thousands of beautiful old books that stretched to the lofty ceiling.

"Since you work in a library," he said, "I don't suppose you'll find this all that extraordinary. But my father was proud of it."

"Are you kidding? This is amazing." The volumes, protectively stored behind tall glass doors, were all bound in leather in a variety of colors. A pair of large portraits hung above the massive hearth, featuring a man who was perhaps in his early forties and a demure young woman, about a decade younger, who were both elegantly attired in eighteenth-century dress. The woman wore an exquisite ruby necklace and matching earrings. "Who are they?"

"The first owner of the house, Lawrence Whitaker, and his wife Alice. Apparently she loved to read, and died rather young. It's said that he was very much in love with her, and so bereft at her passing, that he filled the library with books in her honor. Every generation after him seems to have added to the collection."

"It's truly outstanding."

"I suppose it is." He glanced around, as if really seeing it for the first time. "I've never spent much time in here."

"How could you stay away? If I lived here, this would be my favorite room."

"My father and grandfather wouldn't let me play in here or touch any of these books—they said they were too valuable. My dad and mum divorced when I was eleven, and after that I've lived elsewhere."

"I see." I couldn't take my eyes off the magnificent collection. My fingers itched to take the books off the shelves and examine them. "You're *really* going to sell all these?"

"I have no choice. My father left a ton of debts. I'll be lucky if I manage to break even after selling this place. But enough talk of doom and gloom." His eyes twinkled a bit mischievously now as he looked at me. "I have a confession to make."

"A confession?"

"After our conversation last night, I was so intrigued by what you said—that there might be a missing manuscript hidden in this house, or at the very least, a guest registry book of some kind verifying that your favorite authoress had once stepped inside these walls—I couldn't resist taking a look around myself."

My heart began to drum. "And?"

"I started by looking through this desk, which turned up nothing." He patted the beautiful antique desk, then gestured for me to follow him to one of the walls of bookcases. "Then I started in on these shelves. I got about a third of the way down this wall—I know I've barely scratched the surface in this room—and sorry, I didn't find a guest book yet—but look what I *did* find."

He stopped and pointed out a particular series of books lined up behind one of the glass doors. The twelve volumes were beautifully bound in dark blue leather and embellished with gold embossing and red and yellow flowers on the spine. I recognized them at once.

"It's the Chawton House edition of Jane Austen's novels and letters!" I said with awe. "There's a similar set at the Huntington

Library in Southern California, in slightly different bindings. What a stunning edition."

Anthony opened the cabinet, gently removed the first volume of *Pride and Prejudice* from the shelf, and handed it to me. "Is it valuable?"

"It certainly is." The book felt wonderful in my hands. I held it up to my nose and drank in its aroma. "I think I'm addicted to the smell of books. It's as comforting to me as Christmas."

Anthony smiled, pleased.

I opened the book to the flyleaf. The pages were crisp, white, and clean. "It was published in 1906. This edition is rare. I've been trying to locate a set for our university library for several years, without success. *If* you can find one, it's usually in the original bindings—and even then it's worth many thousands of dollars."

"What do you mean, 'original bindings'?"

"Before industrialization, books were often published in simple, plain cloth covers, with the assumption that buyers would have them rebound. The books were pretty ugly, to be honest. Private collectors with money generally had them bound in leather and beautifully embossed. This collection is gorgeous and would be worth a lot."

"It's nice to learn that members of my family had taste and were discriminating about the books they acquired." Anthony gazed around the room again with what seemed like newfound appreciation. Then, nodding toward the book in my hands, he added, "I admit, I couldn't resist taking a peek."

"A peek? What, you read *Pride and Prejudice*?"

"Just half a dozen chapters. I thought I'd be bored to tears—but to my surprise, you were right. It wasn't bad. I would have probably kept going if I hadn't been so tired."

I couldn't stop my smile. *Wasn't bad*—it was a funny way to describe a brilliant classic—yet how many times had I heard skeptical students make a similar comment at the beginning of a semester? "*Pride and Prejudice* has that effect on people. For many, it's their favorite Austen novel." Reluctantly, I returned the volume to the shelf.

"What's your favorite?" he asked.

"*Persuasion.* It was the last novel she completed before she died, and I think it's her most heartfelt and passionate work."

"What's it about?"

"It's about regret and second chances. The heroine is considered a washed-up spinster at age twenty-seven. She was persuaded years ago to turn down a proposal from the penniless naval officer she loved—a decision she greatly regrets. He returns a rich captain, so filled with bitterness that it takes a while before he can admit that she's still the love of his life."

He nodded politely, without comment. I could see that it was going to take some doing to bring this man around to my way of thinking.

Looking around the vast room with its many thousands of volumes, he said, "Well, I guess it's on to business. We have an ancient guest registry to find."

"If they had one," I mused, "you'd think they'd make it accessible, wouldn't you?"

"That's what I thought—that it wouldn't be buried too deeply, or shelved too high. I went through all of *these* cabinets last night, as far up as I could reach. How about if I continue on from here, and you start at the opposite corner." If our first go-through failed, he added, we could use the library ladder to search the upper shelves.

We got to work. I made a thorough investigation of the books on the lower shelves of the left side of the room. Most of the volumes were very old and looked like they hadn't been touched in decades. We worked slowly, handling everything with the greatest of care. Anthony soon discovered an ancient family Bible, inscribed with the records of his family history. Lawrence Whitaker's wife, Alice, died in 1789, only four years after the house was built. Lawrence was born in 1757 and died in 1814, leaving Greenbriar to his eldest son. There was a whole family tree listed after that, which Anthony had never seen before, and we both sat marveling over it for a while.

We then returned to our respective search areas and worked in relative silence for the next two hours. I coveted every beautifully bound volume I saw. They covered the gamut from classical fiction and poetry to history, biography, geography, medicine, and science. Many had been bound and shelved as matching sets, sometimes more for the sake of appearance than by subject.

I had just turned a corner and started on the next side of the room, when I discovered it.

A slim volume, it was bound in burgundy leather, with no markings on the cover or spine. It was stowed at the end of a row of scientific journals of a similar color and size. When I opened it to the first page, I yelped with excitement. Handwritten in ink, and obviously with a quill pen, were the words *Greenbriar—Guest Ledger.*

Anthony, who was sitting cross-legged on the floor halfway across the room, deeply interested in one of the many volumes he'd piled up beside him, looked over at me distractedly. "Did you find something?"

"Yes, this is it! Greenbriar—Guest Ledger!" The pages were filled with long lists of names and dates, inscribed in a variety of different hands. "It begins in September 1785, and has entries continuing up through 1940. It looks like they stopped using it around World War II, which is probably why your parents never mentioned it."

In seconds, Anthony was at my side. "Well done, you."

We crossed to the nearby couch and plunked down side by side. I thumbed through the volume, with him reading over my shoulder, to the entries for 1801.

And there it was.

> 6 July, 1801. Mr. and Mrs. George Austen, and daughters.

"George Austen was Jane's father!" I exclaimed with amazement.

Anthony uttered an expletive of shocked disbelief. "Oh my God. You were right. You were right!" Then he frowned. "Wait, I thought the letter said she lost the manuscript in 1802."

We stared at each other. I flipped ahead to the summer of 1802. There was another entry.

> 15 July, 1802. Mr. and Mrs. George Austen, and daughters C & J.

Score!

Anthony eagerly insisted that we check further, to see if there were any more Austen entries. But although we went back to the beginning and studied every page through 1817, the year Jane Austen died, we only found those two.

"She was here twice," I said excitedly. The entry didn't mention how long they'd stayed, but, I explained to Anthony, travel at that time was so difficult, time-consuming, and costly, that visitors generally came for at least a couple of weeks, often much longer.

"I wonder how they knew Lawrence Whitaker," he mused. "He wasn't a relative. Maybe he was a friend of her father's. George Austen knew all kinds of interesting people."

"This is incredible. Truly. I can hardly believe it. One of my ancestors actually knew Jane Austen. She slept in my family's house!" He grinned. "And now we have the thrill of the hunt."

"The thrill of the hunt?"

"Yes. Now that we know she was here, we move on to the larger question: where's that missing manuscript? What did Jane say? Let me see that letter again."

I took out the copy of the letter, and we studied it together.

"'*Do you recall my theory as to how it came to be lost? I still maintain that it was all vanity, nonsense, and wounded pride*,'" he read aloud. "What does she mean?"

"I don't know." I continued reading: "'*I should never have read it out to you that night during our stay but kept it safe with all the others.*' Maybe," I theorized, "in taking it out to read to Cassandra, she somehow misplaced it, and blames herself."

"If that's true, wouldn't she have asked Lawrence Whitaker to help her find it?"

"Not necessarily. She says to Cassandra, '*You did persuade me to tell no one about it while I was writing it.*' As if for some reason, she wanted to keep that manuscript a secret."

"Why, I wonder? And more to the point, after she left, wouldn't you think that *somebody* would have found it? And if so, knowing it was a work by Austen, why didn't they sell it?"

"They wouldn't have known it was hers. It wouldn't have had her name on it. This was 1802. Jane Austen didn't publish her first book until 1811, and even then, all her books were published anonymously. When she came here with her family, she was nobody—just the unmarried, twenty-six-year-old daughter of a retired clergyman. The manuscript, if someone found it, wouldn't have had any monetary value at the time."

"So . . . if someone in this house—one of the servants, a maid or a footman, or even Lawrence Whitaker himself—came upon an anonymous manuscript that wasn't worth anything, what would they do with it?"

"I suppose they'd read it—if they could read. They'd keep it if they liked it, or burn it if they didn't."

He grimaced. "Let's hope it's not the last option." After a paused, he added, "What would a Jane Austen manuscript look like?"

"From the few manuscripts we have as evidence, mostly of unfinished works, it seems, in Jane's mind, that they had to look like a book. She used to write on ordinary sheets of writing paper that she folded in half and hand-stitched along the spine. So it'd be a series of small paper booklets, each about eight pages in length."

"Do you think—presuming said person did *keep* the manuscript—there's even the remotest chance that it might still be stashed somewhere in this house?"

My heart leapt at the thought. "It's possible. But we're talking two hundred years. It could have been found, later, by someone who had no idea what it was, and moved any number of times." I glanced around the vast room we were sitting in. "How many rooms does this house have?"

"You don't want to know." We both sat lost in thought for a moment. "Where do people usually stash things?" he said.

"In the bottom of a dresser, or locked in a desk drawer, or in a box at the back of a closet. If it's valuable, in a safe."

He sighed. "There is a safe, in my father's old study, but it only contained his important papers and my mother's jewels. And if there *was* anything secret in a drawer or a closet, I would have found it decades ago."

"Really? Why's that?"

"I loved reading mystery novels growing up, and solving puzzles—things like the Rubik's cube—and I used to play detective in just about every room but this one. Looking for hiding places was my *raison d'etre.* I crawled under furniture and into wardrobes, I investigated every nook and cranny of this house. I found all sorts of things to spark a young boy's interest—but nothing remotely resembling a stack of old, handwritten manuscript booklets."

"Did you look in the attic or the cellar?"

He stared at me. "Now there's an idea. The attic and cellar are both huge. I didn't like going into either one when I was young and haven't seen them in ages." He stood abruptly. "Let's go take a look. I'm going to have to clear them out anyway at some point. I'll find some torches."

He returned a few minutes later with two flashlights. Anthony had to duck through the doorway as we climbed down the narrow, ancient staircase to the cellar. Adrenaline rushed through my veins. We were halfway down when I said, "I can't believe I'm here, and we're actually doing this—looking for a missing manuscript by one of the most beloved writers in history."

He stopped and turned, his eyes serious. "Samantha. Before we go any further, I should probably make sure we're clear about one thing."

"What?"

"We both know how unlikely it is that we'll come across anything. But if we do—you realize that whatever we might find would belong to me, right?"

The question took me by surprise. "Of course," I said, a bit offended that he'd even felt the need to ask.

He nodded, then moved on down the stairs. I followed him, frowning, wondering for a moment if Anthony's sudden interest in Jane Austen sprang not from excitement about the possibility of a newly discovered work, but instead from the money that it might bring. Because, undoubtedly, such a manuscript would be worth a great deal.

I shook off the thought, determined not to let it infect my mood. Whatever Anthony's motivation might be, at least he was on board—and he seemed to find the pursuit as exhilarating as I did. For the next two and a half hours, as we went through the cellar (cold, dark, creepy, and more or less empty) and the attic (warm, dark, musty, and very cluttered), I concentrated on the "thrill of the hunt," as he'd put it—filled with anticipation about what we might uncover.

There were electric lights throughout, but we used our flashlights to look in the dark corners. Anthony came upon all sorts of mementos from his childhood that unexpectedly stirred up fond memories. We found old furniture, family photos, boxes of toys, children's books, dusty Christmas decorations, discarded appliances, obsolete electronics, ancient camera equipment, an old telescope, bolts of fabric, and trunks of lovely vintage clothing and hats . . . but no bricked-up hiding places, and nothing resembling a manuscript.

"Bollocks," Anthony said at last, sitting down on one of the trunks.

"It was always a long shot," I admitted, "but I enjoyed looking. You have a wealth of wonderful family history here."

"I had no idea."

As we traipsed back downstairs, he looked at his watch. "It's two o'clock. No wonder I'm starving. Let's have lunch. I dashed out early this morning and picked up some groceries—I'm sure I can whip up a couple of fairly edible sandwiches."

I figured it was time to call it quits. "Thanks, but you don't have to feed me again—I've already taken up most of your day. Don't you need to get back to London tonight?"

"No, I've taken tomorrow off. I have a lot to do around here before I go home—but to tell you the truth, I've lost interest in it. How long were you planning to stay in the area?"

"I need to go back to London tomorrow, too."

"Well then, we're on the same timetable. We have to eat—we might as well do so together. And I think a ham sandwich on a bakery bun is the least I can do for the woman who proved that a world-famous authoress once spent the night at my childhood home."

I laughed. "All right, a ham sandwich it is."

We retreated to the kitchen, which was large, serviceable, and relatively clean although outmoded. "As you can see, it hasn't been updated in sixty years," Anthony said, as if in apology, "but everything still works."

I loved the look of the old cabinets, stove, and other appliances, and told him so. "I think it's quaint, and fits with the mood of the house. I'd hate to see it modernized."

"Well, that's the first thing the new owners will do, I'm sure—rip all this out and start over."

"Do you already have an offer?"

"No, but I listed it for sale yesterday, and I have my fingers crossed that something will come through soon."

The thought of his selling Greenbriar depressed me, so I changed the subject. We made lunch together, and sitting at the kitchen table, we chatted about this and that, comparing notes on our various travels, and on movies we liked. He loved the same mysteries, thrillers, and action films that I did, as well as many of the historical dramas and romantic comedies that I had watched many times. Yet somehow, he'd never seen a Jane Austen film—he admitted that he'd intentionally avoided them—and I told him he was really missing out.

Eventually, the conversation circled back to the quest at hand.

"I still can't get over the fact that we found Jane Austen's name in the family guest ledger," Anthony said as he sipped his Coke.

"If you let it be known, that little tidbit of information will be added to every Austen biography—and I wouldn't be surprised if the house *is* added to all those bus tours from London and Hampshire."

He grinned. "You're right—I hadn't thought of that. But the ledger isn't the finish line. I'm not done searching for the manuscript."

"You're not?" I said, surprised.

"I'm determined to find the thing. Aren't you?"

"Well, yes. But—"

"Can you imagine if I sold the house, and the new owner was to come upon the manuscript someday? I'd want to shoot myself."

I laughed. "You know *I'm* game. But where else should we look? We don't have a thing to go on."

"True. It's like looking for a needle in a haystack."

We both lapsed into thought as we finished eating. All at once, an idea occurred to me. "If the manuscript's in this house, I think I might know where it is."

"Where?"

"In the library."

"Why?"

"You said you used to play detective in every room in the house except that one."

"So?"

"So—it's unexplored territory."

"We spent three hours this morning looking through the library."

"We just looked at the *books*—and not all of them, not even close. It's a huge room. I can't explain it, but I have a feeling the manuscript is somewhere in that room. It's like when I bought that book of poetry the other day—something about it called out to me. I just knew I was supposed to buy it."

"Well, it's as good an idea as any I've come up with."

We cleaned up from lunch and returned to the library. My eyes were drawn to the series of cabinets with carved-oak doors that were built in beneath many of the bookcases.

"What's in those cupboards?" I asked.

Anthony admitted that he'd never looked inside them in his life.

We opened the first set of doors and found a cabinetful of old maps, covering not just Devon and the British Isles, but many countries in Europe and places farther afield including Asia, Africa, and the Americas. Many of them dated back to the 1800s and were truly remarkable, with fine engraving, beautiful hand coloring, and decorative floral or ivy borders. Recognizing their value, we carefully set them aside.

"Is it okay to be touching these?" Anthony asked. "I read somewhere that you're supposed to wear latex gloves when reviewing old documents."

"I never wear gloves to handle old books and paper—none of the conservators that I know do, either. We sometimes use cotton gloves when handling metal or photographs, to avoid leaving fingerprints—but they don't fit well, and they're clumsy. As long as your hands are clean, and you work gently, the oils on your fingers don't do all that much damage to paper. You'd do far more mechanical damage by fumbling with latex gloves."

The second and third cupboards contained ancient film canisters from what we guessed to be home movies, and more old photograph albums. One of the albums was from Anthony's childhood. We glanced through it, smiling at his baby pictures and shots of his parents and himself as a boy. These seemed to stir up memories, both good and bad. At the back of the album, he came upon a handful of letters and dozens of colorful greeting cards he said he'd handmade as a child.

"All the birthday and Father's Day cards I made for him over the years," Anthony murmured in quiet surprise. "And my letters . . . I had no idea he kept them." Frowning, he put them back in the album and moved on.

The fourth cabinet was stuffed with old file folders full of documents. It was the closest thing we'd seen to a manuscript, and our hopes rose.

"Some of these go back a long time," Anthony said, awestruck, as we started looking through them. "Look, here's one that's a hundred years old."

We spent half an hour sitting on the floor, carefully sifting through the old documents, and separating out the ones that looked the most valuable. They included hunting licenses, deeds, old letters, and even ancient, architectural records for the house—but no manuscripts.

"These are fascinating," I said. "Many are worthy of being in a museum."

Anthony agreed. "Still—they're hardly what we were looking for."

We sat in disappointed silence for a moment. Just then, my

cell phone rang. I pulled it from my pocket. There was a text message from Stephen. We had the following brief text conversation:

How's it going?

Found proof! Austen was here!

U serious?

Yes!! Guest ledger shows she visited twice.

Wow! Amazing.

Sadly . . . no ms.

Oh. Sorry. Will I C U tomorrow?

Yes.

Ok. Later. Bye.

Bye.

I texted a similar, brief update to Laurel Ann, then put my phone away.

From our seats on the floor, Anthony glanced at the portraits of Lawrence and Alice Whitaker, the first master and mistress of Greenbriar. "If only paintings could speak. I'd swear they know something."

The couple gazed down at us as if in possession of some great secret. "Wait," I said. "Didn't you say Lawrence Whitaker built this library in his wife's memory?"

"So I was told."

"If he loved her that much, he must have kept some precious mementos to remember her by. Do you have anything like that? Her jewels, or maybe love letters?"

"Not that I know of."

"Maybe he hid them for safekeeping behind a secret panel."

"A secret panel?" He sounded both amused and skeptical.

"Why not?" I returned lightly. "Doesn't every old English manor house have a secret panel?"

"In all my searching as a child, I never discovered one." Anthony paused, his eyes widening with sudden interest. "But then, I never searched *this* room, did I?"

We leapt to our feet. The floor-to-ceiling bookcases were all made of oak, there were large wooden pillars at each corner of the room, and practically every surface that wasn't a window was paneled.

"You start at that end," he said, "and I'll begin here."

As I moved through the room, looking for any sign of a line or crack that might indicate a hidden door, pressing here, there, and everywhere to see if a panel might reveal itself and spring open, I felt a bit ridiculous—but at the same time, I couldn't help smiling. It truly felt like a treasure hunt, and I knew the prize, if there was one, would be beyond our imaginings.

We studied every pillar, post, and panel. We checked out every inch of the mantelpiece. We looked behind all the pictures on the walls. Nothing.

I sighed and moved to the couch, where I sank down wearily.

Anthony dropped into a chair, equally discouraged. "If Jane Austen really did lose or misplace a manuscript here, either someone found it and took it to God knows where, or they tossed it ages ago, having no idea what it was."

"I'm sorry to have wasted your time."

"It wasn't a complete waste. It was fun." He smiled at me, a look that openly revealed how much he'd enjoyed these moments of camaraderie we'd shared.

I couldn't deny that I returned the sentiment in kind. The expression on his face was so captivating, it made my heart beat a little faster. It was like we were coconspirators in a quest for a precious Austen relic. "It *has* been fun. It was lovely to think, for a little while at least, that we *might* actually find something."

"And in the process, look how many interesting things we've

come across." He gestured toward the piles of stuff we'd emptied from the cupboards, most of which were still strewn across the floor.

I stared at the empty cupboards. A sudden prickle ran up my spine. "Anthony: did you check the back of any of those cabinets?"

"The back?"

"Yes. The back."

We exchanged a look. In unison, we darted to the last cupboard we'd searched through—the one that had held all the old documents—and fell to our knees. I half crawled inside, then felt all along the smooth wooden surface of the rear wall to see if there was evidence of an embedded door. I couldn't find any.

"Press on it," Anthony said.

I laid my palm flat against the back wall and pressed. Still nothing.

"Let me try."

Anthony wedged himself into the small, confined space beside me, until our faces were inches apart, and his lean, muscled arm and the length of his torso were pressed against mine. My heart began pumping loudly in my ears—an effect, I told myself, that had nothing to do with his proximity but was due entirely to the excitement of the search and the anticipation of what we might find.

"I think I feel a crack," Anthony said. He pressed hard on the far right side of the back wall.

Suddenly, as if by magic, a previously invisible door in the rear wall of the cupboard began to swing open toward us, revealing a recessed alcove. We gasped in astonishment as we backed away.

"Dear God in Heaven," Anthony said.

Within the hidden alcove lay two wooden boxes. Anthony

took them out and set them on the carpet before us. The first box looked like a jewelry case. It was about the size and height of a fat, hardcover book, was veneered in figured rosewood with brass embellishments, and styled in the form of a small sarcophagus with a hinged lid.

The second box was much larger—about the size of a man's shoe box—and was intricately inlaid on all sides with a marquetry design made up of different colors of polished wood.

I was nearly paralyzed with excitement. "They're beautiful. I wonder how long they've been in there."

"A long time, I'd wager."

Neither box appeared to have a keyhole or other visible lock, but the rosewood box had a little brass latch. Anthony gently lifted the lid. The inside was lined in royal blue velvet that appeared extremely old although it was in excellent shape. Nestled inside was a small, hand-painted cameo portrait of a young woman who looked like Alice Whitaker, along with a lock of hair, and a stunning ruby necklace and earrings.

I gasped. "It's Alice! And the jewels she's wearing in the portrait!"

"They're incredible," Anthony said, as we studied the rubies.

We paused and exchanged a glance, wordlessly sharing the same thought. *What was in the other box?*

I picked it up. It was completely sealed shut, with no visible opening. "How on earth do you open it?"

"I bet I can figure it out." Anthony began working at the inlaid wooden design meticulously with his fingertips. "I think it's a puzzle box. I had several of these when I was a boy."

I watched in suspense, mystified, as he continued to press on the sides of the box, turning and twisting it this way and that, until, to my surprise, a series of narrow wooden strips that had been hidden by the design began to materialize and slide left and right.

To my amazement, miraculously, the lid suddenly loosened and slid all the way open, revealing its hidden cargo:

A stack of small paper booklets.

Dozens and dozens of them.

Booklets made of ordinary sheets of white writing paper, folded in half, and hand-stitched along the spine. Booklets in remarkably pristine condition, all covered in a small, neat handwriting that I instantly recognized.

The hair stood up on the back of my neck. I could hardly breathe.

I picked up the first booklet in the pile. Atop the title page, penned by quill in black-brown ink, it read: *The Stanhopes*.

The neat, flowing hand of the prose below was unmistakable. Although it included cross-outs, insertions, revisions, and capitalizations of some words in a manner no longer in common practice, the text was eminently legible. I read the first paragraph aloud.

My heart seemed to be leaping inside my chest.

"Oh my God . . . It sounds like her. It *has* to be hers!"

"Well, what are we waiting for?" Anthony said, sitting down on the floor beside me, beaming. "Let's read it."

The Stanhopes

VOLUME ONE

....

CHAPTER I

For nearly all of her twenty-one years, Rebecca Stanhope had lived very happily in the same house on a quiet, tree-shaded lane in the tiny village of Elm Grove, a situation so pleasant and comfortable that she had no desire to alter it in any way. A lively, intelligent, handsome, and accomplished young woman, Rebecca awakened every morning to glimpse the same prospect from her casement window—a lovely view of the grassy slope behind the rectory down which she used to roll as a child—a sight which never failed to make her smile.

Rebecca loved every thing about Elm Grove Rectory. It was not a perfect house; the walls had no cornices, the ceilings were plain plaster without a single ornately carved cherub, and the doorways were so low that many gentlemen had to stoop to move from one chamber to another. But with its balanced, two-storeyed Georgian front, it maintained a dignified, orderly appearance, and it had enough bedrooms, parlours, pantries, offices, and attic chambers—resulting from the many improvements which her father had made over the years—to comfortably accommodate a household of eight, with ample space for guests. It included a glebe of sufficient size for one cow to graze, a neat, enclosed garden for the growing of fruits and vegetables, and surrounding woods which were very picturesque.

Rebecca loved the village of Elm Grove, too, and was content in the belief that she would spend all the days of her life within the confines of its borders, continuing in blissful ignorance of its many deficiencies. The village was very small, and at first glance, had little to recommend it. Its population numbered a mere twenty-seven families, and it was comprised of but a few outlying farms and a single row of cottages scattered for half a mile along a rutted lane. Only two houses were superior to those of the yeomen and labourers,—the manor-house and its park at one end, and the rectory (adjacent to the church) at the other. There was no inn, and not a single shop. Its residents were obliged to go to Atherton, three miles away, to find an apothecary or to buy cloth, ink, drawing paper, or a pair of gloves; and as the Stanhopes had no carriage, the women of the household had to make the most of infrequent visits from travelling salesmen to buy lace and stockings. The Stanhopes' only true companionship in the parish were the Mountagues, who were first in consequence, wealthy, and much respected. None of these aspects, however, were seen as evils by Rebecca. To her, Elm Grove, with its many comforts, familiar walks, and friendly neighbours, was and always had been all perfection; an idyllic place which could not be superseded by any other—and her father shared her opinion.

Rebecca was the second daughter of the Reverend Mr.

William Stanhope, an amiable, scholarly, highly principled man with a bright and hopeful disposition. The only child of a country surgeon, whose money upon his death (through carelessness in not altering his will) had all gone to his second wife, the young Mr. Stanhope had not allowed his destitute position to dampen his spirits. As a young man, he travelled, worked where and when he could, and lived much in the world. At age two-and-twenty, through the grace of a Fellowship, he entered Oxford; and three years later, by joining energy of character to superior abilities, he earned a divinity degree.

Mr. Stanhope might have stayed a Fellow of St. John's for ever, if not for his desire to marry; and though it took more than eight years to come about, through the patronage of an old school friend, Sir Percival Mountague, he was offered an incumbency at Elm Grove. He then sought the hand of the woman he loved, and married her. Margaret Parker was as beautiful and clever as she was kind; a gentle, well-informed woman of pleasing address and considerable conversational powers, who shared his values and interests, and returned his affections. She bore him two children; first Sarah, and three years later, Rebecca.

Mr. Stanhope was a model parish priest, entirely devoted to his community, and an excellent husband and father. Only two faults stood in the way of his being considered a truly flawless individual: he possessed a tendency towards being overly fastidious (which manifested itself in a rare disgust of dirt); and he had no head for finances, giving himself to acts of impulsive, unthinking generosity, which put his own family in difficult straits at times. The Elm Grove living, at three hundred pounds, was not large, but could be improved by the collection of tithes; however, Mr. Stanhope, sensitive to the difficulties of his parishioners, was averse to such collection. Fortunately, his wife brought an inheritance, the interest of which added to his income; this he further embellished by teaching schoolboys he took in as boarders—a practice which profited his daughters, as they, in turn, received the benefits of his tutelage.

Life went on quite happily in this manner in the Stanhope household for many years. Mr. Stanhope and his wife esteemed a tidy household, and were enthusiasts of music, writing, and literature. He was proud of his ever-increasing collection of books, which filled the shelves of his study. Mrs. Stanhope happily performed all those duties expected of a rector's wife, raised their girls, and served as house-mistress to the succession of boys who lived and schooled with them. Sarah and Rebecca, being very close, chose to share a bedroom, and many a night was spent whispering away to each other in the darkness. The two girls did, however, have very different interests.

Sarah was an obedient student, but far more interested in drawing, needlework, and gardening; and she had no aptitude for music. Rebecca loved music from an early age. She was accomplished at playing the pianoforte by age eight, and later the harp; and she possessed a fine voice, which her family and their friends loved to hear. She was skilled at drawing, and good with languages; but more than any thing else, Rebecca adored reading. Every lesson entranced her, and made her eager to learn more.

When Rebecca reached twelve years of age, a small tremor shook the foundations of her carefully ordered life. Mr. and Mrs. Stanhope decided that their daughters required more accomplishments and a more worldly edification than could be taught at home, and sent them off to boarding-school.

The experience proved less than satisfactory. The establishment, situated at a remote country house some ten miles distant, was, to Rebecca, nothing more than a place at which young ladies, for an exorbitant price, attained heightened vanity and elegant accomplishments, without any actual learning. She felt she had achieved more in six days via her father's tutelage than in six whole months at school; and she and Sarah both missed Elm Grove and their parents dreadfully. After a year, the exercise was thankfully ended, and they were brought home.

At age eighteen, Sarah married one of her father's former pupils, Mr. Charles Morris, a clergyman who had received an appointment in Buckinghamshire. This loss to Rebecca was very great, for it took away her best friend and confidante; but additional sorrow lay on the horizon. Her mother fell seriously ill. It became Rebecca's responsibility to nurse her, a task which she took on with devotion, bestowing on Mrs. Stanhope all the tender care which a loving heart can provide. Although the advice of the local surgeon was strictly followed, along with that of two physicians in town, Margaret Stanhope did not rally. When she died, the family grieved long and deeply. Mrs. Stanhope's place could never be filled; yet somehow they must go on.

Without his wife to assist him, Mr. Stanhope closed down the school. Without the company of the boys who used to tread up and down the stairs, and enliven their dinner table with boisterous conversation, the rectory was very quiet; but Rebecca and her father became accustomed to it, and grew to prefer it. At age fifteen, Rebecca was mistress of the house, proving herself useful, and assisting her father just as she ought, as she continued her education under his guidance. Over the course of the next six years, a strong bond formed between them. Despite the disparity in their ages (he was now sixty years of age, having not married early), they became each other's dearest and closest companion. She was her father's prime source of comfort, and he hers; they had much in common intellectually; they loved and admired each other with all their hearts.

Twice a month, she and her father dined at Claremont Park, the elegant home of their patron, Sir Percival Mountague, with whom her father enjoyed a weekly game of cards. On occasion, they dined with friends from the adjacent parishes, where she was asked to play and sing. But most evenings, they spent alone at home, either reading aloud from the paper, or from whatever book had been newly purchased or acquired from the circulating library.

Each and every newspaper and volume seemed to Rebecca like a window to the world, which fascinated her with its many cultures and diversities; yet, she had no desire to move beyond the safety and comfort of that window. She had never undertaken a journey longer than ten miles—had never even seen her sister's house, it being too distant for a day's excursion—and the pleasure of her sister's company was now restricted to but a few weeks at Christmas or midsummer, when Sarah and her husband and family came to them. These visits, which filled the rectory with the happy bustle, noise, and confusion peculiar to children, and obliged Mr. Stanhope to give up any attempt at household order, made Rebecca very happy. She wished they could occur more frequently; indeed, she dearly missed her sister, and their regular, intimate correspondence could never make up for the joys of a face-to-face conversation; but she contented herself with what was offered.

Although there were no longer any young ladies of

Rebecca's age with whom she could keep company in Elm Grove (the Mountagues' youngest daughters, like Sarah, having been removed by matrimony), Rebecca was busy and content. Every morning before breakfast, she practised her music. She took daily walks in the nearby meadows. She worked in the garden and the poultry yard, sewed her father's shirts and household linens, made clothes for the poor, visited the cottagers when they were sick, and read to their children (teaching many to read).

Sarah understood and honoured Rebecca's affection for her home and its environs, yet she worried.

"The true difficulty in the neighbourhood," Sarah had pointed out on her last visit, "is the complete lack of eligible young men." How, she wondered, was Rebecca ever to marry? The balls at the assembly room in Atherton were sparsely attended, by men with no pretensions to culture. The curate-in-charge of Farleigh was married. The vicar of Calderbury was a widower of fifty. The Mountagues had only one son, who was promised to one of his cousins. Was Rebecca destined to be an old maid, dependent on her father all her life, never to give her heart to any one, or to know the joy of raising a family? Rebecca calmly insisted that if she *was* never to marry, she would graciously accept her fate, for her life and heart were full in caring for her father, and in her activities and associations in the parish; and as to children, one must never discount the importance of being an aunt.

It was now a mild evening in early August, the sun hanging low in the sky, the air redolent with the fragrance of roses in bloom and the gentle sound of the breeze brushing the trees. Rebecca sat with her father on a garden bench beneath a large elm, listening to him read aloud from *The Female Quixote*. She loved to hear him read; he was highly skilled at the activity, imbuing his performance with spirit and feeling. When Mr. Stanhope finished a chapter and closed the volume, she gave a happy sigh, drinking in the quiet of the surroundings, thinking how fortunate she was, and how happy and content.

"What a thrilling and amusing story!" commented she cheerfully. "Such refined language and wit—and such an astute imitation of Cervantes!"

"The plot is meticulously constructed," agreed Mr. Stanhope, "and the book has great moral vision. Every time I read it, I find something new to appreciate."

Some minutes were given over to further discussion of the merits of Charlotte Lennox's work, a conversation which brought pleasure and gratification to both parties. Then Rebecca said, "Mama would be pleased to know that we are reading *The Female Quixote* to-night. I can see why it was her favourite book."

"Your mother did, indeed, have exquisite taste in literature," returned Mr. Stanhope with a smile. A handsome man, he was every where admired for his white and glossy hair, which curled above his ears. "Did I ever tell you, my dear Rebecca, the story of how I met your mother? It is a most delightful and amusing tale."

Rebecca had heard the story so many times ever since she was a little child, that she could recite every word by heart;—but being of a sweet and benevolent nature, and knowing how much pleasure her father had in the telling, she only smiled, and answered, "I would love to hear it, papa."

They stood and walked along the gravel path between the lawn and the shrubbery encircling the garden, as Mr. Stanhope recited the anecdote in all its minute details, animatedly recounting how beautiful her mother had looked that day, the colour and style of the dress she had worn, and how he had made it his business to lay wooden boards across a muddy road so that she might cross it unsullied.

"I have never seen such a quagmire as I did that day—truly frightful!" said he at the conclusion of the tale.

Rebecca, who had come to regard to her father's peculiar antipathy to dirt with fondness and good humour, yet could not prevent herself from saying in a tender and teasing voice, "I am sure it was a very dreadful pool of mud, papa! How gallant it was of you to preserve mama's delicate shoes from absolute ruin. No wonder she fell in love with you."

Her father, not detecting the gentle irony in her statement, said with great seriousness, "It was but the work of a moment. One never can tell when a spontaneous action, entirely unpremeditated, might change one's life. I was very lucky, Rebecca, to have found your mother. I only hope you are as lucky one day, to find your life's mate."

"I hope so, too," returned Rebecca with a smile.

"If only your mother were here with us to-day," added he, sighing. "There is something I would very much like her to know."

"What is that, papa?"

"Mr. Fitzroy has just informed me that after counting the proceeds from Sunday's collection, we have at last amassed the sum required to purchase our new bells for the church tower."

"Papa!" cried Rebecca with delight. "I knew you had nearly approached your goal, but I had no idea of your reaching it already. You truly have the amount entire—one hundred and fifty pounds?"

"I do. It was that last generous contribution from Mr. Brudenell, our neighbour at Farleigh, which helped put us over the top. I cannot tell you how delighted I am.—After two long years, to have the money at last! Your mother would be very proud."

"Indeed she would." Rebecca could not forget how often and how earnestly Mrs. Stanhope had applied to her husband on the subject, insisting that their existing bells were too small and too ancient, and so badly cracked as to be unsightly. Three brand-new bells, she said, would be a welcome addition, and far more sonorous than two. To that end, and in her memory, Mr. Stanhope and the churchwarden had been working tirelessly the past two years, to raise the money for their purchase.

"There is just one matter that distresses me," said Mr. Stanhope. "To commission the bells, I am obliged to go to the foundry in London, John Warner and Sons, and deliver the required sum in advance."

"Oh." Rebecca understood his unexpressed concern; for in the years since she had been born, Mr. Stanhope had never once left the county of Hampshire.

"It requires a journey of two days in each direction," added Mr. Stanhope, "with an overnight stop en route, *and* a night in town—which means I shall be gone five full days."

"What is five days?" said Rebecca, in an encouraging tone. "Truly, papa, it is nothing. You will be gone and back again before you know it."

"But travel subjects one to all kinds of dirt. The roads are so dusty, and there is the danger of the vehicle overturning, or becoming stuck in mire. The beds in the coaching inns have been slept on by countless strangers, and as to dining—I hate to think of it."

Rebecca was pained to see him so distressed. "You can bring your own plate and linens, papa. And I could accompany you, if you wish—if I might be of any help, to keep your things tidy and ease your burden."

"Oh! No, child! I would not think of it. Naturally, I would be glad of your company, but I should never subject you to the rigours of a long journey. You would not like London. It is a very dirty city. And in any case, it is impractical. If you came, it would more than double the expense. We should require *two* chambers or a suite of rooms at the inns, and I should be obliged to hire a post-chaise. On my own, I can travel by stage."

"By stage! Papa, you detest public coaches."

"I do, but I must practise economy wherever I can. I am still in debt for all the recent improvements to the house. That new bow window," said he, pointing, as they passed, to the fashionable addition which provided both space and light in his study, "cost a pretty penny, not to mention the repairs to the roof."

"Well, if we cannot afford it," said Rebecca, truly very relieved that she did not have to go, "then I suppose you *must* go without me. And papa, consider that although you may be obliged to undergo some discomfort, it is all for a good purpose."

"How right you are, my dear Rebecca," said he with a nod, his smile slowly returning. "Pray, forgive the complaints and peculiarities of an old man. I have a duty, and I shall perform it. I am humbled by the sacrifices which our parishioners have made on the way to this achievement, and comforted by the knowledge that we shall at long last realise your dear mother's dream."

Rebecca cheerfully plunged her energies into assisting Mr. Stanhope with the preparations for his journey, and learning what she must do while he was away. Although the greatest portion of the money for the three new bells had been raised in coin, Mr. Stanhope had been regularly changing the money into pound notes at the bank. He corresponded with the foundry, and a fortnight later saw Rebecca kissing him good-bye on the door-step, where a hired gig was to take him to Atherton, from whence he intended to catch the public coach.

"Your plate and linen are packed in your trunk," said Rebecca, "and I made a small luncheon for you; it is in your bag."

"Thank you, my dearest," said he, giving her an affectionate embrace. "Do not worry about me. I shall return on Friday night."

As he boarded the conveyance, Rebecca realised how much she would miss him during his absence, for in the past eight years, she had not been parted from him for so much as twenty-four hours; and she began counting the days until she would see his smile again.

To her surprise and dismay, the event occurred far sooner than anticipated. On Tuesday evening—the very day after his departure—Mr. Stanhope returned in a state of great anxiety. A calamity had struck. He had broken his journey, as planned, with an overnight stay at the King's Arms at Leatherhead, Surrey; his progress there by stage had been uneventful; he had enjoyed a good dinner, and had slept soundly in a chamber that was surprisingly clean. But that morning, when he went to pay his bill, he discovered that nearly all the money in his pocketbook was gone!

....

Chapter II

"Dear God!" cried Rebecca. "Gone?"

"Gone! Not only my money, but the hundred and fifty pounds belonging to the church. Only a single one-pound note remained."

"Papa, this is terrible! Could the money have been stolen while on the stage-coach?"

"No." Mr. Stanhope paced back and forth in the parlour, wringing his hands as he spoke, his eyes quite wild with anguish. "I had it with me when I arrived. I distinctly recall it, for I paid for my dinner, and—" He hesitated, blushing slightly. "Afterwards, I played a game of cards with two well-dressed, congenial fellows."

"Could you have accidentally left the money at the card-table?"

He shook his head. "All day, and all evening, I was very conscious of the fact that I had the church's money with me, and was very protective of it. We only played speculation, and only for an hour, for I was tired. I bet very little—less than the price of my meal. I know I had my pocketbook with me, and all the money intact, when I returned to my room."

"Let us think this through together, papa," said Rebecca, striving to be calm. "Did you place the money somewhere for safe-keeping, before you retired?"

"No."

"Perhaps you did, and have just forgotten. Did you search the room?"

"I checked every inch of the room. I went through all my pockets and my bag, but could not find the money anywhere. And I tell you: it was in my pocketbook."

"When was the last time you saw your pocketbook?"

"I cannot recall exactly. I may have placed it on the bedside table before I slept—although I might have left it in my coat pocket."

"Well then, some one must have stolen the money while you slept."

"That is impossible, for I made certain to lock the chamber door, and I slept with the key beside me. It is a mystery, Rebecca. I applied to the innkeeper this morning, and made enquiries of the chambermaid, and all the guests at breakfast. No one knew a thing about it. Dear God! What am I to do? All those people's hard-earned money—vanished! An hundred and fifty pounds! Two years it took to raise it! I had barely the resources to pay my bill. I am obliged to the innkeeper, who took pity on me, and was kind enough to loan me my return fare."

"Oh, papa." Rebecca sank down onto a chair, very distraught. "This is a horrible turn of events."

"What am I to tell the parishioners? How can I face them?"

"You will; you *must*. Papa, it is not your fault."

"Indeed it is. I am entirely responsible for this misfortune."

"But how can you be, if the money simply disappeared?"

He stared at the carpet, a mortified look on his countenance. "Over supper at the inn, I chatted with the people at my table. They asked the purpose of my journey, and being in a conversational mood, I recounted it—all about the new bells, and how much money we had raised. Any one could have overheard. I engaged in a similar conversation with the gentlemen at the card-table. I suppose I should have been more discreet; but I was not. Somehow, this morning,

I cannot think how or when, the money was taken from me." Shaking his head in perplexity, he added, "I must tell Sir Percival immediately."

That evening, Mr. Stanhope went to Claremont Park to secure an audience with his patron. Rebecca waited in a state of such fevered anticipation, that she was unable to concentrate on her needlework, or on the book she attempted to read.

The clock in the hall was just striking nine when Mr. Stanhope returned. Rebecca ran to meet him in the entry hall. The drawn look on his countenance, and the hunched attitude of his shoulders as he hung his hat, were so out of the ordinary, and conveyed such mute distress, that Rebecca knew at once he had received no positive reception, and she acutely felt his pain. She embraced him and led him into the parlour, where she ensured that he was seated comfortably before asking what had happened. It was some moments before he was composed enough to speak, and when he did, she learned thus:

He met with Sir Percival. He gave him a full and honest account of all that had occurred. In view of the circumstances, he felt it would be honourable to offer to tender his resignation—fully expecting that his patron would refuse such a notion outright, and respond with sympathy and support. To his dismay, the opposite took place.

Sir Percival, after a lengthy silence, during which time he seemed to be processing the news with both surprise and deliberation, issued the following pronouncement: that it was a very sorry business, but he believed Mr. Stanhope's offer to be entirely correct and proper; that his tenants, in view of the circumstances—in particular, the fact that Mr. Stanhope had *played cards* the night of the money's disappearance—would no doubt demand it; that Mr. Stanhope was rapidly approaching the age of retirement in any case; that he himself had thought for some time that the infusion of fresh, young blood to run the parish would not be a bad idea; that a new man with new ideas, who did not gamble, and who would not be averse to collecting tithes, would improve the value of the incumbency; and that, in short, Mr. Stanhope *should* resign, and as soon as possible.

Rebecca listened to all this with astonishment, and when he had finished, cried,

"I cannot believe it! After all that you have done for this community—after an unblemished twenty-eight-year career in the parish, where you are loved by one and all—Sir Percival wants you to resign at such an early age, over some stolen funds? You are only sixty! Many clergymen retain their positions well into their seventies or eighties. It is most unfair! It was bad enough to complain about the tithes—for why should *he* care if you enrich yourself or not, by taxing his tenants? But to cite, as an example of unacceptable behaviour, that you played at cards—when you and he have engaged together in that harmless entertainment every Thursday evening for nearly three decades, at his very own house—it is unconscionable! With this ridiculous invective, papa, Sir Percival did not directly accuse you of incompetence, but he very clearly implied it!"

"Yes," replied her father, frowning, "and yet I understand his position. There are many who will agree with him. Even though I have never in all my life lost more than six shillings at any game—for you know that is where I stop, say good-night, and go home—there is in general a prejudice against clergymen who gamble. Suspicion will be aroused. But that is not the worst of it; the worst is not *how* the money came to be lost, but that it is *gone*. I am sure I shall never be forgiven for this. I could never hold my head up in church again. I have no wish to resign, Rebecca; yet it is clearly time for me to go. Which is why I have acquiesced to Sir Percival's demands."

"You did not!" cried Rebecca in anguish.

"It is done. Sir Percival insisted that he himself will find a new man to take charge in a timely fashion. I admit, I am very much grieved. I admire the good people of this parish. I love my work here. I will greatly miss it." With a deep sigh, he continued, "My other regret is on your account, my dear: for in giving up my post, I must also give up this house."

Rebecca nodded and lapsed into a brief, unhappy silence. To leave the rectory, where she had lived all her life! To leave Elm Grove for ever! It was unthinkable! Tears started in her eyes, and she looked away, not wanting her own suffering to add to her father's pain. "Surely you will not be out of work for long, papa. You will find a new post somewhere."

"That is unlikely. Oxford and Cambridge are producing more ordained clergymen to-day than there are positions to fill. Another benifice will be difficult, if not impossible to find, particularly in the circumstances in which I now find myself. How can I apply to a bishop or any other person of influence and power, with my career and reputation so blemished?" His face was so haggard, it seemed that ten years had been added to his age. "No, my dear Rebecca; I am afraid that my clerical career is finished."

Rebecca hardly knew how to reply; her mind was in a whirl, and she was filled with grief. "Where will we go?" asked she at length, her voice catching.

"I hardly know. I have very little in the way of savings.

Without my regular income, our circumstances will be severely reduced. We will not even have enough to rent a house."

"Oh!"

He was silent a moment. Then, exerting himself, with resolution he said, "The Lord giveth, and he taketh away. This is indeed a great blow; but he has a plan, which we can not comprehend now, but shall understand in time. Somehow, we shall make do."

"No!" cried Rebecca, rising and shaking her head. "We shall *not* make do. I will not stand for this, papa. It is not just! I shall speak with Sir Percival myself, and see what can be done."

Although Mr. Stanhope attempted to dissuade her from a pursuit which he deemed to be fruitless, Rebecca was determined: she would go to Claremont Park the next morning, confront Sir Percival herself, and plead their case.

....

Chapter III

Walking briskly, Rebecca covered the distance to the gates of Claremont Park in a quarter of an hour; from there, it was another quarter mile through the park to the manor-house itself. The sun was shining, and birds sang in the trees, but Rebecca was insensible of it, her thoughts entirely consumed by the ill treatment her father had received at the hands of his patron. Mr. Stanhope was normally so self-assured and buoyant. To see him cast down, possessed by worry and doubt, was distressing indeed. She was angry, very angry;

and she meant to make her feelings known to the instrument of all the evil, with a view to changing the dreadful conclusion which had been drawn.

The park lane curved in its downward slope towards the magnificent edifice of brick and stone. Rebecca took her customary shortcut across the great lawn, and was halfway to the residence when she perceived three men approaching from the woods beyond, having just gone fishing. The first was Sir Percival himself, a tall, robust man with thick grey hair, dark, piercing eyes, and a red face.

He was accompanied by his only son and heir, Brook Mountague, a boisterous man of three-and-twenty, who had a predilection for sport, and was well liked by his peers for his friendly disposition and easy, unaffected manners. By no means a scholar, Mr. Mountague had devoted the majority of his time at Oxford to cultivating his social life, and embarking on a riotous career of pranks, dares, and wagers, which had resulted in his being suspended and rusticated for part of several terms—a consequence he had always laughed off, while happily spending his free time hunting and fishing. He had managed to graduate, and was then established by his indulgent father in comfortable gentleman's lodgings in the West End of London. Mr. Mountague currently divided his time between country and town, enjoying the life of the well-bred and financially independent bachelor, until that day, a year or two hence, when it had been decreed that he would settle down and please his parents by marrying a particular, selected cousin.

The third man was Mr. Philip Clifton, the handsome, youngest son of Sir Percival's favourite sister;—who must be visiting, Rebecca reflected, as she knew he lived in West

Sussex. She had met Philip Clifton on occasions too numerous to count over the years, when he had visited at Claremont Park with or without his family. As children, she and Sarah had played often and happily with him and the other Mountague and Clifton offspring, who made up a sizeable group when all assembled.

When Rebecca was nine years old, however (and Philip a lad of thirteen), he had done two things which were now carved into her memory. Her family had been invited to the manor-house for a Christmas party. While gathered with the other girls and engaged in drawing, Philip had made fun of her picture, calling it a terrible scribble. Later, he behaved even more poorly. Rebecca had been asked to sing. Although self-conscious and uncertain at that young age with regard to her ability, she stood up before every one, and sang as well as she could. Throughout her performance, Philip and Brook made rude faces at her; and when every body else told her how well she had done, Philip said she had sounded like two cats fighting. Both boys had run away laughing. Rebecca was mortified and went home in tears.

In the years that followed, Philip did his best to avoid her whenever he came to visit at Claremont Park. He appeared to be amiable around others, but while in her presence he was moody and silent. She did not understand from whence this dislike sprung, for *she* had done nothing that she could recall to offend *him*.

When the young men went off to Oxford, Rebecca saw less and less of them. Having matured herself, she could now laugh at those early incidents as merely foolish acts of youth, although it still made her smart *just a bit* to think of them. Whenever she encountered Brook at the manor-house, she smiled at his lively behaviour and took no offence at his jokes. Of Philip Clifton, she had also hoped to form a new and more favourable opinion, but she had not seen him these three years past; she only knew that he had finished at university, had been ordained, and was settled in a curacy some distance away.

Upon catching sight of her, the group exchanged a discomfited glance, which conveyed to Rebecca that the young men were already acquainted with her father's misfortune. How, she wondered, had the subject been broached? Had Sir Percival made her father the villain in the piece? She prayed that the words she had practised in her mind through a sleepless night should come to her aid and prove both civil and persuasive.

A few minutes more brought them all within speaking range.

"Miss Stanhope!" cried Mr. Brook Mountague, holding up his catch, as bows and a curtsey were exchanged. "If you have come for dinner, you are too early; these fish were still swimming just moments ago."

"I had no idea of dining with you, sir," replied she, in as cheerful a tone as she was able. After greeting Sir Percival, she added, "How nice to see you, Mr. Clifton. I had not heard of your coming to Claremont Park."

Mr. Clifton only briefly met her gaze. "I arrived this morning. I had business in Winchester, and thought to stop and see my uncle before returning home."

"I see you have made a fine catch."

"It is a fine day for fishing," said Sir Percival.

"Every summer day in these parts is a fine day for fishing, when you employ the best bait and hooks!" cried Brook Mountague with animation, clapping Mr. Clifton on the back. "As my cousin well knows from our many expeditions in our youth, and will rediscover for himself soon enough!"

"Oh? Do you plan on a long visit, Mr. Clifton?" enquired Rebecca.

Mr. Clifton blushed and darted a sharp, silencing look at his cousin, which Rebecca could not account for. Mr. Mountague, however, caught some meaning in it, for his eyes widened, and he seemed to be at a loss for words. "He—that is to say—" Mr. Mountague began, but his father interrupted,

"Miss Stanhope, what brings you out this way? Is Lady Mountague expecting you? If so, we would not wish to delay your visit further."

"She is not expecting me, sir. I have come with another purpose entirely. I wish to speak with you, if you please."

"Indeed? Very well, then." Sir Percival instructed his son and nephew to take their catch to the house, in which direction the two set off immediately. Turning his full attention to Rebecca, he said, "Let us make the approach together, shall we? I think I can guess what this is about. Your father has told you the unhappy news, I expect?"

"Yes," admitted she, as they walked together across the lawn, adding warmly, "Sir! You cannot mean what you said yesterday evening. You cannot intend my father to resign from a position he so greatly values, and in which he has proved, through years of selfless devotion, that he is very capable and highly respected."

"It is true that your father has, for the most part, very ably carried out his duties in the past. But in view of recent events, I have no choice, Miss Stanhope. Surely you can see that."

"I cannot see it, sir. He has done nothing wrong. My father was the victim of a theft. It was not his fault!"

"I comprehend that you wish to support your father, my dear," replied Sir Percival calmly, "and that you place great trust in him; as his daughter, it is only right that you should feel this way. But you were not there when this supposed 'theft' occurred. Perhaps it was not a theft at all."

"What are you implying, sir?" demanded Rebecca, her ire rising.

"Your father admits that he was gambling that night."

"As he has done at your very own table, sir, every Thursday evening for nearly three decades! You know how mild is his temper; you also know how conservative is his style. Can you truly imagine that he would bet and lose *an hundred and fifty pounds* at a single game of cards?"

"He said he met up with a couple of wealthy aristocrats at the inn that night. Playing in such company, I find it entirely conceivable that he could gamble away such a sum."

"It is *not* conceivable. My father is too highly principled. He would never behave in such a disreputable manner, and he would never use a penny of the parish's money for gaming. The new bells were to honour my mother. He would have done nothing to stand in the way of their commission—nothing."

"So you say; but we have only your father's word for it."

"His word is gold! He is the best of men. He is incapable of uttering a falsehood."

"Even the best of men can be led astray, Miss Stanhope, or commit an act of folly." He shrugged his shoulders. "Perhaps we shall never know the truth of it. But the sad fact is, the money is gone, and the new bells with it. I see it as a sign that it is time for your father to move on as well. And it is too late to reconsider. I have promised the incumbency to my nephew."

"Your nephew?" gasped Rebecca. "You do not mean—Mr. Clifton?"

"Several years ago, I promised Philip the living of Elm Grove when it became vacant. I did not expect the event to occur very soon; but this episode has brought matters into a new light."

Rebecca now understood Mr. Clifton's reticent and uncomfortable behaviour when they had spoken earlier; he knew that he was to be the means of dispossessing her father of his benefice and her from their home. "Mr. Clifton is young, and newly ordained," cried she. "Surely he should be more experienced before taking charge of a parish on his own."

"Philip has served as a curate for over a year—at a very meagre wage, barely enough to afford food and lodging. He is a good, hard-working, and devoted priest. He will be good for this community."

"Cannot he wait a while longer to advance to this benefice? You and my father were at school together, Sir Percival. You have known him more than forty years. You cannot turn your back on a friendship of such long standing!"

"Blood is thicker than water, Miss Stanhope," was Sir Percival's curt reply.

They had reached the veranda now, where Lady Mountague, having issued from the door in time to hear the last portion of this exchange, was standing with a disagreeable look on her face.

"Miss Stanhope," said she, "do give up these foolish entreaties; they only fall on deaf ears. My husband has made a promise to our nephew, and I assure you, he will not go back on his word."

Rebecca was silenced. She quickly curtseyed and took her leave.

....

Chapter IV

When she got home, Rebecca found her father walking through the house, his hands behind his back, fondly studying the pictures on the walls, as if silently saying good-bye. All his former strength and cheerfulness seemed to have returned to him; but although it did her good to see it, her mind still revolted at the injustice done to him.

"It is an outrage!" asserted she, after relating all that had transpired. "Clearly Sir Percival is taking advantage of your misfortune as an excuse to remove you from office, for the benefit of his nephew."

"That may be; but there is nothing to be done about it."

"He gives no thought to the sufferings which we will endure—and neither will Mr. Clifton."

"Why should Mr. Clifton think of us, my dear?" returned her father generously. "Surely he has aspirations of his own. I myself waited eight years for this benefice to fall vacant, wishing all that time that the incumbent would pop off, so that I might take his place and at last be allowed to marry your mother."

"Papa! You never did."

"It is true. When a man is young and ambitious, it is natural that his own interests should take precedence in his heart. I quite understand Sir Percival's wish to promote his nephew. I should hate to think of a young man like Mr. Clifton being obliged to wait as long as I did to establish himself."

"You are too good, papa; truly you are. You always think the best of every body. But surely, in this instance, you will allow me to hate Sir Percival and his nephew just a little?"

"No, Rebecca; you must not think ill of them. I have given this a great deal of thought, all through the night and morning, and I have come to believe that every thing has happened for the best. We have lived long enough in this village. It is time for a change."

"I do not wish to change. I love our life as it is, papa."

"No one actively *wishes* to change a circumstance which is pleasant, comfortable, and rewarding, my dear; but in the end, change is inevitable. It *will come,* whether we wish it or not."

"But what are we to do?"

"We shall follow Goethe's advice: 'The only way to make sense out of change is to plunge into it, move with it, and join the dance.'" With a comical face, and a little flourish of his wrist, he straightened, and said, "We shall travel."

Rebecca could not help but smile at his antics. "Papa, you hate travelling."

"Lately, yes; and this last journey certainly did nothing to improve my taste for it; but I quite enjoyed rambling about in my youth. I have grown too old and set in my ways, Rebecca—and I have been remiss. By remaining always at Elm Grove, by never taking you anywhere, I have neglected you."

"Oh, no! You never neglected me, papa."

"I have. To shew you and your sister our fine country, to introduce you to its many wonders—this *should* have formed one of the basic foundations of your education. It is a shame, now that we have the opportunity—or should I say, the *obligation*—to go forth, I have no longer the means to do so as I would *like*. And yet, somehow we shall overcome this obstacle and find a way. We shall begin by going to your sister."

"To Sarah? But Medford Vicarage is too small. Sarah has made it clear that there is insufficient space for guests."

"The house cannot be half so small as she claims. When I write to her and explain our circumstances, I am certain she and Charles will make room for us, if only for a little while. We should not impose on them for long, only until I can make some other arrangement. After that—who knows where the road might take us?"

Rebecca felt a rush of shame. To think that they must give up their independence, and would be for ever obliged to live off the goodwill of others—it was dreadful! But when she perceived her father's resolve, and the new light of interest in his eyes, it kindled within her a tiny, unexpected glimmer of expectation and hope. Yes, they must give up their beloved home and leave Elm Grove; this would be very hard, and cause them both pain; their lives would never be the same again;—but perhaps *some* good might come of it. Certainly, she welcomed an opportunity to enjoy her sister's company, and that of her little niece and nephews. Furthermore, she was curious to see Sarah's house, as well as the village of Medford and its inhabitants, which she knew of only by her sister's regular and detailed reports.

Rebecca did have one particular regret in removing thither; it was the knowledge that a relation of Sir Percival's—his older sister, Mrs. Penelope Harcourt—was the primary landholder in Medford, and a very rich old widow. It was through Sir Percival's influence with his sister that Sarah's husband Charles had been appointed to his benefice as vicar; and for that Rebecca was grateful. But in view of present circumstances, she had rather not be obliged to deal with any body connected with Sir Percival ever again. It seemed, however, that they had no alternative. They could not afford a house of their own; nor could she think of any other friends or relatives with the means to take them in. Nodding, and summoning new-found strength of resolve, she said more cheerfully,

"I suppose that is an excellent proposal, papa. From all we hear, Medford is a charming village—and I would dearly love to see Sarah and our family."

"There's a good girl. I am glad to see that smile again."

Looking about the house, Rebecca asked, "What shall we do with all our belongings?"

"The furniture will be too expensive to move. I shall ask your sister if she wants any of the smaller things; whatever she cannot use, we must sell."

"Can we keep nothing?"

"Only your clothes and a few personal possessions."

Rebecca's heart caught at this. "But papa—your books! Our pictures! My pianoforte! My harp!"

"I doubt your sister has room for such things, my dearest;—and we ought to travel as lightly as possible. We may keep only what we can each fit into one trunk."

"One trunk?" Rebecca repeated softly; and in despair, she nodded, promising to be as useful in this endeavour as she possibly could.

Confirmation soon arrived from Sarah, commiserating in their misfortune, and welcoming them to Medford Vicarage with open arms, for as long as they wished to stay. Sarah gratefully accepted the gift of her mother's linen, plate, and china, which were of a superior quality to any she possessed. These were dutifully packed and sent. A fortnight later, the rest of the Stanhopes' prized family possessions had been disposed of, all sold at a significant loss. Rebecca could not help but feel a pang when her beloved pianoforte, the harp which had given her so many years of enjoyment, and the bulk of her music were carted away (after retaining only a few favourite sheets as a memento).

It was very hard indeed to let go of her father's precious collection of over four hundred books, particularly when the best offer came from the new occupant of the house, the odious Mr. Clifton. It made Rebecca's blood boil to think that he, at age twenty-five, should become the owner of a collection which had taken her father a lifetime to acquire! The new rector bought most of the furniture and pictures as well, as theirs very nicely fit the proportions of the rooms, and he had nothing of his own. The funds for said purchases, he told Mr. Stanhope, would come from the interest on money given to him by his father, which had helped support him at Oxford, and had supplemented his income the past year. Rebecca heard this with disdain, recalling that Sir Percival had made it seem as though Mr. Clifton was barely able to make ends meet in his prior position.

Rebecca could not comprehend how her father could conduct these transactions with the very man who was stealing away both his home and position. Although Mr. Stanhope insisted he felt no antipathy towards Mr. Clifton, and that the man had paid very generously for every thing, she could not be so magnanimous. While they concluded their negotiations, she kept herself away in the shrubbery, unequal to the task of witnessing the selling of every tangible thing she knew and loved. As she strolled about the garden, she tried to commit to memory every beloved flowerbed, tree, shrub, and herb, and every winding path. At length, she took refuge in the shelter of her favourite elm, a spot to which she had often ventured when she wished to read, or escape notice; for the trunk was so large that it shielded the occupant of its bench from view of any one walking by. With a sigh, she recalled sitting in that very spot only a short time ago, reading with her father, under much happier circumstances;—and she spent a quarter of an hour indulging in melancholy reflections.

Soon hearing approaching footsteps on the gravel path, and thinking it to be her father, Rebecca stepped out from behind the tree and put on a smile. It was not Mr. Stanhope, however, who halted in surprise before her: it was Mr. Clifton. Quickly removing his hat, he stared at her in confusion; then, with grave propriety, he said,

"Miss Stanhope. Good afternoon."

"Are you out to inspect your garden, sir?" replied Rebecca coolly but politely. "If so, I hope you find it to your liking."

"It is a very nice garden. But—I only thought to cut across the lawn and through the gate to gain access to the fields."

"That is not the most expeditious route to the manor-house, Mr. Clifton."

"I enjoy a long walk, and the neighbourhood is very fine."

"Indeed it is. I have traversed one or another of its many walks nearly every day of my life." To her vexation, as she spoke, her voice broke.

He glanced away, and said abruptly, "Generally, I believe these transitions go rather smoothly—out with the old, and in with the new—but I imagine this will be a very big change for you."

"It will, sir, and I dislike change with all my heart."

"Do you? Why?"

"This is my home. I am surrounded here by all the things I know, and the people I love. I have no wish to leave it."

"Great joy *can* be found in all that is familiar," concurred he, meeting her gaze once more. "Yet, I have discovered there can be even more merit in change. Change often brings unimagined opportunity."

"It can also bring great struggle and hardship."

"If there is no struggle, Miss Stanhope, there is no progress. To live in a safe cocoon—to never step outside one's accustomed boundaries—I believe that is not truly living. It is stagnation."

"Stagnation?" cried Rebecca. "How dare you call my life here stagnation! It has been very full and happy!"

"That was not my intention, Miss Stanhope. I am sorry if I offended you, and sorry you are obliged to give up your home."

"If you are truly sorry, sir, then I beg of you: ask your uncle to reconsider, and allow my father to remain in his position."

"My uncle is doing what he believes is best for the community. Even his daughter must agree, that a clergyman ought to acknowledge and remove himself, if he is discovered to be unfit for service."

"Unfit? You malign my father unjustly, sir! If any one is unfit, I believe it is you, Mr. Clifton. A single year as curate is hardly experience enough to qualify you as rector of this parish."

He coloured slightly. "Forgive me, I have said too much. Pray accept my best wishes for your and your father's health and happiness. Good day." Replacing his hat on his head, Mr. Clifton turned and walked away.

Greatly vexed, Rebecca returned to the house, where she passed the rest of the afternoon and evening packing up her few remaining possessions, while mentally disparaging the new rector.

Her distress increased the next day when, after paying off

his debts, Mr. Stanhope announced that he had turned over the preponderance of the proceeds of the sale of their furniture and possessions, to Sir Percival and the churchwarden, to replace the lost funds for the church bells. They were, Rebecca reflected miserably, now nearly penniless; and if not for the goodness of Sarah and her husband, they would be homeless as well.

Rebecca and Mr. Stanhope spent their final days in the area calling on the poor cottagers and farmers' wives and their children, with whom they'd become close these many years, to say good-bye. By now, every one in the parish knew why Mr. Stanhope was leaving; yet in not a single household were they received with recrimination or cold civility—only with sympathy and profound regret on their departure.

Perhaps the most difficult parting was between herself and their cook, Martha, who had been with them since before Rebecca was born, and for whom Rebecca had great affection.

"Oh, ma'am," cried Martha, as she dabbed at her eyes with her apron, "how sorely we shall miss you. You and Mr. Stanhope have been kindness itself to us, you have, and you've become as dear to me as my own daughter. How we shall get on without you, I can't say."

"You may take comfort in knowing that the new rector is retaining you all," said Rebecca, referring to their maid and man-servant, "and *you* will not be obliged to leave this house."

"I'm grateful, to be sure, ma'am, that he's keeping us on," replied Martha. "As a single gentleman, his needs should be few. But I can't forgive him for taking away your place. I'm not sure we can ever get along."

"I hope you will, Martha," said Rebecca sincerely. "You

have always been goodness itself, and I would not like to think of you unhappy."

On their last night, as Rebecca walked through the rooms of the rectory, she keenly felt her impending loss, knowing that it was the last time she would live there, as mistress of that house; the last time she would ever gaze out the windows at her favourite prospects, or sleep in her own bed. In the privacy of her chamber, she shed a great many tears.

....

Chapter V

They made an early start the next morning, as Mr. Stanhope was determined to make the entire journey in one day; a proposition made easier in that it was still summer. They were to travel post.

A light rain was falling, adding an even more melancholy note to their departure, as, from the misty window glasses of the chaise, Rebecca bid a silent adieu to Elm Grove Rectory. A multitude of scenes passed through her mind, of times enjoyed within its walls, from her early childhood onwards, including particular memories of her mother, which appeared doubly precious to her now.

Rebecca and Mr. Stanhope spoke very little at first, each wrapped in their own contemplations; but once seven or eight miles had been traversed, and new, unseen vistas presented themselves, Rebecca's thoughts turned from what they had left behind, and began to focus on the features of the journey itself, in which every object was now fresh and interesting. Even the changing of horses was something new. Although the day was long, they both found much in the passing scenery to remark upon. Soon, the rain let up. The inn at which they stopped to dine was clean, and the meal surprisingly good, entirely exceeding Mr. Stanhope's expectations.

When they had covered three-and-twenty miles, they were so far away from every thing familiar, that it seemed to Rebecca as if they had entered an entirely new country, a sensation which was not entirely displeasing. When, in late afternoon, they had travelled nearly twice that distance, they entered Medford Valley, a spot so beautifully wooded, and so rich in pasture, that Rebecca's spirits rose even further.

"It is a very picturesque country," observed Mr. Stanhope, "although these bottoms must be very dirty in winter."

In time they passed a pair of fine iron gates, through which Rebecca could perceive a long drive leading through a leafy, green park to a magnificent house, which her father deduced must belong to Mrs. Penelope Harcourt, the wealthy widow to whom Charles Morris owed his benefice.

A mile further on, they entered Medford itself, a large, pleasantly situated, and populous village. As they drove down the broad but irregular main street, Rebecca observed a great deal of bustle. A donkey-cart and a farmer's wagon passed them, followed by a horseman. Moments later, a gentleman walked hastily by, and yet another gentleman came out of an office door. She saw a pair of children chasing a ball, a man cleaning a shop window, and two ladies chatting gaily; all of whom paused to gaze with curiosity at their passing carriage.

"Look, papa, how busy it is! Why, there is a drapery store. And an inn!" As they drove on, Rebecca named with wonder all the shops they passed. "A baker. An optician. A solicitor. A butcher. An apothecary! My goodness. Sarah did not exaggerate in her description of the place. It is a very fine village indeed."

"Why, it almost amounts to a town," said her father with equal satisfaction.

The church was old but stately, with a tower that looked newly built, within which a set of three handsome bells were now ringing out the hour of four, a circumstance which Mr. Stanhope observed with a little sigh. Immediately after the church, the main street became again a lane; and just beyond, at the very end of the town, before the open fields began, lay the vicarage.

The chaise drew up to the small gate. As Rebecca and Mr. Stanhope alighted, they had but a moment or two to take in the exterior features of the house itself—a compact edifice, enclosed in its own small garden, with a vine trained round its casements—when the front door opened and Sarah and Charles appeared with their three little children, and hurried down the gravel path to meet them. In a moment they were all in each other's arms, rejoicing and exchanging greetings and embraces.

Sarah was pretty and pleasingly plump, a woman content in her role as wife and mother, whose gentleness and generosity of heart shone in her bright eyes, blooming cheeks, and ready smile. She carried eighteen-month-old Arabella in her arms, while her husband held the hands of their two fine boys, George and Christopher, who were five and three years old. Rebecca happily took the baby into her arms, as she and Mr. Stanhope admired the children's beauty, remarking upon how much they had grown since their last meeting. After their trunks were unloaded and brought to the front steps, and the vehicle drew away, the party remained outside, engaged in the animated chatter of affectionate people who have not seen each other in several months' time.

"We are very happy to see you," said Charles, "yet grieved by the circumstances which occasioned it." Charles Morris was seven years older than his wife, a man of good understanding who was a thoughtful husband and father; by all accounts, he discharged his duties very ably in the parish, and Rebecca found much to admire in him.

"Dear papa," said Sarah with emotion, "I can scarcely conceive that we shall never return to Elm Grove again—it is too, too hard."

"One can never tell what is waiting for us round the corner," was Mr. Stanhope's cheerful reply, "but we have our health, and now the joy of your company, and we count our blessings."

They all took a turn round the garden. The gentlemen, as always, must have their say about the details of the journey undergone; they immediately fell into an animated conversation, beginning with the costs incurred in hiring the equipage, tipping the post-boy, &c., and moving on to the state of the roads, which in turn prompted a debate as to whether it was worse to travel in winter, when one was plagued by frost and snow upon beds of stones on the rough lanes about the villages, or in spring, when every thing was flooded. The ladies, meanwhile, took delight in studying the flowerbeds and potatoes which Sarah and the children had planted, while little Christopher shyly held down his head against his mother's skirts, and George danced about, alternately throwing himself on the lawn and jumping up to play. Charles then invited them to admire the view of the fields and surrounding hills, which Rebecca and Mr. Stanhope agreed was very fine.

They were about to enter the house, when two lively voices hailed them, and Rebecca looked round to discover a pair of women hastening up the road in their direction. At first she thought her eyes deceived her; for the ladies were absolutely identical in appearance, not only in face and form, but in dress as well, wearing every thing exactly the same, from their bonnets to their shoes.

"It is the Wabshaw sisters," whispered Sarah.

"Good afternoon, ladies," said Charles, as the two in question breathlessly hurried up and stopped before them with bright smiles.

Rebecca recalled what her sister had told her about the Wabshaws: they were the twin daughters of a man of property in a neighbouring county, whose estate had been entailed away from the female line. Since the death of both their parents, they had removed to Medford, where they lived in reduced circumstances in a small cottage. They were no longer young; their features suggested that they had never been handsome; and they were indistinguishable, one from the other, although one was introduced as Cecilia, and the other as Cordelia.

"We saw your carriage pass by," said one of the Miss Wabshaws, in a tone of great enthusiasm, accompanied by a shrill laugh. "We see every thing from our front window, you know, for it overlooks the street."

"Yes, it overlooks it quite directly," said the second Miss Wabshaw, with equal animation and identical laughter.

"Mrs. Morris said you would arrive to-day, and we simply could not prevent ourselves from coming at once to bid you welcome."

"We simply could not prevent ourselves!"

"I am the eldest," said the first Miss Wabshaw, "born five minutes before my sister, but no one can tell us apart—"

"—even our mother and father could not make the distinction—"

"No, they never could—"

"—so you may address us both as Miss Wabshaw."

"Every body does."

"We do not mind."

"Well then, Miss Wabshaw, and Miss Wabshaw, I am very pleased to make your acquaintance," said Rebecca, restraining her own urge to laugh; and her father repeated the sentiment.

The sisters each carried a basket which they thrust at Rebecca and Mr. Stanhope. "Pray, allow us to present you with a little welcoming gift. Here is a cake we baked ourselves."

"And muffins. We could not agree on which you would prefer—"

"We discussed it endlessly, and could not agree—"

"So we made both."

"Thank you kindly," said Mr. Stanhope, as he and Rebecca accepted their offerings. "I am sure we shall enjoy them, for I am equally fond of cake and muffins."

"Equally fond, sister!" cried one of the Miss Wabshaws, as they exchanged a look and a smile.

"Equally fond! So we were both right!"

"We were both right!" This seemed to please them both no end. Turning back to Rebecca and the others, the twin continued, "We know you have just arrived, and we do not wish to impose on you—"

"No, we do not wish to impose—"

"So we shall take our leave. But we do hope you will call on us very soon."

"Yes, very soon! We live in Rose Cottage, immediately adjacent to the apothecary, you cannot miss it, there are pink roses trailed round the door."

"Pink roses! You cannot miss it."

"We may not live elegantly—"

"Indeed we do *not*, for our cottage is very small, but we can offer good cake—"

"The very best cake!"

"And attentive company!"

"You will not want for conversation with the Wabshaws, we assure you!" The sisters laughed in unison.

"Thank you kindly for the invitation," said Rebecca. "My sister and I shall be sure to call on you soon."

Parting remarks were exchanged, and the twins returned in the direction from whence they came.

"What congenial ladies," said Mr. Stanhope, beaming.

"They are precisely as I imagined them to be," whispered Rebecca to Sarah, sharing a look of amusement, "for you wrote of them most descriptively in your letters."

"Did I happen to mention in my letters that they are the worst cooks in England?" whispered Sarah in return. "We will be obliged to feed their cake and muffins to the chickens."

This statement was met with general laughter; and they all issued within the vicarage.

"It is a very old house, I am afraid, and far too cramped," apologised Charles, as he and Sarah guided the newcomers through the tiny entrance hall into the sitting-room, and on a tour of all the chambers. "I have not had the money to make the improvements I would like."

The place was, indeed, even more compact than Rebecca had anticipated. Many modest extensions, Charles explained, had been made before his tenure, but none too well, and no two rooms were on the same level.

"The vicarage is so small," said Sarah, smiling, "that Charles often likens it to a carriage with a basket and dickey. But it is large enough for me, and satisfies all my wants."

"You have made it very comfortable," observed Rebecca truthfully, taking care not to trod on the children's playthings, which lay strewn about. She was pleased by the brightly-coloured drapes at the windows, and the pictures which added cheer to the walls. "It is gratifying to see where you have been living all these years. I see why you are so happy here."

The sleeping arrangements were soon gone over, and Rebecca learned what pains had been undergone to accommodate them. There were only three bedrooms, and a tiny chamber adjacent to the offices which housed their manservant;—as such, it had been determined that the nurse maid would move in with the maid and cook, and Rebecca would sleep with the children.

Rebecca swallowed back her dismay. For six years, she had slept alone. While she had missed Sarah's company at first, she had come to enjoy the privacy. Never had she envisioned herself sharing a room with an infant and two small boys. At the same time, she was ashamed for feeling any thing less than grateful, and suffered a pang of guilt on behalf of the poor maid and displaced nurse maid, who (unlike herself) would be obliged to share a bed. "Thank you," said she sincerely.

"Dear Charles insisted that papa must have a room of his own," said Sarah. "Wait until you see what he has designed."

They were led to Charles's small study, where he proudly demonstrated his newest acquisition: a shut-up bed, which unfolded from a cupboard simulating a wardrobe, and when set up for sleeping, left just space enough in the room to walk between it and the desk and the wall.

"I saw it advertised in the paper," explained Charles proudly, "as one of the articles at an estate sale. I sent for it immediately. It was only just delivered and installed yesterday."

"Did not Charles have a bright idea?" enthused Sarah from just inside the doorway, where she and the rest of the party looked on in admiration. "Is not it very grand? You shall feel quite at home, papa; I have outfitted the bed with your very own linens, which you sent from Elm Grove. I took care to wash them and air them on the line especially, so they will smell very fresh."

"You shall have all your privacy by night, Mr. Stanhope," added Charles agreeably, "and I shall regain the use of my study by day—a perfectly cordial arrangement."

Mr. Stanhope agreed that the bed would suit him very well, and told Charles how obliged he was to him. Rebecca could see in her father's eyes, however, and infer from his tone, that he felt the burden which their presence imposed on the household, and wished it could be otherwise.

After a late dinner, the new arrivals, weary from their journey, were glad to retire. It was the first time in many years that Rebecca had slept in a bed and a room different from her own, and it felt very strange. Arabella woke twice in the night, and Rebecca sang her a lullaby as she rocked the infant in her arms. It seemed to Rebecca that she had only just gratefully laid her head down once more, when she opened her eyes to find sunlight streaming in beneath the curtains, and George and Christopher standing at the side of her pillow, staring curiously at her.

With her pianoforte and harp no longer in her possession, Rebecca was unable to practise her music, as had been her daily custom for more than fifteen years; and all through breakfast she felt out of sorts. Although her father generally kept a smile on his countenance, Rebecca observed him covertly wipe his knife and fork on the tablecloth before eating; and she saw him shake his head at the state of clutter in the vicarage itself.

When Sarah invited Rebecca to accompany her on a walk into the village on an errand later that morning, Rebecca was happy to comply.

"Barlow's Store is the principal haberdasher's shop in the village," explained Sarah, as she and Rebecca strolled down Medford's Main Street, arm-in-arm. "You can find nearly any thing you require there. Oh! But it is hot to-day."

Rebecca agreed that the day was warm, but so thrilled was she to be walking through the bustling village, with so many diversions to choose from, and so many scenes inviting her eye—all within a ten-minute walk from the vicarage!—that she was insensible of any real discomfort.

They entered Barlow's. It was a well-outfitted store, busy with customers; and it was warmer within than without.

"What colour ribbon do you think would suit Arabella's new bonnet?" asked Sarah.

"I think pale lemon would nicely complement her fair complexion and golden curls," answered Rebecca.

They had not taken five or six steps towards the counter, when Sarah paused and held her hand to her temple, wavering unsteadily on her feet. "Oh, dear! I feel quite light-headed."

Alarmed, Rebecca reached out to support her sister; but before she could act further, aid came from another quarter. A tall, good-looking young man of most gentlemanlike appearance, dropped the gloves he was examining at a nearby counter, hastened over, and cried,

"Mrs. Morris, you are ill. Pray, allow me to assist you."

"Please, sir," was all Sarah could manage, before she fainted dead away into the man's arms.

....

Chapter VI

"A chair for this poor woman, if you please!" called out the gentleman to the proprietor. "And a glass of water!"

A flurry of activity ensued; the customers all gathered around, chattering with concern; a chair was brought, and Sarah deposited in it. Within a minute, she was sensible again, and gratefully sipping a glass of water, under the gentleman's watchful eye and dutiful ministrations. Rebecca observed all this with astonishment, gratitude, and awe, all the while wondering who the handsome man was, and how he knew her sister. When she wished aloud that *she* might be of some service, he instructed her to remove Sarah's bonnet, which Rebecca did accordingly.

"How do you feel, Mrs. Morris?" asked he kindly, bending down before her.

"Better, thank you, sir," replied Sarah.

"Are you still light-headed?"

"No, sir."

"Do you have any pain, or feel ill in any other way?"

"No, I am only hot and a little fatigued. I do not know what happened. One moment I was fine; the next—"

"This heat is quite oppressive. It is not uncommon for a lady to faint in weather such as this. May I?" He gestured towards Sarah's hand. She nodded; immediately, he took her wrist between his fingers and paused thoughtfully.

Rebecca realised that he was taking her pulse; and from this action, and his preceding words, she presumed him to be a medical man.

"A few minutes' rest is all you require, Mrs. Morris. You will be fine." He straightened and smiled at Rebecca, then glanced back expectantly at Sarah, who took his silent meaning and, fanning herself with her bonnet, said weakly,

"Dr. Watkins, may I have the honour of presenting my sister, Miss Rebecca Stanhope. Rebecca: pray allow me to introduce Dr. Jack Watkins."

Rebecca was surprised. She had heard from Sarah of a Dr. Watkins, who used to attend Mrs. Harcourt whenever she went to town. Mrs. Harcourt liked him so well that, five years previously, she had asked if he might be amenable to caring for her exclusively in the country. Her offer was apparently so generous, as to convince him to close down his practice in London and remove permanently to Medford, where he and his wife had resided ever since. Based on this information, Rebecca had always imagined Dr. Watkins to be a much older man. This gentleman, however, looked to be no older than twenty-five or twenty-six.

Bowing, he said, "Miss Stanhope, I am very glad to make your acquaintance."

"And I yours, sir," answered Rebecca, curtseying. "My sister has mentioned you, Dr. Watkins, in previous conversations and in her letters—always with the greatest respect. You are, I believe, Mrs. Harcourt's private physician?"

"No," replied he, "that honour belongs to my father, Dr. Samuel Watkins."

"Your father?"

"I was only recently licensed by the Royal College of Physicians. I was preparing to open a practice in town, when my grandmother fell ill. My father and mother were obliged to go to her at once. He asked me to fill in here while he was gone, and to provide such care as Mrs. Harcourt required, until he could return."

"Oh! I am very sorry to hear about your grandmother," replied Rebecca. "I hope she will be well soon."

"As do I, Miss Stanhope."

He looked at her with a directness and a smile that were captivating. She felt her cheeks grow warm under his gaze. "Your presence here was fortuitous to-day, sir. Thank you for helping my sister."

"I was very glad to render the service."

Rebecca had never met a physician in her life. There had, of course, been no man of that distinction within miles of Elm Grove;—although she recalled that her father had thought highly of the physician with whom he had consulted about her mother's illness years ago. She was disposed to think well of men in the medical profession in general, as her grandfather had reportedly been a country surgeon; and she thought Dr. Watkins an interesting man. He had a good figure, and a fine countenance which was both lively and intelligent. His air and address were unexceptionable, and his ease of manner reflected his education and good breeding. She had not been in his presence but a few minutes when she knew that she would like him; and the expression in his eyes conveyed that he might share a similar interest in her.

Sarah, feeling herself again, thanked Dr. Jack Watkins once more and took leave of her chair. In a few minutes' time, she and the doctor had both completed their purchases, and he accompanied the ladies as they issued outside together.

"You are only recently arrived in Medford, I believe, Miss Stanhope?" enquired Dr. Watkins.

"Yes. My father and I came only last night."

"I have heard about your—circumstances," added he in a low voice, his tone and expression conveying his sympathy. "May I say how sorry I am. It must have been difficult to give up your home of so many years."

"It was; yet, we are fortunate to be welcomed at my sister and brother's house."

"Indeed, and you will find that Medford has many charms. If the neighbourhood could support the practice of another physician, I would happily settle here myself; but with only one client, and *she* retained by my father, that is quite impossible." Motioning to a curricle nearby, he added with a smile, "May I offer you ladies a ride home? I believe we can squeeze in three; and you ought not to walk in this heat, Mrs. Morris."

"Thank you kindly, Dr. Watkins," replied Sarah, "but I am perfectly recovered, and it is but a short walk to the vicarage."

"If you insist. Pray forgive me. I must be on my way. It was a pleasure to meet you, Miss Stanhope. Good day, ladies."

Sarah and Rebecca replied in kind; and with a tip of his hat, Dr. Jack Watkins climbed into his vehicle, put the horses to, and drove off.

"Such an amiable and clever gentleman," observed Sarah, as they began towards home.

"What a shame that a man of his education and profession cannot find occupation here, if he desires it."

"I agree. But Charles calls in Mr. Pearson whenever we are ill; and our apothecary is also very good with medicines and advice. Who but the wealthiest could afford the services of a physician?" With a sharp intake of breath, Sarah touched her sister's arm, and said, "Oh, look! There is Miss Davenport!"

A low phaeton was progressing up the street, and seated within was a pretty young woman, with light eyes and a fair complexion, expensively dressed in a gown of deep violet. Catching sight of Sarah and Rebecca, she broke into a smile, and said something to the driver, who stopped the vehicle.

"Mrs. Morris!" cried the young lady, as she descended the equipage and crossed the street to them, beaming. "You are looking very well. And Miss Stanhope! I am in such raptures! Mrs. Morris has frequently spoken of you with great affection these many years. How often have *I* thought of you, since that one, happy time we met, so long ago. We were children, of course; I must look very different now—but tell me that you remember me!"

Rebecca did remember her. Amelia Davenport was Mrs. Penelope Harcourt's niece—the daughter of her departed husband's brother. Miss Davenport's parents died when she was five years old, and ever since, she had lived under her aunt's protection, growing up at Grafton Hall with every advantage. Mrs. Harcourt had lost two children at birth, and an adored son had not lived to see his third year; and so she poured all her energy and affection into her niece. As her estate was not entailed away from the female line, she had named Amelia as her heir.

"Of course I remember you," replied Rebecca, so affected by the young woman's sincere enthusiasm that she could not help but smile. "How nice to see you, Miss Davenport."

"What fond memories I have of that Christmas when I visited Aunt and Uncle Mountague at Claremont Park—the chief delight of which was my association with you! I had no friends at home—no girls with whom I was allowed to associate.—My cousins are all much older than I; they are more your age, Mrs. Morris; and although the age difference means nothing now, when you are young, you feel it quite distinctly, do not you think? Brook and Philip were terrors at the time, teasing us girls, as I recall, at every turn. If not for you, Miss Stanhope, I should have been quite miserable and had no one with whom to play. Do you remember the tea party we held in honour of my new doll?"

"I recall it perfectly," responded Rebecca. "Your aunt Mountague was so kind as to allow us to use her daughters' play tea set, despite *their* objections that we would injure it."

"Yes! And nothing happened, except that we had a lovely afternoon! My only regret was that we had to come away so soon, after only a fortnight. I feared I should never see you again—and so it seemed to prove, for we never did return to Elm Grove. Only think how vastly happy I was, Mrs. Morris, when you came to live in the neighbourhood, and brought regular reports of your sister; and now to have *you* join us, Miss Stanhope! I am quite beside myself! I am still terribly cut off, you know, living in that great house. You *will* stay a long while, I hope?"

"My father and I have no firm plans at present."

"Our home is open to my sister and my father for as long as they like," said Sarah, glancing at Rebecca with affection.

"What felicity is this!" cried Miss Davenport, linking her

arm through Rebecca's as she walked back to her carriage. "I cannot tell you what it means to me, Miss Stanhope, to have you at last in Medford. You and I are going to be great friends, I am certain of it. I can hardly wait to introduce you to Aunt Harcourt."

The next morning, while all were at breakfast, the maid entered with a note for Miss Stanhope.

"It come from Grafton Hall, ma'am," explained Mary. "The servant says he must wait for an answer."

Rebecca took the missive and read it aloud.

Grafton Hall

My dearest Miss Stanhope,

It is all arranged! I have spoken with my aunt, and our hearts are set on it; you and your sister must call on us this very day! Pray forgive us for not coming to you first; but my aunt has a horror of small rooms, and insists that it will be quieter and more comfortable here than at the vicarage, with all your children running about. I am sure you cannot disagree. The weather is so fine, we will receive you in the garden. Aunt Harcourt is most particularly interested in seeing you again, and please tell Mrs. Morris how much we always delight in her company. Shall we send the carriage for you at one o'clock? Do let me know at once. We have so much to talk about. I am counting the hours!

Yours most truly,
Amelia Davenport

"That is odd," said Sarah, frowning. "She invites—or rather, *commands*—us to call this morning, and just the two of us. I thought we should all be asked to dinner."

Charles said, "I am in no hurry to dine again at Grafton Hall. We have been there twice this month already."

Rebecca turned to her father, conflicted. "I have no wish to leave you, papa. If we were to go, what should you do to-day?"

"Do not worry about me," replied Mr. Stanhope. "I have had my eye on several books in Charles's study, and I mean to sit in a corner and read all day, if there is no objection."

"None whatsoever," replied Charles.

"In that case, I should love to accept," said Rebecca, "but *must* we go by carriage? How far is it, to Grafton Hall?"

"On foot, taking my usual shortcut, it is not a mile and a half," answered Charles.

"That is nothing. On such a fine day, I should much rather walk."

Sarah agreed, and a note was sent to that effect. But at noon, as the sisters were putting on their bonnets, Sarah began to feel ill again and was obliged to lie down. Making her apologies to Rebecca, she said she could not go after all.

"Shall I call the surgeon?" asked Rebecca.

"No, it is only a recurrence of the mild complaint I felt yesterday. This heat does not agree with me. A little rest is all I require, and I have Mary to attend me. *You* must go, however—you must not disappoint Miss Davenport and Mrs. Harcourt, they are expecting us." Calling out to Charles, she added, "Will you accompany her, Charles dear, and show her the way?"

Charles agreed that he would, determining to make the walk do double duty by calling on several of the cottagers who were ailing or in want of company on his way back. Rebecca took her parasol, and the two set out. The walk was lovely. She enjoyed witnessing the activity in the village as they passed through, but was particularly entranced once they had left the main road and entered the country-side. Walking was one of Rebecca's favourite pursuits; crossing field after field, climbing over stiles, and strolling past scattered dwellings and farms, were to her, one of life's chief delights. All around her was fragrant beauty, brilliant and alive in the summer sunshine; and as she admired the colourful, waving flowers in the foreground, and the high green hills in the distance, Rebecca recalled similar sights in Elm Grove with a little, heartfelt sigh. Although she missed home, for the first time in many weeks, she was not at all unhappy; and she determined that to-day she should *be* happy, if she possibly could.

"Charles," said Rebecca, "I have only the vaguest of memories of Mrs. Harcourt, from the one time she came to visit the Mountagues at Claremont Park in my youth. Over the years, you and Sarah have painted very different pictures of her. Sarah finds her amiable and wise, while you seem to have no great affection for her. What shall I expect?"

"Well," replied he with a smile, "from the first moment of your appearance, you shall surely be treated to her latest affliction and complaint. You shall be criticised and given the benefit of her *lifetime of knowledge*, as she puts it, about something or other. Over the course of your visit, she will no doubt say one or two things very offensive; but have courage, for in the next moment, she will be kindness and charity itself, and so sympathetic, that you cannot help but forgive her, aware that every thing was said with the very best of intentions."

"An interesting description indeed," said Rebecca; and she looked forward to the meeting.

....

Chapter VII

Rebecca and Charles parted at the main gate. A long, shaded lane brought her to the house, which was indeed the very estate they had passed on their journey to Medford. It was, Rebecca noticed with equanimity, equally as grand as Claremont Park, and nearly the same size, yet with even more windows.

She ascended the steps and was admitted to an ornate entrance hall of fine proportions. Immediately, the servants ushered her to the rear of the house, whence she was taken outside to a wide brick veranda overlooking a landscaped garden which bordered an immense green lawn. At a table in the shade of a large, canvas shelter, sat Miss Davenport and Mrs. Harcourt. They were both attired in dark-coloured silk gowns, which although expensive-looking and attractive, appeared too warm for the season.

Rebecca was presented. Mrs. Harcourt (whose strong features bore some resemblance to her brother, Sir Percival) stood and received her with dignity. Rebecca had remembered her as being tall; but clearly that had been a little girl's impression, for the woman before her was but of moderate height, and now several inches shorter than Rebecca herself.

Miss Davenport more enthusiastically cried, "Miss Stanhope, how delighted I am to see you again!"

"Where is Mrs. Morris?" declared Mrs. Harcourt, resuming her seat, and indicating with a gesture that the young ladies should do the same.

"Please accept my sister's apologies. Sarah was most appreciative of your invitation, but at the last moment she felt ill, and thought it best to remain at home."

"What is her complaint?" enquired Mrs. Harcourt with interest. "Is she feverish? Does she suffer a sore throat? Only two weeks past, I was stricken with a fever and a very bad sore throat; several of my tenants have complained of it. I feared it should be of the putrid infectious sort, or worse yet, quinsy, and that if I lived, I should be laid low for the remainder of the summer. I was obliged to take several very expensive medicines. Thankfully, as you see, I have fully recovered."

"I am very glad to hear it, madam." Rebecca smiled to herself, thinking how accurately this speech met with Charles's prediction. "Sarah's throat is fine, however, and she has no fever. It is only a touch of fatigue and dyspepsia."

"Fatigue and dyspepsia? Well." In a lowered tone, Mrs. Harcourt added confidentially, "We know what *that* means in a woman of Mrs. Morris's age and circumstance, do not we? I cannot say I am surprised. Her youngest is how old now—eighteen months?"

Rebecca, blushing, caught Mrs. Harcourt's meaning—the idea of which had not occurred to her before. She was so astonished at Mrs. Harcourt's mentioning such a delicate and private subject, particularly on so short an acquaintance, that she could not immediately reply; however, a response was apparently not required, for her hostess continued,

"Young women breed entirely too often. A few young ones can be a fine thing, but you so often find families of eleven or twelve to-day. It is not healthy to have so many children."

Although Rebecca found these remarks equally astonishing, she could not help but admit that in private moments, she had often thought the same thing herself. "I am certain my sister and brother will welcome another child," replied

Rebecca earnestly. "A large family can be a source of much happiness and comfort."

"Yes, but at what risk to the mother? Not to mention the financial burden imposed on the father. Had my darling children lived, *I* should have taken care to stop at three." Glancing at her niece, she added, "Amelia, pour our guest some lemonade."

"Yes, aunt."

A few minutes were devoted to the serving and consuming of refreshments, and remarking upon their quality, of which Mrs. Harcourt was very proud. The ham had just been cured, the fruit, the last of the season, came from her own orchards, and as every one of taste knew, her cook, Mrs. Graham, made the best lemonade and lemon cake in the country. Rebecca found every thing to be delicious, and pronounced it so.

As she sipped her beverage, Mrs. Harcourt surveyed Rebecca critically. "You are very flushed, Miss Stanhope. Are you ill yourself?"

"I am quite well, Mrs. Harcourt. If I am flushed, it is only the result of my exertion, in my walk from the vicarage."

"Do you mean to say that you *walked* all the way hither, in this hot weather?"

"I did."

Mrs. Harcourt was astonished. "Amelia, I said very expressly that you were to send the carriage."

"I made the offer, Aunt Harcourt," replied Miss Davenport quickly, "but Miss Stanhope graciously declined. Do forgive me if I neglected to mention it."

"Thank you for the offer," said Rebecca, "but I prefer to walk when I can. Your country-side is very picturesque, and I enjoyed the exercise."

"You did not walk alone, I hope?"

"No. My brother accompanied me. He had other, urgent business to attend to, or he would have stopped in."

"Well, I always say a little exercise is beneficial to one's health—I myself *always* take a turn about the garden in fine weather," said Mrs. Harcourt, setting down her glass, "but to walk all that way, in this sun and heat? Never! Too much sun is not good for any body. If you are not careful, you will come out all over with freckles. I once fainted dead away at a party held out of doors, where insufficient shade was provided. I remained in a stupour for three days entire. Dr. Watkins feared I might never recover."

"And yet you did," said Amelia with a smile.

"Do you refer to Dr. Watkins junior, or senior?" enquired Rebecca.

"Are you acquainted with them?" asked Mrs. Harcourt.

"I have met Dr. Jack Watkins."

"Oh? Where did you meet him?" asked Miss Davenport curiously.

"At Barlow's Store, yesterday—just before we saw you. My sister was unwell, and Dr. Watkins took charge of the situation most capably. He is—we are—very obliged to him. He was every bit the gentleman."

"A gentleman?" Mrs. Harcourt frowned. "No, on that score, I beg to differ, Miss Stanhope. I can never think of a physician as a *gentleman*."

"Why not?"

"What is a physician?" responded Mrs. Harcourt with a shrug of her shoulders. "He is not a landholder, he has no title, and no family connections whatsoever. He is but one tiny step above the surgeon and the apothecary, who are held very low, and with good reason; for the apothecary is nothing but a merchant, and it is not so long since *surgeons* were formally linked with *barbers* in the guilds."

"Certainly your judgment with regard to surgeons and apothecaries is sound," replied Rebecca, "but is not a physician different, and more respectable? He has gone to university, after all."

"Any one with means to-day can advance his station through education," replied Mrs. Harcourt, "but it does not make him a gentleman."

"After meeting Dr. Jack Watkins, I must say that I found him to be as much a gentleman—if not more—as any one I have ever known who was born to that designation," replied Rebecca boldly.

"I feel exactly the same!" cried Miss Davenport warmly. "Aunt Harcourt, you always say that Dr. Samuel Watkins is a sensible man. I have heard you state on innumerable occasions that you do not know *what* you should do without him—and that the son will take after his father. I do wish you would think better of them."

"I admit, I *like* Dr. Samuel Watkins," replied Mrs. Harcourt. "He is an excellent practitioner, and a cheerful, independent character with a fine, active mind;—and his son does seem to shew good natural sense. But no matter how many colleges he attends or licences he acquires, the physician will always be no more than an educated tradesman to me. Why it is considered appropriate to-day to accept men of that breed into our circle, is beyond my comprehension;—however," added she with a sigh, "it is every where done now."

Rebecca determined it best to remain silent.

"We shall never agree on this subject, aunt."

"Let us move on to a new topic, then. Miss Stanhope, I remember you as a very thin, ordinary-looking child, but I am pleased to observe that you have filled out. Your deportment and air are very good, and you have grown up into a handsome young woman."

"Thank you," replied Rebecca, somewhat taken aback, yet suppressing a laugh.

"I know your mother died some time ago, and you do not have her to guide you. I hope you will not be offended if I offer advice with regard to your apparel?"

"My apparel?"

"I have a lifetime of acquired knowledge on many subjects, and I feel that my duty in life now is to educate others whenever I can. When it comes to ladies' fashions, I am particularly discerning—both my gown and Amelia's were made up from my own design—and yours, I am afraid, is too plain and not at all practical."

"Indeed?" said Rebecca.

Miss Davenport blushed at her aunt's remark. "I think Miss Stanhope's gown is lovely."

"There is merit in simplicity, but Miss Stanhope is a rector's daughter, and can do better without giving offence to those of higher rank. That pale shade of lavender will shew spots, and I dare say the muslin will fray and require a great deal of maintenance. How often have you washed it?"

Reluctantly, Rebecca admitted, "I have washed it several times, Mrs. Harcourt, and—you are correct. This gown *does* stain rather too easily, and I have been obliged to repair it several times."

"I shall recommend you to my mantua-maker."

"Thank you, madam, but I cannot afford a new gown at present."

"Well then, you must work with what you have." Studying Rebecca's gown with narrowed eyes, she added, "Appropriate embellishments can serve to mask many an evil, and not at a very great expense. A bit of black lace at your neck and hem, I think, would make all the difference—and perhaps some adornments on the sleeves. You would be surprised what an improvement a black lace can make."

"I appreciate your advice, and I will surely consider it."

Mrs. Harcourt nodded with satisfaction. "I am glad of one thing: that you have not fallen prey to this ridiculous notion of wearing white, which seems to be so much in vogue to-day."

"Oh! How I should *love* to wear a white gown," enthused Miss Davenport, followed by a little sigh.

"I would not waste good money on a white gown. You cannot keep it clean for two minutes, and it turns yellow with just a few washings, at which point it must be entirely remade or thrown away. It was not so long ago that a party or ball was a brilliant spectacle, reflecting every shade of the rainbow in male and female alike; but now there is a shocking lack of colour in a room."

Mrs. Harcourt sighed and lapsed briefly into reflection. All drank their lemonade. After a moment, Miss Davenport looked at her aunt with raised brows and a silent, eager expression. Mrs. Harcourt, apparently discerning some hidden meaning therein, turned to Rebecca, and said,

"Miss Stanhope: I have heard from Mrs. Morris that you are quite a proficient at both the pianoforte and the harp, and that your voice is very fine."

"Pray, do not believe every thing my sister says," returned Rebecca modestly. "I admit, I do love music very much. It is one of my particular enjoyments."

"My mother played the harp," interjected Miss Davenport. "I do not remember her well, but I remember the music she played. We still have her instrument in the drawing-room. I should so *love* to hear the harp again."

"You could hear it every day, Amelia, if you would only *practise*," admonished her aunt, adding, "I sent Amelia to the first private seminary in town, but to my disappointment, she returned no more accomplished than when she left."

Miss Davenport coloured violently. "I have no ear for languages, Aunt Harcourt—truly, I do not—and no talent for music. Surely *you* will play and sing for us some time, Miss Stanhope?"

"I should be happy to oblige, if the occasion arises."

"Where were *you* educated, Miss Stanhope?" enquired Mrs. Harcourt.

"I attended school for a year, but primarily I was educated at home. My father ran a small boarding-school for boys, and my sister and I studied with them."

"You studied with *boys*? What did you learn?"

"We read the best of literature, and studied history, geography, mathematics, and a little Latin and Greek."

"Upon my word! What can your father have been thinking? A refined young lady ought to be proficient in music and needlework, and know a phrase or two in French and Italian. Other than this, the most important principles she can learn are prudence, modesty, and economy. Of what use are these *other* subjects to her?"

"The same use as they are to a man, I suppose."

"Explain yourself," replied Mrs. Harcourt.

"Well, my knowledge of history, geography, and languages has afforded me an excellent appreciation of the classics, which in turn provide an interesting contrast to and commentary on the current affairs we read about every day in the papers. This gives me a fuller understanding of the world, and greatly increases my conversational abilities. You prize economy, Mrs. Harcourt; which by definition requires a woman to learn to live within her means;—and is not she also obliged to run a household, maintain accounts, and pay bills? Mathematics, then, is a very useful skill to a woman."

Mrs. Harcourt did not immediately reply. Under her steady gaze, Rebecca felt that some new criticism must be coming; instead, Mrs. Harcourt only said with a smile, "I declare, your answer surprises and delights me. You seem to me an intelligent and accomplished young woman. You have a very sensible head on your shoulders."

"You see, Aunt Harcourt? I *said* you would like her!" cried Miss Davenport, with a hopeful and expectant expression.

Mrs. Harcourt's smile now vanished; and from the look she gave her niece, Rebecca began to realise that there had been an underlying purpose to her visit;—a notion which Mrs. Harcourt confirmed with her next stern pronouncement.

"Miss Stanhope, for a great many years, I have heard flattering reports of you and your father from Mr. and Mrs. Morris and from my brother. However, ever since I learned the details of a certain—event—I have been in a quandary as to whether or not it is proper to receive your father, much less for Amelia to associate with *you*."

Rebecca bristled indignantly. "You may decide what you like about me, ma'am, but where my father is concerned, I assure you that he is the best of men."

"And yet, according to my brother's report, your father has behaved most irresponsibly; he gambled away a large sum of money belonging to the Elm Grove church."

"That was *not* the case. If you will permit me, I should be happy to apprise you of the real facts."

"Go on then; speak, Miss Stanhope, and I shall listen."

With animation, Rebecca ventured into a thorough explanation of the history of her father's efforts to raise funds for the new bells, all that had occurred on his ill-fated journey to London, and every thing which had transpired since. Mrs. Harcourt and Miss Davenport heard her with interest, asking questions at intervals, and making discerning comments along the way. "I am sorry to speak ill of Sir Percival," said Rebecca as she came to the end of her discourse, "but he has treated my father very ill—and all for the benefit of his nephew, Mr. Clifton."

"Oh!" cried Miss Davenport. "What a terrible story! When I heard of my cousin Philip's appointment, I was happy for him, not thinking how *his* good fortune had so adversely affected you."

Mrs. Harcourt sat for some moments, thinking, then said, "Gambling is a terrible sin, particularly in a clergyman, whose chief duty is to uphold the highest standards of behaviour for his parish. My brother believes in your father's guilt, my dear; that much is clear. Yet, it is quite possible he *deceived* himself into believing thusly, to promote Philip's interests; for our nephew has always been a great favourite of his." She sighed, and with genuine sympathy continued, "Miss Stanhope, if all is as you say, and *if* your father is truly blameless, then I am sorry for him—and for you as well. You have lost your home, your very way of life. It seems your father has done all he could to make up for the injury, as he repaid the entire sum out of his own pocket, quite impoverishing himself in the process. This is commendable, indeed."

"Can you help my father, Mrs. Harcourt? Will you write to Sir Percival on his behalf?"

"I will," answered she, "but I doubt it will do any good.

Mr. Clifton is established at Elm Grove, and from what I hear, discharging his duties most admirably; and I have rarely known my brother to change his mind about any decision."

"Is it possible, then, for you to help my father secure a new post?"

"I regret to say that I have no influence in *that* quarter, either. In truth, I think it highly unlikely that any one will employ your father—not only in view of his questionable circumstances, but because he is of an age when many might think it fit and proper for him to retire. Perhaps he should live a quiet life now, and find contentment in it."

"That would be easier to do, had we greater means; but we cannot even afford a house of our own."

"Well," returned Mrs. Harcourt pointedly, "I am certain that you, with your fine mathematical skills, can discover a manner in which to make a small income go a long way."

Rebecca laughed. "I shall try my best."

"In the meantime," pronounced Mrs. Harcourt, "I am happy to say that *you* are welcome at Grafton Hall at any time during your stay at Medford."

"Oh!" cried Miss Davenport with delight and relief.

"As for your father," continued Mrs. Harcourt, "I must make out his character for myself. I am holding a dinner party on Thursday next. Mr. and Mrs. Morris shall be invited, of course. I hope you and Mr. Stanhope will attend, and I should be delighted if you would play and sing."

"Thank you, ma'am. I will, if you wish it."

"The dinner is in honour of my nephew, Brook Mountague. He is coming to visit. You are acquainted with him, I believe?"

"I have known him all my life."

"Then you know he is Amelia's intended."

"I do."

"A very great match it will be; for he is a fine, polite, well-bred young man with excellent manners, who will inherit his father's estate; and one day, Amelia will inherit mine."

Several minutes more were devoted to Mrs. Harcourt's fond descriptions of her nephew, happy memories of his past visits, and the eager anticipation of the two families with regard to the future alliance, which was expected to take place within the next two years. Although Mrs. Harcourt clearly took great pleasure in the subject, Rebecca could not help but notice the disconcerted expression on her niece's countenance, which—although she struggled to contain it—suggested she did not think likewise.

Mrs. Harcourt soon expressed her intention to return to the house to rest. Formal good-byes were exchanged, and a promise from Rebecca extracted that she would agree to allow Mrs. Harcourt's carriage to deliver her home; and the two young ladies were left on their own for a private tête-à-tête.

"I do hope you will forgive my aunt's directness," said Miss Davenport, as she and Rebecca strolled in the shade between two hedgerows. "I am often mortified by the things she says, but I must bear it all with a smile, for I am her heir, and she has been every thing to me: my mother, my aunt, and my grandmother all in one."

Rebecca acknowledged that she thought Mrs. Harcourt to be an interesting and knowledgeable person, and found her honesty surprisingly refreshing.

"Oh! I am relieved to hear it! I have only had the opportunity to enjoy the society of other young ladies when we are in town, and more often than not, my aunt says something so impertinent or offensive, that they never call again! But I see that *you* will not be so easily dissuaded, Miss Stanhope. You *will* be my friend, will not you?"

"I should be honoured to be your friend, Miss Davenport."

"I am so glad! All my life, I have *dreamt* of having a friend who lived nearby, and here you are. Why, we can see each other every day. I simply cannot *wait* to hear you play and sing! Although in every other respect, I admit, I am *not* looking forward to my aunt's party."

"Will not you be happy to see Brook Mountague?" asked Rebecca in surprise.

"*He* is the reason I most particularly do *not* look forward to it."

"But—my dear Miss Davenport, you are engaged to him!"

"Engaged? Good heavens! No, Miss Stanhope! We are not *engaged*, not yet. No formal words have been spoken, and no promise has been made between Brook and myself—thank God. There is only the general *expectation* of a union, which has been designed and anticipated by my aunt and my uncle ever since I came to live here, when I was five years old."

"Oh. I see. But—do not you like him?"

Miss Davenport hesitated. "If I share a confidence with you, Miss Stanhope—something I have never shared with a living soul—will you promise to say nothing of it to any one?"

"You have my word."

"Well then, Brook is good-looking and rich, and as Aunt Harcourt constantly reminds me, he is well-bred and—" (with a smile) "—he comes from the *best* of families. But—" She made a face. "—he seems rather silly to me at times. He jokes a great deal. He is very proud of the pranks and reckless deeds in which he engaged at Oxford, and seems to be living the same sort of life in town now as a merry bachelor.

We hardly saw him at all, when we were in London earlier this summer, he spent so much time at his club and at Tattersall's. He talks a great deal about dogs and horses, and guns and hunting, which I find quite tedious. I only pray that he will improve with age. Fortunately, he believes that we are too young to marry—that he ought to be five-and-twenty at *least* before he will settle down—which gives me two years to see if a better offer comes along."

"Miss Davenport!"

"I see I have shocked you. But we are friends now, are not we? I cannot hide any thing from *you*, Miss Stanhope. I hope I may speak plainly and openly with *you*."

"You may. But if you do not love Mr. Mountague, if you do not wish to marry him, would not it be better to be honest with him—and to tell your aunt, as well?"

"Oh, no! I could never do that, Miss Stanhope. Every body expects me to marry Brook; my aunt, in particular, has her heart set on it. I would not wish her or any one else to have the slightest suspicion of my *private* reservations, for it would only trouble them, and I may never meet another man who will suit, or meet with my aunt's approval."

"I understand your hesitancy," said Rebecca, frowning, "but I still say you should share your feelings. My father always says that no good ever comes from an untruth—and *withholding* the truth is the same as a lie."

Miss Davenport blushed slightly and looked away, but made no comment.

"I do not know how you can conceive of marrying some one you do not love," continued Rebecca. "I could never do it. Before I promise to spend my life with a man, I must love him with all my heart."

"I quite agree with you, my dear Miss Stanhope, in *the-*

ory," replied Miss Davenport with animation. "I do *hope* to love my husband, more than any thing else on earth. But in *practice*, I am afraid I do not have the same freedom of choice as you; for how could I think of disappointing my aunt?"

....

CHAPTER VIII

Rebecca returned to the vicarage to find Sarah much improved, and playing in the garden with the children. That evening, while they were alone over their work in the sitting-room, Rebecca asked Sarah how she was feeling.

"I am well."

Rebecca gave her sister a long look, and said quietly, "May I wish you and Charles joy?"

Sarah lowered her gaze and her needle, colouring slightly. "It is not yet confirmed; I have said nothing to Charles, and I have yet to call Mr. Pearson—but I have my suspicions." Her glowing countenance reflected genuine contentment. "Four children would be a blessing. Three is such an awkward number; some one is always left out. I am hoping for another girl—a playmate for Arabella, just as you and I had each other."

Embracing Sarah, Rebecca said, "I could wish for nothing better. I am very happy for you, my dearest."

"I am happy, too."

Rebecca communicated to her sister the chief details of her visit to Grafton Hall.

"What do you think of Mrs. Harcourt?" inquired Sarah.

"I found her a woman of great understanding. I did not agree with all her ideas—she regards physicians as no better than barbers, and she treats her niece rather too severely—but she was kind enough to advise me as to the value of adding black lace to a plain gown."

Sarah laughed. "Charles is constantly complaining about something Mrs. Harcourt has said—which I suppose, coming from the lips of any one of less consequence, might be considered rude or impertinent. But while it is true that, at times, her views are old-fashioned, and she could show more tact, I think her sensible, elegant, and refined. We are indebted to her, for had not she given Charles his incumbency, we should not have been able to marry."

"Has Mrs. Harcourt been a long time a widow?"

"Nearly two decades. She manages all the affairs of her estate and the community very capably and nobly. She often thinks of the comfort of others, and sends food to neighbours subsisting on insufficient incomes. She took in her niece—the daughter of her husband's brother, and therefore no blood relation of *hers*—and has raised her up since a small child as if she were her own—a kind and generous act."

"Miss Davenport is a very amiable young lady."

"Her sincere enthusiasm for an association with *you* cannot be denied." Sarah smiled. "It will be nice for you to have a particular friend of your own age in the neighbourhood."

The promised invitation to Lady's Harcourt's dinner party arrived the next morning, and Charles promptly accepted on their behalf.

A visit from Mr. Pearson confirmed their suspicions, and all the family rejoiced over the impending event, which was still many months distant. Although Sarah was often indisposed in the mornings, it did not preclude Rebecca and Mr. Stanhope from enjoying a daily stroll. As the week passed, they visited together many of the principal walks of the neighbourhood, on one occasion accompanied by Miss Davenport. In the afternoons, they read to George and Christopher, an activity equally enjoyed by all parties; and Rebecca chased butterflies with the boys and played with the baby.

Sarah and Rebecca delighted in each other's company as they worked in the kitchen, poultry yard, and vegetable and flower gardens, and sewed shirts for the boys. They called on the Miss Wabshaws and passed an agreeable half-hour in their company, listening to their gossip; and although consuming very little, they complimented the baked goods on offer with such enthusiasm, as to give their hostesses real pleasure.

Despite these moments of companionship and felicity, not all was perfection. Rebecca deeply missed her music. She overheard the nurse maid complain that her new bedfellow kicked something fierce, and was wont to snore, which increased Rebecca's feelings of guilt in having displaced her. She herself found it a challenge to obtain a full night's sleep, for the three children, although very good (and she loved them dearly), made noises of their own, and were wont to rise much earlier than the hour to which she was accustomed.

Her father was equally weary, as he was obliged to stay up later than his customary bedtime, to allow Charles time to work in his study. On several occasions, Rebecca discovered Mr. Stanhope dozing in a chair—something he had rarely if ever done at home. On those evenings when Mr. Stanhope was allowed to retire early, Charles was obliged to give up his evening plans.

One morning, as Rebecca and her father were out walking, she could not prevent herself from saying, "It is lovely here, papa, and I am very grateful to Charles and Sarah for taking us in; but what I would not give to be back home in Elm Grove! How I miss my bedroom, our sweet dining-room and parlour, and all the daily walks which were so familiar and beloved."

"I miss them, too," admitted he. "We are in the way here, and every day it becomes more evident; but your sister and brother have been very accommodating. I am afraid we have no alternative but to remain for the present. In time, I believe, it will feel more like home. After all, what do we really need to be happy, other than the affection of our family, a few good friends, a comfortable home, food on the table, and a worthwhile occupation to fill our days? To love, to be loved, and to be useful: these are the most important elements in a happy, meaningful life, and they can be achieved anywhere."

Rebecca agreed with this sensible assessment, which was indicative of her father's eternally positive outlook. She remembered how light of heart she had felt on the morning she walked to Grafton Hall;—and she determined to be melancholy no longer. She would not look back in sorrow. She would look forward, and concentrate on all the good that had come of their removal to Medford—most particularly, on the interesting people she had met.

While helping Miss Davenport to select a new hat at Barlow's Store, Rebecca asked who was to make up the remainder of the dinner party at Grafton Hall two days hence.

"Oh, it will be the same people from the neighbourhood who always come," replied Miss Davenport, as she twisted a bonnet this way and that, and considered her reflection in the looking-glass. "I dare say, I have seen every one so frequently, and heard all the same stories so many times, I should go quite mad if *you* were not present to relieve the tedium. My cousin Brook will be there, of course, and the Wabshaw sisters, and no doubt Dr. Jack Watkins."

At the mention of this last name, Rebecca's cheeks grew warm. She had not seen Dr. Watkins since their encounter at Barlow's Store, although she had often thought of him. "Does your aunt truly mean to include Dr. Watkins?"

"Of course. Why do you sound surprised?"

Not wishing to betray an excess of interest in the matter, Rebecca said with composure, "After the lack of enthusiasm Mrs. Harcourt expressed for mixing with physicians in general, I did not expect her to invite him to her party."

"She has generally been obliged to include Dr. Samuel Watkins and his wife at all our engagements, as there are rarely enough people of quality to make up a sizeable gathering. With them both away in town, she would naturally invite the son. Most people do not share my aunt's opinion with regard to physicians, so it would look very bad if she did not ask him. What do you think of this purple hat? Do you like the grapes and cherries? Is the feather too large?"

Although Rebecca shared her view that the feather was precisely the right size, and the hat and decorations most becoming, Miss Davenport was not satisfied until she had tried on every other bonnet in the place, some of which were covered with an acre and a half of shrubbery, complete tulip beds, and clumps of peonies, and others which featured such a large quantity of fruit as to resemble a kitchen-garden. At length, expressing her wish to honor Nelson's great victory in Egypt, she settled on a red Mamalouc cap adorned with a Nelson Rose feather.

On Thursday evening, as Rebecca and her sister separated

to prepare their toilette before the dinner party, Rebecca teased, "Take care to wear your best gown, dearest, so that Mrs. Harcourt should not find it wanting."

Sarah laughed good-naturedly. "I suppose I should have warned you similarly before your first visit to Grafton Hall."

Rebecca told herself that the reason she took extra time dressing her person and her hair was to avoid censure from Mrs. Harcourt; but in truth, she knew there was more behind it, and could not help but smile at the thought that she would be meeting Jack Watkins again.

Entr'acte I

I GENTLY LAID THE JUST-FINISHED MANUSCRIPT BOOKLET onto a mahogany tray atop the coffee table, with the stack of others we'd already read. "I can hardly *believe* we're reading this!"

Anthony and I had been taking turns reading aloud. He was a quick study and had a marvelous gift for bringing characters to life. Hearing Jane Austen's words in his delectable British accent was divine. He now sat up on the couch, where he'd been stretched out listening to this particular section. "It's good. Far better than I expected."

"Can you *imagine* how excited Jane Austen fans will be when they learn about this?"

"Yes—but only if it's really hers."

"Oh, it's hers. I'm sure of it."

"How can you be so certain?"

"Well, the handwriting for starters. It's a perfect match to Jane's. The idiosyncratic spelling of certain words—alternating between show and shew, or enquire and inquire, for example—Austen did that. And it's her writing style."

"The style is certainly very similar, but I don't think it's identical to what I read in *Pride and Prejudice*."

"That's not surprising. If all the facts line up, this manuscript is one of Austen's earlier works, probably written in 1801 or 1802. She didn't revise and publish *Pride and Prejudice* until 1813—more than a decade later."

"So you're saying this was Jane Austen's more youthful writing style?"

"I think so. I think it's a transitional piece from her juvenilia to her mature works. Besides, this was clearly just a first draft. Who knows what it might have become, if she'd had a chance to revise it. Look at all the insertions and deletions—and there was that one page where she'd crossed out so much, she started a page again and actually pinned it in."

"I see what you mean."

"They say there are two kinds of writers—the ones who pour everything out in one great, inspired moment, and the kind who go back and endlessly rewrite. Jane was clearly one of the latter—a tinkerer. This is really a marvelous, evocative document. It shows us her mind at work."

"*If* it's hers," Anthony persisted. "The title—*The Stanhopes*—that doesn't sound very Jane Austen."

"Oh, but it does. Most of her early titles were simply the names of her characters."

"Her characters?" he repeated, surprised.

"*Sense and Sensibility* was originally *Elinor and Marianne*. *Northanger Abbey* was going to be *Susan*. The working title of *Persuasion* was *The Elliots*. Jane Austen's brother Henry retitled the last two after her death. The book she was working on before she died, the fragment we know as *Sanditon*, was going to be called *The Brothers*. And then, of course, there's *Emma*, and *The Watsons*."

"Interesting. I never knew any of this," Anthony admitted.

"Speaking of character names—here's another way I know this is her work. Jane Austen often reused the same names across different books, and I recognize almost all of these, many from her juvenilia. *The Three Sisters*, an epistolary short story she wrote as a teenager, had a family named Stanhope. So did *Sir William Mountague*—which gives you another name right there. As I recall, there were Rebeccas in *Mansfield Park* and *Frederic and Elfrida*, Sarahs in *Persuasion* and *Northanger Abbey*, several Jacks and Harcourts, and too many Williams and Charleses to count."

He laughed. "I see you really do know your Austen."

"That's not all." I shot him a teasing smile. "I seem to remember a Whitaker in at least one of her novels."

"A Whitaker?"

"I think it was a very rigid housekeeper who turned away housemaids for wearing white gowns—which is pretty funny when you consider that she often named characters after people she knew."

He laughed again. "So Jane Austen lost a manuscript at Greenbriar and got her revenge by naming a servant after her host."

"Maybe. She took mischievous delight in human folly."

"Okay, but even given all that, we don't know for certain *when* this manuscript was stashed here, or why. All we know is that Austen once stayed at this house, and according to that letter, she lost a manuscript. It could just be a coincidence that this manuscript resembles hers. It could be the work of someone else."

I shook my head. "No way. This smacks of Austen to me. So many aspects of the story and characterization are right out of her own life."

"Such as?"

"Jane spent the first twenty-five years of her life happily living at Steventon, a tiny village in Hampshire, very much like the fictional Elm Grove. Her father was rector, and their house was similar to Elm Grove Rectory. Sarah reminds me of Cassandra, Jane's older sister, who she considered as wiser and better than herself. Like Rebecca, Jane loved literature and music and daily walks in the countryside. She prized a comfortable and settled home. It's said that when George Austen abruptly announced his intention to retire and move to Bath, Jane was so distraught that she fainted. She was devastated that they had to sell all their books and possessions."

"Okay, okay, you've convinced me," he acceded, grinning.

"They say, 'write about what you know.' It must have been therapeutic for her to write this. The subject was clearly very meaningful to her. Two of her other books—*Sense and Sensibility* and *Persuasion*—also begin with the heroine being forced to give up her beloved home. I bet Jane began this novel after learning that she was being evicted from Steventon, and wrote most of it during their first year or two in Bath. She was probably homesick at the time."

By now, it was well past the dinner hour. We both admitted we were starving. Anthony said he'd bought a couple of steaks that morning, some potatoes and veggies, and the makings of a salad. He added that his dad had an excellent wine cellar. A good meal at this point in the evening sounded wonderful, and I told him so.

I hadn't cooked with a guy in years—not since my last boyfriend in grad school—and it was fun working together. Anthony really knew his way around a kitchen and was a master when it came to spices.

"Why do you think Jane kept this manuscript a secret from her family?" he said as he placed the steaks under the broiler.

"Maybe she felt it was too close to home. In the letter I found, she mentioned a 'valued family member' who might have been troubled by it. It could have been her father."

"Her father? Why?"

"Jane seems to have been close to him, just as Rebecca is close to hers. The physical description of Mr. Stanhope, and his personal history and Fellowship at Oxford, are similar to George Austen's. He was a literary enthusiast, and proudly owned a library of five hundred volumes—and when Jane was young, he also supplemented his income by running a boarding school for boys. But I wonder: how was he at handling money?"

"You mean," Anthony nodded, catching my drift, "did he play cards?"

"Everyone at the time played cards. There's no evidence that I know of that Mr. Austen ever gambled recklessly, but what if he *did* lose money at the table on at least one occasion—enough to give the family financial problems?"

"They no doubt would have been too embarrassed to mention it, and he would have been mortified if his daughter put it into a book."

"Exactly! This is exciting. It raises new questions about George Austen. Were Mr. Stanhope's flaws inspired by fact, or was that pure invention on Jane's part? Scholars are going to have a field day with this!"

Anthony went quiet at that. As we finished the dinner preparations, he seemed to be in a world of his own. We sat down and ate in silence for a while. I wondered if this discussion about George Austen had made him think of his own father. I was curious about Reginald Whitaker and the rift between them.

"You mentioned that you've been estranged from your father for a long time," I said at last, sipping my wine. "What happened? Or would you rather not talk about it?"

He shrugged. "I don't mind. It's a tale as old as time, unfortunately. My dad married my mum for her money—money he needed to keep the house going. I think my mum loved him, but he spent her entire inheritance, and then he wasn't even faithful. He cheated on her for years. Finally, when I was eleven, she got fed up. She took me, moved to London, and filed for divorce. In many ways it was a relief to get away. I'd sensed the discord the entire time I was growing up. He was a very controlling, dictatorial man. I was the only child, and I always felt like I was a disappointment to him. I was so angry with him for what he did to my mother, and for breaking up our family—but I think what hurt the most is that he didn't even try to get partial custody, and he never came to visit me."

"I'm so sorry."

"Yeah well, that's life." His casual words belied the hurt in his voice.

"Did you ever see him again?"

"Just twice. The first time was years later, when I was at university. He showed up one day out of the blue—found out where I was living from my mum—and said he wanted to take me to lunch."

"Did you go?"

"Yes. I suppose I was curious to see what he'd have to say, or hoping maybe he'd apologize. He never did, not in so many words. He just gave me lots of excuses, and said he felt bad about neglecting me."

"At least he acknowledged his mistake where you were concerned. Sounds like he was trying to reach out to you."

"I think he was just trying to ease a guilty conscience. He asked what I was studying. If I'd answered 'history' or 'the arts,' I guarantee he would have given me an angry lecture and walked away. But when I said finance, his face lit up. He was thrilled. All at once, he was my best friend. He said I'd chosen an excellent major that would lead to a successful career. He offered to help pay for my education—which astonished me, since he'd always held very tight to his purse strings. He said he'd have me down to the house soon, and we ought to keep better in touch. Better in touch? This, from a man who hadn't picked up a phone or sent a single birthday card in eight years? I was dubious. And to me, it was that controlling thing again—offered only because he happened to approve of my already-chosen path. But I never said as much. I just thanked him and told him that would be very nice."

"I take it he didn't follow through."

"He sent a check a week later. A much smaller one a month after that. I wrote to thank him both times, and when I didn't get a response, I wrote again—a friendly letter, trying to keep the line open. But I didn't see or hear from him again until the day of my mother's funeral." There was deep bitterness in his tone.

"How sad. You and your father both missed out on so much." I sighed, shaking my head. "And yet . . . it appears he didn't stop thinking about you. He kept all your cards and letters. And more importantly, he left you this house."

"Yes he did. I admit, it came as a surprise. I expected him to cut me out of his will entirely and leave everything to his newest lady friend, or to charity. I was shocked and touched, at first, that he left Greenbriar to me. But when I came back and saw the condition of the place, and fully understood the financial complications, I realized he hadn't done me any favors. All I could see was one big headache, and I couldn't wait to get rid of it."

"Do you still feel that way?"

He paused and looked at me, his features softening. "Not so much. Not at the moment." The warm glow in his blue eyes suggested that he wasn't thinking at all about the house, or even about the manuscript we'd found buried here.

I blushed and glanced away, my heart doing a little unexpected dance. I couldn't deny it any longer: I was smitten with Anthony. I gave my brain a silent, forceful kick to move on. I *had* a very nice, very handsome boyfriend, after all, and crushing on this man just wouldn't do.

"I think your father was proud of you," I said quickly, determined to stay on track. "I think he wanted you to have the house, and he hoped, in your line of work, you could figure out a way to save it. I can see why. I can hardly stand the idea of your selling this place."

"Well," he said, with a pointed smile, "if that manuscript really is an Austen . . . maybe I won't have to. How much do you think it's worth?"

"I don't know—probably a lot." I was still overwhelmed with disbelief at our discovery. "It's unique. None of the original drafts of Jane Austen's published novels survive, just a couple of discarded chapters. The last sale that was in any way similar was her unfinished manuscript *The Watsons*. It sold at auction for nearly four times its estimated value—for $1.6 million—and it was just a fragment of a known work that had already been published for centuries."

"I wonder what's the most expensive manuscript ever sold?"

Anthony whipped out his cell phone and started surfing the Web.

I had to admit, I was curious, too. I *had* my precious literary discovery; I knew the reading world was going to eat it up. If Anthony made a fortune out of it—if it meant he could save Greenbriar—that only made it more exciting.

"Okay, here it is," he said, reading aloud off his phone, "'Shakespeare's *First Folio*, including more than a dozen of his plays etc. etc., only 750 copies ever made, sold at Sotheby's of London in 2006, adjusted price for inflation: $5.5 million . . . James Audubon's *Birds of America*, adjusted sale price would be close to $11 million . . . A manuscript of the *Magna Carta*: $21.3 million . . . The *Gospels of Henry the Lion*, written by Benedictine monks, sold through Sotheby's in 1983, adjusted price today: $25.5 million."

"Oh my God."

"It gets better yet. Listen to this: 'Leonardo Da Vinci's *Codex Leicester* holds the record as the most expensive book ever sold to date. This journal contains the famous artist's notes about the link between art and science . . . The manuscript is handwritten in Italian on 18 separate sheets of paper that are folded in half and double-sided to create a 72-page document. In 1994, Bill Gates purchased it for $30.8 million. Today, this is comparable to almost $44 million."

"Forty-four million dollars!"

Anthony's smile took over his face. "What we have is every bit as valuable, wouldn't you say?"

"It could be! And it's longer, too." We hadn't counted the booklets yet, but I guessed there were at least forty of them. "This manuscript is probably over three hundred pages. Plus, it's an entirely *new novel*. It's never been seen before! But Anthony:

you can't sell it to someone like Bill Gates. This has to go to a library or university, where it can be viewed and studied."

He hesitated, then raised his wineglass in a toast. "Wherever it goes, if all the stars align, it looks like I might become a very wealthy man. And I owe it all to you."

"And to your father, and to all his fathers before him," I pointed out, toasting him in return.

"To Dad, and the Whitakers of yore," he conceded, raising his glass heavenward with unexpected reverence. "Thanks!"

As we drank our wine, it suddenly occurred to me that I hadn't told Laurel Ann or Stephen about our discovery. I asked Anthony if it was okay for me to call them and share the news.

"I'd appreciate it if you'd keep this to yourself for now," he said. "I still need to get it formally authenticated. And even then, I won't want to draw any attention to me or to Greenbriar."

"Oh. I see." Although I knew it was going to be hard to keep mum, I understood. I agreed to keep our secret safe from anyone else for the moment.

We cleaned up from dinner and returned to the library. As Anthony sat down beside me on the couch, he asked to see Jane's letter, the one that had started this whole adventure.

"There were a couple of things at the end that I've been wondering about." After glancing over it again, he said, "Here. She's talking about reading a manuscript aloud to her sister, then she says something that seems totally out of context: 'What banner years for me—two proposals!' What proposals is she referring to?"

"Well, we know that Jane Austen received an offer of marriage from a family friend, Harris Bigg-Wither, in December 1802. She famously accepted him, but after a sleepless night, changed her mind and refused him."

"Who was the second proposal from?"

"A good question."

"Another thing—what's this reference to *Plan of a Novel*?"

"I've been thinking about that. I've only read Austen's *Plan of a Novel* a couple of times. It's a brief outline that scholars have always thought was a parody of novels in general—a wink wink to the overly dramatic books of the time, which it *is*—but with this new evidence, we know it was more than that."

In the Austen collection on the shelf, we found a volume including *Plan of a Novel*, and read it through together. The comic outline described a beautiful, accomplished heroine, the daughter of a clergyman, who was driven from his curacy by a vile and heartless young man, forcing them to go forth on all sorts of adventures. Jane Austen included footnotes, attributing a few story elements—some of which were very silly—to hints from friends and relatives.

"The *Plan* does have a lot of similarities to what we're reading," Anthony noted.

"Yes, but thankfully, some of the more ridiculous plot points don't seem to be included. Jane admits in her letter that she wrote *Plan* in a mood of wit and wistfulness, making fun of the manuscript she wrote and lost, and had half forgotten. All of which is revolutionary when it comes to Austen lore, and incredibly exciting."

"I have to admit, I'm enjoying the story. I like the characters. Rebecca is brave and spunky. Mr. Stanhope is a good old soul. Dr. Jack Watkins is a first-rate hero—I look forward to seeing more of him. The whole setup is like a little mystery-adventure. Where will they go next? And what happened to all that money?"

"I can't wait to find out."

We locked gazes.

"Shall we get back to it?"

....

Chapter IX

On the evening of the dinner party, Mrs. Harcourt sent her carriage to the vicarage; and in due course, Rebecca, Mr. Stanhope, Sarah, and Mr. Morris arrived at Grafton Hall. They were shown into a grand drawing-room of fine proportions and finished ornaments, where several guests were already assembled. Mrs. Harcourt welcomed every one with handsome cordiality, and Mr. Stanhope presented such a composed picture of genteel civility, intelligence, and sincerity, as to do Rebecca proud.

Rebecca and Sarah greeted the Wabshaw sisters, the first of whom murmured quietly, "Mrs. Harcourt is such a dear friend—so good of her to always include us."

"Yes, so good of her," added her sister. "We did not know a soul except her when we first removed to Medford."

"Not a soul! She was great friends with our dear mother and father, you know."

"Yes, very great friends. We worry about her, you know."

"Worry about who?" asked Rebecca.

"Why Mrs. Harcourt, of course. Dr. Watkins visits the house so often now. We see him drive by in that smart-looking curricle of his."

"Such a smart-looking vehicle!"

"She is so often ill. We cannot help but be concerned."

"I would not worry about Mrs. Harcourt," interjected Sarah with a smile. "She has a fine, healthy frame for a woman of two-and-sixty, and is as strong as an ox. I predict she will outlive every one of us."

"I pray you are right, Mrs. Morris." Then, with a gasp of delight: "Oh, sister! There is Mr. Spangle!"

"There he is! Miss Stanhope, are you acquainted with Mr. Spangle?"

Rebecca admitted that she was not.

"He is a very gallant gentleman," said a Miss Wabshaw.

"Mrs. Harcourt should introduce you," said the other. The sisters made it their immediate business to speak with their hostess on the matter, and the introduction soon took place.

Mr. Humphrey Spangle was a diminutive, heavy looking widower who was more than twice Rebecca's age. His air was extremely courteous and effusive; immediately after presentation, he welcomed Rebecca and her father to the neighbourhood, and proclaimed what an honour it was to meet them. When Mrs. Harcourt, Mr. Stanhope, and the Wabshaw sisters moved off to converse with other guests, he paid Rebecca and Sarah a host of compliments with regard to their gowns and shoes, the style and colour of their hair, and their beauty, remarks which they insisted were far too generous.

"There is merit to moderation in many things, what what?" countered Mr. Spangle. "But, however, my experience with my dear departed wife, Mrs. Matilda Spangle, who was I assure you the loveliest, the gentlest, the most modest and discreet creature on this earth, has taught me that, where a lady is concerned, one can never be too generous in praising her outward appearance and articles of dress. Whereas for a gentleman, one's congratulations can never be too demonstrative with regard to his personal property, be it a horse, a hound, or a house."

"You make many excellent points, Mr. Spangle," said Rebecca. "I wish I could have known your wife; I am sure I would have liked her."

"Oh, to be sure, Miss Stanhope; never was a truer word

spoken. To know my dear Matilda *was* to love her. She passed on some eight years ago, and she is sorely missed, very sorely missed. I built my house, you know, expressly to please her, and she did love every alcove and corner of it. It is a very quiet place now without her, a very quiet place indeed."

"But it is a *lovely* house," said Sarah, adding to Rebecca, "Finchhead Downs is just beyond the village of Bolton, only two miles distant. Mr. Spangle has beautiful woods and a pretty little lake."

"I am honoured and humbled by the compliment, Mrs. Morris," said Mr. Spangle with a bow. "Miss Stanhope: I believe it is not idle flattery to say that my home is *one* of the finest in the country; but, however, I do not pretend that Finchhead Downs holds a *candle* to the elegant and imposing residence in which we now stand."

"Is it true what I hear, Mr. Spangle," enquired Sarah, "that you are installing a new fountain in the garden?"

"I am, Mrs. Morris; a splendid fountain, if I do say so myself, which I have erected in my dear Matilda's honour, and expect to be completed in the next few days. It is a truly magnificent work, with all manner of statuary around it, just the way she would have liked—Greek gods or some such, all spouting water, eh what what? And giant fish—you know, dolphins—carved from marble. My wife always delighted in the splish splashing of water. Whenever we passed by a brook or river, she used to say, 'Mr. Spangle, listen to that splish splashing, is not it divine?'—and I cannot say that I do not find equal enjoyment in it. Splish splash, splish splash—a very pretty sound, eh what, what? I am promised that with my new fountain, splish splashing will be heard from every corner of the house and grounds."

Rebecca replied that this would be very nice indeed,

when Miss Davenport suddenly seized her by the arm, allowing her to utter only the briefest of parting words to her sister and Mr. Spangle, before being drawn away to the other side of the room.

"Thank goodness *you* are here," cried Miss Davenport. "I was never so glad to see anybody in all my life! What a relief to have some one new to converse with at one of these dreadfully boring parties!"

"Mr. Spangle is a *very* interesting conversationalist," returned Rebecca with a smile.

Miss Davenport laughed. "I declare, Mr. Spangle is so excessive in his manner of expression, it is all I can do not to laugh every time he opens his mouth! I do feel sorry for him, though. He misses his wife dreadfully, which is very sad. And he is a nice man, and very rich—although he inherited his wealth from a father who prospered in trade, and is only newly made a gentleman—a fact which my aunt cannot quite forget."

"A newly made gentleman is as good as any other, in my book," replied Rebecca. "He is even more worthy perhaps; for he has had to work for all he has, rather than being born to it."

"I feel precisely the same!" cried Miss Davenport. "If only more people thought as we do—but so many cling to the old ways." With a heavy sigh, she added, "Where on earth is Brook? I never knew a man to take so long getting dressed. Oh! Look who is here!"

Rebecca turned her attention to the door.—All at once, she was all agitation and flutter. Dr. Jack Watkins had just arrived. He was taller and possessed even more fine a figure and countenance than she had remembered. She watched as he greeted their hostess and several others with equanimity; overheard him inquire solicitously after Mrs. Morris's health; observed as he was presented to Mr. Stanhope; and then caught her breath as he turned to Rebecca and her companion.

"Good evening, Miss Davenport."

"Dr. Watkins."

"Miss Stanhope, how very nice to see you again." His eyes found hers, and his smile was charming.

"And you, sir," replied Rebecca, with a curtsey.

He seemed about to say something else, when, of a sudden, approaching footsteps resounded in the passage, along with male voices deep in argument. Seconds later, Mr. Brook Mountague burst into the room, accompanied by—to Rebecca's complete astonishment—Mr. Philip Clifton.

"I only missed that last shot because the sun was in my eyes; otherwise, I would have brought home three brace, not two," cried Brook Mountague, so enthused by his subject, that he seemed unaware of where he was, or of the presence of any one else. "You bagged not two, but one and a half; and the half is in such a mangled state as to be inedible, so it should not count."

"I accede," replied Mr. Clifton, in a tone far more subdued than his cousin, as he lowered his eyes in embarrassment. "You won the match, fair and square; and we may speak of it no further."

Brook Mountague smiled broadly and clapped Mr. Clifton on the back. "There is a good fellow; I knew you would see reason. I only wish you had seen fit to bet with me beforehand, as I wished; I would have won a tidy sum off of you."

Rebecca observed this spectacle with great surprise, then inquired of Miss Davenport softly, "What is Mr. Clifton doing here?"

"He came to keep his cousin company."

"You made no mention of his visit."

"Did not I? Well! They so often come together, I suppose I did not think of it."

"Miss Stanhope," said Dr. Jack Watkins, "is something wrong?"

"No," replied Rebecca, with a tight little smile.

"I have seen very little of my cousins since their arrival," said Miss Davenport. "They went out early this morning in a couple of shooting jackets, and did not return for such a long while, I nearly forgot they were here. Philip cares nothing for hunting, you know; he only goes to please Brook."

"I did not know."

"From their argument, it seems they fared better to-day than yesterday, when they killed nothing at all."

Brook Mountague was working his way through the room, shaking hands gregariously with the men and bowing to the ladies. Philip Clifton followed a step behind him, performing the obligatory rites with decorum. Rebecca could not see that gentleman without the slight sting of resentment; his presence was a painful reminder of all that she and her father had been obliged to give up—and she could not forget that he had called her father *unfit*, and her life *stagnation*. However, as she watched Mr. Stanhope shake Mr. Clifton's hand in a manner of utmost geniality, she silently vowed that *she*, too, should rise to the occasion; she should not allow Mr. Clifton's presence to ruin her evening; she should be equally as gracious.

Mr. Clifton greeted Miss Davenport and Dr. Jack Watkins;—and all at once he was standing immediately before her.

Bowing, with all his customary reserve, he said, "Miss Stanhope. I hope you are enjoying your stay in Medford?"

"I am," replied she.

"It must be pleasant to be with your sister?"

"Sarah and her family have been most welcoming."

"And you find the village to your liking? You are enjoying it here?"

"It is a very agreeable place."

"I am glad you find it so." Mr. Clifton bowed again, and without further comment, moved on to greet another guest.

Rebecca let out a breath, relieved that the encounter was over.

"I knew Philip Clifton at Oxford," said Dr. Watkins. "A very quiet, dutiful fellow, as I recall."

"He is far too fond of books," said Miss Davenport, making a face. "He is always trying to persuade me to read something or other."

Rebecca glanced across the room, and to her surprise, found that Mr. Clifton was looking at her. She could not read the expression on his countenance; but upon meeting her gaze, he quickly looked away. At that moment, a servant entered with the announcement that dinner was to be served.

All proceeded into the dining-room, led by Mrs. Harcourt and Mr. Mountague. A splendid repast was laid out, attended by a great many servants, with every article of china, crystal, and plate on view, and every imaginable kind of food on display, from salmon and sweetbreads to curry of rabbit and goose. Mrs. Harcourt sat at the head of the table, with her niece on one side, Mr. Mountague on the other, and next to him Mr. Clifton.

Rebecca smiled upon observing her father take a seat next to Miss Davenport. Perhaps, she mused, such proximity to Mrs. Harcourt would give that lady opportunity to "make out his character" during the meal. Rebecca attained a situation which greatly pleased her; for although Mr. Humphrey Spangle immediately sat down to her left, on her right sat Dr. Jack Watkins.

As the soup was served, Dr. Watkins declared to Rebecca in a low tone, "I must say, I could not have asked for a better spot at the table, or a more preferred dinner companion."

His smile was so sincere and congenial, and his sentiment so welcome and reciprocated, that Rebecca immediately felt a lift in spirits, and an easing away of that tension which had filled her earlier. "I, too, am pleased as to the *right*," whispered she playfully;—adding, with a private glance towards Mr. Spangle, "although perhaps not quite so much as to the *left*."

"Pray allow me to disagree, my dear Miss Stanhope; for from my position, the left leaves nothing to be desired."

She smiled; but her satisfaction wavered upon catching sight, at the other end of the table, of Miss Davenport's expression. Her friend was frowning.

"What is it?" asked Dr. Watkins. "Your lovely smile just fled. I hope I have said nothing to offend?"

"You have not, sir. I am only concerned about Miss Davenport. She seems unhappy."

"Does she?" He looked round to study the young lady in question, who acknowledged their inquiring glances with a comical face. "Well, she does not seem unhappy *now*. If she was before, perhaps it is because she is accustomed to thinking herself the most handsome woman in the room, and she knows that she has been outshone by you to-night."

"Dr. Watkins!" Rebecca blushed.

"I speak only the truth. I think Miss Davenport rather vain. She seems to enjoy being the centre of attention."

"Please do not say such things to me, sir. She is my friend."

"Is she? Pray, forgive me, and allow me to reinterpret her earlier unhappiness as a sign of her dissatisfaction with her *own* dining partners. Were I seated with an elderly, infirm aunt and two dreary cousins, I should hardly be in a good mood myself."

Rebecca laughed.

"I say!" boomed Mr. Spangle, "may I inquire of what you are speaking? I delight in any thing humorous!"

With only the slightest pause, Jack Watkins replied, "We were just discussing Miss Stanhope's favourite book, which she finds most amusing."

"Oh? What book is that, Miss Stanhope?" asked Mr. Spangle.

Rebecca, giving Jack Watkins a look that was half gratitude, half reproach, considered for a moment how best to reply, when she was saved from that action by his interjection: "*The Female Quixote; or, The Adventures of Arabella.*"

Rebecca's eyes widened in amazement, at his making such an appropriate choice, and saw that her reaction produced a delighted smile from Dr. Watkins.

"It is indeed a remarkable book, Mr. Spangle," said Rebecca, "and one which has made up my family's evening entertainment over numerous readings. In fact, my sister is so enamoured of it, that she named her daughter Arabella after its heroine."

"A well-deserved tribute," said Jack Watkins, raising his wine-glass, "to Charlotte Lennox's art."

The soup was now removed, and a large saddle of mutton carved, as the first course began.

"Are you well acquainted with the work in question, Dr. Watkins?" inquired Rebecca.

"I admit, without the slightest embarrassment," replied Jack Watkins, as he helped himself to the dish in front of him, and offered it to Rebecca, "to having read a few novels in my day. I did not get through the whole of *The Female Quixote*, but as I recall it was most entertaining, and the character of Sir George Bellmour very amusing."

"And thus," proclaimed Rebecca to Mr. Spangle, "the impetus for our mirth! Have *you* read the book, sir?"

"Read it? Good God! No," replied Mr. Spangle. "I say! What is the point in *reading* a book? A great, tedious expenditure of time, that—particularly these new things, what did you call them, novels? All manner of nonsense about people who never existed and places one will never see! Far better to be up and doing things yourself—riding, fishing, shooting, eating, what what?—than to sit in a chair reading a made-up story about *other* people doing things. No, I do not *read* books—but my dear Matilda did, God rest her soul—she liked books *very* well. I collect them in *her* honour. Books lend such a scholarly air to a man's library, do not you think? My Matilda always said that I have the finest library in the country—and I defy any one to prove otherwise."

Rebecca was about to respond, when Mr. Mountague remarked to all the table, "I would like to propose a toast to my aunt Harcourt's health. Is not she looking very well this evening?"

A chorus of well-wishers voiced their agreement and raised their glasses, after which Mr. Morris said, "I am pleased to see you so fully recovered from your recent indisposition, Mrs. Harcourt."

"Thank you," replied she gravely. "I was saved only by the timely emetic Dr. Watkins prescribed"—(a glance here to Jack Watkins, who graciously nodded in return)—"from the complaint escalating into a serious illness. Mrs. Martin, you know, who I visited shortly before I fell ill, is still confined to her bed."

"The air in those houses is very bad!" declared one of the Miss Wabshaws.

"Very bad!" added her sister. "We have long discouraged you from calling there, Mrs. Harcourt."

"I must shew myself at regular intervals," asserted Mrs. Harcourt, "to offer my advice and counsel. It is my duty, however bad the air may be. The cottages are often dirty as well, a circumstance which incurs my constant reproof."

"Cleanliness," said Mr. Stanhope, "is not only a virtue, but a great facilitator of good health."

"Indeed, I am quite of your opinion, Mr. Stanhope," replied Mrs. Harcourt with enthusiasm. "I have long insisted that there is a connection between good health and good housekeeping."

"An amusing notion," whispered Dr. Jack Watkins to Rebecca, "but I am afraid there is no medical support for it."

Rebecca held back a smile. Mrs. Harcourt and Mr. Stanhope exchanged remarks with regard to the best way to wash window glass; and when he complimented her on her sparkling casements, she appeared extremely gratified.

The dinner proceeded, with the second course equally as fine and elegant as the first.—Although, to Rebecca's frustration, Mr. Spangle so monopolised her in conversation on matters of little interest or import, to which she felt obliged to reply, that she was unable to speak to Dr. Jack Watkins again.

After the table-cloth was removed to reveal the fine polished table, and the nuts, fruits, and other desserts were laid out, Rebecca was rescued from her private dialogue with Mr. Spangle, when her father turned to that gentleman, and said, "Sir, did I hear you mention earlier that you are in possession of a fine library?"

"Indeed!" cried Mr. Spangle. "You heard correctly. I flatter myself to admit that I have acquired more books than you have ever witnessed in one location. Every volume in my library is printed with the best quality paper and ink, and I have had them all handsomely bound with the finest leather and gilding."

"Do you perchance have *Life of Johnson*?"

"Life of who?"

"*Life of Johnson*. The biography by James Boswell is a great favourite of mine. I was just thinking the other day, how much I should like to re-read it. Dr. Samuel Johnson is, in my humble opinion, the most distinguished man of letters in English history—he was an adept literary critic, his poetry and essays are remarkable, and as a lexicographer, he remains unparalleled."

"My good man, I have such a vast quantity of books," averred Mr. Spangle, "it is quite impossible to memorise the titles of them all, what what? You must come to Finchhead Downs and see for yourself. If I have it, it is yours for the lending."

"Thank you, sir."

"You must come, too, Miss Stanhope," continued Mr. Spangle. To all assembled, he proclaimed, "I say, it occurs to me that it has been quite a while since I did any entertaining. Let us rectify that by celebrating the installation of my new fountain with a little party, eh what, what? Shall we say

Saturday next? You are all invited to Finchhead Downs for lawn bowling, refreshments, rowing on the lake, and a tour of my library, where you will each be welcome to borrow a volume of your choice."

This announcement was met with a general outburst of applause and many approving comments.

Turning back to Rebecca, Mr. Spangle added confidentially, "I have the most bewitching barouche and four in all the world, Miss Stanhope. Have you ever ridden in one?"

"I have not, sir," admitted she, "although I have often heard it said that it is an unexceptionable vehicle."

"There is no finer way to see the country." With a wink he added, "I shall dispatch the conveyance to Medford Vicarage to convey you and your family to my affair."

"We should be much obliged, sir, I am sure."

Mrs. Harcourt soon rose, signaling the end of the meal, and the moment when the ladies were to leave the room.

....

Chapter X

As the ladies made their way through an ante-chamber, Mrs. Harcourt declared the meal to have been a success, and told Sarah and Rebecca, "Mr. Stanhope seems after all to be a very sensible and genteel sort of man. I for one am pleased to have made his acquaintance, and I shall let it be known that he is always welcome at Grafton Hall."—a pronouncement which was met with happy murmurs of gratitude from his daughters.

Entering the drawing-room, Rebecca's attention was immediately captured by a pianoforte prominently situated, and beside it, a beautiful harp, which she could not help but stop and admire.

"You will find both of our instruments to be very fine, Miss Stanhope," declared Mrs. Harcourt. "I should be gratified if you would play and sing when the gentlemen join us. Begin with the pianoforte, then move to the harp."

"As you wish, ma'am." In reviewing the music on the stands, Rebecca was relieved to discover several pieces with which she was familiar.

She took her seat beside Sarah and Miss Davenport, where they looked through picture books while Mrs. Harcourt spoke with the Miss Wabshaws. For some minutes, Mrs. Harcourt listened to the minutiae of the sisters' lives, and delivered information on a great many topics, from the ordering of meat, and the best time of year to plant potatoes, to the proper way to toast bread over the fire without singeing its corners. At length, Mrs. Harcourt turned to Rebecca, and said, "I observed at dinner, Miss Stanhope, that you were very animated in your conversation with Dr. Jack Watkins and Mr. Spangle."

Rebecca, colouring at this unexpected remark, said only: "The time passed very pleasantly, ma'am."

"The young Dr. Watkins is a congenial enough young man. I ascertain that you like him. For some one of your station, particularly in view of your present circumstances, he might make a good match."

Rebecca's cheeks grew even rosier. "Please, ma'am; I have only just met Dr. Jack Watkins. I do not know him well enough for it to be said that I like him, and I assure you, I have no aspirations in that regard."

"Well then, what do you think of our Mr. Spangle?" asked Miss Davenport with a smile.

"Mr. Spangle is an interesting gentleman," responded Rebecca, "who dearly misses his wife, and is apparently the proud owner of a fine library full of books he will never read."

This observation was met with general laughter. Even Mrs. Harcourt could not suppress a smile. Not long after the tea and coffee were brought in, the gentlemen joined them. A gesture on Mrs. Harcourt's part made it known to Rebecca that it was time for her to perform. Gracefully, she moved to the pianoforte, sat down, and, without any introduction, began.

So accustomed had Rebecca become to playing and singing at dinner parties over the years, that it was no great feat for her to perform before this small crowd. The only distinction was that, in the past, she had generally known every person in the audience, and they had all been so familiar with her particular talents that they had seen nothing remarkable in them. Now, as Rebecca played and sang, for the first time in her life, she felt a different *something* in the hush that fell over the room. The gentlemen quietly took their seats and listened. The ladies leaned forward in their chairs. All attention was focused on her.

At the conclusion of the song, there came a round of sincere applause. An encore was requested and delivered, and received with equal enthusiasm. Afterwards, Rebecca moved to the harp, where she played several pieces in succession, each of which was met with similar accolades. Rebecca stood and curtseyed at the end, blushing at her reception, both thrilled and humbled to be surrounded by so many admiring faces.

"An excellent performance, Miss Stanhope," remarked Mrs. Harcourt with a nod. "You are indeed a highly skilled musician, and your voice is very fine. Thank you for indulging us."

"I say!" cried Mr. Spangle with enthusiasm. "That was very well done, what what? Such an elegant display! Such lilting tones! Such a voice—like music from heaven! I declare, I have never in all my life heard any thing to equal it!"

"You are too kind, sir," replied Rebecca.

He seemed prepared to go into further raptures, but was interrupted by Miss Davenport, who grasped Rebecca's hands in hers and exclaimed, "Amazing!"—adding with a sigh, "I would give any thing to be able to play and sing like you."

The Miss Wabshaws paid their personal compliments, as did Rebecca's family. A final tribute came from Dr. Jack Watkins, who smiled, and said quietly, "Miss Stanhope, you have a truly lovely voice, and you play like an angel."

Rebecca glowed with pleasure; for some time after, she could not stop smiling.

The card-tables were promptly made up. There were exactly the right number for three tables of four. Under Mrs. Harcourt's direction, one group took their seats to play Quadrille, and another Commerce; and before Rebecca knew it, she found herself at a distant table with Miss Davenport, Philip Clifton, and Brook Mountague, who elected to play Casino. There was no alternative but to sit down. The game began.

"I have nothing that matches," protested Miss Davenport, studying her cards and the board. "Oh! Wait! Three and four makes seven, does not it?"

"The last time I checked," joked Mr. Mountague, "except when expecting change from a street vendor."

"I will build sevens then," stated Miss Davenport, placing her three upon a four.

Mr. Mountague was next, and promptly captured the build with a seven of his own.

"Villain!" cried Miss Davenport. "How dare you steal the spoils I had so clearly marked as my own?"

"In the same manner in which I stole your heart," replied Mr. Mountague teasingly. "Boldly and directly, without regard for the consequences."

They both laughed. Rebecca could not help but join in, and even Mr. Clifton smiled—an expression which did wonders to improve his looks. As the game continued, Mr. Mountague made additional amusing observations, Miss Davenport complained about her hand, and Mr. Clifton played in silence, exclaiming only once, when Rebecca triumphantly cleared the board.

"I see that we may add card-playing to your other, many talents, Miss Stanhope," said he.

"I claim no talent for card-playing, sir," replied Rebecca. "It is merely an amusement."

"And yet, to play cards well does require a certain amount of skill—this game, for example, requires strategy and mathematical ability."

"Abilities that even the smallest school-child should possess," responded Rebecca.

"I think Mr. Clifton was attempting to give you a compliment," said Mr. Mountague with a laugh, "an event so rare, I urge you to accept it with good grace."

"Speaking of compliments," interjected Miss Davenport, "we are playing with two very insolent gentlemen, Miss Stanhope. I believe they are the only people present who did not offer flattering remarks earlier in praise of your playing and singing."

"I assure you," insisted Rebecca quickly, "that I have received enough accolades this evening to last my entire life, and could not bear to hear more; and a commendation is not worthy when pressed, but only if freely offered."

To which Mr. Mountague replied, "I freely proclaim to have heard Miss Stanhope perform so many times since we were children, that I cannot pretend to be astonished. However, I *will* acknowledge that her pipes are as pretty as any of the birds I have heard in town, and she moves her fingers over the keys and strings with great speed and agility."

"Shame on you, Mr. Mountague!" cried Miss Davenport. "To speak of speed and agility, rather than *ability*. I declare, you have no appreciation for music whatsoever."

"I appreciate music as much as the next man," returned he, "as long as it comes after a fine meal and port, and does not go on longer than a quarter of an hour."

"And what have you to say to this, Mr. Clifton?" persisted Miss Davenport.

Mr. Clifton did not immediately reply. Rebecca grew warm with mortification, wishing that her friend would give up the subject; but finally he said, "It is a long while since I have heard Miss Stanhope play and sing. She was skilled as a youth; and her talents have indeed improved since then."

"I cannot decide if that is a compliment or not," said Miss Davenport, "since you do not say how *much* her talents have improved, or if you enjoyed her performance, then or now."

Mr. Clifton seemed about to reply, but was interrupted by Rebecca's uttering emphatically, "I implore you; let us talk of something else. Pray tell me, Mr. Clifton, what news have you of Elm Grove? How was the dear village when you left it?"

"All was well, and quiet," responded Mr. Clifton.

Starved for news of her old friends and surroundings,

Rebecca could not prevent herself from continuing. "How are Martha and Eliza, and Mr. Gower?"

"Very well, and capable. I am grateful for their services."

"And Mrs. Wilson? How does she fare? She had hurt her arm just before I left, and two of her children had the croup; I have been concerned about them."

"I am not yet acquainted with Mrs. Wilson or her family."

"She lives at Long Meadow Farm."

Mr. Clifton shook his head apologetically.

"Have you met Mr. Coulthard? He and my father are great friends."

"Good God!" cried Mr. Mountague. "Are we going to talk about Elm Grove all night? Who cares about a yeoman and a farmer's wife?"

"I have the greatest respect for yeomen and their wives," responded Mr. Clifton. "They are the salt of the earth. Where would you be if they did not work your father's land and pay their rent?"

"Let them pay their rent, then, and let *us* play cards."

Dutifully playing a card, Mr. Clifton asked Rebecca, "Is Mr. Coulthard a tall man with dark hair, of about forty years of age?"

"Yes."

"Ah. I believe he introduced himself at church on Sunday—he seems a very decent fellow—but we have not yet had a chance to chat."

"I used to stop in once a week at the Wilsons' farm, weather permitting. I was teaching their oldest, Susan, to read. Both the mother and daughter enjoy having the Psalms read to them."

"Thank you, Miss Stanhope; I shall try to remember."

"You cannot expect Philip to be bosom friends with every body already," commented Miss Davenport. "He has barely been in Elm Grove two weeks."

"True," replied Rebecca. "I admit, Mr. Clifton, I am surprised that you were able to leave the parish so soon after having become employed. My father was rarely absent in the eight-and-twenty years that he was rector." Rebecca felt all the impertinence of her remark, and knew she ought not to have said it, particularly when she had *vowed* to be gracious; yet she could feel no regret.

"Oh!" interjected Mr. Mountague with a renewed smile. "Now *there* is a well-placed barb. How will you reply, cousin?"

Mr. Clifton coloured slightly, and answered, "It was my uncle's particular wish that I accompany Brook here, and Aunt Harcourt was also most insistent. I found a suitable substitute to conduct the Sunday services while I am away."

"I hope you do not resent Philip for retaining his position, Miss Stanhope," observed Mr. Mountague.

Rebecca could vouchsafe no answer.

"My father was obliged to appoint *some one,*" continued Mr. Mountague. "He could hardly allow Mr. Stanhope to continue as rector after what happened. Your father brought his misfortunes upon himself."

Rebecca found her voice. "He did no such thing!"

"You ought not to disparage Mr. Stanhope," remarked Miss Davenport. "Miss Stanhope assures me that he was a victim, not a perpetrator."

"I wish that were so," said Mr. Clifton quietly. "It would be preferable to the truth."

"What makes you think *you* know the truth, sir?" demanded Rebecca.

Mr. Clifton hesitated, then said, "Forgive me. I see that you are distressed, Miss Stanhope; let us speak of this no further."

"Pray, *do* speak of it," insisted Rebecca. "I wish to hear what you think is the *truth*, that I may offer a defence on my father's behalf."

Mr. Clifton reluctantly went on in a lowered voice, "It is common knowledge that Mr. Stanhope is guilty of behaviour unbecoming to any man, but particularly a clergyman—that he indulged his proclivity for gambling and behaved very recklessly with church funds which had been entrusted to his care, resulting in a disastrous loss."

"That, sir, is a malicious fallacy," said Rebecca with rising anguish. "You have met my father on numerous occasions. He is a good and responsible man! How can you think he would behave in such an infamous manner?"

"I do not like to think it; and yet he did," replied Mr. Clifton calmly.

"A mistake of some kind has been made. I insist upon it. If you had only seen how distraught my father was when he came home that day! So confused and uncertain. 'All those people's hard-earned money—vanished!' he cried. He was utterly beside himself!"

"Is that his claim?" said Mr. Clifton, surprised. "That he has no idea what happened to the money?"

"No idea at all. He went to bed with the funds in his pocketbook, and when he awoke, the money was gone."

"My uncle said nothing of this," mused Mr. Clifton.

"Yet your father admits to engaging in a betting game with a group of gentlemen earlier in the evening, does not he?" said Mr. Mountague.

"Yes," admitted Rebecca, "but his stay was brief, and involved only the smallest amount from his own pocket." She explained how long it had taken her father to raise the money, and what its sacred purpose had been. "He would never, *could* never dispose of it in one ill-conceived night of gambling. Some one must have stolen it—how or when, I cannot say; but it *must* have been stolen. It is not in my father's character to behave as you have suggested. And yet, despite his innocence in the matter, he felt it his duty to pay back every penny of the lost funds before we left Elm Grove."

Mr. Clifton frowned as he listened to this impassioned discourse, and looked particularly surprised by her last statement; but he made no further comment.

Mr. Mountague, however, shook his head with impatience, and said, "You insist that it is not in your father's character to behave thus, Miss Stanhope; but how can you be certain? Even a man of the greatest integrity can be susceptible to a lapse of judgment." With lifted eyebrows and a tilt of his head, he gestured across the room towards the card-table where Mr. Stanhope was engaged in a game of Commerce—and was at that very moment betting heavily on a hand, with great enthusiasm.

"Perhaps," said he, "you do not know your father quite so well as you think."

VOLUME TWO

....

Chapter I

During the return journey from Grafton Hall, as the conveyance jostled her companions to sleep, Rebecca sat in silent confusion, brooding over all that which had just transpired. For the first time, doubt began to creep in beneath the solid layer of confidence which had pervaded her every thought regarding her father's innocence.

Could her faith in him have been misguided? Could there be any truth at all to the dreadful accusation against him? If so, it would mean that her father had been lying to her these many weeks, about all that had happened that fateful night—that he was the worst sort of gambler, a man without scruples, and a discredit to his profession! This, Rebecca could not accept nor believe; yet when she tried to regain her former resolve, she encountered only increasing confusion, anxiety, and uncertainty.

Sarah, opening her eyes sleepily, glanced at Rebecca, and whispered, "Dearest, what is wrong? Are you ill?"

Rebecca softly replied that she was only tired. The distressing subject consumed her thoughts all night, however, and still weighed heavily on her mind at breakfast. After Mr. Stanhope left with Mr. Morris on church business, Sarah sent the children out to play in the garden with the nurse maid, and proposed that she and Rebecca take a walk.

No sooner had the two ladies set off, than Sarah said, "It was a lovely party last night—quite a success for *you* in particular. Every body loved your performance. I believe you have made a new conquest."

"A new conquest? What do you mean?"

"Any one with eyes could see that Dr. Jack Watkins is interested in you. Regardless of what you said to Mrs. Harcourt, I believe you like him, too?"

"I do like him," admitted Rebecca, colouring slightly.

"There! I thought so. I am very happy for you. He is a charming young man. It would be an excellent match."

"Please do not speak of matches! I barely know him."

"Well then, it is a good beginning." Sarah paused, and with a gently inquiring look said, "Something is troubling you—something quite apart from this. What is it?"

Unable to keep her worries to herself any longer, Rebecca shared the details of the conversation which had ensued the evening before, with regard to their father.

"No wonder you looked so distressed when we took our leave. But my dear Rebecca: surely you do not agree with this interpretation of events?"

"I never before considered that it could be so, but ever since last night, the question has tormented me! What if it *is* true? What if papa *did* invent the story about the money's being stolen?"

"I cannot believe that."

"I have only the greatest respect for papa; you *know* I love him with all my heart. But if he *is* guilty, it would explain why he was so ready and willing to leave Elm Grove without a fuss; he believed he did not deserve to remain. It *is* a fact that he enjoys playing cards, and always has. It is *also* a fact that we have long had money problems at home. We always attributed it to insufficient income, and his habit of giving so generously to the poor. But what if he did not tell all? What if, all these years, the troubled state of our finances actually derived from another source?"

"Are you implying that papa has had a gambling problem of long standing?"

"It is possible, is not it?"

"No. *No*; it is *not* possible. He is too good a gentleman; too highly principled; too worthy."

"I have always thought the same; but perhaps our unwavering faith in his good nature has blinded us to the truth.

How do we know what went on at all those weekly games of cards over the years? If papa had a tendency to bet too heavily, and if Sir Percival was privy to it, surely that would explain his immediate proclivity to believe in papa's guilt in *this* affair."

"I refuse to accept that. We have known papa's sterling character and unselfish heart all our lives."

"Even the best of men can make a mistake, Sarah."

"Why are you losing faith in papa, over the unfounded accusations and suppositions of others? They do not know him as we do."

Rebecca hesitated, then said, "You are right, as always. There is no proof of his wrong-doing; none whatsoever! Dear God, Sarah. What *can* I have been thinking?"

"Mrs. Harcourt was very taken with papa last night, and very approving—and the community will follow her lead."

Rebecca sighed with relief, ashamed now of what her thoughts had been. "I hope that is true. In the meantime, I shall pray that one day, the true facts of the affair will come to light, and papa will be fully exonerated."

On the morrow, a note arrived from Mr. Spangle, making good on his promise, and requesting the company of Rebecca, Mr. Stanhope, and Mr. and Mrs. Morris, to a garden and boating party to be held at Finchhead Downs a week from Saturday. The invitation was accepted.

Shortly thereafter, as Rebecca happily ran after the children up and down the passage in a chasing game, she found Mr. Stanhope writing a letter at a small table by the sitting-room window.

"To whom are you writing?" inquired she, stopping to catch her breath, as Christopher clutched at her skirts, and

George struggled to seize his grandfather's pen from his hand.

"To a cousin of mine," replied her father, shaking his head calmly at little George.

"A cousin? Who? Have I met him?"

"No. Nor have I. He is called Thomas Newgate. He is distantly related to me, on my father's side." To the children, he added, "Be good boys. Run along now."

There was a sharp edge and a grimness to his tone that alarmed Rebecca. "George, Christopher, go out to the garden. I will catch up with you in a moment, and we shall continue our game." With squeals of delight, the children raced out the door. "Papa," continued she quietly, once they were alone, "why are you writing to a man we have never met?"

"I think you may guess, my dear." He finished inscribing a line and dipped his pen. "I am grown too old to live in a house full of young children. The vicarage is not as clean and tidy as I would like—there is dust and clutter every where, and I am constantly sneezing or tripping over something—and my peace of mind is daily disrupted by all the noise and bustle. But more importantly, I keenly feel how much *our* presence is a disruption to those who reside here. We are in the way."

"And so—you are writing to find some one else who might take us in?"

"Yes."

Rebecca's cheeks burned with shame. "If only we were not so dependent on the charity of others, papa. If only there was some way in which *I* could earn a living. I do so wish that I could help!"

"You are a great help to me every day, my dearest Rebecca.

Just your presence makes me smile. I cannot think what I should do without you. Now do not worry your head about any of this. I *will* find us another place to live, and soon."

Rebecca went out to play with the children, but her thoughts were now distracted, and her heart no longer in it. To be obliged to leave Medford—to undergo yet *another* substantial change in their lives, just as she was growing accustomed to and fond of *this* place—it was disheartening indeed. And where should they go? Upon what new family—what strangers—would they be obliged to trespass? No matter who or where it was, she could not imagine that she should feel as welcome as she did here, in her dear sister and brother's home.

As the week wore on, Rebecca tried to dismiss these unhappy thoughts from her mind, and to enjoy what little time she might have left in Medford. She and Sarah called again on the Miss Wabshaws. Accepting a kind offer from Mrs. Harcourt and Miss Davenport, Rebecca and Mr. Stanhope made two visits to Grafton Hall, where Rebecca played for an hour or two on the pianoforte and the harp, and Mr. Stanhope read aloud from a book of poems, exercises which afforded both performers and listeners a great deal of enjoyment.

Rebecca looked forward to the impending party at Finchhead Downs with anticipation. She had always loved going out in a boat on the river at home, but could not recall the last time she had been on a lake. Even the knowledge that Mr. Clifton and Mr. Mountague would be in attendance could not dampen her spirits, for Miss Davenport had confirmed that Dr. Jack Watkins would be there.

On the morning of the party itself, a parcel arrived at the vicarage for Mr. Stanhope. Its contents were received by him with the greatest surprise and delight: for it was none other than a copy of *Life of Johnson*. As there was no card or note accompanying the book, and no return direction on the wrapper, there was no way to determine who had sent it.

"Why, it is the very book which you have been so desirous of obtaining!" observed Rebecca. "What a fine edition."

"Some one must think very highly of you, papa, to send such a lovely gift," said Sarah.

"But who can have sent it?" said Mr. Stanhope, puzzled. "If it is a gift, why have they not put their name on it?"

"Perhaps it is from Mr. Spangle," conjectured Rebecca. "You expressed your wish to him so eloquently at dinner on Thursday last. He must have found the book in his library."

"Why should Mr. Spangle go to all the trouble and expense of sending it to me, when we are visiting his house this very day?" countered Mr. Stanhope.

"Mr. Spangle does not strike me as the sort to give anonymous gifts," added Charles. "If *he* was your benefactor, he would surely delight in letting you know all about it."

"I agree. Moreover—forgive my impertinence—but I should be rather surprised if Mr. Spangle had the facility to recall the title of the book I mentioned the other night. He is not—he did not *seem* to me—the most literary of men."

Rebecca laughed. "You both make excellent points. But if it is not Mr. Spangle, then who can it be?"

"Who else was privy to our conversation, other than ourselves?"

"The Miss Wabshaws are kind women, with good hearts," suggested Sarah.

"The Miss Wabshaws could not afford to purchase such an expensive edition as this, my dear," returned her husband.

"What about Mrs. Harcourt?" asked Rebecca. "She has an excellent library."

"She was busy talking with her niece and nephews, at the other end of the table," said Charles. "I doubt she overheard."

With a little gasp, Rebecca exclaimed, "Oh! It must have been Dr. Jack Watkins. He was sitting directly beside me, and he is an enthusiast of literature."

"Dr. Watkins?" repeated Mr. Stanhope with a nod. "Now there is a thought."

A few minutes further discussion convinced them that the gift could have come from no other person. Rebecca glowed with pleasure. What a considerate gesture on the part of Jack Watkins—such an example of gallantry and generosity! She had liked him before, but this act recommended him to her all the more.

They dressed for the party, and an hour later, a handsome barouche landau with its top down drew up to the vicarage, pulled by four elegant white horses. The vehicle was spacious and comfortable, a tribute to its designer in both looks and performance; and the ride through the lush green countryside to Bolton was every thing that Rebecca could have hoped for. Although it had rained the day before, prompting grave concerns that the anticipated event would have to be abandoned altogether, the sun at last made an appearance, and the weather proved to be fine. As they drove, the blue sky formed a pleasant canopy amongst billowy white clouds, and the breeze felt refreshing against Rebecca's face. Moreover, she was in the company of the three people she loved best; what greater felicity could there be in the world?

....

Chapter II

In contrast to the older, often rambling and irregular manor homes in the area, which bore tribute to the long-standing gentility of the families residing therein, Finchhead Downs was more recently erected. Its gleaming red brick and marvelous symmetry bore testimony to the recent acquisition of wealth by its owner. The size of the house was respectable, and it was becomingly situated on a small rise above well-tended gardens, with an excellent prospect stretching down to meadows bordering a small but pristine lake.

All the expected members of the party, with the exception of Jack Watkins, arrived almost within the same moment, creating a confluence of horses and carriages at the front of the house. Every one alighted and greetings were exchanged. A great many large dogs were about, panting and seeking attention. Mr. Spangle proudly led the members of the party on a tour of the interior of the residence, which boasted more than half a dozen immense portraits of the departed Mrs. Spangle in various presentations and modes of dress. The place had all the rooms that it ought, furnished with every thing new and fashionable; but which, Rebecca thought, reflected a shew of conspicuous affluence rather than taste. The only room she could admire was the library, for it was indeed grand and impressive, and filled from floor to ceiling with books of every size and description.

When they entered, Rebecca found herself and her father standing next to Mr. Clifton, who was surveying the room and its contents with appreciation and admiration.

"A truly remarkable library," murmured he.

"Of all the things I was obliged to part with at Elm

Grove," said Mr. Stanhope quietly, "it is my books that I miss the most."

Rebecca blushed, embarrassed by this candid reference to their personal troubles, which Mr. Clifton had clearly overheard. Hoping to ease her father's anguish, she said in a low tone:

"We are most fortunate, however, papa, that your library remains intact," continuing, with a look at Mr. Clifton, "at least I presume that is the case, Mr. Clifton?"

"You may rest assured, Miss Stanhope," stated Mr. Clifton discreetly, "that no one could esteem or value your father's excellent library more highly than I." To Mr. Stanhope, he added, "I will make it my business, sir, to retain and care for it, and I shall peruse its literary wonders as devotedly and comprehensively as you would yourself."

"That is a great comfort, sir," replied Mr. Stanhope.

Mr. Clifton seemed to wish to say more; but the conversation was put to an end as Mr. Spangle addressed the assembled group.

"This collection is the work of two decades," announced Mr. Spangle proudly, while patting the head of one of his hounds with vigour, "for I began buying entire libraries from any place I could, from the moment the house was built. I have a man, you know, who is very good at that sort of thing—he sends me all the newest volumes just as they are published, as well. I have had the preponderance of them handsomely bound, and shelved as you see, in accordance with my dear Matilda's exquisite sense of taste and style—with all the larger books in this section, the red books in these cases, the green here, and there is black, blue, and brown."

At that moment, a deep, teasing voice spoke in Rebecca's

ear. "What an interesting arrangement. I had never thought to catalog my books by size and colour."

Rebecca turned to find Dr. Jack Watkins beside her. She could not contain her smile. "While it is true that it might be difficult to find a particular author or title under such a system," murmured she in return, "the display has its merits, for it is very pleasing to look at."

Jack Watkins laughed. Mr. Clifton moved away with a frown.

Turning to her father, Dr. Watkins said in a more audible tone, "Mr. Stanhope, the book you mentioned on Thursday last must surely be contained somewhere within these walls. *Life of Johnson,* was not it? May I offer my services in helping you to locate it?"

"There is no need, Dr. Watkins," answered Mr. Stanhope, with a knowing smile, "for I am pleased to state that I am already the proud owner of that volume—quite an excellent edition. I received it this very morning. As there was no note or direction attached, I can only deduce that it was a gift from a person who wished to remain anonymous."

"Anonymous? Is that so?"

"It was a very handsome present," added Rebecca, "and there has been much speculation as to the identity of the giver."

"If it is as excellent an edition as you say, then surely it must have come from Mrs. Harcourt," said Dr. Watkins, his eyes seeming to dance.

"That name was considered," replied Rebecca, "but rejected."

"Indeed? Well then, perhaps it is from Mr. Spangle himself; he sent it ahead so that it might be accepted as a gift, rather than a loan."

"That is possible," said Rebecca," but we think improbable."

"If the book did not come from either of these two sources, I cannot think who it could be," said Jack Watkins lightly. "What a delightful mystery."

Mr. Stanhope said, "It *is* a mystery, sir. But if I could know the name of my benefactor, I would tell him how much I appreciate the offering, and give my utmost thanks."

Eyeing Mr. Stanhope with grave penetration, Dr. Watkins said, "Clearly, whoever sent the book desires neither your thanks nor recognition, sir. Just knowing that you are happy—and that your daughter shares in your delight—must be recompense enough."

His conviction seemed real, and the self-satisfied look on his countenance assured Rebecca that he was indeed their mysterious patron.

Rebecca now entered into the general ongoing conversation, which was filled with admiration for Mr. Spangle's achievement.—"Such an imposing room! (a Miss Wabshaw)—Truly imposing! (the other Miss Wabshaw)—Did you ever see so many books? (Sarah)—Look at the gilding on this one (Charles)—This title intrigues me (Mr. Clifton)—I should love to read that one (Mr. Stanhope)—My library is equally fine, if not as large; and I am sure I do not approve of this habit of collecting books for their own sake, according to colour and number (Mrs. Harcourt)—Did you see the view from this window? (Miss Davenport)—Such a delightful prospect, all the way down to the lake! (Dr. Watkins)—Excellent grounds for sport, and that black bitch pointer of his is a real beauty (Mr. Mountague)."

A quarter of an hour passed in this manner, at which point Mr. Spangle reminded every body that at the conclusion of the festivities, they were all welcome to return and borrow any volume that interested them. He then invited the assemblage to adjourn to the grounds, where they were followed by all the dogs, and he eagerly presented his new fountain, which stood in the centre of his landscaped gardens. A large and rather ostentatious circular structure, it was ornamented *not* with dolphins but with spouting whales, fish, cherubs, a variety of birds, and a representation of Neptune cavorting with the three Muses, one of whom (the most modestly clad), due to her striking resemblance to the woman in the portraits within the house, must have been modelled after none other than the departed Mrs. Spangle.

"It was erected after my own design," explained Mr. Spangle, "in the memory of my dear Matilda, and I am assured that it splishes and splashes such a vast quantity of water every hour, as to rival the sound and productivity of Aysgarth Falls themselves."

A round of applause and congratulations followed, with many pretty compliments, which Mr. Spangle received with blushing modesty; at which point he invited his guests to enjoy the many and varied delights of his property, promising them a picnic on the lawn at one o'clock.

Although it was a mild morning, Mrs. Harcourt and Sarah retreated to a shady grove bordering the pleasure grounds, where they sat on a bench talking and fanning themselves. While Mr. Mountague and Mr. Morris engaged in a game on the lawn, the rest of the company began walking along the short avenue of limes which stretched beyond the garden on its way down to the meadows and the small lake. Every where were bounding dogs.

Mr. Stanhope and Mr. Clifton were at the head of the party; from the few words which Rebecca caught, they seemed to be engrossed in an earnest conversation about Elm Grove and its population. Behind them ambled the Wabshaw sisters in the company of Dr. Jack Watkins. Rebecca heard one of the twins enthuse as they passed by,

"What a fine-looking place. Such a lovely house and grounds!"

"Lovely!" agreed her sister. "One rarely sees such elegant furniture. Mr. Spangle has very refined taste."

Rebecca felt an arm slip through hers; it was Miss Davenport. Beneath the shade of their parasols, her friend said, "Did you ever see any thing so horrid as that fountain?"

"It does make a very pretty splish splash," replied Rebecca, smiling.

"'The splish splashing can be heard from every corner of the house and grounds, what what?'" quoted Miss Davenport, mimicking Mr. Spangle's unique manner and inflection, then sinking into laughter. "Those statues were nearly naked! One was clearly Mrs. Spangle!"

"And why were ravens and sparrows cavorting with whales and fish?"

"I have no idea! It *is* very endearing, though—that he built it for his wife."

"I quite admire him for that."

Miss Davenport sighed. "I would love it if a man built a fountain for me."

Just then, heavy, hurried footsteps were heard behind them. Rebecca looked round to find Mr. Spangle himself hastening in their direction. The ladies exchanged a silent, conscious glance, and ceased their conversation.

"Miss Stanhope," cried he, "Miss Davenport! I beg you, attend, attend."

Dropping arms, they allowed their host to catch up to them.

"I cannot express what delight it gives me," cried Mr. Spangle, gasping and perspiring profusely as he drew near, "to have you lovely young ladies at my humble home. I hope every thing meets with your approval?"

"It does indeed, sir," replied Miss Davenport.

"Do you like my fountain?"

"Oh! Yes, sir," enthused Miss Davenport. "It is a truly lovely fountain. I like it more than I can say."

"And you, Miss Stanhope? What do you think?" asked he, as they all walked on together.

"It is a fine tribute to your wife, sir," responded Rebecca sincerely. "And the house and grounds are very beautiful. You should be justly proud."

"Just so, just so, Miss Stanhope! Do you know that when I bought this property—I chose this precise location expressly, out of all of England, and for good reason—I said to myself: this is not only a very beautiful piece of land, but a very well situated parcel as well. It has every thing one could wish for.—As my dear wife always said, it has many attributes which do not at first meet the eye—will you allow me to point them out, Miss Stanhope? You no doubt saw that it is close to the church, a very, very good thing on a Sunday in bad weather, for I assure you the walk is not troublesome at all; and neither is it far from the village, which delighted Mrs. Spangle, for there is an excellent butcher; very convenient, what what? I say! A far cry from what the residents of Thornton and Bleglsey must endure, for *they* are obliged to send four miles for their meat. Look, just there you see the stew-pond, which I put in for Mrs. Spangle, who always delighted in fresh fish; and for me, I have the dovecote, for there is nothing like a good pigeon-pie, eh what what? And I trust you saw my fruit-trees planted just inside the garden wall? Although they are not as ancient as one might wish, some are quite the best in the country, for the quantity of harvest they bear."

Rebecca replied that she thought the house very well situated indeed, and that the grounds, trees, and gardens were any thing which a man could want. These compliments seemed to gratify him exceedingly. They had by now reached the meadow at the edge of the lake, where a pair of small row-boats were tethered and bobbing at a small wooden dock.

"What pretty boats," said Rebecca. "I like nothing better than a water party."

"Oh! Do let us take a stroll instead," protested Miss Davenport. "I see a nice path along the lake edge, through the trees."

"I think Miss Stanhope had rather go *out* on the lake, than to walk around it," said Mr. Spangle eagerly. He paused to shout an order to several hounds who were milling nearby, and barking at the ducks. As the dogs obediently ran away up the hill, Mr. Spangle added, "That little blue row-boat is a very sturdy vessel, and was quite a favourite of Mrs. Spangle. I am sure you would like it, Miss Stanhope."

Rebecca hesitated, unsure how best to reply. Her friend had requested her company on a walk, and at the same time, although Mr. Spangle had not worded it specifically, his meaning was clear: he wished for her to go out in the boat with him.

All at once, Jack Watkins intervened, and said, "I understand why your wife would have been partial to that little blue boat, sir; it looks very snug. I, however, admit to a preference for the *green* one. May I have your permission to borrow it? That is, if Miss Stanhope will do me the honour of allowing me to convey her out onto the lake?"

Mr. Spangle's face fell; his mouth opened and closed in a manner resembling a fish, as he emitted a small, disappointed sound; then, slowly recovering himself, he said, "Why, why, certainly young man; that is what the boats are for, to be borrowed and taken out, eh what what? And, if that is what Miss Stanhope wishes—" He was unable to continue.

"Miss Stanhope?" enquired Jack Watkins with a charming smile.

Rebecca felt all the awkwardness of the moment. Although she was keen to go boating with Dr. Jack Watkins, she had no wish to disappoint either her friend or her host—and she felt particularly bad on Mr. Spangle's account. "There are three seats in the boat," said she at last. "Perhaps Miss Davenport or Mr. Spangle would like to accompany us?"

"Certainly," replied Jack Watkins smoothly, "there is room for one more."

"You know I hate going out on the water!" cried Miss Davenport with irritation. "It always makes me ill!" Then, eyeing Rebecca and Jack Watkins, she added more softly, "Well, perhaps you did *not* know. But now you do."

"Perchance some one else would be amenable to walk with you, Miss Davenport," suggested Jack Watkins.

Philip Clifton immediately strolled up to Miss Davenport, and said, "I would be happy to join you on your walk, cousin. The woods at the water's edge look most inviting."

Miss Davenport did not look happy; but she smiled and thanked her cousin for his offer. "Are you sure you will not come with us, Miss Stanhope?"

"I—thank you," replied Rebecca, who, if she had considered walking with Miss Davenport before, certainly had no wish to do so *now*, under her present company, "but—if you will forgive me—"

Miss Davenport sighed and turned, and, with a brief backward glance, she and Mr. Clifton walked away.

Jack Watkins then pronounced, "Mr. Spangle, I have observed Mr. Stanhope and the Miss Wabshaws studying your lake with the greatest interest and anticipation. I believe they would be most grateful if you took them out for a ride in the other boat."

"Oh! Yes!" cried one of the Miss Wabshaws with enthusiasm.

"We should like nothing better, Mr. Spangle!" agreed the other.

"It has been quite a while since I enjoyed a water cruise," admitted Mr. Stanhope, "if you do not object to rowing for a bit, sir."

"Well, well, I say!" returned Mr. Spangle with a formal bow. "The pleasure would be mine." He then escorted his party down towards the dock, bestowing upon them a detailed description of the fine workmanship of the boat in question.

Jack Watkins and Rebecca followed at a small distance behind them. The whole matter had been resolved so quickly, that Rebecca was too amazed to speak. As the others boarded the blue vessel, Jack Watkins handed her down into the green one. Once he had assured himself that she was comfortably situated, he untied the boat from the dock, settled onto the seat facing her, and took up the oars. Before she knew it, they were gliding away.

....

Chapter III

As they proceeded out into the glassy green water of the lake, Rebecca could not help but smile at how smoothly Dr. Watkins had arranged it; for the two of them were now quite alone together. He made a fine figure as he rowed.

"What does that look signify?" asked Jack Watkins, gazing at her. "You smile; yet there seems to be some deep meaning behind it."

"I am thinking that this was very wicked of you, Dr. Watkins," said she. "You must be aware that Mr. Spangle wished to take me out on the lake."

"Would you have preferred to be with Mr. Spangle?"

Rebecca smiled again, then caught herself; and said nothing.

"Are you happy in present company?" persisted Dr. Watkins.

Rebecca blushed and did not reply.

"I will perceive this intriguing silence as an affirmative," said he, laughing. "I hope you forgive me for being so forward? I thought only to rescue you from an uncomfortable situation."

"You did, sir, and I thank you, but—I admit, I feel guilty for disappointing Mr. Spangle."

"He seems to taking his disappointment very well," replied Dr. Watkins indifferently, nodding towards the other boating party, who were gliding in the opposite direction.

Catching sight of Miss Davenport and Mr. Clifton, as they strolled along the path surrounding the lake, he added, "I wish I could say the same for your friend, however. She seems rather—how shall I put it—perturbed."

Rebecca glanced thither, intercepting a look from Miss Davenport, whose countenance indeed looked pained. "I wish it were not so. I surmise she feels that I have abandoned her."

"That is Miss Davenport for you; always thinking of herself and her own pleasures first. She wanted your company, and could not have it. She is pretentious and spoiled—the sad product of her upbringing with her aunt."

"I wish you would not speak ill of her. I like her, and I am flattered that she likes me and enjoys spending time with me. She is not perfect, Dr. Watkins, but who amongst us is without flaws?"

"You are absolutely right, Miss Stanhope. I have been rude. Consider me properly chastised. Again, I beg your forgiveness."

"Granted. But will you please try to be nice to her, in future—for my sake?"

"For your sake, I shall. You have my solemn promise: in all future encounters, I shall endeavour to think and speak more highly of Miss Davenport."

"Thank you." Rebecca removed a glove and, balancing her parasol against her shoulder with one hand, she trailed the other in the refreshing water as they rowed along. They were quiet for a moment, listening to the sounds of the insects and the gentle breeze which ruffled the distant trees. "It is lovely here. If I close my eyes, I can almost imagine I am back in Elm Grove, floating down the river in my neighbour's boat."

"You are fond of Elm Grove."

"I am."

"Tell me about it. What was it like?"

Rebecca hesitated, uncertain if she wished to talk about a place so dearly missed, lest it give her pain; but as she began to speak, she found the conversation unexpectedly cheering. She shared fond memories of the village itself, their friends, her family, and her years growing up there; and he listened to all with the greatest interest.

"It sounds like a very nice neighbourhood, indeed."

"I never imagined that I would leave it, yet here I am."

"Are you sorry to be here?"

Her answer surprised her.—"No."

"No?"

"No," repeated she, marvelling at the discovery. "I was quite miserable when we first went away, and I miss home very much. But—I have enjoyed my time here. It has been pleasant to see new places and meet new people."

"Meeting new people *can* be most agreeable." A pause ensued, during which Dr. Watkins gazed at her in a very penetrating way, which seemed to be equal parts admiration and approval. This study made Rebecca colour.

"Sadly, I believe our stay in this place may not be much longer. My father has spoken to me of his desire to move on."

"Oh? I am sorry to hear that." He said no more, but frowned and lapsed into contemplation.

Rebecca glanced down, scrambling for something else to say. "I understand that you grew up in London, Dr. Watkins, and went to Oxford. What was *that* like? Oxford, I mean?"

"It was the same as any university, I suppose."

"As I have never had the pleasure of attending university, I should really like to know—details, if you please."

"Well, we had chapel at eight, meetings with our tutors in the mornings, and lectures in the afternoon. We dined in Hall at five, were obliged to be back in college by nine, and any one who returned late was fined. Servitors were publicly distinguished from those whose rich fathers paid their way, and—" (a little bitterly) "so were those whose family had no property or title. Some undergraduates shamefully caroused and got into debt; others, like me, avidly pursued their studies."

"But what about the *classes*? What did you learn?"

"The usual: Latin, Greek, the higher workings of mathematics, history, literature, philosophy. We read the classics in their original languages, and translated them."

"How exciting it must have been, to have all that knowledge at your command, and to hear lectures by such learned men! I studied all the same subjects, but in far less detail I am sure, for I was taught at home by my father."

He appeared surprised. "You were fortunate in your education. It sounds very rare for a young lady."

"I believe it was." As the lake was small, they now glided past the party in the other boat, and exchanged friendly waves. "Most of my sex are allowed only a few years of schooling, *if* any. The establishments, according to my experience, are appalling, and girls are taught only the most rudimentary subjects."

"What *should* women study, in your opinion, Miss Stanhope?"

"Why, every thing that men study! There should be no distinction. Women should be allowed to advance to higher learning, just as men do."

He smiled. "An unusual outlook, Miss Stanhope. I can just imagine the confusion and disorder which might ensue, were the female line introduced at Oxford or Cambridge! A woman in a roomful of men would be a powerful intoxicant. No man would ever attend to his studies again."

"How do you know? It has never been tried."

"And I dare say it never will."

"You men do not know how fortunate you are, to have all the fruits of a formal education at your disposal, and the freedom to choose a profession along with it."

"That *choice* is not always as free as you might think, Miss Stanhope."

"Oh?" She looked at him. "Are you saying you did not wish to be a physician, Dr. Watkins?"

"*Wish* is not the proper word. I have always known that I was *meant* to be a physician."

"How so?"

"Since I was a small child, it has been my father's express desire that I follow in his footsteps. For him, there was no question but that I would be the next Dr. Watkins. It was only under those terms that he agreed to finance my education."

"Are not you pleased with your profession?"

He hesitated. "I hope I can do some good. But—had not I been obliged to obey my father's design, who knows what other route I might have chosen? Perhaps I would have been a painter."

"A painter!" Rebecca thought he must be joking—but his eyes were serious.

"I studied with a master for several years as a young man. It was said that I had talent for drawing and painting, and might have a future in it; but my father would not countenance such a thing, and my lessons ceased."

"I, too, used to be fond of drawing as a child," admitted

Rebecca, "but I always considered it as a hobby. Can a man truly earn a living at it?"

"It is difficult, I am sure." He sighed. "My dearest wish has always been to live in the country. A physician must live in town. Had I been an eldest son, Miss Stanhope, born to wealth and property, I might have enjoyed a country life and indulged my passion. But that pleasure has been denied me—just as you, as a woman, have been denied the formal education you seem to desire."

"Perhaps so, Dr. Watkins; but there is a difference. *You* may still paint if you wish, and you have the power to earn your pewter; while I can never go to Oxford or Cambridge, and can only ever earn a living as a governess, companion, or teacher in a school—all occupations which I shudder to think of."

"Judging from the musical talents I saw on display the other evening, Miss Stanhope, you could earn a good living, if you chose, on the London stage."

Rebecca's cheeks coloured at the compliment, and at the look in his eyes, which was warm and flattering. "That, sir, is unlikely ever to happen," replied she with a laugh.

The water party soon concluded, and all assembled beneath a shelter on the lawn, where a long table was set and a cold repast was served. Miss Davenport sat down immediately beside Rebecca and Sarah, and they engaged in lively conversation throughout the meal. As her friend's manner no longer betrayed any trace of hurt or malice, Rebecca deduced with some relief that her apparent offence had been forgiven.

When all had eaten their fill, Mrs. Harcourt proclaimed that, as her nephews would be in Medford only a few days more, she had decided to hold a ball on the evening before their departure. The announcement was met with approbation on the part of the men, praise from the older women, and delight on the part of the younger ladies.

"A ball!" cried Miss Davenport with enthusiasm. "How lovely, Aunt Harcourt! It has been an age since we have had a real ball at Grafton Hall!"

Mrs. Harcourt nodded with pleasure. When she and Mr. Spangle stood, and all were permitted to leave the table, Miss Davenport drew Rebecca off into the privacy of the shrubbery, and said, "My aunt mentioned nothing to me about a ball; how cunning she is."

"Cunning? Why?" asked Rebecca.

"She has been complaining that I have neglected Mr. Mountague all week; that I ought to have spent more time in his company. Clearly, she is holding this ball so that we might dance and be *seen* together."

"Oh! I understand."

"I do love a ball! But have you danced with Mr. Mountague?"

Rebecca paused, a smile tugging at her lips. "I have, many times over the years, both at Claremont Park, and at our assembly rooms back home."

"What is your opinion of his performance?"

"Well," Rebecca began, and then paused, not wishing to speak ill of any one.

"Is not he the *worst* dancer who ever lived?"

"He does make a rather appalling spectacle," admitted Rebecca.

"He is all left feet, and he is for ever stepping on mine! He goes this way when he should go that, forward when he should go back, and does a half turn when a full is required. He could no more tell the difference between a Figure of Eight, a Hey, a Chassé, and a Pousette if his life depended on it!"

"On one occasion when we were neighbours in a Mad Robin, he moved so clumsily that I ended up losing my partner entirely."

"And *this* is the man I am to marry!"

"Surely an aptitude for country-dancing is not a requirement for matrimony, Miss Davenport."

"If a man cannot dance, how can I love him?"

"I believe many excellent unions have been founded between persons with a disparity of talent for, or interest in, the amusement. My father, for example, is not a good dancer; yet my mother was; and they were very happy together."

Miss Davenport sighed. "I shall keep that in mind. And now on to more important matters: what shall we wear?"

"That is easily settled in my case. I have only the gown I wore to your house for dinner on Tuesday."

"Oh, dear. That will not do. You cannot wear the same dress again. Have you nothing else?"

"No—at least, nothing appropriate for a ball."

"Well, I have loads and loads of frocks, and we are about the same size. I will loan you one of mine. You must come to me on the morning of the ball, and we will find the one which suits you best. I want nothing but the finest for my dear friend! My maid is good with a needle; I will have her make any small alterations necessary for a proper fit."

....

Chapter IV

"You and Dr. Watkins appeared to be very deeply engaged in conversation yesterday, whilst out upon the lake," said Sarah the next morning, as she and Rebecca pulled weeds in the garden.

"We found a great deal to talk about." For some reason, Rebecca's cheeks warmed. She worked more vigorously at the earth with her trowel.

"You have a lot in common, I believe."

"Perhaps we do. We both appreciate music and drawing, and apparently share similar taste in literature. At our second meeting—it was rather astonishing—he guessed *The Female Quixote* as one of my favourite novels."

Sarah laughed. "It was no guess, Rebecca, and not quite so astonishing as you think. Some months ago, I told Dr. Watkins of our family's partiality for that novel, in response to his inquiry about my daughter's name."

"Oh! The rogue!" cried Rebecca. "He made it seem as if he knew by instinct!"

"Do not be vexed with him. Clearly he was attracted to you, and wished to make a good impression. He is a charming man, do not you think?"

"Yes, very charming."

"And intelligent, *and* good-looking."

"Three things every gentleman *ought* to be, if he possibly can," said Rebecca with a smile.

"Would you like to be a physician's wife?"

"Sarah!"

"I am only thinking of your happiness, dearest. I have

watched you two together—the way he looks at you—the way you look at him. I think he loves you."

Rebecca could find no words to reply.

"Do you love him?"

"I hardly know. I admit, I like him." Rebecca wiped her hands on her apron distractedly. "There have been a few foolish, private moments when I gave way to the conjecture of what it might be like to be married to him, and whether I could be happy with him, were he to ask. But—Sarah, I have only been in his company three times!"

"I have known people to fall in love at first meeting."

"*You* did not. You knew Charles for years and years before you accepted his hand."

"Because I was just a child when we first became acquainted. He is seven years older than I. But he was papa's favourite student. I admired him."

"How did you know—when he was ordained and came back for you—that you loved him?"

"I cannot say. After a few days in his company, I just knew that I did."

"I have formed my own ideas with regard to marriage, by observing the unions of others, and in particular my own parents' union. I promised myself that if I ever did marry, my relationship must be akin to *theirs*; that it should be founded on mutual admiration, respect, trust, shared interests, and affection."

"Dearest Rebecca, how wise you are. You have solved the mystery of love, with one simple equation!" Smiling thoughtfully, Sarah added, "Perhaps that is why Charles and I fell in love. All these elements apply."

"But do they apply to me and Dr. Watkins?" murmured Rebecca uncertainly.

"You admire and respect him, do not you?"

"Yes."

"And you trust him?"

"I have no reason not to."

"You have shared interests—we ascertained that. Do you feel affection for him?"

Rebecca paused. "I suppose I do."

"There you have it. All the ingredients for love."

Rebecca laughed, and blushed.

"I have known Jack Watkins's father and mother for five years now—they are very good people. I have often wondered what might happen if you and he were to meet and get to know one another. And now, it has come to pass! How happy I should be, to see you settled down and married—and to such a fine man. The timing could not be better, Rebecca. I know papa is thinking of moving on—that he has been writing to people—"

"To a cousin we have never met. God only knows where we shall end up."

"If you marry Dr. Watkins, there will be no need for that. You will have a house in town, and sufficient space for papa to live comfortably with you. You will never want for money again. Your children will receive fine educations. And you may visit *us* whenever you wish, and stay at the Watkins's house in the village. It will be ideal!"

The picture Sarah presented sounded like perfection itself. But Rebecca cautioned, "I fear you may be allowing your emotions to run away with you, dearest. Jack Watkins has not admitted to any feelings for me, and I have no expectation that he will make a declaration any time soon."

"Did you mention that you may be leaving Medford?"

Rebecca nodded. "He seemed disappointed to hear it."

"Well, then! He knows the clock is ticking. I should not be surprised if he asks for your hand this very week, perhaps on the night of the ball itself."

Whether or not Dr. Watkins intended to propose to her at the ball, Rebecca could not be certain; but she began to hope that he would. Having never before had an offer of marriage, she pictured the scene in her mind, imagining what he might say, and how she ought to reply. For several days her head was full of Dr. Watkins; she could think of nothing but him.

On the morning of the ball, Rebecca arrived at Grafton Hall in very high spirits. It was astonishing to think that, if events transpired according to her sister's prediction, her life might change in the most dramatic of ways *that very evening*!

To Rebecca's surprise, she was not shewn up to Miss Davenport's sitting-room for a fitting, as she had anticipated, but instead to the drawing-room. As the servant announced her and she entered the room, Rebecca found her friend seated on a comfortable chair by the hearth, with her outstretched foot, bereft of shoe or stocking, resting upon a footstool, and Dr. Watkins kneeling before her, examining said foot with his hands. Mrs. Harcourt looked on from the nearby sofa, glowering.

Dr. Watkins rose gracefully and uttered a good morning to Rebecca, which she returned in kind.

"Miss Stanhope," said Mrs. Harcourt. "Please take a seat."

"Pray forgive me for being obliged to receive you in this manner," said Miss Davenport. "There was no time to send a note. It seems I have twisted my ankle."

"I am so sorry. How did it happen?" said Rebecca, curtseying to Mrs. Harcourt, and crossing to sit beside her friend.

"I encountered a patch of low ground during my morning walk, and took a false step; suddenly, I was lying on the ground myself! I am in *such* pain—I cannot begin to recall how I returned to the house."

"You should not have walked at all, without assistance," said Dr. Watkins. "It does not appear that any bones are broken, thankfully, but it is rather a sprain."

"What a horrid thing—and to-day of all days!" cried Miss Davenport. "I suppose I shall not be able to dance at the ball to-night?"

"I am afraid you will not be dancing for several weeks," insisted he. "You must rest, and not place any weight upon your foot." Glancing at Rebecca now, he gestured with a silent inclination of countenance and eyebrow, which declared—*Do you see? I am being nice to her, just as you requested*.

Rebecca struggled to suppress a smile. Mrs. Harcourt shook her head, and said with a frown, "Well! This is an unhappy circumstance indeed. I cannot cancel the ball at this late hour."

"Aunt, I would never wish for you to cancel the ball on *my* account. Think how disappointed every one would be!"

"The ball was to be for *you*, Amelia."

"It was a most thoughtful gesture on your part," replied Miss Davenport softly, "and I sincerely appreciate it. I cannot tell you how distressed I am, to know that I shall miss out on all the fun."

"You and Mr. Mountague were to be partners for at least two of the dances. He will be very disappointed."

"When Mr. Mountague returns from his ride and learns

what has happened, I have no doubt that he will receive the news with equanimity. He will find plenty of other partners. I am certain the evening will be a great success."

Miss Davenport spoke with sincerity, as if she truly meant all that she said. Even so, the injury seemed so specific and convenient, that Rebecca could not help but wonder if her friend was affecting it, to get out of dancing with Mr. Mountague. "I am very sorry," said Rebecca, "that you will have to sit out to-night."

"Do not worry about me," replied her friend. "I shall be content to sit in a corner and watch. It is *you* I am concerned about. We must find you a gown."

Dr. Watkins, after giving instructions for Miss Davenport's care, took his leave, agreeing to check back on the patient later in the day. The invalid was carried upstairs and placed upon her bed, and from that vantage point, directed her maid in the process of bringing out a great quantity of gowns and accessories, and helping Rebecca to try them on. Although there were no white gowns in evidence, there were so many colourful frocks to choose from, and they all fit so well, that it was difficult for Rebecca to make a choice; but in the end she decided on one in a becoming shade of blue, which was manufactured with such a profusion of delicate pleats, ribbons, lace, and embroidery, as to be truly splendid.

Only the most minor of alterations was required; and while the maid took away the garment to attend to her task, Rebecca passed a pleasant hour talking with her friend. As they chatted, Rebecca tidied up the chamber, putting away all the unnecessary combs, feathers, shawls, and gloves which she had tried on. In opening a particular drawer, she noticed a small locket which contained a lock of hair, and commented,

"I have never seen you wear this locket. It is very pretty."

"What locket is that?"

Rebecca held it up for her view. "Whose hair is it?"

Her friend made a face. "Oh, that—it is my cousin Brook's."

"The hair seems too light to be Mr. Mountague's."

"Well, he gave it to me a long time ago, when we were children—when it was first mentioned that we should marry one day. His hair has grown darker since then. I do not like to look at it. Please, bury it beneath my shawls."

This reference to matrimony, a subject which was very much on Rebecca's mind, gave her the courage to ask if her friend could keep a secret, to which Miss Davenport replied that of course she could. Rebecca admitted that there was a gentleman in the neighbourhood whom she liked—a good, respectable, amiable sort of man, who she thought liked her in return.

"I know just the gentleman to whom you refer!" cried Miss Davenport. "I am certain you are right!"

"Are you?" answered Rebecca with rising excitement.

"Yes! Any one could see that he was smitten with you the night you all dined here. And he made his feelings *quite* clear at the party at Finchhead Downs, when he so particularly sought you out. I would not be at all surprised if he made his intentions known to you at the ball."

Rebecca felt she could not breathe. "Sarah said the very same."

"She is very observant, as am I. Why do you think I am going to such effort to ensure that you look ravishing to-night? Why else would I loan you my favourite gown? I want to give you every possible advantage, to encourage his suit, and to help bring about the most favourable conclusion."

Rebecca smiled in surprise. "I appreciate your efforts, and the gown. So, you like him, then? You think he is a suitable match?"

"Oh, yes! Most suitable, indeed. He is not the sort of gentleman of whom my aunt would approve; but for a woman in *your* position, you could not hope to do better."

"I am pleased that you think so. Your approval means a great deal to me." With a sigh, Rebecca sat down on the bed and added, "If he *does* mean to ask me, I hope it is to-night, or it might be too late."

"Too late? Why?"

Rebecca shared her concerns with regard to her father's growing discomfort with their accommodations at the vicarage, and his intentions to leave the neighbourhood as soon as another situation could be found. Miss Davenport exclaimed in distress and regret,

"Oh! Tell me it is not so. I will quite die if you move away! What shall I do without you? I have never had a friend like you before, Miss Stanhope. I feel I could tell you any thing. I think of you as quite the sister I never had."

"You are becoming as dear to me as a sister, as well."

"If that is the case, Miss Stanhope, do not you think we ought to call each other by our Christian names?"

"Yes, if *you* are amenable to it."

"I am." Miss Davenport took Rebecca's hands in hers. "My own particular friend, from now on I shall address you as nothing but—*Rebecca*."

"And I shall call you *Amelia*." The young ladies smiled as they squeezed hands.

"As I have shared a confidence with you, my dear Amelia, will you satisfy my curiosity about something—in complete confidence of course?"

"What do you wish to know?"

"Your ankle: is it really sprained?"

With a flutter of eyelashes and a little half smile, Miss Davenport replied, "I am shocked, quite shocked by your inquiry. What motive on earth could induce me to *invent* such an injury, on the very morning of a ball?"

Her statement rang with such amusing disingenuousness, that, although Rebecca was appalled, she could not help laughing. "Oh! You are too horrid for words! I cannot, in good conscience, condone such bad behaviour."

"My dear Rebecca, I do not comprehend your meaning," insisted Miss Davenport, still smiling.

"Do you intend to sustain an injury every time there is a dance, once you are married?"

"Perhaps I shall not marry my cousin Brook. Some good-looking stranger might take notice of me this very night—a man of such fortune and rank, that my aunt will prefer me to marry *him*."

"Amelia! You are impossible."

Their conversation was interrupted when the hairdresser arrived, and immediately set to work arranging the tresses of both young ladies—a luxury which Rebecca, who had only ever had her housemaid's help, enjoyed for the first time. Soon, they were dressed and ready for the evening's entertainment. When Rebecca glanced in the looking-glass, she felt in remarkably good looks; and Miss Davenport, resplendent in the gown her aunt had selected for her, hopped on one foot as her servant helped her from the chamber and down the stairs.

....

Chapter V

A great deal of bustle was in progress below, as the servants engaged in final preparations for the evening's entertainment. Mrs. Harcourt, who was waiting in the drawing-room when Rebecca and Miss Davenport arrived, immediately sent the servant off to fetch more flowers for Amelia's hair.

When they sat down to table, Mr. Mountague and Mr. Clifton joined them. Although Rebecca felt the prick of awkwardness at their presence, she could not deny a flutter of pleasure at the look in the young men's eyes, which assured her that both she and Miss Davenport were approved.

"Cousin!" cried Mr. Mountague, taking his seat. "Imagine my astonishment and distress when we returned from our ride, and heard the terrible news. An ankle, sprained? Is it true?"

"I am afraid so, Brook. Forgive me, but I cannot dance; both the pain, and the doctor, forbid it."

"Alas! What a tragedy. And you looking so pretty, too."

"What is the prognosis?" asked Mr. Clifton with concern.

"I am promised that rest will produce a full recovery in time."

"Thank heavens for that," said Mr. Mountague. "But as for to-night—Aunt Harcourt said we were to lead the way and open the ball." Turning to Rebecca, he said, "Miss Stanhope, will you do me the honour of promising me the first two dances, in my cousin's stead?"

Rebecca was startled. When considering her friend's feigned injury (and the purpose behind it), it had never occurred to her that *she* might be obliged to dance with Mr.

Mountague, and even worse, to begin as his partner! But there was nothing she could do, other than to nod and reply with a grateful affirmative. Miss Davenport gave her a private, apologetic look. Rebecca saw the humour in the situation, and could not feel resentful that she should be its object.

Mrs. Harcourt dominated the conversation throughout the meal, naming all the people in the surrounding neighbourhoods who were expected at the ball, the latest news about them and their families, advice which she had given them in previous encounters (some events occurring twenty or thirty years in the past), and how in each case they had acted upon that advice with gratitude and advantageous results.

After dinner, as they waited for the carriages, Mr. Mountague made jokes, and they all laughed. Rebecca felt gay of heart and filled with anticipation for the coming festivities—all the while, keeping her secret hopes to herself.

Mr. Spangle was the first to arrive. He was extravagant with his compliments, insisting that Miss Stanhope was a shining example of feminine beauty, and that she must promise him a dance. The party from the vicarage came next, followed by a great many people whom Rebecca did not know. Mrs. Harcourt received them all with pleasure. Amelia Davenport, seated regally in a chair with her foot wrapped and raised, was the centre of much attention, as every body stopped to inquire about her injury, and to offer their condolences and advice as to treatment.

Sarah and Rebecca regarded the door expectantly, waiting for Dr. Watkins to make his appearance; and when he did, his eyes immediately found Rebecca's across the crowded room, with a look which seemed filled with significance.

"Surely he *does* mean to speak to you this evening!" whispered Sarah.

"If only my first two dances were not promised to Mr. Mountague," returned Rebecca regretfully.

In no time at all, the company was moving into the ballroom, and Rebecca lost sight of Dr. Watkins. How, she wondered, would it be possible for a man to perform an act so intimate as to offer his hand in marriage, in a room so filled with people? Would he contrive to get her alone, as he did at the lake? If so, when and how?

She heard the violins. Suddenly, Mr. Mountague was before her, offering his arm. They moved to the top of the room; the rest of the couples joined them, forming several lines; and the first dance began. To Rebecca's consternation, Mr. Mountague went left instead of right, causing a disruption. Laughing with apology, he rushed into the proper place, only to step on Rebecca's foot. He continued to dance with good-natured but incompetent zeal. The second dance was equally painful to endure—but Rebecca smiled patiently throughout, feeling more sorry for *him* than for herself. The moment of her release, she thanked him and sought out a chair in a quiet corner, to gain respite for her injured toes.

While sitting out the next two dances, Rebecca was able to look around with ease. On the opposite side of the ballroom, she observed Dr. Watkins bringing a cup of punch to Miss Davenport, who was settled in a chair by the wall. The two fell into an animated discussion; *she* seemed irritated, and *he* was doing his best to soothe her. Rebecca perfectly comprehended why Amelia was unhappy; her injury—even *if* contrived—prevented her not only from dancing with Mr. Mountague, but from participating in any of the evening's entertainment.

Of a sudden, Rebecca became aware that Mr. Mountague and Mr. Clifton were conversing nearby; and although they were partially obscured from her view, she overheard the following:

"I knew it had to be you who sent it to the old man," asserted Mr. Mountague. "Who else would give such a dull book?"

"Well, now that you know, I would appreciate it if you would keep it to yourself," replied Mr. Clifton.

"Whatever you wish; but from all reports, he is delighted with it. A costly edition, I am told. Why you should wish to keep it a secret—indeed, why you sent it in the first place—is beyond me, unless it was to impress his daughter. She is a lovely creature."

"Do not be a fool."

"Wait! I know what it is—You think to make recompense for taking over the poor old man's living, do not you!" Mr. Mountague laughed.

"Keep your voice down, will you?"

"You are the fool, cousin. There is no call whatsoever for guilt or remorse, and *certainly* no need for such an extravagant, conciliatory gesture—particularly if it is anonymous!"

There was a pause; then Mr. Clifton said, "If it eases the mind, what harm can it do? Except, perhaps, to the pocketbook."

Mr. Mountague laughed again.

Rebecca's cheeks grew warm with disappointment and indignation. To discover that Mr. Clifton apparently did, after all, feel *some* measure of guilt with regard to her father's removal from Elm Grove, was satisfying; but to learn that the book Mr. Stanhope received did not come from Dr. Watkins after all—that it was the result of such a low motive—that all the imagined generosity and goodwill which she had attached to the person behind the gift, was entirely false—*that* was a real blow.

In this state of heated vexation, Rebecca observed Mr. Mountague walk round the perimeter of the room. When the music stopped and the dancers separated, he had caught up with Dr. Watkins and Amelia on the other side. Dr. Watkins now glanced over, and, whether by accident or design, caught her eye. He smiled. All notion of Mr. Clifton and his transgressions left Rebecca's mind. Certainly, she thought, Dr. Watkins means to cross to me *now;* but at that moment, she heard Mr. Clifton's voice at her elbow.

"Miss Stanhope: may I be allowed the honour of the next dance?"

Rebecca was too astonished and piqued to reply; to her consternation, he was accompanied by her father.

"Come, my dear Rebecca," said Mr. Stanhope congenially, taking her hand and urging her to her feet, "after having been obliged to dance with the worst possible partner in the room, you cannot refuse to dance with the *best*. Never were two cousins more unlike, to my mind! Mr. Clifton feared that you might turn him down, but I said you never would."

Rebecca had no wish to dance *now*—and even if she did, of all the gentlemen in the room—Mr. Mountague included—Mr. Clifton was the *last* person whom she would choose as her partner. But how could she refuse, without offending her father?

The couples were already assuming their positions. Mr. Stanhope smiled. Mr. Clifton nodded graciously, and without a word, led her to their place in the set. Without knowing quite what she did, Rebecca allowed herself to be led.

They stood opposite each other in line, in perfect silence. From the calm look on his face, it was clear to her that he had no idea of what she had just overheard. Why he had bothered to ask her to dance was a matter she could not fathom. Too infuriated to initiate any conversation, and afraid she might say something she would regret, she resolved to hold her tongue. As the music began and they performed the customary steps, he took the burden upon himself, and asked if she was enjoying the ball.

"It is too early to tell," replied she. "I have only danced one set."

"And that with great patience and forbearance, from what I observed. As your father said, my cousin Brook has more enthusiasm for the dance than ability."

"Mr. Mountague has great enthusiasm for many things."

"Certainly, he enjoys every kind of sport."

"And he enjoys making sport of others."

Mr. Clifton seemed troubled by this remark, but made no answer.

Rebecca could not resist the temptation to go on. "Mr. Mountague always speaks his mind; that is one thing I admire about him. Even when the truth might be painful, he keeps no secrets; he is very straightforward."

"Perhaps too straightforward at times."

"Perhaps; but at least one knows where one stands with him. Whereas you, Mr. Clifton, have always been an enigma to me."

"An enigma, Miss Stanhope?"

"I have known you, or known of you, for much of my life; and yet we have never had a meaningful conversation—unless you count the day we disputed the merits of change, while standing in the rectory garden at Elm Grove."

He did not comment.

"I feel that I know your sisters and brother better than I know you, sir, although I have had far less occasion to see *them*."

In a constrained manner, he said, "It is only natural that you should gravitate to my sisters—they are lovely young women, and you have much in common."

They made their way down the rest of the line and back without uttering another word. It was not until they were well into the second dance, that Mr. Clifton asked her if, since coming to Medford, she had been afforded any other opportunities to play the pianoforte and the harp. The question was so unexpected that Rebecca could not hide her surprise.

"I have, sir. Mrs. Harcourt has allowed me to make use of her instruments on two occasions."

"That is generous of her. However, you must be accustomed to practising every day."

"I did practise very regularly when I lived at Elm Grove."

"You must miss it."

"I do."

"Your performance at the dinner party here was truly exquisite. You gave pleasure to a great many."

His compliment, which seemed very sincere, caught her unawares; but she reminded herself of the source. "Thank you."

"Your voice is particularly fine."

"You believe it has improved, then, since our early days? You no longer think I sound like two cats fighting?"

"I beg your pardon?"

"You said so at a Christmas party at Claremont Park when I was nine years old. You and Brook sat with your fingers in your ears while I sang, and afterwards made fun of me."

He blushed slightly. "Did I say that? Forgive me. I hate to think of how I acted then. Pray tell me you do not still hold a grudge. It was just youthful antics."

"Was it just *youthful antics* again to-night, sir—the conversation you two held not more than half an hour ago, with regard to a particular book? 'If it eases the mind, what harm can it do? Except, perhaps, to the pocketbook.'—I believe that was your remark?"

A deep shade of crimson now overspread his features. He seemed incapable of a reply.

"Do not worry, Mr. Clifton. I will not tell my father who sent him that volume, or that the only reason you did it was to assuage your conscience. *He* thinks an admirer wished him enjoyment of the gift, and I would not rob him of that pleasure."

Mr. Clifton said no more, nor could he look her in the eye. Thankfully, the dance was soon at an end, and they parted in silence.

Once again Rebecca fled the dance floor with relief, this time with a pounding heart, due more to the anxiety of the meeting, than from her exertion. What an unpleasant encounter that had been! She was very annoyed with herself, and could not decide if she was glad she had spoken, or if it would have been better had she remained silent.

As she caught her breath and looked round the room, she noticed Dr. Watkins still standing beside Amelia, his attitude suggesting the unwilling performance of a duty. He turned now, and gazed directly at Rebecca with such intensity, that a flush came over her. This was the moment, she thought; and, deciding to take matters into her own hands, she returned his look with an encouraging smile, then glanced meaningfully towards the side-door, which she knew led to the veranda. She proceeded thereto, hoping he would follow.

Stepping outside, Rebecca was immediately refreshed by a light breeze and the coolness of the evening air. The ballroom windows were open, and the illumination from within, coupled with that of a bright, full moon, cast a pleasing glow upon the brick terrace. Crossing to the low rail which overlooked the gardens, she stopped, gazing down at the immense expanse of lawn, trees, and shrubbery beyond, all shrouded in shadowy darkness. Had Dr. Watkins comprehended her meaning? Would he join her here?

Her wishes seemed answered; for just as the music started up again, the sound of the door opening met her ears.

....

Chapter VI

Rebecca's heart drummed in anticipation; she retained her posture and waited as footsteps approached.

"Miss Stanhope?" uttered a male voice.

Her spirits sank. It was not the voice she had hoped for. It belonged to Mr. Spangle.

Straining not to show what she felt, she turned to face him. "Mr. Spangle: sir."

"I have been earnestly desiring an opportunity to speak to you all evening," said he, hastening to her side. "Imagine my delight when I intercepted your most demure, most welcome signal just now, alerting me to your objective to go without, and inviting me to join you."

With great discomposure, Rebecca comprehended what a mistake had been made; he must have been standing not far from Dr. Watkins, although she had not noticed him. "Forgive me, sir, but I did not venture outside with a view to effecting a private meeting with you."

"Indeed? Well! If I mistook your intentions, I am glad of the result. May I deduce that you stepped outside only to admire the moon? A beautiful moon it is, too, what what? A full moon is always agreeable on the night of a ball, for even the brightest torch or lamp of a carriage does nothing to light one's way. My wife used to awaken me from a sound sleep to look at the moon, particularly a full moon, which made her think of a great cabbage in the sky. 'Does not it look like a great, white cabbage, my dearest?' Mrs. Spangle would say in that sweet, engaging voice of hers. The morning after a full moon, she quite often had a taste for produce from the garden."

"It is a lovely moon, sir," said Rebecca, looking rather desperately at the door to the ball-room, through which she expected Dr. Watkins to appear at any moment.

"But, however, let us speak no more of moons, Miss Stanhope. I believe—I feel certain that after our delightful conversation at Finchhead Downs, you can be in no doubt as to the direction in which our next discourse would tend."

"Sir?" replied she, in some perplexity.

"You expressed admiration for my humble domicile—this did not escape my notice—and I could not agree with you more, for it is indeed a most desirable place. I have there every thing a man could want in terms of money and life's comforts. My dear Matilda managed our household effortlessly, with a success which even the most skilled housekeeper in the world could never hope to attain. Since her passing, however, the very air in the house seems changed. It is a solitary, may I say, lonely existence now. My home is very much in need of a woman's touch, and I have determined that you, Miss Stanhope, are the very woman to fill my departed wife's shoes."

Rebecca, in astonishment and incredulity, stared at him, coloured, and struggled for words.

"I realise that there is a disparity in our ages," continued he, "but, however, I trust you will not see that as an impediment, any more than I find your father's recent—shall we say—*unfortunate circumstances*, an impediment to *me*. A man, on occasion, is wont to make little errors of judgment, and a good Christian will not allow these small transgressions to blind his opinion to all that is good in a man's character."

"Mr. Spangle; I beg you—"

"I appreciate your eagerness," interrupted he, "but pray allow me to continue, so that when you express your gratitude, you will be apprised of all that which has been offered." Leaning one hand briefly on the rail in an attitude of forced casualness, he went on, "You shall of course have all of my dear wife's jewellery at your disposal, and any of her clothes and personal effects which appeal to you—I kept every thing she owned, bonnets and gowns and caps and shawls and shoes and silk stockings and gloves and fans and feathers and combs and reticules and handkerchiefs of every sort, and each item is I assure you of the finest quality. My carriage and four will be at your disposal. One of the smaller parlours will be made available as your sitting-room, and you may refurbish it as you please. I like roast beef every Sunday, and pigeon-pie on Thursdays; but otherwise the menu will be left entirely to your discretion. I think I have said all; I have only to pronounce the formal words which are required to make my intent complete, and which will pave the way towards that felicitous union, which will bind us together for ever: Miss Stanhope, will you do me the greatest honour which woman can bestow on man, by consenting to be my wife?"

At that instant, Rebecca heard the slight sound of a startled intake of breath; and looking past Mr. Spangle, caught sight of a tall man standing in the shadow of the doorway: Dr. Watkins!

Rebecca's discomfort and embarrassment were beyond expression. That Dr. Watkins, of all people, should have witnessed this unwelcome offer from a man so clownish—and to-night of all nights! Blushing more furiously, and with barely concealed desperation, she said quickly, "Mr. Spangle, sir, I thank you for your offer. I am honoured by it—"

"A very pretty reply," interrupted Mr. Spangle, straightening up with a satisfied smile, "and I am equally honoured to receive it—but, however, it occurs to me that I have forgotten to mention three important things: you may have your own mare, and when my pointer Popsy has her litter, you may choose any puppy you like as your very own. Moreover, as soon as our engagement is announced, I shall have your portrait painted, and it will hang directly beside that of the first Mrs. Spangle in the entry hall for all to admire. *Now* I have said all, and may I reiterate that it is with—" This statement never reached its conclusion, for as Mr. Spangle reached out again to lean upon the rail, his hand missed its mark; he lost his footing, and tumbled to the ground.

"Mr. Spangle! Are you injured?" cried Rebecca in alarm.

"Perfectly fine, no bones broken, nothing amiss, no help required." Recovering himself, and refusing the gloved hand offered to him, he managed with some bustle to return to his feet, dust himself off, and resume his formerly dignified air. "As I was saying, Miss Stanhope: it is with considerable joy and happiness that I anticipate our alliance, which I trust will take place very soon, you have only to name the day."

"Sir," said Rebecca, "you have misunderstood me. When I said that I was honoured by your proposal, I did not wish to imply that I had accepted it. Indeed, I cannot." She glanced back at the doorway, hoping that she had spoken loud enough for Dr. Watkins to hear, but to her dismay, he had vanished.

"Cannot?" repeated Mr. Spangle in utter astonishment. "But—why ever not?"

Rebecca, who desired nothing more than to get this discourse over with, and to return to the ball-room with as much expediency as possible, said quickly, "There are many reasons, sir. But first and foremost: in your very elegant proposal, although you spoke of money, jewels, clothes, ornaments, puppies, and your requirement for a housekeeper, you never once mentioned *love*. You cannot love me, sir; nor do I love you—and I must love the man I marry."

"Forgive me, Miss Stanhope—I have perhaps lost the knack of saying just the right and proper thing which would convince a young lady such as yourself of my affections; but, however, pray allow me to assure you that I have only the highest regard for you. Love will surely follow, as it did with the first Mrs. Spangle and myself. We were strangers when we wed—yet as the years unfolded, we became quite inseparable."

"That may be, sir, and I am very happy that your first marriage was so affectionate and fulfilling. But—may I speak frankly, sir? In truth, I believe you are still in love with your first wife, and that there is no room in your heart or home for any one new."

"Believe me, Miss Stanhope, when I tell you that my heart is open, and my intentions could not be more sincere."

"I am sorry to disappoint you, sir. Again, I thank you, but I cannot consent to be your wife."

"I see. I see." His face went quite red. "Well then. Well then—there is nothing left for me to do, but to—to bid you good evening." He bowed stiffly, and with dignity walked away and disappeared through the ball-room door.

Rebecca waited impatiently a few moments, then flew towards the same entrance. A dance was in progress, the lively music keeping time with the rapid pace of her heart. Anxiously, she surveyed the room, and saw Dr. Watkins dancing at the centre of a line. Her mind was in a tumult. She felt certain he had overheard Mr. Spangle's proposal—but he had not stayed long enough to hear her refusal. What must he be thinking? Were her chances of hearing from *him* this evening, or any evening, now ruined for ever?

Some distance away, she noticed Amelia Davenport seated alone and eyeing her particularly and with great interest. Her friend beckoned urgently. Greatly vexed, Rebecca moved through the crowd and sank into the chair beside her. Before she could utter a syllable, Miss Davenport cried,

"Well? Did he speak to you?"

"Did who speak to me?"

"Why, Mr. Spangle, of course."

"How did you know Mr. Spangle meant to speak to me?"

"I saw him follow you outside just now and return forthwith. But we talked about this earlier!"

"Did we?"

"Surely you cannot have forgotten! It is why I loaned you

my gown! I *told* you he meant to make his intentions known to-night, and I have been waiting anxiously for some sign of it. But why are you all nerves and agitation? You must keep me in suspense no longer! Did he ask for your hand?"

Rebecca was incredulous. Had not she been already seated, she should have been unable to support herself. To think that she had so entirely misunderstood her friend's meaning! That all the time she had believed Miss Davenport to be advocating a proposal from Dr. Watkins, she had in fact been speaking about Mr. Spangle! Rebecca struggled to take a breath. "He did make me an offer."

"Oh! But how marvelous! How absolutely thrilling! You are engaged!"

"I am not! How can you think so? I turned him down."

"You turned down Mr. Spangle?" Miss Davenport stared at her.

"Amelia, how can you think I would even consider marrying a man so ridiculous?"

"But—why should not you? You said you liked him!"

"I was talking about some one else."

"What? You were? Who?"

"It hardly matters now."

"Rebecca: Mr. Spangle is very rich. He has a beautiful home, a fabulous carriage, and a place in society. You will have more gowns than you can wear!"

"I am most conscious of the merits of wealth, status, and a comfortable home, but I can think of no greater horror than to acquire them deliberately through a marriage which would be a subjugation of all self-respect and feeling. I do not love Mr. Spangle! I never *could* love him. And *he* can only love his first wife, about whom he can never cease to speak, even while proposing to some one else."

"I admit, he is overly devoted to his first wife, but this should only be a recommendation to you: for one day he will surely regard *you* with that same high esteem."

"I think not. Whoever marries Mr. Spangle will always rank a distant second in his heart, and will be obliged to listen to a litany of praises about his dear Matilda every single day for the rest of her life. His house is overrun with dogs; he is twice my age; he does not read or think; and he is an idiot."

"*You* are an idiot to refuse a man of Mr. Spangle's consequence, particularly in your present circumstances."

"Perhaps I am. But I would rather be poor all the rest of my days—be a governess or a teacher or a ladies' companion if necessary—than to tie myself for life to a man I can neither like nor look up to."

"A governess! A companion! A teacher!" cried Miss Davenport, wrinkling her countenance in disgust. "My heart goes out to such women. I can think of nothing more degrading than to serve in such lowly occupations."

"Nor can I; except to marry without love. *That* would be a misery I should be unable to countenance. Surely *you* can understand that, Amelia."

Miss Davenport fell silent as she studied her gloved hands in her lap. At length, she shrugged her shoulders, and said, "My circumstances should not influence yours. I still say you should take him. If you apply to him, and say you have given the matter more thought, and would now look favourably on such a union, I am certain he would still be agreeable to it."

"I will make no such application."

Miss Davenport sighed. "Well, that is a shame. But—pray tell, if it was not Mr. Spangle, from whom did you *think* you might receive a proposal to-night?"

Rebecca blushed and covered her face with her hands. "I cannot tell you."

"Cannot or will not? I will get it out of you sooner or later! Oh! But what is wrong with my aunt?" Miss Davenport's voice was diffused with sudden worry.

Rebecca uncovered her eyes and, following the direction of her friend's gaze, saw Dr. Watkins helping an unsteady Mrs. Harcourt to her feet. "Is she ill?"

"It seems so. I must go to her. Will you help me?" asked Miss Davenport.

They stood. Rebecca assisted her friend with her charade, the latter leaning heavily on her and hopping on one foot, as they began their way around the perimeter of the ball-room. Rebecca was soon relieved by both Mr. Mountague and Mr. Clifton, who came rushing to Miss Davenport's aid. When the group reached the entry hall, they encountered Dr. Watkins and a servant assisting Mrs. Harcourt up the stairs. Dr. Watkins gave them the intelligence that Mrs. Harcourt was adversely affected by the heat in the room, and feeling very faint—she must lie down—they should not worry—he would attend to her.

The party returned to the ball-room, where Miss Davenport was settled in her former position by her two cousins, and Charles asked Rebecca to dance. Feeling it would be rude to refuse her brother, and better to remain occupied, she danced two sets with him, and four more with eager gentlemen she had never met. She did not catch sight of Jack Watkins again until, winded and nearly at the end of her resources, she observed him talking with Mr. Clifton and Mr. Mountague at the front of the room.

Sarah drew Rebecca off the ball-room floor, saying, "Dr.

Watkins assures us that Mrs. Harcourt is sleeping peacefully, and in no danger."

"Thank goodness."

"Now that I have you to myself for a moment, you must satisfy me," said Sarah, with a gleam in her eyes. "Did any thing of import occur this evening? Did you receive an offer?"

Rebecca answered that she did, however, it was not from the gentleman they had anticipated. She had just filled her in on the barest of details, prompting a burst of surprised bewilderment from Sarah, when Charles came up and said that Mr. Stanhope was tired and wished to go home. Accordingly, they made their apologies and withdrew.

• • • •

Chapter VII

"Well, well!" cried Mr. Stanhope at breakfast, after reading a letter which had just arrived in the morning post. "I have heard from my cousin, Thomas Newgate, and it is good news indeed."

"I have never heard of a Mr. Newgate," said Sarah, as she gently caught hold of her son's foot to stop him from kicking the leg of the table, and adeptly rescued a spoon which dropped from her infant daughter's hand.

"What does he have to say?" enquired Charles.

"Pray, read it aloud, my dear." Mr. Stanhope handed the missive to Rebecca, who took it with a sense of foreboding, and read it out for all to hear.

Pulteney St., Bath

Dear Mr. Stanhope,

It was with the greatest surprise that I received your letter, which was forwarded to me here at Bath. I had not, I admit, heard your name mentioned before by any of my own family. I was obliged to peruse our family Bible to discover that connection which, some generations back, indubitably binds us by blood. What felicity to discover, at my age, a new relation—and a clergyman, at that! I have always held the members of that honourable and venerable profession in the highest esteem. Before I go further, I must say, that the information you shared with regard to your present state of affairs is truly shocking. After your many years of devoted service, that your patron should deign to dismiss you so abruptly, against your will, is unforgivable. Whether you mislaid those funds, or were the victim of a theft, as you say, or lost the money at gaming, as he believes, what difference does it make? You have paid back every penny! You do not say who he appointed in your stead, but may I venture to guess that it was his son, or some other favoured relation? My dear sir, rest assured that you shall receive no censure from me on this subject; indeed, we need never mention it again.

And now to your enquiry. My wife Edith and I very much look forward to meeting you and your daughter—however—we are not at our country house at present, but at Bath for the season. Our house here is not large, but it is comfortable, and on an excellent street. We would be pleased to have you stay with us for that extended period which you will no doubt require, to adjust to your new financial circumstances, and to determine whether or not you wish to make Bath your permanent home. If you are looking for a good place in which to live out your retirement, I assure you, you could do no better than Bath! There are many houses available, and the expense of living is quite reasonable. Although it rains more than one might wish, we like to pass the winters here. In contrast to our quiet life in the country, the amusements of the city are a refreshing novelty, the shops have every thing one could need, and the society is invigorating. We are blessed to have made a great many friends, some quite high—the Dowager Viscountess Carnarvon has just come to town, prompting a flurry of events to which, naturally, we are always invited, and which have proved most entertaining; and we are always welcome at the residence of Lady Hermione Ellington. Please inform me of the date of your arrival, so that we may have all in readiness. You may come at your earliest convenience. With the greatest respect and best wishes to you and Miss Stanhope, I remain, your cousin (thrice removed, but no less sincere),

Thomas Newgate

Rebecca lowered the letter with a sinking heart. She had no desire to leave Medford, particularly now—yet she knew her father's inclinations. Surely, they would go to Bath.

"He sounds like an admirable fellow," remarked Charles.

"He does," agreed Mr. Stanhope. "He is very generous and appears to be most sympathetic. We are indeed fortunate. How delightful to discover that he is at Bath. I have fond memories of Bath—I visited there once in my youth. The pavements there were very clean."

"But—surely you are not thinking of leaving us so soon, papa?" said Sarah, with an anxious glance at her sister.

"I am afraid we must. I shall write to my cousin at once to accept his kind offer, and say that we will leave Medford in five days' time."

"Cannot we wait another week or two?" asked Rebecca. "I love it here, papa."

"Truly, there is no hurry for you to leave, father," said Charles.

"We have trespassed on your goodwill long enough, Charles. It is high time we moved on."

Rebecca left the table very distressed. When she later met with Sarah privately, they shared their disappointment with regard to this event; and Sarah expressed her grave concern that Rebecca should be parted from Dr. Watkins at this early juncture.

"If papa were made aware that you might receive an offer of marriage from a man you highly esteem, I am sure he would remain longer. You ought to tell him of your feelings for Dr. Watkins, and your expectations."

"I hardly know what my feelings are, Sarah. And as to expectations—how can I speak of something about which I have not the slightest shred of proof? Dr. Watkins has never once mentioned his regard for me, *if* such a regard exists. Miss Davenport knows him well, yet has no inkling of it; *she* thought me destined for Mr. Spangle! Oh! I blush now to think of it. This *expectation* might be something which you and I have invented entirely in our minds."

"I do not think so, dearest."

"If only Mr. Spangle had not intervened at such an inopportune moment last night! Dr. Watkins might have spoken then."

"I feel certain that was his intention."

"If he thinks me engaged, he will never speak at all."

"He can think no such thing. News travels fast, and you told Miss Davenport all. If you do not wish to bring papa into your confidence, we must pray that Dr. Watkins will have—or make—an opportunity to speak to you before you leave, since otherwise you will not even be able to correspond."

Rebecca immediately sat down and wrote a note to Miss Davenport.

My dearest Amelia,

What a lovely ball last night! You looked beautiful, and I know you broke the heart of many a gentleman by depriving him of the pleasure of dancing with you. Thank you so much for loaning me your gown. I hope and trust that your aunt Harcourt has recovered from her indisposition; please let me know how she is feeling, for we are most concerned.—And now I must share some unpleasant news, which will not surprise you, as I alluded to it in some detail yesterday. My father has received an invitation from a cousin who currently resides in Bath, and we are to leave on Monday. It is with the heaviest of hearts that I am obliged to go. When and if we shall ever return to this neighbourhood, I cannot say. Please extend my best wishes to your aunt. I hope to see you soon, so that I might say a proper good-bye. I remain your friend,

Rebecca Stanhope

A reply arrived the next morning.

My dearest Rebecca,

I cannot bear it! I am all agony! Tears are spilling down my cheeks even as I write this letter! Do you see how the ink is smeared? I had learned to be content with my life before you came, but now that I know the sweet pleasures of true, heartfelt friendship, how shall I get on without you? I am vastly furious with your father, who I blame entirely for this unwelcome turn of events. It is too much to be borne! To think that we shall be separated, perhaps for ever! Please return my gown tomorrow. I trust it will be in the same con-

dition in which you borrowed it, without any rips or pulled threads, and with a clean hem. My aunt is somewhat better to-day, although she still feels very languid. Excessive heat has never agreed with her, and it does get so very hot in a ball-room. However, I do not think Dr. Watkins knows all. He is not her regular physician. She is very old. I suspect there might be something terribly wrong with her, which he has not yet discovered. But I cannot go on—speaking of such things makes me cross and anxious.—My cousins left yesterday. I cried prettily, as one ought, and my aunt will be sorry to see them go; but I may confess to you that I was not. Philip did nothing but read and talk about books the whole of his visit, except when he was obliged to go hunting or fishing with Brook. The conversation at tea was so tedious! (Promise me you will burn this letter after you read it!!) I will send the carriage for you at noon tomorrow. Bring my gown.

Amelia Davenport

P.S. Do not forget to return my two pearl combs and the ribbon which you wore in your hair.

When Rebecca alighted from the carriage outside Grafton Hall, carrying her friend's hair ornaments and gown, another vehicle was standing in attendance, and she recognised it as belonging to Dr. Watkins. She caught her breath as, seconds later, Dr. Jack Watkins himself emerged in some haste through the front door of the domicile. Upon seeing her, he paused briefly, then hurried across the gravel drive to stop before her with a bow. There was an element of anxiety and reserve in his manner which she had never before perceived.

"Good morning, Dr. Watkins." She struggled for equanimity, wondering what he was thinking.

"Miss Stanhope.—Miss Davenport said that you might be arriving shortly. I have been attending Mrs. Harcourt."

"How is she?"

"Fully recovered from her previous ailment. However, she is not a well woman." In a lowered tone, he added, "I believe she is plagued by more varied and diverse nervous complaints than any one in the country. I have written out several new prescriptions, which I hope will do her good—and now my father can take over."

"Your father? Is he returning, then?"

"In a few weeks, yes. I have just received word that my grandmother died."

"Oh! I am so sorry."

"Thank you for that. I regret that I do not have time to chat long; I am on my way to town. I hope to arrive in time for the funeral. Once my parents leave, I intend to stay on."

Rebecca's heart sank. "You will stay in London?"

"Yes—I mean to open my new practice."

"I do hope that all will go well with your new venture."

"Thank you," said he again.

"It is a time for removals, it seems. My father and I are also to leave a few days hence."

"So I heard. You go to Bath?"

"We do."

"You are not to marry, then?"

"Marry?" repeated she in surprise. "No—no!"

"I heard—Miss Davenport mentioned that you had received a proposal from Mr. Spangle, but that—you refused him."

"Yes. I mean, I did refuse him."

There was a brief pause. "If only—" he began; then caught himself. To her distress, he made no further comment, but only bowed, and said, "Forgive me, I must take my leave. I wish you all the best on your journey, Miss Stanhope, and I hope we shall meet again one day. Good-bye."

Rebecca returned his farewell. He climbed into his waiting carriage without looking back, and she stood for a full minute, watching in great distress as the vehicle drove away. Clearly, Dr. Watkins had been in a hurry, and this was neither the time nor the place to express delicate feelings; yet his behaviour had been strange and reticent. Had she and her sister been wrong about his regard for her? Knowing she was not promised to Mr. Spangle, he had still said nothing. Had he ever meant to propose at all? Or had something occurred to change his mind? It seemed now that she would never know. All was over between them; they were going their separate ways.

It was in this state of depressed spirits that Rebecca entered the Hall, where she was received by Mrs. Harcourt and Miss Davenport. The former, although still feeling rather indifferent, insisted that she would not let it stop her from seeing Miss Stanhope.

"I am sorry you are leaving," said Mrs. Harcourt. "Amelia and I have both enjoyed your company."

"As I enjoyed yours," returned Rebecca with feeling.

Amelia, whose ankle appeared to have made a miraculous recovery, directed her servant to take the borrowed gown and have it washed, and took Rebecca's hands in hers. "It will not be the same here without you. I shall write to you every morning, and cry with loneliness every afternoon and evening."

Rebecca also promised to regularly correspond, while expressing a wish that her friend would not be so inconsolable as she predicted.

"A shame you are to go to Bath," said Mrs. Harcourt with a frown. "I daresay that nothing good can come from a visit to Bath."

"Indeed, madam?" said Rebecca. "You are not fond of Bath?"

"Not at all. I do not mind London. The amusements and society *there* are so superior, as to make up for the crowds, the noise, and the traffic. Bath was tolerable in the old days, but it is now an affront to one's nerves. You will find it overrun by husband-seekers, individuals who seek to elevate their status, and all manner of the sick in search of a cure they will never find. There is no benefit to immersing oneself in that water of which they think so highly, nor from drinking it—I have proved its inefficacy any number of times."

"Well," said Rebecca, refusing to be alarmed by this warning, "I shall take your advice about the water; but I must look on the experience as a new adventure, for I have no choice. To Bath I am to go, whether I like it or no."

Half an hour later saw the parties expressing their sincere wishes for each other's health and happiness, and then all said their good-byes. Rebecca and Amelia hugged, shed tears, and again promised faithfully to write.

A similar scene was repeated at the vicarage on the day of Rebecca's and Mr. Stanhope's departure, with equally as many tears shed, and just as many good wishes. From the window of the carriage, Rebecca watched with a heavy heart as her family and the vicarage disappeared from view.

Entr'acte II

THE ANTIQUE CLOCK ON THE LIBRARY MANTEL CHIMED the eleventh hour, startling us back to reality. Anthony had read the previous two chapters aloud, and his rendition of Amelia Davenport's last letter and Mr. Spangle's proposal were both so hilarious, they'd reduced me to tears.

"The scene before the ball," I said, "where Rebecca and Amelia were talking at cross-purposes—that was *so* Austen. She had verbal miscommunication scenes like that in at least two of her other novels."

"I think that may have been my favorite proposal scene ever," Anthony said. "Not that I've read many proposal scenes."

"Austen was definitely a fan of the awkward offer of marriage. She never wrote before about a widower who couldn't stop talking about his dead wife—but the idea of a comical man proposing is similar to her ridiculous clergyman, Mr. Collins, in *Pride and Prejudice*." I paused as a thought occurred to me.

"I wonder if Mr. Spangle might be an early version of Mr. Collins?"

"What do you mean?"

"Maybe, because this manuscript was lost, Austen took aspects of these characters and used them again later. Mr. Spangle must have still been in her head when she revised *Pride and Prejudice* before publication. Mr. Stanhope may be modeled in part after George Austen, but his fear of dirt is in some ways a literary forerunner of Emma's father, Mr. Woodhouse. Who knows—we might find other similarities between this story and her other books, plot points she felt she could reuse because *The Stanhopes* went missing. For the first time, we're actually seeing through a peephole into Jane Austen's thought process. It's fascinating!"

Anthony nodded and agreed. After a moment, he stood up and stretched, glancing at the clock. "Let's take a break, shall we? There are lights in the garden, and there's a bit of a moon. Are you game for a walk?"

It was my first view of the rear gardens of the estate. They were immense, and looked as though at one time they'd been quite beautiful, with long gravel paths meandering past overgrown flowerbeds bordered by high hedgerows. The night air felt crisp and clean, and the sky was alive with twinkling stars. As we strolled, Anthony nostalgically pointed out familiar spots where he used to play as a child.

"Jane Austen must have loved Greenbriar," I mused. "She adored the country. It's very fitting that she's sending the Stanhopes to Bath, since it seems she lived there when she was writing this book. The city figures in two of her other novels as well."

"Did Austen like Bath?"

"I think she found it exciting as a youth and tried to find things to like about it when they first moved there. But she was stuck there for years, dreaming of the country, and found the social life in Bath very superficial. When they finally left, she said it was with 'happy feelings of escape.'"

"Wasn't Bath some kind of medical mecca at the time?"

"It was. It's interesting, isn't it, to see Jane's portrayal of a medical man? It's so different from the doctors of today."

"What exactly *was* the difference in Austen's time, between an apothecary, a surgeon, and a physician?"

"Apothecaries were the poor man's doctor. They were basically what we Americans call a pharmacist, and you call a chemist—they sold remedies, but they also gave medical advice. Surgeons were one step up: they treated illnesses, set broken bones, and performed surgeries like amputations. Because both worked with their hands and were paid for their services, they were on the lower social rung and considered tradesmen."

"Didn't physicians also charge a fee?"

"No. As gentlemen, physicians couldn't *ask* for money, but you can bet they *accepted* their pay in some discreet manner. Their training at university was all theoretical—they couldn't even dissect a corpse for instruction—that would mean doing manual labor. When it came to treating patients, they rarely touched them. They just listened to a list of symptoms, made observations, and prescribed medications."

"They sound totally ignorant."

"I'm sure they generally were. But surgeons and apothecaries weren't any better. There was no understanding of hygiene then—bleeding with leeches was a common practice—and drugs were rudimentary at best, and often toxic. Many people died from the very treatments that were intended to save them."

Anthony shook his head in disbelief. "From now on I'm

going to count my blessings every time I see my physician, no matter how long he keeps me waiting."

We laughed and walked on.

The conversation drifted back to our personal lives. We shared memories of our college days. Then Anthony asked me what I had enjoyed most about teaching English.

"Working with the students—that was my favorite part," I told him. "I tried to make my love of literature relevant, to show how important it was to learn about human nature from fiction—to see how it might be to stand in someone else's shoes for a while, whether that someone was an impoverished, batty old woman, a mistreated child, or a murderer. Sometimes our discussions were so spontaneous—the students really *wanted* to talk about what they'd read. And when I could bring in critical perspectives or historical data to give the reading more context, it was like opening up a new book every time."

"I wish I'd had you as my English literature teacher—it sounds like you made learning fun."

"I tried. I loved it when a student could find a new way to look at a work I'd read and taught many times. It reminded me that good literature is alive—always reinterpreted and reunderstood every time it's read anew. I often talked about how a good story works on us, even if we know the outcome. Even though we know Romeo and Juliet will die, we're pulling for them not to every time we encounter their story. 'No!' I want to shout when I read that scene in Act Five. 'She's not really dead!'"

"It's a potion—don't kill yourself, Romeo!" Anthony cried with enthusiasm. "But he always does."

I nodded, thrilled that he understood. "It's wonderful that we can get so caught up like that and care from deep down inside us about fictional characters."

His eyes found mine in the moonlight. "Yes . . . wonderful," he said softly. His appreciative expression, and the way he emphasized the word *wonderful* as he looked at me, implied that he wasn't thinking about literature when he said it. He quickly looked away.

I lowered my eyes as well, my heart beating faster, searching for something—anything—to say, that would get my mind off how attracted I was to him.

"So," he said, after a brief pause, "what was your thesis about? The one you never finished?"

Grateful for the distraction, I answered, "It was called *Grounding the Figure of the Heroine: The Other Women in the Novels of Jane Austen*."

"Other women?"

"I focused on the minor female characters in the books, such as Miss Bates and Maria Bertram—they're the equivalent of the Miss Wabshaws and Amelia Davenport in this manuscript. Even if they play smaller roles, Austen created them for a reason—part of which is to show us something about the heroine."

"It sounds like an interesting topic."

"I could write three dissertations about it! I looked at characters in the books of other women writers of the era as well. Being in England while I worked on it was invaluable. I thrive on research, so every minute I worked on that thesis was a thrill for me."

"Is it really too late to come back and finish it?"

"I've thought about it—but that was four years ago. A lot has changed since then. I've moved on. I have a wonderful job now at Chamberlain University."

"As a Special Collections Librarian, you said?"

"Yes."

"What do you do, exactly?"

"I do a lot of everything. I catalog rare books and anything else we happen to have in the vault. I create descriptive records for rare materials that we've digitized and posted online. Sometimes faculty bring their classes to me for an hour or two, and I talk to them about using special collections for their research. I prep exhibits for our gallery and supervise our student assistants. Occasionally, I get to do collection development—buying rare books. And I spend at least two or three hours a day in the reading room, where I'm basically a reference librarian—answering questions and helping people find research materials—and a security guard, making sure they don't steal anything or razor pages and maps out of our rare books. Oh, and last but not least, I serve on fourteen different committees."

"Fourteen committees?" He seemed astonished.

"Some committees take more of my time than others, but they're all important—committees do everything from testing out the library's new mobile app to planning regional workshops to writing the cataloging rules for the English-speaking world."

"My God. All this time, I just thought librarians shelved books and checked them out to people at the front desk."

"Unfortunately, that's what a lot of people think. It's why so many schools are slashing the budget and laying off librarians—they think the Internet has made us obsolete. But we couldn't possibly digitize every book we have, and you'd be amazed at what students don't realize they don't know about doing online research."

"I hope you find the work fulfilling?"

"I do. As I'm sure you can tell, I'm a book geek. I love the craftsmanship that went into the older books, and I get to be around them all day—even if, sadly, I don't have time to read them. When I can help students find the primary sources they need—to see them get excited about items that are a hundred or two hundred years old, that enable them to research and write a stellar paper—that's rewarding."

"I imagine it is. Although . . ." His voice trailed off. His expression and tone were polite but suggested skepticism.

"Although?"

"Forgive me—I don't mean to be rude. I'm sure you're very good at what you do, and that you make a difference in the lives of a lot of people. But—you said you love reading and doing research—that you *thrive* on it."

"Yes."

"In your current position, it sounds like you're surrounded by wonderful books that you never get to read. You're helping *other* people find resources to support their research, but you don't get to do much original research yourself."

I felt little prickles of resentment run up my spine. "That's true, I guess. But as I said, it's a rewarding occupation."

"You don't miss teaching?"

"Well, yes," I admitted. "I do miss it. But I don't want to teach high school. I'll never teach at community college again. And going back to Oxford would be very expensive. It'd take me a couple of years at least to finish my doctorate." Leaving the country might affect my relationship with Stephen, too, although for some reason I didn't want to bring that up. "I just, *finally*, finished paying off my mom's medical bills. I still have an outstanding student loan. I don't want to take on any new debt." Why did I feel like I was babbling, making excuses for staying in a job I truly enjoyed?

"I appreciate all that." His smile was sincere. "The thing is . . . we all have an inner passion that drives us—the thing we feel we were born to do. I have no doubt that you're an excellent librarian. But when you talk about *teaching* literature—about interacting with students—it's just obvious how much you love it."

"Well, that ship has sailed," I said firmly, "and anyway, positions for university professors aren't that easy to come by." Intent on rerouting the direction of the conversation, I added, "Now, enough about me. Tell me about *your* passion. You must have gone into finance for a reason."

He gave the question a lot of thought before answering. "I guess . . . I appreciate the opportunities that money can bring. I've always dreamt of owning my own company. I'm not quite there yet, so I help other people finance theirs."

"Any favorite stories?"

"Lots of them. For one, there's the Bowery Museum in London."

"That lovely little museum in Greenwich, in the beautiful, eighteenth-century building?"

He seemed delighted that I knew of it. "Yes—have you been there?"

"It's fantastic! What a great collection of art and porcelain, and all those beautiful fans from around the world. I loved the Japanese Tranquility Garden."

"Ten years ago, it was about to go under. I helped save it."

"How?"

"I arranged for bonds to be sold to finance not only its comeback and the building's restoration, but to put it on sound footing and allow for expansion. I did something similar for the Manheim School for the Arts—I got major donors to sponsor it, and now it's one of the most prestigious small arts schools in southern England. I'm on the board of directors of both institutions."

"Anthony—how wonderful."

"As you said, it takes a lot of time, but—you have to give back. And I enjoy it."

The image of Anthony as a philanthropist was very appealing. I admired him, and was about to tell him so, but my attention was suddenly diverted by a sight ahead of us.

"What's that?" I asked. We were approaching a huge, old fountain in the middle of the garden. It wasn't running, and the water in the man-made, circular pond looked stagnant. Although it was hard to see in the semidarkness, I could make out scantily clad maidens and some kind of fish in the intricately carved marble.

"I almost forgot about this old monstrosity," Anthony said. "According to legend, it was built by Lawrence Whitaker in the late 1700s, in his wife's memory."

The moment the words left his mouth, I saw his face light up with a dawning thought—the same idea that had just occurred to me.

"Mr. Spangle's fountain!" I cried.

"What does it mean? Do you think Jane Austen based Mr. Spangle on Lawrence Whitaker?"

My pulse pounded with rising excitement. "I'll bet she did—at the very least, he could have been the inspiration for the character."

"Now that I think about it, Mr. Spangle's library *does* sound an awful lot like the library here at Greenbriar."

"All the way down to the way the books are shelved!" So many thoughts tumbled into my brain that I could barely keep up with them. "Lawrence Whitaker was born in 1757, so he would have been a forty-four-year-old widower in 1801—about the same age as Mr. Spangle—the first time Jane came to visit."

"And Lawrence Whitaker was equally in love with his deceased wife."

"I'll bet he asked Jane to marry him on her first visit here in 1801—and *that's* the other marriage proposal Jane was referring to in her letter!"

Anthony nodded excitedly. "It must have been an amicable and civilized refusal since the family was invited back a year later."

"Maybe she never told anyone about it except Cassandra."

"Then Jane—with comic flair—lampooned his proposal."

"Lawrence Whitaker must have overheard Jane reading the manuscript aloud to her sister."

"Either the scene of that very proposal, or any of the other scenes in which she ridiculed him."

Our eyes met in astonishment and understanding. "This manuscript didn't go missing!" I cried.

"It was stolen!"

"Mortified that people would recognize *him* in the character of Mr. Spangle if it were ever to be read or published, Lawrence Whitaker made sure it would never see the light of day."

"But his vanity at seeing himself so well portrayed wouldn't allow him to destroy it."

"So he locked it in a box and stashed it behind a hidden panel in his library, where it's been ever since."

"He died in 1814," Anthony recalled. "When did you say Jane Austen died?"

"Three years later—1817."

"So he never knew that she was the author of some very popular novels."

"His secret died with him."

"Mystery solved."

"Poor Lawrence Whitaker!"

We laughed, stopped, and turned to face each other. We were standing just a few feet apart. Mutual excitement and the thrill of our discovery seemed to charge the very air between us with electricity. Anthony's blue eyes sparkled with wonder, admiration, and joy. Answering sensations welled within me, and I felt a magnetic pull toward him.

He reached out and tentatively touched my hand. I didn't pull away. He wrapped his fingers around mine. My pulse began to pound. We stood that way for a long, heart-stopping moment, hands entwined, just looking at each other. The expression on his face, and the touch of his fingers, sent a little shock wave reverberating through me. I felt an almost overwhelming impulse to walk into his arms and kiss him—and I sensed that he felt exactly the same way.

It was all I could do to resist. With burning cheeks, I withdrew my hand and my gaze.

Without another word, we walked in the direction of the house, and returned to the library to continue reading.

....

Chapter VIII

The two-day journey from Medford to Bath was accomplished with suitable quietness; neither robbers nor storms nor accidents marred their progress; and the inn at Marlborough, despite Mr. Stanhope's concerns, proved comfortable and clean—Rebecca could find no evidence of the dirt which he found so alarming in their glasses at dinner.

As they approached the striking outer limits of Bath, Rebecca's melancholy began to lift. Having never visited a city, her surprise and amazement at all she saw was considerable, and she gazed through the window with rising eagerness and delight. Soon, they had crossed the River Avon and were driving down broad streets, past tall rows of limestone buildings of such architectural beauty that she could only stare in wonder. It reminded Rebecca of the pictures she had seen of Paris. Indeed, it seemed to her as if she had left England behind and arrived in one of the great capitals of Europe.

Never before had she seen so many people on the streets. Every where Rebecca looked were well-dressed ladies and gentlemen strolling, conversing, looking in shopwindows, or exiting one of the many fine edifices. Some rode in enclosed, black-painted leather chairs on poles, carried aloft by pairs of men; these, her father explained, were sedan chairs, to accommodate the city's many steep streets. The noise, as Mrs. Harcourt had warned, was considerable: the dash of other carriages, the deep rumble of carts and drays, the plodding of horses' hooves, the steady clink of pattens on the pavement, and the bawling of milkmen, muffin-men, and newsmen. Although the many sounds *did* grate on Rebecca's ears, she could not help but think it all very exciting.

They now found themselves on a dramatically wide, handsome street called Great Pulteney, on the very outskirts of Bath, at the edge of open country-side. The street was lined with broad pavements and long rows of classical townhouses, all similar in appearance. The coach drew up before one of them, and its passengers were soon shewn into an elegant residence and introduced to their new host and hostess.

Mr. and Mrs. Newgate were every thing that could be expected, from reading the former's letter. A fat, merry, middle-aged couple, they strongly resembled each other in every respect: their dress and appointments, which were expensive, and reflected their high regard for beauty, grace, and style; their manners, which were outwardly warm and congenial; their propensity to talk a great deal; and a total want of talent and information with regard to any thing other than their own personal history, and that which society produced. This confined their conversation within a very narrow compass. They both liked to be in company—it was necessary to their happiness—as such they never missed a morning at the pump-room, or an evening's entertainment; and the opportunity to introduce their guests to the many delights of Bath, was something very agreeable to them.

"I cannot tell you how pleased we are!" cried Mr. Newgate for the tenth time, after Rebecca's and Mr. Stanhope's trunks had been brought up to their rooms, and they were settled with refreshments in the drawing-room. "To think we share the same blood, and all these years I knew nothing of it! Extraordinary! I am so pleased, cousin, that you tracked me down."

"We are indeed thrilled that you have come to us at Bath," put in Mrs. Newgate, "for it is very dull at our house in the country. You would have been bored to death had you visited us there. We are so far from every thing, quite tucked away—very few families with whom we can dine, and nothing to do. It is seven miles to the nearest village. Lord! To order meat in winter can be quite a challenge. Here in Bath, it rarely snows, which is a great blessing. And such a variety of amusements—an evening need never go by unoccupied! There is the theatre, the concerts, the balls, the shopping—and every thing so convenient. The shops are second only to those in London; the merchandise is quite unexceptionable;

and being grouped so closely together, they are far more convenient for shopping on foot than those in town. Why, you can walk outside and in ten minutes get any thing you wish!"

"We used to come whenever I suffered from the gout, and Mrs. Newgate so enjoyed it, she was always on the look-out for any sign of illness. 'Mr. Newgate,' she would say, 'are you feeling gouty again? Please say you are!' When we did come, six weeks was never long enough. 'Let us stay another month!' she would plead. At last I said, let us remove to Bath for the winter. And so we have done, these past four years."

"It was not *just* for the waters and medical men we came, even in those early years—although I do think the hot baths were of some help to Mr. Newgate—would not you say so, dear?"

"I would, I would; it is impossible to enumerate all the diseases cured by Bath Water, internally taken or externally used. I often came away quite stout."

"But in the main, we came for the society. One is able to make such esteemed acquaintance here."

"Indeed! The honourable Lady Carnarvon never fails to invite us to her parties, and she is but one of our many good friends of rank."

Smiling at Rebecca, Mrs. Newgate added, "We have two daughters, you know, both grown and married now; and where, Miss Stanhope, do you think they got their husbands?"

"I could not say," replied Rebecca.

"Why, right here at Bath, of course!" cried Mrs. Newgate with a laugh. "Bath is just the place for young people—and people of any age, mind you—but *the* place to catch a gentleman. Living where we did, our girls were never wont to meet any body, except the rector's son, and *he* was a half-wit—not right in his head since the day he was born, that one—talked all sorts of nonsense, yet his parents insisted he was right as rain, and *would* bring him with them every time they came to call. We quite despaired of our girls ever marrying at all, until we thought to bring them here."

"Our first season at Bath, they both fell madly in love."

"With perfectly suitable gentlemen," added Mrs. Newgate; and the couple treated their guests to a lengthy expository regarding the qualifications and attributes of said gentlemen, the beauty of their daughters, and the charms of their new grandchildren, all of them more beloved, intelligent, and talented than any other beings in the history of creation. "We must get you a husband next, Miss Stanhope," added Mrs. Newgate with a happy smile. "You are a very pretty girl. There are four balls a week here, two each at the Lower and Upper Rooms, and a great many dashing officers in Bath just now, with nothing to do. I assure you, you will not want for partners."

Rebecca assured *her* that she was not in the market for a husband (thinking all the while, with a little pang, of Dr. Jack Watkins); but despite her continued protestations, Mr. and Mrs. Newgate would hear none of it. Over dinner, they said many witty things on the subject of husbands and matrimony, which caused Rebecca to blush in vexation; and she went to bed in very low spirits, armed with the information that breakfast was always served precisely at ten o'clock and cleared away by eleven, and that should she arise late, she would miss it.

Rebecca awoke the next morning to a grey sky and low-hanging fog, which did nothing to improve her mood. Arriving at the appointed hour for breakfast, she found their hosts' conversation to be limited to a lengthy discussion of the weather—(a shame it was not better for the Stanhopes' first day at Bath—although at least it was not raining—when it rained, a man could walk out if he chose, but a lady simply could not go out for the day entire—far too wet and dirty—a carriage or sedan chair was required—one was so limited on a rainy day—impossible to shop or even stop in at Molland's to enjoy a pastry—never venture out without an umbrella—) followed by an equally lengthy recounting of all the new arrivals listed in the *Bath Chronicle*. When they had read out each name, and exclaimed with delight over the people of interest and those who were familiar to them, Rebecca said with astonishment,

"Does the newspaper truly announce every single person who arrives at Bath?"

"Oh! No, my dear," replied Mrs. Newgate, "only those persons of *consequence*. To learn about the *rest*, you must check the book at the pump-room."

"You must make certain, Mr. Stanhope," added Mr. Newgate, "to write your name and place of abode in the book at once. Such information is absolutely required, you know."

"Required?" repeated Mr. Stanhope in surprise.

"Yes, by the order of 1787."

"I had no idea. It has been nearly thirty years since I was at Bath. If you will be so kind as to guide me in that direction, I should be much obliged."

The Newgates promised to escort them to the pump-room that very morning, insisting that it was *the* place to *rendezvous*, and not too distant, a mere stroll across the bridge. If they wished to explore much further than the closest streets beyond it, they must do so unescorted. They chose to live on Great Pulteney Street because it was so flat, and in such proximity to Sydney Gardens, as to make it convenient for regular outings. Many shops and parades Mrs. Newgate did not hesitate to walk to, but some destinations in Bath were along such steep hills—the Crescent and Upper Rooms, particularly—that they were obliged to use the carriage or call for a chair.

Soon after, they all left the house together. Exposed to the wonders of Bath on foot, Rebecca's spirits rose. All around her were buildings and sights of interest and delight. Their route took them down Great Pulteney Street, through Laura Place (a very expensive and truly elegant place, explained Mrs. Newgate—one of the houses had two water-closets!) and across Pulteney Bridge, which did not appear to be a bridge at all, but like a street itself; for it was lined entirely on both sides with shops, one of them offering ice-creams and plum and saffron cakes. In no time at all they reached the Abbey Church, an immense Gothic edifice surmounted by all the requisite battlements, pinnacles, and parapets, and featuring a fine tower and a profusion of windows.

Immediately beyond the Church Yard, was the entrance to the pump-room. They issued within the large public room, to find a sizeable crowd gathered and milling about in stylish elegance, the hum of their conversation mingling with the efforts of the musicians performing in the west apse. Through the throng, Rebecca glimpsed a counter at the far end, where an attendant was dispensing glasses of water to a line of patrons. Rebecca's admiring study of the room itself, which was impressively constructed of Bath stone and lined with tall, arched windows on one side, was impeded by

Mrs. Newgate's continuous stream of chatter, and her determination to introduce her new guests to every person she recognised or had ever met.

"The water should always be drunk hot from the pump," said Mrs. Newgate. "Some prefer to drink it in the morning fasting, between the hours of six and ten, that it may have time to pass out of the stomach, before introducing food; but Mr. Newgate and I have never adhered to that notion—indeed, we cannot venture from the house until we have eaten a good breakfast—and we find it equally as beneficial to drink a glass at noon. Oh! Look there—it is Mrs. Worsted! *She* is quite high up, the wife of an admiral. I say, Mrs. Worsted! How nice to see you! Pray, allow me to introduce you to our new visitors who have only just arrived—they are cousins, thrice removed, on Mr. Newgate's father's side, and they know not a soul at Bath."

Mr. Stanhope was the picture of patience and delight through these many introductions, which Rebecca, although grateful, found more overwhelming than any thing. While the gentlemen talked over the politics of the day and compared the accounts of the newspapers, the women gossiped about who had said and worn what at which party. Rebecca was aware of receiving stares from some of the ladies, as they studied her clothes; and she was disconcerted to note that their hats, gowns, and cloaks were newer and of a somewhat different style from hers. Nevertheless, she smiled and curtseyed, said what needed to be said, and graciously accepted promises of future invitations from one person after another.

The water, when Rebecca drank it, was rather unpleasant. She could only smile in wonder that any body should charge for it, and understood Mrs. Harcourt's doubts as to how any one could derive a curative effect from it. After Mr. Stanhope signed the book, they met several additional people, one of them a very fashionably attired woman called Lady Ellington, who cordially invited Mr. and Mrs. Newgate, herself, and her father, to a soiree that evening, at her home.

"Well," cried Mrs. Newgate with satisfaction, as they left the pump-room, "this is a lucky meeting, indeed; for Lady Ellington knows people in the best circle."

Passing under a great stone colonnade, they emerged on a busy street, where they stopped for refreshment at a pastry shop. Although it was as spotless a place as any Rebecca had ever encountered, and Mr. Stanhope was delighted to see gooseberry tart on the bill of fare, he was suspicious of his fork, and requested another before he would deign to take a bite.

"I declare," said Rebecca, greatly enjoying her first taste of the famous Bath Bun, and gazing about the shop in awe, "I have never dined out so often in my life as I have the past two days, since we left Medford."

"In the country," commented Mrs. Newgate through a mouthful of gooseberry pudding, "nearly every thing we eat is grown, raised, baked, preserved, or churned at home. What a tedious job it is to supervise all that! Here, we do not have to worry about any of it."

"The food here is something wondrous," agreed Mr. Newgate. "The principal markets are kept on Wednesdays and Saturdays, and supplied with every kind of provisions."

"Is the butter fresh?" inquired Mr. Stanhope.

"Oh yes, fresh butter, equal to any in England, is brought in from the country every single morning."

"And the meat? Is it of good quality?"

"Our butchers supply us with the best of meat every day. We get fish three times a week. And the prices are generally quite moderate."

The threat of rain prevented them from doing any more exploring; and they had no sooner returned to the house, than a drizzle began to fall. While Mr. Newgate and Mr. Stanhope sat down to a game of backgammon in the study, the lady of the house asked Rebecca what she thought to wear to the party that evening. Rebecca showed her the gowns in her possession. Mrs. Newgate frowned, and said,

"I did not want to say any thing before, Miss Stanhope; but your gowns and other *accoutrements*, while perfectly fine in the *country*, are not quite up to the style expected in *town*. We must get you some new things at the earliest possible moment."

Rebecca blushed. "I am afraid that will be impossible, madam. We have not the means for any new additions to my wardrobe."

"I understand that, my dear. Mr. Stanhope represented your circumstances in his first letter to us. But pray, let us not allow *that* to stand in our way! My daughters have got rich husbands to buy their clothes now, so I am denied the pleasure. I shall make you a project, and purchase your new things myself. I am acquainted with all the best shops, and have an excellent dressmaker."

"That is very kind of you," said Rebecca, astonished, "but I cannot allow you to go to such expense on my behalf."

"I can afford it, my dear—and what is money for, if not to spend on pretty things? I have all I need, and I love to shop—only think what fun it will be! We need not go over-board; but a stop at the linen-draper's tomorrow will be a good beginning. You must have two new gowns, one for day and for evening; a bonnet I think—yes, of cambric muslin—and new gloves, these are quite frayed. Perhaps a black gauze cloak—they are very much worn here now."

"Mrs. Newgate! This is too much!" protested Rebecca. "My old cloak will do just fine."

"If you intend, as we hope and wish, to accompany us to all the parties, concerts, balls, &c., over the ensuing weeks, then you must look your best. We are sure to be invited to drink tea with the Dowager Viscountess Carnarvon one evening next week, and we cannot have you making the wrong impression—to be thought of as the poor relation—oh! that would be mortifying, it would not do, particularly if you have any hope of catching a husband."

The party that evening was like many other parties Rebecca had attended in Elm Grove, in that it involved a group of people gathered in a room, who passed the time conversing, drinking tea and coffee, listening to young ladies playing the pianoforte, and playing cards; but in every other respect it differed. There was no dinner (almost nobody in Bath, Mrs. Newgate explained, served dinner); Rebecca was not asked to play or sing; and other than her father and the Newgates, she knew not a single soul, which made her feel out of sorts and uncomfortable.

The only person who seemed to take more than a passing interest in her was a young officer by the name of Salisbury, who, although handsome in his red coat, was far more ready to talk about himself, than to receive any information about her. It was with relief that, when the hour of departure came, she was allowed to thank their hostess for including her, and made her escape in the company of the Newgates and her father.

....

Chapter IX

It rained the next day, but Mrs. Newgate was so determined that Rebecca should have new clothes as soon as possible, that she would not let the weather impede their shopping expedition. They proceeded to the linen-draper's shop on Milsom Street by carriage, to begin looking for her gowns, which Mrs. Newgate promised could be made up in a short time by her dressmaker. The shop was busy, but they were quickly served, as Mrs. Newgate was well-known at that establishment. Rebecca was taken by the vast array of colours and patterns of cloth on display, but Mrs. Newgate insisted that the shopkeeper begin by showing them nothing but muslin, and only white.

"All the young ladies are wearing white now," said Mrs. Newgate, "and muslin is the very thing."

No sooner had the muslins been laid before them, than Mrs. Newgate saw an acquaintance across the room, and with delight, hurried over to greet her. The shopkeeper soon excused herself to help some one else, leaving Rebecca to her deliberations. There were several viable alternatives, including plain white, spotted, and sprigged, and she could not decide.

"Which one is best?" murmured Rebecca to herself.

"I think the plain white is the nicest," said a soft, feminine voice beside her.

Rebecca turned in surprise, to find two fashionably attired young women standing close by. Both had fine figures and an air and countenance which at once reflected good breeding and real elegance. One was tall, fair, pretty, and smiling; the other was shorter, dark-haired, reserved, and so beautiful, that Rebecca could not help gaping at her. They looked to be Rebecca's age or perhaps a year or two older, and were so unlike in features and complexion that Rebecca concluded they could not be related. "I beg your pardon?"

"Oh! I thought you were speaking to us," said the fair-haired young lady. "Forgive me."

"There is nothing to forgive. I was talking to myself, which was poor company indeed, when making such a choice, for other views are greatly valued." Rebecca smiled, adding, "You prefer the plain, then?"

"It is fresh and clean," said the fair-haired young woman, with quiet grace. As she spoke, she studied Rebecca in an enquiring manner, as if attempting to place her. "I own two plain white muslin gowns. They are ideal for day or evening, can be worn with any colour of bonnet, and adorned with any shade of ribbon."

"That is excellent advice. Thank you." Rebecca immediately felt drawn to the young lady, for her manners were neither shy nor affectedly open, but something in between, which felt warm and genuine; at the same time, she looked vaguely familiar, although Rebecca could not think why.

She was about to solicit a second opinion, but the other young lady was frowning with disapproval, and in a cool and distant manner said, "Catherine, we ought not to be speaking to her. We have not been introduced."

"I suppose that is true. I did not think of it," replied her companion with chagrin, exchanging an awkward and apologetic look with Rebecca.

Rebecca had never been overly concerned with such formalities, yet did not wish, on such new acquaintance, to make a social faux pas; and all three glanced round in uncomfortable silence. Mrs. Newgate, faced away from them, was still engaged in lively conversation with a woman on the other side of the shop; and no one else appeared interested or available to intervene. All at once, the fair-haired young lady said gently,

"Wait a moment. Are not you Miss Rebecca Stanhope, of Elm Grove?"

"I am." The answer now came to Rebecca as to why *she* believed she knew the lady, although it had been many years since she had seen her. "And you are Miss Catherine Clifton!"

"The very same!"

Rebecca had met Miss Clifton when they were children, and once or twice since, whenever her family stayed with their relations at Claremont Park. Although Rebecca could not at present think of *Mr. Clifton* without negative feelings, she harboured no ill-will towards his *sisters*—and she recalled Catherine Clifton, the youngest, as a sweet, affable girl.

Miss Clifton smiled with pleasure at this unexpected encounter, as she introduced her companion and particular friend, Miss Laura Russell, and they all shook hands.

"I always enjoyed our trips to Elm Grove," said Miss Clifton, "and wished I could have gone more often. But once my older brother, sisters, and cousins were married and gone, my aunt and uncle showed little interest in me; it was only Philip they invited to Claremont Park for the summer and holidays, to keep company with their son Brook."

"It is no wonder your aunt and uncle were partial to him," said Miss Russell. "Mr. Clifton is very amiable."

"Indeed he is," agreed Miss Clifton. To Rebecca, she added, "I have the most delightful memory of a particular Christmas, when I was ten years old or so, and we were all gathered at Claremont Park for a grand celebration."

"I recall it perfectly," said Rebecca. "The older girls looked so lovely in their gowns. We younger ones had great fun playing together; and there was such food and music and dancing."

"*You* stood up and sang very beautifully; and on Sunday, your father gave the most interesting sermon I had ever heard. I cannot remember now what he spoke about, but it was the first time I had ever really *listened* to what was said at church."

"My father did excel in that regard," replied Rebecca proudly. "He took pleasure in writing his own sermons whenever he could, instead of simply reading from a text."

Miss Clifton turned to Miss Russell, and explained, "Mr. Stanhope was the rector of Elm Grove before Philip took over the—" She paused and coloured, a thought seeming to come to her, which prevented her from continuing.

"Pray, do not be distressed," said Rebecca quickly. "My father is now retired, and wishes Mr. Clifton well in his curacy."

"I am pleased to hear it," was Miss Clifton's relieved reply. The quiet look which she directed at Rebecca was imbued with kindness and sympathy, as well as a mild confusion, revealing without words how little she understood, and yet how much she felt, with regard to that event. A brief pause succeeded; then she said, "Philip has often spoken of you, Miss Stanhope, and mentioned you in his letters."

"Indeed?" Rebecca was surprised to hear that Philip Clifton ever thought of her at all, much less had spoken to or written about her to his sister. Wishing very much to change the subject, she enquired, "How long have you been at Bath?"

"Two weeks. We are here with my mother and father, who

is suffering from a stomach ailment. Thank goodness Laura agreed to come, to keep me company, for papa thinks to stay another two or three weeks at least. He drinks to-day at the Hetling Pump, is to bathe tomorrow, and try electricity on Friday." Lowering her voice, Miss Clifton added, "I expect no advantage from it; but he and my mother are hopeful."

"I pray that it has good effect."

"Thank you. What brings *you* to Bath? I hope your father is well?"

"He is. We are not here for the waters. We have come to—to visit a distant cousin, Mr. Newgate and his wife." Rebecca pointed out Mrs. Newgate, who was still chattering with another lady at the front of the shop, and now turned slightly, allowing her countenance to be viewed from a better angle.

Miss Clifton's eyes grew wide, and she smiled. "It is a small world, Miss Stanhope. I am well acquainted with Mrs. Newgate, and the lady with whom she is speaking is my mother."

The new friends made their acquaintanceship known to their elders, who shared their delight in the circumstance. Rebecca recognised Mrs. Clifton from the few occasions when they had met at Claremont Park. A good-looking woman, she was as gracious and agreeable as her daughter. The two parties then assembled to share opinions and advice as they completed their purchases—two gowns for Rebecca (one plain white muslin, one pink silk) and one for Miss Clifton (in sprigged yellow)—after which they made their way, under cover of umbrellas, to several nearby shops, where Rebecca had the pleasure of four (sometimes conflicting) views to guide her selections of a new hat, gloves, slippers, and shawl.

At last, finished with their shopping, they all stopped for buns and tea; and a very merry party it was. While Mrs. Newgate and Mrs. Clifton conducted their own conversation, the younger ladies became better acquainted. Miss Russell was intelligent and refined, although too vain for Rebecca's taste. From a wealthy family, she had travelled a great deal, had been to the Continent many times, had studied with the best masters of music and the arts, and was apparently (an opinion generously echoed by her friend) the very best at every pursuit, despite demonstrating not an ounce of genuine affection for any of it.

With Miss Clifton, Rebecca felt more on a par; for they discovered they shared many interests, including a deep love of reading (and of novels in particular); a real taste for music; a disinclination for needlework and riding on horseback; and a great enthusiasm for walking.

"There are so many wonderful walks, both in and outside of Bath," said Miss Clifton. "Have you seen all the great buildings yet—the Circus and the Crescent?"

Rebecca admitted that she had not had a chance to see much of any thing beyond the pump-room and the shops; nor had she had an opportunity to venture beyond the city limits.

"We must rectify that immediately. What do you think, Laura? Shall we take a long walk tomorrow, and shew Miss Stanhope the sights?"

"We must, indeed," replied Miss Russell. "I am quite an authority on all the best walks in Bath."

"May I bring my father?" asked Rebecca. "He enjoys walking, and I know he would appreciate a knowledgeable guide."

Her friends agreed that they would be pleased to have Mr. Stanhope join them. They parted company with promises, on the part of the young ladies, to meet the next morning, if it did not rain.

That night, as Rebecca lay in bed on the verge of sleep, she hugged her pillow to herself with a happy smile. She could not recall the last time she had experienced a day quite so fulfilling or exhilarating, or enjoyed the society of a woman so like-minded as Miss Clifton. In Elm Grove, once her sister moved away, Rebecca had been starved for friends her own age. In Medford, she had enjoyed the companionship of both Sarah and Amelia; and now, to have three new friends! For Mrs. Newgate was kindness and generosity itself. Miss Russell, despite her self-important airs, *was* very interesting. And Miss Clifton was both sweet and sincere, and of an even, unaffected temperament which Rebecca found extremely pleasing. By comparison, Amelia now seemed disingenuous and a bit pretentious; she had often expressed exaggerated feelings, from ecstatic delight to extreme vexation, over the most trivial matters, which Rebecca had tried to overlook, but which in truth had become a bit tiresome.

These negative thoughts filled Rebecca with guilt and remorse, for she believed that one ought not to judge people against the merits of others. She reminded herself of how good Amelia had been to her, how very *fond* she was of Amelia, and how much she missed her. At the same time, she could not ignore the deep satisfaction she felt in the new, meaningful connections she had just made.

How pleasant Bath seemed to her, now that she had friends here!

....

Chapter X

Great Pulteney Street, Bath—Monday

My dearest Sarah,

Thank you for your letter. Please pardon me for not writing again sooner; I have barely had a minute to myself all week. As we are passing a rare, quiet evening at home, I have given myself permission to sit down by the fire and fulfill my duty as a proper correspondent. A great deal has happened since I wrote last. Forgive my penmanship. To prevent this missive costing you the earth, I shall be obliged to write in my smallest hand. At one of the shops on Milsom Street on Thursday, I made two new friends. You will hardly believe it when I tell you the identity of one of them: it is Miss Catherine Clifton, the youngest sister of Mr. Philip Clifton! She is here with her mother and father, and a beautiful but conceited creature called Miss Laura Russell, who I am trying to like, without much success.

You will be happy to hear that Miss Clifton is nothing like her brother. She is sweet, sensible, intelligent, gentle, useful, and well-informed; and she is a great walker! The young ladies, on two succeeding (and quite exhausting) days, have shewn me and my father all the major sights and buildings of Bath proper, from the River Avon and High Street to Marlborough buildings, and the Paragon to St. James's Square, and every thing of interest in between. Did you know that Bath, like Rome, was built on seven hills? Hence it affords a variety of remarkable prospects if one is strong enough to attempt its steep slopes. To describe it all is beyond my power; you must wait until we next see each other; and even then, to appreciate it truly, you and Charles must make the trip here yourselves. Papa is particularly enamoured of the Circus, Camden Place, and the Crescent (the masterpiece of John Wood the younger, said to be the most beautiful terrace of houses in all of Europe), edifices which are constructed in a circular, quarter moon, or half-moon shape—truly magnificent—although he found the walks to the latter tedious, for they involved steep climbs.

Apart from walking, we have kept very busy—there is so much of interest to see and do. Shopping, and looking in shopwindows, is a great entertainment. Saturday night, we went to the Theatre Royal—my first time at a real theatre, and I cannot describe how exciting it was! The auditorium is perfectly rectangular, and lined with boxes which all have a good view of the stage. For 3s each we saw Charles Dibden's The Birthday, *with Bluebeard as an afterpiece—a long evening that proved to be both shocking and entertaining. I have the highest respect for the company, who play here on Tuesdays, Thursdays, and Saturdays, and at Bristol the other three days of the week. Think what an exhausting routine it must be for the actors, to move between neighbouring cities—particularly as a different pair of plays is performed on each night of the week! We went to church twice on Sunday at Laura Chapel, a neat and commodious building very conveniently located, and after evening service, walked for a little while in Crescent fields, a wide green slope in front of the Royal Crescent, which was very crowded. I mean to say that the slope was crowded, not the Crescent. The Newgates, who regularly enjoy the parade, were delivered thither by carriage, of which my father took advantage; I preferred to walk.*

This morning, my father and Mr. and Mrs. Newgate and I attended the public breakfast at Sydney Gardens. What a magnificent place. Again, I fear that words cannot do it justice, for it is, I am told, not surpassed by any garden in the kingdom. I shall, however, attempt to describe it as best I can. The gardens are large, about sixteen acres, and conveniently located on flat ground East of Bath, at the termination of Great Pulteney Street, very close to where we reside. The whole is laid out with lovely serpentine walks, waterfalls, grottos, and shady bowers. The Kennet and Avon Canal passes right through, over which are two elegant cast iron bridges, after the manner of the Chinese. There are also bowling greens and an enormous labyrinth, which is said to be twice as large as Hampton Court's, with classical pavilions and swings. I would surely have lost my way, had not the Newgates been there to guide us, with a little map. The breakfast is held once a week, outside in especially designed dining booths, and offers an excellent repast of cold meats, cheeses, eggs, buns, and tea cakes. As it was a warm and sunny day, we afterwards enjoyed a pleasurable stroll through the gardens. Every amusement costs money, of course; my father paid a month's subscription for us at 2s 6d each. If only I could share the delights of the place with you, I should be truly content. I mean to return again, and often.

Mrs. Newgate says that, before attending a ball, I must wait for my new gowns. The first is to be brought over on Wednesday morning; it will be a round gown of white muslin, with short sleeves and a handsome lace around the neck and hem. The other is to be a pink silk, very elegant. Tomorrow, weather permitting, Miss Clifton and Miss Russell and I intend to take a walk into the country-side outside of Bath, to Beechen Cliff, which is apparently famous for its view. Wednesday, papa and I attend a concert with the Newgates. I am all anticipation. Have you heard any news of Dr. Watkins? I wonder how he progresses with his new practice in town. I love and miss you. Hugs & kisses to Charles and the children.

—Yours very affectionately, your sister, R.S.

The next morning, Mr. Stanhope excused himself from the outing to Beechen Cliff, having been warned by Mr. and Mrs. Newgate that the climb was so very steep, as to recommend itself only to the young and stout, or the most robust of walkers. The party was reduced even further when Miss Clifton arrived at Great Pulteney Street, and explained that Miss Russell was laid up with the headache. Rebecca, although sorry to hear of any one's being ill, was not dismayed to find that Miss Clifton was to be her only company, for it would give them a chance to have a real tête-à-tête.

It was a beautiful day. Beechen Cliff, with its green, overhanging, wooded precipice, rising sharply and immediately to the south of the River Avon, could be seen from almost every vantage point in Bath. It was so striking, as to have been the object of Rebecca's interest and admiration ever since her arrival in the city. As she and Miss Clifton left behind the white pavements and tall buildings, and exchanged them for the quiet openness of a path and green meadows, Rebecca gave a sigh of relief and contentment.

"How I love a walk in the country," said she, breathing in the familiar, pleasant scents of fresh earth and grass, and smiling at the sounds of the insects and bleating sheep.

Miss Clifton was of the same opinion. While both had come to enjoy and appreciate the pleasures of the city, they could never compare with the beauty and tranquillity of the country-side. As they walked, Rebecca found her mind and body recovering a sense of peace, which she had not even been aware was missing.

Their exertion in climbing the steep hill made conversation difficult, so it was put off until they reached the summit, where they found a dry, grassy expanse upon which to sit, rest, and admire the view.

"I have been to Bath half a dozen times, and I always make sure to take this walk," said Miss Clifton, smiling as she looked out over the city below, and the surrounding verdant country-side. "Laura finds fault with it—she compares it to prospects in Italy and Switzerland she has witnessed, which she insists are far more beautiful and expansive. I should love, one day, to see those places which she describes; but even if I never do, I am quite content with this."

"It *is* lovely," concurred Rebecca with enthusiasm, "and worth every step." As she drank in the view, she said slowly, "Do you know, I am beginning to realise that my life before this was very small indeed."

"Small? What do you mean?"

"I have travelled so little. I had never been anywhere, really, until—until my father's retirement. I was averse to leaving Elm Grove;—I dreaded any alteration in my daily routine. I do miss home dreadfully, every day—but to my surprise, I find that I cannot entirely regret our removal. My stay at Medford, although different from the life to which I had been accustomed, proved to be most gratifying. And Bath, in pictures and by report, can be only an idea in one's mind—even the most vivid imagination cannot conjure the true aspect of all its wonders. One must experience the city in person fully to appreciate and comprehend it." Rebecca plucked a blade of grass and twirled it in her fingers, as she gazed at the scene before her. "It is the same for this view. I used to get such contentment every morning gazing through the window of the rectory at our own green slope—but it is nothing compared to this! How much I was missing!"

"I understand you completely. When I was younger, I rarely wished to leave home; but my brother Philip always said that a little variation can be a very good thing. He was right. Every time I come away, I discover something new which delights me, and I am so happy I undertook the journey."

This mention of Philip Clifton, brought back to Rebecca's mind the conversation she had held with him on this very subject, some weeks previously, while standing in the garden at Elm Grove Rectory. At the time, she had violently disagreed with his opinion of change, and had thought him both discourteous and impertinent. Now, she was beginning to think very differently; and she began to wonder if, on that *particular* matter at least, she might have judged him a little too harshly.

Miss Clifton's voice broke into her thoughts. "From Philip's letters, I gather that you saw him quite often at Medford?"

Rebecca's cheeks warmed slightly. On their previous outings, she had successfully avoided any discussion of Mr. Clifton, not wanting to infect her friendship with his sister, by any mention of her feelings towards *him*, which could only deteriorate into a lengthy and unhappy review. Being now compelled to answer, she said,

"We had occasion to meet several times."

"I envy you. I have not seen him in months, ever since he removed to Elm Grove. Even then his visit was brief." She sighed. "It has been so long since I have had the pleasure of spending any real time with him. His first position, after he was ordained, was so far away, that he was rarely able to come to us; and before that, the whole time he was at Oxford, he was so devoted to his studies, I was obliged to rely on his regular correspondence to keep apprised of what was happening in his life." There was no mistaking the genuine affection in Miss Clifton's voice and countenance as she spoke.

"It sounds as though you and your brother are very close."

"Oh! Yes, we have always been close, for we are the youngest of six children, only three years apart from each other.

Growing up, we had such fun running about the country, and engaging in all sorts of games together—do you know, we used to write little plays with only two characters in them, and perform them for our entire family in the barn?"

"My sister Sarah and I did exactly the same!" cried Rebecca. "We insisted that our cook, maid, and man-servant attend every performance, along with my mother and father, or we should never have had an audience large enough. I am certain if I were to find and read those early works of our youth now, I should find them dreadful! But at the time, we considered ourselves quite brilliant."

"Certainly my parents let us *think* we were." They laughed; and then Miss Clinton said more soberly, "Of course, they were right about Philip. He *is* brilliant in so many ways. He is, and always was, the best person I know. He is so good, kind, thoughtful, and considerate; ever since he was a boy, he has always thought of others before himself; and when he puts his mind to something, it becomes his entire focus. I have never met any one as hard-working or devoted."

These positive remarks about Mr. Clifton gave Rebecca pause; but then she said, "I suppose if I had a brother, I should be equally partial to him."

Miss Clifton looked at her. "You think me *too* partial to him—that I am guilty of a sister's prejudice, and blinded to his faults."

"I did not say that."

"You did not need to," responded Miss Clifton in a teasing voice. "I see it in your eyes; I hear it in your voice. But I am not the only one who thinks well of him. Every one in my family loves him dearly, and for good reason. Here, I shall prove it to you, by telling you something of him as a child." She resettled herself on the grass, and said, "When Philip was nine years old, one of our horses was very badly injured in its hoof. It was not Philip's favourite horse, nor even the best in the stable, but when told that the beast must be put down, he refused to allow my father to do it. It was not right, he said. The animal deserved to live. So sternly and violently did he protest, that papa at last relented. Philip stayed up all night soothing the poor beast, and rarely left the barn for days. The animal was never able to be ridden again, but remained under Philip's care for many years afterwards, spending its time in the pastures, until at last it died a natural death."

Rebecca agreed that it was a good story.

"There are many other stories I could share, of acts of great kindness which my brother has performed, which are reflections of his good character. One occasion in particular stands out in my memory: it was perhaps six or seven years past. My mother had commented, with great regret, upon a bonnet which she lamented not buying on a previous outing to London. Philip travelled all the way to town deliberately to procure it for her, for her birthday."

"How thoughtful," said Rebecca sincerely.

"Indeed it was. I cannot begin to describe how thrilled and grateful my mother was! Ever since, that hat has been her favourite." Smiling, Miss Clifton added, "Oh, and I can never forget the time, several years ago, when I was very ill. My brother rode all the way home from Oxford—a distance of an hundred and twenty miles—in a single day, in order to see me, and to bring a medicine which he thought might do me good. To this day, I believe that it was his visit which cured me, rather than the remedy—for time spent in his company always lifts my spirits."

Rebecca listened with wonder to these anecdotes, which

presented Mr. Clifton in a very different light from that in which she had formerly held him.

As the two ladies rose, and made their way down the incline, Rebecca reflected upon the inconsistencies of human nature. How interesting it was, that the same young man who had been so unsympathetic with regard to her and her father's plight, should be so much more generous when dealing with his *own* family and friends. But it was not surprising, really. What was it that Sir Percival had said? *Blood is thicker than water.*

It seemed Mr. Clifton shared that conviction.

....

CHAPTER XI

The first ball Rebecca attended at Bath was a great success. She felt pretty in her new white muslin gown; her hair, thanks to Mrs. Newgate's hairdresser, was put up in a becoming style; and she was asked to dance by so many gentlemen, that her only opportunity to converse with the Newgates, her father, and Miss Clifton and Miss Russell, was at supper. At the next ball, a week later, freshly attired in pink silk, Rebecca received a proposal of marriage from a young, florid gentleman with whom she had danced only one set, and to whom she had spoken five sentences at most—an offer which she firmly refused. When she told her friends about it, the young ladies shared her amusement; and Mrs. Newgate solemnly agreed that Rebecca had done right and should hold out for a better offer, as the young man in question was not from one of the best families.

The proposal, coming as it had at a ball, made Rebecca

think of Mr. Spangle, and with more generosity and regret, of Dr. Jack Watkins. She wondered how Dr. Watkins was faring in London, and fondly replayed their conversations in her mind. It saddened her to think that their friendship—and what might, at least in *her* mind, have amounted to *more* than a friendship—was over entirely; that she would, most likely, never see or hear from him again.

With longing, she thought of Elm Grove—of the house which was so dear to her—and she wondered how Martha, Eliza, Mr. Gower, and Mrs. Wilson were faring. She missed her sister a great deal, and was grateful for the regular letters which Sarah sent, relating all the events in her life. Every detail was of interest to Rebecca: Sarah's garden had stopped blooming; George had scraped his knee; Charles had acquired a new book from the circulating library; they had experienced an early frost; Mrs. Harcourt had been ill again, but it did not appear to be any thing serious. To Rebecca's disappointment, she did not receive a single letter from Amelia, despite writing to *her* twice.

As time went on, however, Rebecca found herself thinking less and less of home and Medford, and more of the many delights of Bath. The same held true for Mr. Stanhope; for one morning he told Rebecca,

"Our life at Elm Grove was very satisfying, and I knew myself to be useful there; but it is as I thought and hoped—leaving has opened the world to our view, and allowed us both to experience a great many pleasures which would otherwise have been denied us."

Rebecca's favourite entertainment—the evenings she looked forward to with particular eagerness—were the concerts, held every Wednesday in the Upper Rooms, under the direction of Mr. Rauzzini, a refined gentleman of great musical taste who was highly regarded in the city. A diversity of musical programs were offered, from a small orchestra to individual singers or a choral group; and while listening to these presentations, Rebecca closed her eyes, and felt as if she were carried away on a blissful cloud. The music continued to ring in her mind for days afterwards; she often found herself humming the tunes. One evening, after a woman sang a lovely Italian song, Mr. Stanhope insisted that Rebecca's abilities were superior, which she immediately discredited; the next week, a masterful performance on the pianoforte both thrilled her and gave her a little pang, for she greatly missed playing that instrument.

Her friendship with Miss Clifton was particularly agreeable. Although Rebecca could not like Miss Russell, she endured her company because it afforded her the opportunity to spend time with her friend. Rebecca continued to hear good reports from both of them with regard to Mr. Clifton. Indeed, Miss Russell seemed quite enamoured of the gentleman, and often spoke as if he were her particular beau.

The only diversions Rebecca did not like were the private parties she was obliged to attend with her hosts—evenings of elegant stupidity, peopled by the snobbish and the dull. They did indeed drink tea, as prophesied, with the honourable Lady Carnarvon, whom the Newgates regarded with the highest degree of esteem. Rebecca, on the other hand, considered the viscountess a disagreeable woman of great self-importance, who judged others entirely on outward appearances, without seeing or valuing any thing which might lie within. Mr. Stanhope enjoyed these soirees more than Rebecca did, for he had a gregarious and forgiving nature, and could fit in any place. For *her*, the games of cards were an obligation rather than an amusement; for *him*, they were a temptation. Once or twice, she felt certain she observed him glance longingly at the Speculation, Loo, and Vingt-et-Un tables; but since they arrived at Bath, Mr. Stanhope had made a solemn pact with his daughter to play only those games which did not involve betting, and he kept his word.

The precarious state of their finances was never far from Rebecca's mind. Although the Newgates continued to be accommodating, she and her father could not stay with them for ever. When she brought up the subject, however, Mr. Stanhope admitted that he hoped to remain another two months—until Christmas, at least.

"What will we do then, papa?" inquired she, worried. "Will we be obliged to find yet another friend or relation who is willing to take us in?"

Mr. Stanhope sighed and nodded. "Unless some one produces a freehold for our benefit, Rebecca dearest—or you were to *marry*—we will likely remain itinerant for life."

His reference to marriage—a subject which they had only rarely ever discussed—was so unexpected, and so weighted with unspoken hope and meaning, that it took Rebecca by surprise. Teasingly, she offered her apologies for having turned down the young officer's proposal at the ball the other night; which made them both laugh.

"I do not mean to imply that you ought to accept the first man who makes you an offer, my dear," said Mr. Stanhope emphatically, "and you should certainly not take a stranger. A comfortable home and income is only one component of the equation, of which love must be the biggest part. Whoever you marry must be a good man who loves and respects you—a true gentleman, who proves his character and worth not with words, but by his deeds. And you must love and respect him equally in return."

Rebecca hugged him, and avowed that she could not agree more.

During their fourth week at Bath, Rebecca and Mr. Stanhope had made plans to join Miss Clifton and Miss Russell on another country walk. That morning, however, he was laid up with a mild cold, the result of a stroll in a frigid wind on the parades the day before. Rebecca left him wrapped in a warm blanket by the fire, with his tea and his reading, and ventured out to meet her friends at Sydney Place. To her surprise, when she arrived at their appointed spot, she found the two young ladies in the company of Mr. Philip Clifton.

"Look who is here!" cried Miss Clifton, as Rebecca approached, and Mr. Clifton bowed and doffed his hat. "Is not it the most wonderful surprise? My brother showed up at our house without any warning yesterday evening. After such a tedious journey, he was so desirous of a walk, that when he asked to accompany us to-day, I could not possibly refuse. I hope you do not mind."

"Not at all. It is a pleasure to see you, Mr. Clifton," replied Rebecca. Her friends did not seem to discern any thing unnatural in her expression, which she hoped was gracious; but on Mr. Clifton's countenance, she read his full understanding of her feelings, and his consciousness of the last, unhappy words which had been spoken between them.

"Is not your father joining us?" inquired he.

Rebecca explained why Mr. Stanhope was obliged to miss the outing, and how sorry he was. Mr. Clifton looked disappointed; both he and the young ladies communicated their sincere regrets and well-wishes, and the four turned southwards, out of the city.

Miss Russell, with a bright smile, asked if she might take Mr. Clifton's arm, and then immediately took possession of said limb, making any reply unnecessary. The pair took the lead, leaving Rebecca to walk a few steps behind with her friend. They began in the same direction formerly taken to Beechen Cliff, but then diverged onto a foot-path.

"The valleys of Lyncombe and Widcombe are very beautiful," promised Miss Clifton. "I think this one of the prettiest walks outside of Bath."

They fell into conversation, the better part consisting of the surprise and joy with which Miss Clifton and her parents had received her brother's unexpected visit, and a recounting of what they had discussed the night before.

"Philip had a great deal to say about the people of Elm Grove, whom he seems to admire very much. He was in a glow all evening; Laura could not take her eyes off him. She has liked him, you know, ever since she moved into the neighbourhood when we were sixteen, and now declares she will marry nobody else."

"Does he return her affections?" asked Rebecca.

"I feel certain he does. He is kind and attentive to her, and in his letters to me, never fails to send her his best regards. Now that he is settled with a house and a good income, it would not surprise me if they were wed by this time next year."

Rebecca had little time to reflect upon this statement; for at that moment, Mr. Clifton paused and said to Miss Russell,

"I have monopolized your company long enough, Laura. I know my sister would love to talk with you. Shall we exchange walking partners?"

Miss Russell looked dismayed; but Miss Clifton, smiling, said, "An excellent notion."

Mr. Clifton left the former's side, walked directly to Rebecca, and offered his arm; which, not wishing to embarrass or offend his sister, she took after some hesitation. In an instant, the two new parties moved ahead.

They were traversing a meadow, on a foot-path only wide enough for two. The sun shone brightly in a clear blue sky, the air was mild, and the landscape serene. For some time, the only sounds which reached Rebecca's ears were the bleating of sheep, the twitter of birds in the trees, and the tramp of their own feet. She was bewildered as to why Mr. Clifton had sought out her company, if he was not to speak; but she was determined to be polite to him.

"I understand your visit to Bath was unexpected, Mr. Clifton?"

"Yes. I decided to come on very short notice."

"I hope you are here for pleasure and to see your family, and not for any reasons of ill health?"

He looked surprised. "Thank you; you are very kind. I remain in good health. I am happy to see my sister and my parents, although that was not my motive in travelling hither."

"No?"

"No. I came to see you."

"Me?"

"My sister had mentioned in her correspondence that you were here."

They walked on. Rebecca was too astonished to speak further, yet bursting with curiosity—why on earth Mr. Clifton should be compelled to travel to Bath to see *her*, consuming all her thoughts. At last, he said,

"Miss Stanhope: I find that I owe you an apology."

This pronouncement was equally unexpected. "Indeed, sir?"

"The last time we spoke, on the night of the ball at Grafton Hall, you accused me of committing an act not out of generosity, but with a selfish purpose: to assuage my own conscience. When I sent that book for which your father had expressed a desire, I thought I was simply doing him a kindness. It did not occur to me to view the act in any other light, until my cousin brought it up that evening. But upon further reflection, I saw that both he—and you—were right. I did have more of my own self-interest at heart in the matter, than his."

Rebecca looked at him. This was, in her recollection, the lengthiest speech Mr. Clifton had ever made to her; and the substance of it was very gratifying. "Thank you, Mr. Clifton. It is noble of you to share these thoughts. But surely, you did not come all the way to Bath, just to tell me that?"

"No; indeed, I have a matter of far greater consequence to impart." A pause succeeded, as he seemed to collect his thoughts. "I considered writing to your father about this, for it concerns him as well—but it is a personal matter, and I thought—I think—that some things are best said in person. I had hoped to speak to you *both* to-day—but I trust you will repeat what I say for his benefit." He paused again. "No doubt you can guess the subject to which I refer?"

"I confess I cannot, sir. Unless, in some way, it involves the—the circumstances of my father's resignation?"

"Exactly so." With a steadiness of manner and calmness of tone, Mr. Clifton went on. "What I wish to communicate is this: when I took over as rector at Elm Grove, I believed I was doing the community a service. I had no reason to question my uncle's depiction of Mr. Stanhope. I accepted the position on offer with gratitude—only a fool would have done otherwise—and I considered it as the most natural of progressions. However, when you defended your father so unequivocally that night over cards, and insisted that the church's money had been stolen, not gambled away—an idea which my uncle had never mentioned—I began to question my uncle's motives. At the party at Finchhead Downs, when I fell into conversation with Mr. Stanhope, I found that I liked him very much. He seemed to me an honourable and decent gentleman. I came away wondering: could he have been telling the truth about the money's loss? After you and I spoke at the ball, the subject would not leave my mind. So I decided to delve into it."

Rebecca's heart beat faster; she was all attention. "What did you do?"

"Upon my return to Elm Grove, I spoke with the servants at the rectory. To a man and woman, they showed only the highest regard for their former master and his daughter." He gave her a brief smile. "They insisted that Mr. Stanhope was the most scholarly, good-hearted, and charitable man in the world. He may have liked to drop a few farthings at the card-table, they said, but he would never stoop to *serious* gambling."

"How good of them to say so."

"I spread my inquiry further amongst the community. Although reticent at first to impart any thing which might make me feel unwelcome, all, at length, came round to sing the praises of their former clergyman. If any one was in trouble and needed a helping hand, Mr. Stanhope was only too glad to lend—or give—the required sum. I found it difficult to believe that a man of such a selfless and giving nature, would so betray his parishioners' trust. Several admitted that they thought it very hard he had been obliged to resign, just because that money went missing. '*Missing,*' said Mr. Coulthard, with absolute conviction. '*Missing, sir, but never gambled away, I promise you: that money was stolen.'* I asked myself: could he be right?"

Mr. Clifton paused, for they had now reached a narrow, shallow stream, and he insisted, in a most gentlemanlike manner, in assisting all three young ladies over the well-placed stepping-stones which crossed it. Rebecca was all anticipation, awaiting a continuance of their discourse.

As they resumed their walk in their established pairs, Mr. Clifton went on, "When I confronted my uncle with the reports I had received, he admitted, rather shamefaced, that he may have *overemphasized the gambling charge a bit*—those were his very words—as an excuse to let Mr. Stanhope go, so that he might make good on his promise to give *me* a living. You can imagine, Miss Stanhope, what agony I felt, upon making these discoveries—and how I blamed *myself* for all the pain which you and your father have suffered on my account."

Mr. Clifton spoke with such animation and sincerity, and was so obviously distressed, that any ill-will towards him which had formerly been lodged in Rebecca's mind and heart, began immediately to soften and dissolve. She had presumed Mr. Clifton to be selfish, cold, and indifferent; yet it seemed he had only been blinded through his devotion to his uncle, and that he did indeed suffer deep feelings.

"Mr. Clifton: I thank you," said she slowly. "Your report relieves my mind on many matters, and I am grateful and honoured for the effort you have gone to on my father's behalf. But pray, do not take the entire responsibility for our troubles on yourself. Your uncle was the instigator of true evil in this affair."

"I am equally at fault, for I should not have accepted my uncle's offer without questioning his intentions. And if you will permit me, Miss Stanhope, I intend to redress this wrong, by seeking the proof of what occurred on the night in question."

"Proof? How do you propose to accomplish that, sir?"

"By appealing to the innkeeper, where your father passed the night, the last time that money was in his possession. Can you tell me, Miss Stanhope, where your father broke his journey, on his way to London?"

"He stayed at the King's Arms, at Leatherhead, Surrey."

"I shall write to the innkeeper this very evening, and see what I can learn. If it is at all within my power, I intend to set things right."

• • • •

Chapter XII

After Mr. Clifton's declaration, so choked was Rebecca with emotion and new-found hope, that she could only utter a quiet, "Thank you, sir," and it was some minutes before she could speak again. Mr. Clifton, seemingly aware of her distress, maintained a respectful silence as they walked along.

They soon reached Widcombe. Although it offered a charming view of the manor-house, parsonage, and church, their visit was cut short by Miss Russell, who complained that she was tired, and wished to return to Bath at once, with Mr. Clifton's arm to lean upon. They exchanged walking partners and immediately turned back.

Miss Clifton was curious to know of what Rebecca and Mr. Clifton had been speaking. Rebecca discovered, with gratitude, that he had been very discreet regarding the particulars concerning herself and her father, with regard to their removal from Elm Grove. Now believing there to be no reason to conceal any thing, she informed Miss Clifton of the whole of the affair. Her friend expressed shock and regret over all that had transpired to date, and shared in the hopes that with her brother's intervention, the matter should be soon resolved in a satisfactory manner.

As they said their good-byes outside the Newgates' house, Mr. Clifton explained that he must return to Elm Grove in two days' time. Miss Clifton invited Rebecca and her father to join them all at the theatre the following evening, and she readily agreed.

No sooner was Rebecca in the door than, finding her father alone in the parlour, she eagerly told him every thing which Mr. Clifton had related that morning. Mr. Stanhope was thrilled beyond expression.

"I pray, papa, that Mr. Clifton's efforts will be successful; that somehow, he will find a way to establish your innocence."

"It is almost too much to hope for," replied Mr. Stanhope. But for the first time in months, Rebecca saw a gleam of hope in his eyes.

As she lay in bed that night, Rebecca's mind was full of the day's events, and her feelings were in turmoil. In a single day, her view of Mr. Clifton had altered considerably. He had gone to great effort to learn the truth about her father. She appreciated all his explanations and apologies. Mr. Clifton was, she realised, an intelligent, thoughtful, and sensitive man. She wondered at herself, that she had never been aware of these qualities in the past. She saw him now as a friend and ally. Even more overwhelming was the new-found possibility, that he might be able to learn some information which might clear her father's name. Oh! If only it could be so! Eagerly, she looked forward to speaking with him again.

However, at the theatre the following evening, Miss Russell monopolized Mr. Clifton's attention before the performance and during the interval, and it was not until the play ended, that Rebecca and Mr. Stanhope at last secured a moment to converse with Mr. Clifton in the lobby.

"I wanted to express my gratitude, sir," said Mr. Stanhope, "for all you have done so far on my and my daughter's behalf. It was very good of you."

"It was both my duty and my pleasure, sir."

"I wish to thank you in particular," added Rebecca, "for seeking us out in Bath to explain your findings."

"I hope to have even better news for you in the very near future," replied Mr. Clifton. "As soon as I know any thing, I shall write to my sister."

They said good-night, and went their separate ways.

A week passed away. Rebecca walked with Miss Clifton and Miss Russell, visited the shops and the pump-room with the Newgates, and attended a concert with her father; but there was no further word from Mr. Clifton.

On the eighth day after Mr. Clifton's departure, just as Rebecca was leaving the house to go walking on her own, Miss Clifton hurried up the pavement to meet her, a distressed expression on her countenance. After they exchanged greetings, Miss Clifton said,

"We are to leave tomorrow. Papa is fed up with Bath, and wants to go home at once."

"Oh! I shall miss you."

"I shall miss you, as well."

Her friend looked so anxious, that Rebecca hoped to

calm her by saying, "You will be happy to be home, I am sure, and we can write to each other."

"Yes, of course. But—it is not only our leaving, that—" Miss Clifton broke off, and with increasing disquiet exclaimed, "Forgive me, Miss Stanhope. I am expected back at the house. I have come on an errand of some urgency.—I received a letter this morning from Philip. He sends information with regard to—I debated whether or not I ought to—but—Philip said you would wish to know."

"What is it?" asked Rebecca, growing alarmed. "Does the information pertain to me and my father?"

Miss Clifton nodded, and, unable to meet Rebecca's gaze, she pulled a letter from her reticule and gave it to her. "It is all in here. You may keep the letter, or destroy it if you wish. I am very, very sorry." Thrusting another small note into Rebecca's hand, Miss Clifton added, "I have written down my direction. I hope we *will* correspond. God bless you." She then turned and fled down the street.

Greatly worried and perplexed, Rebecca ran back into the house and up to her room, to read the letter in privacy.

Elm Grove

My dearest Catherine,

It was a great pleasure to see you at Bath last week. I only wish I could have stayed longer, but duty calls. As I write, I have two parishioners waiting to speak to me, a baptism to officiate, and a meeting with the churchwarden to attend. As such, I am obliged to keep this letter brief and to the point. You may recall the circumstances of Mr. Stanhope's departure from Elm Grove, which we discussed before I came away. I shared my dissatisfaction with the manner in which the matter was handled, and my determination to seek the truth. I have since made my inquiry. The intelligence which has just come into my possession is of such a distressing nature, that I hesitate to put it down on paper. Although I did promise to make Miss Stanhope acquainted with my findings, I leave it to your judgment as to whether or not it is best to reveal it.

The long and short of it is, I wrote to the innkeeper at the King's Arms, Leatherhead, Surrey, which was the seat of Mr. Stanhope's misfortune, requesting information with regard to the proceedings that night. The man's reply—not the most literate of epistles—written in a disdainful tone, and containing some very colourful terminology—insisted that Mr. Stanhope had played cards with three rough characters until the wee hours of the morning, that a great deal of money had exchanged hands, and—in the innkeeper's own words, "when the old gentleman at last stumbled upstairs to bed, he looked most ashamed and distraught." I know this news will greatly distress Miss Stanhope. I cannot express how sorry I am to have learned it; I wish now I had never written—but I fear this rather settles the matter, as to Mr. Stanhope's guilt. I still think him to be a good man, who sadly suffered a lack of judgment on this particular occasion, with quite disastrous results.— And now, I must sign off. I hope you are well, and that your journey home is free from incident. Please give my mother and father my best wishes for their health and happiness, and as always my regards to Laura.

I remain, Ever Yours, your brother, Philip Clifton

Rebecca stared at the page in her hands, horrified. Her stomach clenched, her mind reeled, and she felt truly ill. The information which Mr. Clifton imparted seemed impossible to believe—and yet it was so! Previously, she had been able to hold her head high despite their difficulties, believing her father to be the innocent victim of a crime; but now that she knew his culpability, she felt deeply ashamed, sick at heart, and angry.

It was bad enough that Mr. Stanhope had gambled with money which did not belong to him; but far worse, in her mind, was that he was guilty of the grossest falsehoods. He had *lied* about it to her, to Sir Percival, to every one! How could he do it? Rebecca had not thought it in his character to be so deceitful! No longer could she blame Sir Percival for insisting on her father's removal from his position; indeed, if the truth were known by the parishioners of Elm Grove as to Mr. Stanhope's behaviour that night, they would have most likely demanded his resignation, just as Sir Percival insisted.

For a long moment, Rebecca sat frozen with fury and indecision. Should she confront her father with what she knew? She wanted to lash out at him, to tell him how much his actions hurt her, and that he had let her down. However, upon re-reading Mr. Clifton's line about her father still being a good man, Rebecca felt all the kindness behind the sentiment, and began to soften. Despite her father's terrible lack of judgment that fateful night, despite his falsehoods in *this* instance, she acknowledged to herself that he *was* and always had been a good man. And he had certainly paid heavily for his mistake. He had lost his home and livelihood, and used the proceeds of all his worldly goods to pay back the debt. Clearly, Mr. Stanhope was as mortified as she by what he had done; so mortified that he could not bring himself to admit the truth even to *her*. With a sigh, Rebecca's heart went out to him. Even knowing that it was his misdeed which caused all their subsequent misfortunes, she still loved him; she would always love him. She pitied him, and she forgave him.

Crossing to the hearth, Rebecca tossed the letter into the fire and poked it until it burned down to ash. She would not—could not—bear for her father to know that she knew.

Two days passed away, and they were very long and melancholy. With Miss Clifton gone, Rebecca had no close friends left in Bath. Mrs. Newgate was a generous and cheerful woman, but she was not some one to whom Rebecca could feel comfortable sharing her troubles, particularly on *this* subject. She considered writing to her sister and unburdening her heart, but it did not seem fair to trouble Sarah with such distressing news by letter;—indeed, it was perhaps better to pretend that *she* had never heard this report, and allow Sarah and Charles, at least, to continue to think well of her father. The fewer people who were privy to this mortifying information, Rebecca decided, the better. She felt particular regret that Mr. Clifton had been the one to find it out, for she had come to regard him as a friend. Now that he possessed this knowledge about her father, she thought bitterly, she would no doubt never hear from Mr. Clifton again.

The soiree they attended that night with the Newgates proved even more tedious than usual, the conversation empty and meaningless. As Rebecca walked the streets of Bath, the delights of the city no longer held any appeal for her. All she observed around her was noise, congestion, and confusion. How, Rebecca wondered, was it possible to feel so entirely alone, in a room—nay, a city—so full of people? She walked out into the country-side to escape, and breathed in its beauties with great longing. She thought of home; but then remembered that she had no home.

Mrs. Newgate invited her out shopping the next morning, but as it was very wet, Rebecca stayed in and played backgammon with her father. She tried to appear as usual, but he sensed her low spirits, and asked more than once if she was ill. She found herself continually watching him and silently questioning his every statement. Was he the man she had always imagined him to be? Could she ever trust him again? Later, when he went to get the money for tickets to that evening's ball, he shielded his pocketbook from her view and appeared hesitant. Concerned, she said,

"Do not we have the money, papa? It is not important that we go."

"But it is important—we *should* go," replied he, and he gave her the money; but she thought she caught hidden worry behind his eyes.

Although Rebecca danced every dance that night, for the first time since coming to Bath, she did not enjoy a single one of them. Outwardly, their circumstances remained unchanged—but inwardly, she felt as if every thing were different. How many of these men would be interested in her, she wondered, were they privy to the shame which her father had brought down upon their family? As far as she could determine, Mr. and Mrs. Newgate had said nothing of her father's history or financial circumstances to any one, but had represented Mr. Stanhope as a respectable clergyman, newly retired. The Newgates' acquaintances at Bath, who had so graciously included Rebecca and her father at their parties and such—how many of them would continue the association, were they to learn the truth?

After breakfast the following morning, when Mr. Stanhope accompanied the Newgates on their daily pilgrimage to the pump-room, Rebecca stayed in, explaining that she preferred to read. She was alone in the drawing-room, and had just picked up her book, when she heard the sound of the door-bell, followed moments later by the maid's announcement that a gentleman had come to see her.

Rebecca rose to greet her visitor, her spirits a little fluttered, for she could not imagine what gentleman of her acquaintance would come to call. Could it be one of the young men with whom she had danced the night before, come to enquire after her? This, however, was not the case.

To her utter astonishment, the man who walked into the room was Dr. Jack Watkins.

VOLUME THREE

• • • •

Chapter I

Dr. Jack Watkins strode across the drawing-room and stopped a few feet away, whereupon he removed his hat with a gentlemanly bow. As he straightened, the eyes which met hers were fraught with emotion. "Good morning, Miss Stanhope."

Rebecca was so surprised, that she was momentarily robbed of the power of speech. To see him standing before her, so unexpectedly, after so many weeks of thinking of him, without hearing a single word! It was incredible! Her heart pounded as she gathered her wits; she hardly knew what she said, but thought it might have been, "Dr. Watkins—how very nice to see you."

"I trust you are in good health?"

"I am, sir. And you?"

"I am well." He spoke quickly, his manner agitated. "Pray, forgive me for intruding on you like this. I only arrived in town last night. I suppose I should have first sent a note to your father, but—" Then, as if an afterthought: "He is well, I hope? Your father?"

"Yes, thank you. He is out with his cousin. Will you sit down, sir?" She motioned to a nearby chair. They both sat. He glanced at the carpet, then at her, as if struggling for words. She broke the silence. "How did you know where to find me? From the book at the pump-room?"

"Your sister gave me the direction."

"Oh. Have you been in London these past weeks?"

"I have."

"I hope that all went as you planned, with regard to the establishment of your medical practice?"

"It—I did not—" With an impatient sigh, he leapt from his chair and walked about the room in an anxious manner. At length, he returned to stand before her, and said with great feeling, "Miss Stanhope: I cannot bear to waste time on idle chatter. I have come to Bath particularly because I have something to say to you. Pray permit me to express it."

Rebecca waited in silence, and was audience to the following:

"It was with the deepest regret that I parted from your company at Medford, Miss Stanhope, with no verbal articulation of my feelings, and no formal connection between us. I thought—I truly believed—that once I turned my attentions to my new practice, I should become too busy for an attachment of any kind, and that I must forget you; but I cannot. All these weeks that I have been in town, I have thought of nothing but you. No longer can I deny those feelings which began from the moment of our first acquaintance, and have grown with every encounter since. I love you, Miss Stanhope. Will you do me the honour of accepting my hand in marriage?"

Rebecca sat mute before him, her thoughts in a tumult, as she struggled to take in this extraordinary speech. She was amazed—stunned—astonished! She knew that she ought to be thrilled and grateful. Was not this the very moment she had once dreamt of? Every thing she and Sarah had once surmised was true: Dr. Watkins *did* love her. He wanted her to be his wife!

To her surprise, however, her heart did not flutter with excitement as it used to do, when she was in his company. Indeed, an unexpected confusion had descended upon her the moment of his arrival, and had only increased when he began to speak. She was now overcome by a strange, frozen feeling, which she could not account for. He stood waiting for her answer with anxious expectancy. A blush rose to her cheeks, and she found that she did not know how to reply. At last she stood and said,

"Dr. Watkins. I am honoured by your proposal, and grateful to you for extending it. But this is all so sudden and unexpected—it has been many weeks since we last saw or spoke to one another—"

"Yes, it has; yet I sensed—when we were last together, you gave me reason to believe that my feelings are reciprocated."

Her blush deepened as she groped for words.

Seeing her response, he stepped back in frustration. "Forgive me; I should not have descended on you so abruptly. I have been too direct, too open."

"I assure you, sir, that is *not* the case. I appreciate directness and openness, almost more than any other qualities."

He started at this, and changed colour himself; then

resumed, without looking at her, "Well then, it was poor manners on my part. Perhaps I should have first applied to your father, to seek his permission, before addressing you. I promise to do so directly. Will Mr. Stanhope be in this evening?"

"I believe he will, sir. But—"

"I shall return. Pray tell him to expect me at eight o'clock. I wish you a very pleasant day." So saying, Dr. Watkins replaced his hat on his head and hastily left the room. A moment later, she heard the sound of the front door to the house closing behind him.

Overcome by emotion, Rebecca sank into a chair. For several minutes she remained thus, so astonished that she could not move. She had received offers before, over which she had not expended an ounce of energy in declaring her decision; this, however, was different. Dr. Watkins had presumed her hesitation to be founded on a break in decorum, but that was unfounded—gentlemen were not *required* to ask the father's permission before courting or proposing to a woman, and based on her recent experience, clearly *many* did not. No;—the problem lay in a different quarter entirely: she truly had no idea how she felt.

Too unsettled to remain indoors, Rebecca retrieved her hat and shawl and went out for a long walk to St. James's Square and back, which time she spent in deep reflection. She was conscious of the importance of this moment in her life; that her future lay dangling before her. If she said yes, she would have a house in London, and an end to her and her father's financial woes. She believed it her duty to tell Dr. Watkins the terrible news she had learned about her father. Once he knew, would he still want to marry her? And if so, did *she* want to marry him?

She recalled her discussion with Sarah, regarding her hopes and expectations on the subject of matrimony. Did she love Dr. Watkins? She had always presumed that if she and a man were truly in love, she would know it with conviction, in the very depths of her being; that a connection should exist which allowed them to be completely honest and open with each other, and drew them closer than to any other living being; that to be *with him* should make her feel happier and more complete, than to be without him; that she should care more for *his* happiness than she did for her own; and that he must feel the same way about her.

Did *he* feel all those things? Did she?

Rebecca looked back on the few occasions which she had spent in Dr. Watkins's company, and began to perceive certain of his actions from a different point of view. When he deliberately stole her away from Mr. Spangle and took her out on the lake, she had been flattered and amused; yet she knew it was selfish and rude to their host. Dr. Watkins, however, had felt no guilt at all. He had spoken unkindly about her friend Amelia, until she had begged him not to. Upon discovering that her father delighted in an anonymous gift, Dr. Watkins had deliberately allowed them to believe *he* had sent it, just as he had wished her to think they intuitively shared a certain preference in literature. Would a true gentleman have behaved thus? No;—he would not.

A true gentleman proved his character and worth not with words, but by his deeds, her father had said. Dr. Watkins had many charms, and she had been captivated by them for a while; but with sudden clarity, Rebecca realised that she had never felt any truly *deep* regard for him. It had been merely a flirtation. She was not—and never had been—in love.

Rebecca returned to the house in a state of great disquiet. She would refuse his offer. Since there would be no connection between them, she was not obliged to reveal her father's secret. Before Dr. Watkins called that evening, she must think of the proper words with which to respond. She hoped that her answer would not cause him pain.

Upon entering the house, however, she received intelligence which sent these ideas scattering to the winds. It came in the form of a newly arrived letter, which lay waiting on the entry hall table. Rebecca caught it up, her spirits rising at the direction therein inscribed: it was from Amelia! Having not heard from her friend these many weeks, Rebecca was very interested in what she might have to relate, and hastened upstairs to read the missive.

Grafton Hall

My dearest Rebecca,

I know what you are thinking: that I am the world's worst correspondent. You have sent me two lovely, long letters, and only now am I replying! You will forgive me when you hear the reason behind the delay. My aunt has been very ill. She has kept to her bed this past fortnight. I have attended her with the devotion of a true daughter, which she avowed yesterday has always been the light in which she holds me. I cannot tell you how I cried at hearing those words from her parched lips! In truth, I do not mind very much when she is ill, for she is then less likely to scold and command me to do things which I dislike or find extremely tedious. However, on this occasion, I have been truly worried. Thank goodness Dr. Samuel Watkins has returned from town. He has been here every single day. He says it is a nervous weakness of the liver, and that bleeding, cupping, and his prescribed medicines will almost certainly restore her to her former state of health. When I look at her, though, and see how vastly pale and weak she has become after his treatments, I do not hold out much hope.

I cannot tell you how much your letters have meant to me, during this time of trial. I wish I could be at Bath with you—or better yet, London! It is so dull here in the country. How I miss the theatre and concerts! How delightful it would be to attend a fancy ball with more than twelve couple! But even a country life can be made tolerable, by the society of a particular friend (of course I mean you), and by a relationship with a man of whom one is very fond. Perhaps you have guessed where this statement is leading, and to whom I refer? If not, all the better, for we did take great pains to be discreet! But now that you are safely away at Bath, I am at last at liberty to reveal the truth about a circumstance of which I have been positively dying to tell you, ever since we met on Main Street!

You seemed shocked that I could never feel any thing for Brook Mountague, but I cannot help it; he disgusts me; and there can never be any thing between us. There is more. Rebecca dearest: I am promised to another. Dr. Jack Watkins and I have had a secret understanding for nearly a year now. We are passionately in love! I would die for him! Do you remember the locket you found in my drawer? The lock of hair is Dr. Watkins's, not Brook's; I sleep with it every night under my pillow, and sometimes, I long for him so desperately, I cry myself to sleep. But of this, naturally, I can say nothing to any one, particularly my aunt. She would never approve of my relationship with a physician. She has made it clear that I will marry Brook, or not get a penny of her money. So Dr. Watkins and I have been forced to keep our feelings private, and be patient. When she dies, I will inherit every thing, and then I shall be free to marry whomsoever I choose.

Dr. Watkins's attentions to you during your stay in Medford were all a pretence. He insisted that it would throw my aunt off the scent. It was unnerving to be forced to watch my own lover flirt openly with you—at times I was very out of sorts—and I could not help but see that you appeared to develop a regard for him—but what woman could not, for is he not the most handsome man alive? Am I not the luckiest woman in the world? Am I correct in my suspicion, that it was he from whom you expected a proposal on the night of our ball, rather than Mr. Spangle?

How I laugh when I think of it—how cleverly we concealed our plot—not even you, my dearest friend, guessed the truth! I trust that your disappointment was not too great, and no harm was done; for now that you are in Bath, and have so many handsome, landed gentlemen throwing themselves at your feet, I am sure you have quite forgotten a country doctor! Not that he will need to be a physician any more after we are married, and Grafton Hall is ours. Of course you must promise not to breathe a word of this to any one, for you know how quickly gossip spreads; I trust I can rely on your discretion. Now I must put this in the post, and return to my aunt's bedside. Dr. Watkins (senior) bled her again this morning, and she is very weak. Whether she is meant to pass from this earth to-night, or tomorrow, or will live another year entire, is in God's hands; in the mean time, I am resolved to remain strong and uncomplaining, and wait until that day when Dr. Watkins (junior) and I can be together for ever. Write to me as soon as ever you receive this! I wish I could see your new pink silk gown, it sounds divine. I long to hear more of the red-haired gentleman you met at the ball.

Your affectionate friend, Amelia Davenport

Rebecca's feelings, as she read this letter, can scarcely be described. At first, she was concerned to learn of Mrs. Harcourt's illness, and distressed by Amelia's callous view of the matter. When she read the third paragraph, however, she leapt to her feet, and exclaimed, "Good God! I do not believe it! It cannot be!"

That Amelia Davenport (who, to all her family's expectations, had long been intended for her cousin Brook Mountague) should have had a secret understanding with Dr. Jack Watkins—for nearly a year! It was inconceivable! Rebecca had never once suspected such a thing. She was horror-struck—incredulous. Was there any chance, she wondered, that it was untrue? After some thought, she decided that it must be so; for why should Amelia fabricate such a story? Further proof presented itself when she recalled the manner in which Jack Watkins had started and blushed that very morning, when she related how much she appreciated directness and openness. He must have been thinking of the lies he had told her, and was ashamed. And yet, Rebecca thought with increased perturbation, if it *was* all true—if Dr. Watkins *was* promised to Amelia—then why did he just propose to *her*?

Rebecca paced back and forth, her mind in a tumult, and divided between three things: her prior conversations with Dr. Watkins and Amelia, in which they had both expressed their contempt for each other—statements which she now realised had all been the grossest falsehoods, deliberate instruments of their deceit; small moments when she had observed the two of them in interaction, which now took on new meaning (such as the way Amelia had behaved on the day of the boating party, when Dr. Watkins had taken Rebecca out on the lake; and the ankle injury Amelia had feigned the day of the ball—no doubt to facilitate a need for Dr. Watkins's attentions); and the offer of marriage which Dr. Watkins had just made, which was unaccountable.

With regard to the first two ideas, in reviewing Amelia's behaviour, Rebecca grew very angry. How could Amelia (whom Rebecca had thought her friend!) have silently allowed this charade to go on, with no regard for Rebecca's growing feelings? How cruel! How disingenuous! That no permanent injury had been inflicted on *her*, with regard to Dr. Watkins, came as a relief; however, it did not excuse Amelia's conduct, for in secretly consorting with another man, Amelia had inflicted injury on both Mr. Mountague *and* their aunt. Moreover—and far worse—was Amelia's admission with regard to her feelings for that very aunt. To think that Amelia had deliberately kept her proposed suitor, Mr. Mountague, in the dark, while lying in wait like a vulture for Mrs. Harcourt's demise—all the while intending to marry Dr. Watkins, the moment she received her inheritance. Shocking! Abominable! Despicable!

When Rebecca moved on to consider Dr. Watkins's part in the equation, she became very perplexed. She could not comprehend it. If all that Amelia purported was true, then he was a veritable scoundrel. Yet he had seemed so sincere in his expression of love to her. Surely, a man of his calibre would not propose to a woman on a whim—particularly if he was already promised to another. Could Amelia somehow be mistaken in her conception of their relationship? Were they really, truly *engaged*? Even though Rebecca did not want Jack Watkins, she wanted to learn the truth behind the affair. She required an explanation from *him*—and she hoped that he would have something to say in his own defence, which would make her think better of him.

All during dinner, while her father and Mr. and Mrs. Newgate chatted animatedly, Rebecca scarcely heard a word that was said. Her gaze kept returning to the clock on the mantel. Mrs. Newgate, noticing Rebecca's distracted manner, and having heard from the maid about Rebecca's visitor, teased her unmercifully about her secret beau, and begged for full disclosure. Rebecca only replied that the gentleman in question was expected at eight o'clock, and that she would be most grateful to be allowed a private interview. This request prompted raised eyebrows from the men, and additional quizzing from her hostess; but every one agreed to make themselves scarce at the appointed hour.

....

Chapter II

At eight precisely, Dr. Watkins arrived. This time, Rebecca was prepared for him. When he walked into the drawing-room, bowed and smiled, and enquired where he might find her father, she replied,

"He is upstairs, sir. However, before you speak to him, there is a matter of great importance which you and I must discuss first."

"Oh?"

"It concerns a letter I received to-day from Amelia Davenport."

His smile fled. Cautiously, he said, "What—did Miss Davenport have to say?"

Rebecca calmly informed him of the contents of the letter, as they pertained to him. He blanched, with an expression of mingled shame and mortification; then, leaning against the mantelpiece, he stared into the fire for a full minute without speaking. When Rebecca could stand the silence no longer, she said,

"Well? Is it true?"

In a quiet voice, tense with irritation, he replied, "This is not the manner in which I intended—"

"A simple yes or no will do."

He let out an exasperated breath as he turned back in her direction. "Hang it all! Fine. Have it your way. What is the point in keeping it from you *now*? Yes! *Yes,* I *did* have—*do* have—a private—*understanding* with that young lady, but we are not *engaged*. I fully intend to break it off with her at the earliest possible opportunity."

"Oh!" cried Rebecca, his admission vanquishing the hope that he might have any thing to say which could redeem him. "You villain! How can you speak so coolly about a matter which will break another's heart? Amelia is in love with you!"

"She will get over it, and as for myself—I am not to blame." His gaze met hers across the divide between them. "One cannot predict or control the direction in which our affections will tend."

"Sir," replied Rebecca warmly, "you seem to transfer your affections from one party to another as lightly and effortlessly as a feather, and with as little emotional attachment."

"I do nothing of the kind. I assure you, Miss Stanhope, my offer to you this morning came from the depths of my heart. I said I love you; and I do."

"I would relish an explanation as to how a man who is promised to one woman, can find it in *the depths of his heart* to proclaim his love and propose to another."

"I will explain—gladly. I *intended* to tell you all myself, in any case, once every thing was settled between us—I am truly sorry you heard of this first from Miss Davenport. Blast it all! This is so very like her!" Taking a breath to compose himself, he went on: "The facts are these: while at university, I often visited my mother and father in Medford. We were frequently invited to Grafton Hall, and I became acquainted with Miss Davenport. It soon became evident to me that she was becoming—enamoured of me. I cannot explain what I saw in her. I suppose I was bewitched by her beauty; and she made me laugh. But looking back, I think I became more captivated by the idea of *being* loved by her—*worshipped* is more the word—than any thing I felt for the young lady herself. Admittedly—I am not proud of this—there was the added attraction of her money. One day, when Miss Davenport inherited her aunt's wealth and property, she would be very rich; if I married her, it would all be mine. I should not be obliged to be a physician after all; I should not have to work hard all my life as my father has, dispensing prescriptions and catering to ridiculous valetudinarians. I could be a gentleman of leisure, and devote my time to drawing and painting, as I have always dreamt of doing. I suppose I had all this in mind when we discussed marriage last year;—but Miss Davenport insisted that her aunt would never approve, so it was best to wait."

His brazen, unashamed account filled Rebecca with disgust. "Wait for what? For Mrs. Harcourt to die?"

"No! No! What sort of monster do you take me for? I am a man of honour, integrity, and feeling, Miss Stanhope. I do not *wish* for Mrs. Harcourt to die! It is true: she is sickly. Miss Davenport did mention once or twice that it might not be long until she passed on, which would clear the way for us to marry;—but from the start, *I* only waited in the hopes that Mrs. Harcourt's opinion of me would improve. I continued my education; as a physician, I knew I would be admitted to her circle. To my chagrin, however, it made no difference." Bitterly, he added, "I know *now* that she will never take kindly to her niece's affiliation with any one whose family history of land and property does not go back at least several generations."

"Yet knowing this, you still maintained your secret engagement."

"I insist, there was no *engagement*—"

"A promise is the same as an engagement, sir, to any man of honour. Did you think to elope?"

"Of course not."

"So you *are* waiting for Mrs. Harcourt to die."

His face grew red. He did not reply.

"And while I was at Medford," continued Rebecca, "you feigned a dislike for Amelia and flirted with *me*, to keep Mrs. Harcourt from guessing your intentions."

His blush deepened further still. His eyes, when they returned to hers, were full of feeling. "What began as a harmless flirtation, turned into something very different. I did not understand what true love was, Miss Stanhope, until I met you. I think Miss Davenport guessed, at the last, that my affections might be changing, for she became incredibly jealous. At the ball at Grafton Hall, she did every thing in her power to keep me at her side—I cannot even be certain her ankle was truly injured. She told me that if I danced so much as one dance with you, our understanding was at an end. I should have jumped at the opportunity to bow out of a situation which was no longer tenable; but I was not prepared, that night, to make so final a decision. I went away to London because I required some time alone to think it through."

"To think it through? *Not* to open your new practice?"

"No—I have put off making those arrangements, in case—"

"In case Mrs. Harcourt died, and there was no need?"

He sighed with frustration. "It has been a difficult struggle. Were you and I to marry, I knew I was giving up any hope of a landed gentleman's life, and should be compelled to earn my own living as a physician in the city. Could I do it? I asked myself. At last, I decided that I could and *would*." Crossing the room, he sat down on the chair beside Rebecca and leaned forward, speaking earnestly. "What I once felt for Miss Davenport is nothing compared to what I feel for you, Miss Stanhope. If I have wronged her, I regret it, but you are, to me, the shining example of all that womanhood should be. Our future is ahead of us. Do tell me that you can forget what is in the past; that you can forgive me; and that you will do me the honour of consenting to be my wife."

If Rebecca had been amazed at his audacity before, she was even more astonished now. "If you thought to flatter me with these declarations, sir, I regret to inform you that you have failed entirely. How can you imagine me to think well of your proposal, after all that you have just said? You call yourself a man of honour; yet you have deliberately deceived me and many others in so many ways, that I should be ashamed to recount them. You call yourself a man of integrity; yet you have maintained a secret attachment in the expectation—the hope—that a good woman would die, and you would profit from it. You call yourself a man of feeling; yet you stand before me and declare your love, with no thought for the young lady to whom you are already promised—a lady whom you are callous enough to cast off without a second thought. You insist that it was a struggle to choose between a life with me, and a life with another, based primarily on the status and level of leisure you might attain with each. Can this be love? I think not."

He was taken aback, and did not immediately reply. "Miss Stanhope, you are angry with me. That is understandable. Given the circumstances, I deserve nothing less. But pray, do not allow that anger to blind you to your own feelings. You do not comprehend your own heart. I know you love me—I have seen it in your gaze, and heard it in your voice—and where true love lies, there must be forgiveness."

"You are mistaken, sir. I may have entertained feelings for you at one time, but I do no longer; and they never amounted to love. Your lack of compassion astounds me; your lack of remorse disgusts me. I am, however, grateful for having had this opportunity to gain insight into your true character." She stood. "And now, this interview is at an end."

Dr. Watkins rose and stared at her in consternation, all affection fleeing from his countenance, instantly replaced by anger and resentment. For some moments, he appeared to search for some reply; but, failing, he at last replaced his hat on his head, calmly walked to the door, and left without another word.

Rebecca sat for some minutes alone in the room, reflecting on what had just passed with great emotion, and feeling that she had made a very fortunate escape. Imagine if she had been foolish enough actually to marry Dr. Watkins, without learning the truth behind the affair! At length, the sound of approaching footsteps made her realise how unequal she was to making any explanation of the preceding events; and, with a brief apology to her startled father and the Newgates, she hurried out of the room and up the stairs.

She lay awake long into the night in very agitating reflections. When she awoke to find sunlight filtering in through the shutters, the clock in the passage was striking eleven. Still troubled by all that had occurred the previous evening, Rebecca rose and dressed, all the while struggling to prepare that elucidation which would be expected by Mr. Stanhope and the Newgates.

However, no such illumination proved to be required, for—as she was soon to discover—in the intervening hours, events had transpired which would alter her and her father's circumstances in a most catastrophic manner.

....

Chapter III

Having risen too late to partake of breakfast, Rebecca ventured down to the drawing-room, where she heard sharp voices issuing from within. As she entered, instead of the kindly greetings she was accustomed to receiving, she was met by a strange and uncomfortable silence. Her father sat in a chair by the fireplace, with a bleak expression on his countenance. Mr. Newgate's eyes were cold and harsh; and his wife, who sat on the sofa engaged in needlework, appeared both furious and mortified.

"Papa!" cried Rebecca, hurrying to his side, all thoughts of the previous evening's events eclipsed. "Are you ill?"

Mr. Stanhope shook his head wordlessly, and looked away.

"What is wrong?" persisted Rebecca, turning to her hosts. "What has happened?"

"We have just come from the pump-room," answered Mr. Newgate, as he rattled his newspaper closed.

"We heard news of the most *distressing* nature," added Mrs. Newgate in a clipped tone.

"What news?"

"It has come to our attention," replied Mr. Newgate, "that you and your father have not been forthright with us regarding your true reason for leaving Elm Grove, and coming to Bath."

"Indeed, you have most gravely misled us!" cried Mrs. Newgate. "We are mortified beyond expression!"

"I do not understand," said Rebecca haltingly, growing very alarmed.

"In your father's first correspondence," alleged Mr. Newgate, "he claimed that he was dismissed for having *lost* a sum of money belonging to his church—an hundred and fifty pounds, that was the aforementioned amount. I was led to believe that he was, at best, the victim of a theft, and at worst, at fault for somehow mislaying the funds."

Rebecca's face grew hot; she could not speak. Could it be that they had somehow discovered the truth about what happened at the inn at Leatherhead?

"There! Do you see how she blushes?" exclaimed Mrs. Newgate. "She knows of his guilt! All along, she was party to the evil!" Casting a scathing look at Mr. Stanhope, she continued, "How could you think to take advantage of my husband's good nature by representing yourself as you did?"

"To seek *me* out in particular—a very distant cousin, who could not be privy to the facts!"

"And then to impose so shamelessly upon our charity!" (To Rebecca) "When I think of all the clothes and things I bought you!"

"To discover that I opened my heart and my home to a common thief!"

"A thief?" Rebecca was bewildered. "Whatever do you mean?"

"Oh, do not play the innocent with me, my dear," said Mr. Newgate.

"You thought the truth would never reach us; but we are now fully acquainted with what occurred: your father *stole* five hundred pounds from church funds which had been raised to build a school!"

Rebecca's astonishment on hearing this was very great. "Five hundred pounds! But—where on earth did you hear such a report?"

"From Lady Ellington," replied Mr. Newgate.

"Lady Ellington!"

"Her maid received the intelligence early this morning from her brother," replied Mr. Newgate, "who works at the White Hart Inn, who heard it last night from the valet of a prominent London physician who was staying there—" (turning to his wife) "what was his name?"

"Dr. Jack Watkins."

"Yes, Watkins. He told his valet the dreadful news in the strictest confidence, which is this: that he became acquainted with you and your father in Medford; that Mr. Stanhope's patron at Elm Grove was Sir Percival something or other—"

"Mountague," put in Mrs. Newgate.

"Yes, Mountague; that Mr. Stanhope stole the church funds, took the entire sum to London, and shamelessly gambled it all away; but as he covered up all trace of his crime, there was no way to prove it."

"Oh!" cried Rebecca, aghast. "That is not true! My father never stole any thing! It *is* true that some of the church's money went missing, but it was the smaller sum that you described; and—" She could not go on.

"If that is so, Miss Stanhope, then why was he forced to flee Elm Grove like a common criminal?"

"We did not flee," Rebecca began, but Mr. Newgate interrupted her by saying,

"You cannot protect him, my dear; only look at his face, and it becomes clear where the truth lies."

Mr. Stanhope was indeed the colour of a ghost.

Rebecca knelt before her father, taking his hands in hers. "Papa," she pleaded, in a hoarse whisper, "tell them what really happened." She looked at him earnestly, hoping that he could read in her eyes the terrible knowledge which she had never been able to voice. But Mr. Stanhope only shook his head. "What is the point, my dear? It is my word against theirs."

"We could *never* doubt the word of Lady Ellington," said Mrs. Newgate.

Rebecca rose, her thoughts in disarray. Should she ask if they might write to Sir Percival Mountague or to Mr. Philip Clifton, who could surely explain what had had happened at the King's Arms? Instantly, she rejected the notion. The truth, she realised, was almost as damning as the lie. Nevertheless, she must find some way to appease her accusers and defend her father, and to remain candid while doing so.

"Sir! Madam! You are too hasty! You base your opinion on an account which I assure you is false, quite false. It is nothing but a vile chain of gossip—you can give it no credence. My father is no thief. The report has changed hands no less than five times in the sending, perhaps even more—and the content of the message has been equally as changed. Either that, or Dr. Watkins has misrepresented the proceedings entirely."

"What possible reason could the gentleman have for inventing such a story?" said Mr. Newgate.

"He had reason," said Rebecca in great agitation. "It was

Dr. Jack Watkins who came to see me last night. He asked for my hand in marriage, and when I refused him, he left very angry. I would never have thought it within his character to—but if, indeed, this is the report he gave—then he has taken out his bitterness in the most vile manner, by deliberately circulating this malicious rumour."

Mr. and Mrs. Newgate exchanged a surprised glance; then he said, "That is not the account which Lady Ellington heard."

"Nothing was said about a proposal," agreed his wife.

"Dr. Watkins told his valet that, hearing you were in Bath, he called on you in friendship, to see if he could be of some assistance to you in your troubles; but you sent him away, begging him to say nothing of the matter."

"No wonder you afterwards took to your bed in such haste, without uttering a syllable to any one," added Mrs. Newgate with a sniff.

"Oh! The villain!" exclaimed Rebecca. All at once, Dr. Watkins's motive in starting this rumour, and in particularly avoiding any mention of his proposal to Rebecca, became clear: having failed to gain *her* affections, he could not risk losing Amelia's. No doubt he was already on his way back to Medford, Amelia, and her anticipated fortune, praying all the way that if Amelia *did* hear any thing of what had transpired at Bath, it would only be of the Stanhopes' loss of reputation and ruin.

Mr. Newgate sighed and rose from his chair. "I see that it is too much to expect an admission or an apology in this affair."

"Sir: how can you accept gossip spread by a man you do not even know, over the assertions of myself and my father?" inquired Rebecca in despair. "You have known *us* for many weeks now!"

"We have known Lady Ellington far longer; and *she* knows Dr. Jack Watkins, having been attended by his father, who is also a physician, on her many visits to town. She assures us that his reputation and character are unexceptionable."

"And yet again I insist: this account is not true!"

"You would say any thing to protect yourself and your father—*that* is all *I* know to be true," replied Mrs. Newgate with a sniff. "With the manner in which gossip spreads, this news will soon be common knowledge all over Bath."

"What will people think, when they hear that we have sheltered a veritable fugitive?"

"Lady Ellington would never invite us anywhere again. The Dowager Viscountess Carnarvon would cross us off her list!"

"The scandal is too great," insisted Mr. Newgate coldly. "You must understand that I can no longer be associated with you, Mr. Stanhope, or your daughter, in any way. It is imperative that you both pack up and leave this house at once."

Mr. Stanhope proudly stood, and said in quiet reply, "If that is your wish, sir. Thank you for the friendship you have shown us heretofore. We shall depart without delay."

Rebecca was now speechless, her throat nearly closed with the threat of tears. Having already said every thing she could think of in their defence, she understood that they had no alternative but to comply with their hosts' demands. Crossing to her father, she promptly led him away.

It was not until they reached Mr. Stanhope's room upstairs that Rebecca was equal to inquiring, in a voice which she struggled to keep even, "Do you need help packing your things, papa?"

"No, my dear—I can do it—I have so little."

She was about to turn towards the door when she stopped and said, "Where shall we go? Shall we return to Medford?"

Mr. Stanhope sighed. "I hate to throw ourselves upon Sarah's and Charles's mercy once again, but—I shall write to them. However—" He stopped, as moisture gathered in his eyes.

"What is it, papa?"

Mr. Stanhope struggled to regain his composure. "To my utter mortification, my dear, I have insufficient funds to cover the journey to Medford, and the requisite overnight stay en route—even if we were to travel by stage."

Rebecca was shocked. "Is it truly as bad as that?"

"I am afraid it is. Our stay at Bath has proved far more expensive than I anticipated. Even though our lodgings and most of our meals have been provided, I have spent a great deal on tickets to the theatre, balls, concerts, and Sydney Gardens. We are nearly at the end of our resources."

Remorse spread through her, as she thought of all that he had so generously paid for. "Why did you never say?"

"You were having such a good time, dearest. Tucked away in the country all your life, I was never able to give you opportunities such as these. You deserved a few luxuries.—I had twelve guineas remaining, which I had hoped, with careful economy, and the benefit of the Newgates' hospitality, to last for some weeks more—but Mr. Coulthard was in such dire straits, we have been corresponding, you know, and he lost his cow, there was no milk for the children—I felt compelled to send him the preponderance of the sum."

"Oh, papa."

"How could I have anticipated that this terrible thing would happen?"

"Can we borrow the money?"

"I have already tried. No bank would advance me a sum, and we have no real friends here to ask."

"Perhaps we can sell something."

"What should we sell? We already divested ourselves of every thing of value before leaving Elm Grove."

"Mama's pearl brooch is real gold; it must be worth something. I could—"

"Never!" cried Mr. Stanhope, aghast. "I gave that ornament to your mother the day we were married. I will not hear of your selling it!"

Rebecca sighed with relief, for the brooch was her favourite possession; it was the only memento that remained of her mother's, and she wished never to part with it. Taking a deep, wavering breath, she said, "Well, I am certain that Sarah and Charles will be happy to assist us. But even if you send a letter by express, it may be several days before we hear back. What are we to do in the meantime?"

"We shall simply have to find an inn that is not too costly."

Mr. Stanhope immediately wrote to Sarah and Charles, apprising them of their circumstances, and requesting that they advance a loan to a local post office, which he promised to repay. Their belongings were packed within the hour, and left with a servant to be claimed once they made new arrangements. Rebecca left most of her new clothes, which Mrs. Newgate had paid for, in the cupboard; but at the last moment, unable to stop herself, she took the pink silk gown. As Mr. and Mrs. Newgate did not deign to make a reappearance, Rebecca and Mr. Stanhope were obliged to depart without so much as a good-bye.

A wearisome survey of inns in the area led them to ascertain, to Mr. Stanhope's horror, that they could only afford lodgings in the lower part of town, which could not in any way compare to the wholesomeness and desirability of the northern slopes. This low-lying section of Bath was immediately adjacent to the arc of slums which housed the majority of the labourers upon whom the comfortable lives of the visitors and leisured residents depended. As Rebecca and her father walked along the crowded streets of that compact area, which included a great many alehouses and workshops emitting foul, repulsive fumes, they were distressed to find themselves surrounded by filthy beggars, children in tattered clothes, starved-looking dogs, and women and men of such low order that Mr. Stanhope insisted they could only be tarts and criminals. To their further distress, the few inns within their means were very close to the river, and dampness clung to the walls of most of the chambers, sending Mr. Stanhope into a paroxysm of alarm.

Rebecca did her best to calm and assure him that a brief stay would not prove ruinous to their health. At length, they settled on an inn not far from Westgate Buildings, which was the least objectionable of those on offer. Although the place was tiny, airless, and none too clean, and was positioned directly above a noisy tavern from which emanated the stink of fish, it had the advantage of being a suite with two tiny rooms, each with a single bed, one of which contained a small table and chair; and the innkeeper, a slovenly woman named Mrs. Riddle, said they could purchase dinner and breakfast at a nominal charge. Being very cheap, Mr. Stanhope could afford two nights' lodging, the first of which he paid in advance.

"How far we have come down in the world!" exclaimed he, sinking down on the edge of the bed in despair. "My reputation is permanently maligned, and we are truly penniless—

two days away from living on the streets." He looked so tired and forlorn, that Rebecca—who felt very despondent herself—had to rally all her inner strength not to burst into tears.

"You must take a little rest, papa. All this walking has tired you out exceedingly."

"Yes, but I cannot bear to lay my head upon this pillow—see you how stained the case is—and the blanket is very dirty and frayed."

Rebecca removed her shawl and lay it over the offending articles, providing him with a clean place upon which to lie. With a small, grateful smile, Mr. Stanhope lay back, and said, "You are a clever girl, my dearest, and I thank you. Can you ever forgive me for bringing all of this shame upon us?"

"Hush, papa," said Rebecca soothingly, sitting down beside him and taking his hand. "There is nothing to forgive. And it is *not* your fault. I think the Newgates have behaved quite heartlessly."

"They have; and I find it hard to believe that Dr. Watkins could have said something so unkind about me. I thought him my friend."

"So did I. Events have proved that he is not at all the man we supposed him to be."

"And yet, perhaps he is not as much a villain as it would appear," mused Mr. Stanhope. "It is possible that Dr. Watkins only happened to mention, in passing to his valet, something about the *true* circumstances of our removal from Elm Grove; and this report grew and altered with each retelling, until it became infamous."

Rebecca shook her head with a sad smile. "This is so like you, papa: always searching for some way to find the good in every body. But it will not do in this case, for even if *that* is true, it does not explain away his denial of his true purpose in calling on me yesterday."

"But it does, my dear. Did he really ask you to marry him?"

"Yes."

"And you refused him?"

"I did."

"There is your answer. After a failed proposal, Dr. Watkins would have been too embarrassed to mention a thing about it to his man-servant."

Rebecca considered this idea, but saw only the barest glimmer of reason in it. "That *might* be the case, papa; I hope it is. But it does not truly answer, for it was said that *I* sent Dr. Watkins away, and begged him to say nothing of our troubles."

"This might be attributed, as you suggested, to a deterioration of language, due to the gossip chain." Mr. Stanhope gave a heavy sigh. "But if it *is* what he said—well, there is no telling what a man will do, when he is disappointed in love." Glancing at her, he added, "Why did you turn down Dr. Watkins's offer? I mean, before all this happened—I thought you liked him."

She hesitated, uncertain whether or not to tell him the reason behind her refusal. Amelia had begged her to keep the details of her relationship with Jack Watkins a secret. Rebecca had no sympathy for either of them;—they had behaved in the most despicable manner, and she hoped that Mrs. Harcourt would live another fifty years, just to plague their hearts out. Yet at the same time, she felt the weight of her burden to remain silent on the matter. And what good could come of revealing it to her father—or to Mrs. Harcourt? Who would believe any thing *they* said *now*? Therefore she only replied, "I sensed that there was something wanting in his character, papa. But more importantly, I did not—I *do not* love him."

He nodded and squeezed her hand. "Well, there is nothing worse than marrying without affection."

In the ensuing silence, Rebecca felt a deep sense of self-pity. She had never in her life been reduced to such sorry circumstances. It seemed impossible that they should receive the required financial assistance from Sarah and Charles in only two days; and when their money ran out, what then? Would they be cast out upon the street, like the common beggars they had passed that afternoon? Would they be obliged to sleep in an alley-way, drink from rain barrels, and eat rubbish? What on earth were they to do?

. . . .

Chapter IV

As Rebecca looked about the wretched little room, she shuddered. There must be some way, she thought, that she could remedy their desperate circumstances; some manner in which she could *earn* money on her own.

An idea now began to form in Rebecca's mind, as to how she might be able to accomplish that very thing. She had never worked for hire or earned a penny in her life. She required something immediate. There must be a situation for which she was qualified—in a shop perhaps—and where better to seek such a post, than in the populous city of Bath, with its vast litany of establishments? The idea filled Rebecca with hope. When she shared her intentions with her father, however, it only added to his grief. He considered such employment very lowly, and tried to dissuade her from the attempt; but Rebecca assured him that they had no alternative.

"I shall first return to Great Pulteney Street and leave our new direction," added Rebecca, "so that our trunks may be delivered this afternoon. I know you will want our linens as soon as possible, to re-make these beds."

"Thank you, my dear. But you must take your shawl, and stop to eat along the way. You have had nothing all day. You must be starved." He took out a few coins from his purse and tried to hand them to her, but although her stomach was rumbling, Rebecca shook her head.

"We need that money for dinner. I will be fine until then, and you may keep my shawl; it is very warm without." She added that she might be gone for some length of time, and that he must on no account be uneasy.

Rebecca made her way back to the Newgates' residence, and after discharging her duty, returned to the main part of town, where she stopped in at the linen-draper's from whence she had purchased her muslins, intending to inquire about possible employment. No sooner had she entered the establishment, however, and uttered a cordial greeting, than the shopkeeper, recognising her and looking at her oddly, motioned for her to step aside to a remote corner, where she said in a hushed tone, "Miss Stanhope: I have just heard the most unaccountable rumour. I try not to set much store in such things; but are you aware of what people are saying about your father?"

Rebecca turned very red. Although well aware of how quickly rumours spread in a small village, she was astonished to discover that the incidence was no different in a city the size of Bath. Very uncomfortable, and hoping the evil was not so bad as she presumed, Rebecca asked what the shopkeeper had heard, to which the woman replied,

"They say that Mr. Stanhope stole six hundred pounds from his own parish."

"Six hundred pounds!" The averred amount seemed determined to grow with each report! Rebecca assured the shopkeeper that the rumour was entirely false, had escalated beyond all reason, and had already caused them a great deal of trouble. Without going into detail, she added that their friends had abandoned them; their circumstances were reduced; and she had come seeking a post. The shopkeeper, taken aback, immediately expressed her regrets, but said that no positions were open. Wishing Rebecca good luck, she quickly and firmly bid her good day.

Although deflated by this rebuff, Rebecca persisted in her endeavour, and spent the remainder of the afternoon calling at shops on Milsom Street, Bath Street, and Bond Street. In an effort to prevent a repeat of the first experience, and fearing that a stigma might now be attached to the name Stanhope, she elected not to use her own name, instead introducing herself as "Miss Clarissa Fitzgerald," a name she had often employed as a child when she and her sister performed their little theatricals for the family. She offered her services to sell every thing from tea and cakes to china, silver spoons, linen, lace, hats, and muslin—all to no avail. Every where she received the same response: "Experience was required—They were not hiring at present—all were full up." There was not a position to be had.

The sun had just set, bringing with it the mild chill of early evening. Rebecca's feet ached with every step, and she was weary in both mind and spirit, an evil compounded by a complete want of nourishment. One shopkeeper, sensing her exhaustion, had taken pity on her and offered her a piece of bread and a glass of water, which Rebecca had accepted and consumed as if they were nectar from the gods. As she was passing a tea shop, where two chattering ladies were just exiting, her head began to swim; and she was obliged to stop and lean against a post to steady herself. Thus positioned, as the ladies approached, their conversation caught her ear.

"Such an interesting variety on the program at the concert to-night," said the first lady. "Did you see the list?"

"I did," replied the other. "I always enjoy the tender Italian love-songs."

"Yes, but I like the gay and the sophisticated music equally as much."

"What a shame Miss Campbell is too ill to perform, and was obliged to cancel."

"My husband will be particularly disappointed. We heard her in London, you know—a lovely soprano. We both so looked forward to hearing her Scots songs."

A pause; then: "Miss? Are you quite all right?"

Rebecca, opening her eyes, discovered the women standing immediately before her and regarding her with concern. Recovering, she said, "Yes—thank you—I am just a bit tired. I will be fine."

Nodding, the ladies moved on, resuming their discussion. Rebecca, however, stood as if fixed to the spot, the intelligence she had just received ringing through her mind like a carillon: "*Miss Campbell is too ill to perform—obliged to cancel—lovely soprano—looked forward to hearing her Scots songs—*."

The solution to her dilemma came to her with the speed of a thunderbolt.

How many times had she been told that she had a superior voice—that she was good enough to perform on the stage?

Had not Dr. Watkins (of whom she hated to think) once told her that she could earn a good living if she chose, by her voice? Indeed, it was said that singers were paid good money—and there was no shame in it, no shame at all! Perhaps—like the proverbial Tommy Thumb in *Mother Goose's Melody*—she might be allowed to *sing* for her supper!

....

CHAPTER V

The question now arose of how to go about securing such employment. It was Wednesday—the night that concerts were always held at the Upper Rooms—yet it was still early. If she was lucky, perhaps the conductor, Mr. Rauzzini, might be there at this very moment.

Filled with renewed energy and purpose, Rebecca hastened up the steep streets in the waning afternoon light until she reached the Upper Rooms. The area was deserted, the entrance door open and unattended. Rebecca slipped inside and made her way through the connecting foyers, where the staff was making ready for the evening's entertainment. Following the sound of instruments and voices in song, she proceeded to the ball-room, which was in the process of being lit. The chairs and benches were already set up, and a rehearsal was in progress, under the direction of Mr. Rauzzini.

From the doorway, Rebecca observed the assembled musicians, the fine-looking couple—a tenor and an alto—presently singing, the elegantly dressed conductor (so highly regarded by the populace of Bath), and his small, studious-looking, bespectacled assistant, who she knew was called Mr. Thurst.

Rebecca trembled at the sight, and began to lose her nerve. Did she really dare approach these accomplished men—she, who had never sung professionally a day in her life? *You must,* she told herself;—and lest any further delay might prevent her from acting, she boldly strode up to the front of the room, where she stood listening with appreciation to the performers, who were very good. When the song had finished, every one turned and glanced at her, and Mr. Rauzzini briskly asked if he could be of service.

"You can, sir.—I have greatly enjoyed all your concerts over the past several weeks, Mr. Rauzzini, and—I am—I have only just heard—is it true that one of the singers on to-night's program, a Miss Campbell, was obliged to cancel due to ill-health?"

"Alas, that is indeed so," replied he with a nod. "A great loss for us, too; for she was to be our featured performer, and I never heard any one sing 'Their Groves O' Sweet Myrtle' like Miss Colleen Campbell."

"I can sing 'Their Groves O' Sweet Myrtle,'" replied Rebecca.

"Can you now?" said Mr. Rauzzini with a tired look which conveyed both his doubt and his complete disinterest.

"I am a soprano. I could happily fill Miss Campbell's place on the program, if you wish. I have been singing ever since I was a girl."

"Have you ever sung on the stage?"

"No, but I have performed countless times before my family and friends, and have oft been told that I have a lovely voice."

He frowned impatiently. "I am sure you delight your friends, Miss, but we have no room for amateurs here. Only professionals with the most sterling reputations perform at Bath."

"Sir," said Rebecca, struggling to keep the desperation from her voice, "if you would only consider allowing me a trial. If you heard me sing, I believe you might have a different opinion."

"Miss," said Mr. Thurst disdainfully, "Mr. Rauzzini has spoken. Cannot you see that we are very busy? Please do not further waste our time."

"We have two more songs to rehearse, and then my musicians are off to dinner," added Mr. Rauzzini dismissively. "I bid you good evening."

Rebecca's heart sank. But before she could turn to leave, the tenor who had just performed, and who had exchanged a few quiet words with his partner during this conversation, said,

"Why not let her sing a few bars, Mr. Rauzzini? She seems very eager. What harm could it do? It will only take a minute. She may have the remainder of our rehearsal time, for we feel quite ready."

Mr. Rauzzini opened his mouth to object; but noticing the acquiescing looks from the musicians, and the kind and determined expressions on the two singers' faces, the conductor reluctantly gave way. With a sigh and an irritated shake of his head, he said to Rebecca, "Very well, then. You may sing one song—let it be 'Their Groves O' Sweet Myrtle.' Stand just over there."

Rebecca crossed to the appointed spot; he gave instruction to the small orchestra to accompany her; and then he, Mr. Thurst, and the other two singers stood watching and waiting.

As the musicians picked up their instruments and got into position, Rebecca's heart beat fast, and her nerve began to waver; a sudden urge to give up this folly and run from the room was so overpowering, that it took all her strength to check it. Glancing up, however, she discovered the tenor regarding her with a kind and encouraging smile; this renewing her confidence, she stood her ground.

The introduction to the song was struck; Rebecca began. Having had no time to warm up—indeed, her throat was very dry—the first bar sounded rough and uneven. Witnessing the disappointment on the other singers' faces, and the disgust on Mr. Thurst's and Mr. Rauzzini's, she was mortified. Drawing on whatever reserves of strength and resolution she possessed, she pressed on; and very soon, to her relief, her voice began to resound with its customary brightness of tone and pitch-perfect clarity. The song was not difficult, but required a certain skill to capture the intent of Robert Burns's lyrics; and this song in particular, about a man musing on the bright summers and perfumed vales of a foreign land, which could not compare to the glorious country-side of the native land he holds dear, held great meaning for her at present. Indeed, it was a mirror of her soul; and she sang from the depths of her heart about "humble broom bowers," "blue-bell and gowan," and "a-list'ning the linnet"—while imbuing the description of the faraway land with the lyricist's disdain.

It was only when she had finished singing the final note that Rebecca dared to look in her judges' direction. The expressions on their countenances were now so altered from those which she had beheld at the start, as to make her feel encouraged. The pair of singers were beaming, Mr. Thurst looked positively thunderstruck, and Mr. Rauzzini's eyes were wide with astonished delight. All applauded, and then Mr. Rauzzini and his assistant came forward eagerly.

"That was extraordinary—truly unexceptionable! I confess, you entirely defied my expectation," said Mr. Rauzzini.

"I daresay, superior even to Miss Campbell!" cried Mr. Thurst.

"What is your name, Miss?"

Promptly, Rebecca answered, "Clarissa Fitzgerald."

"Well, Miss Fitzgerald," replied Mr. Rauzzini, "I must say, you do have a lovely voice. I should be delighted to have you perform to-night in Miss Campbell's stead. Are you familiar with any more Scots songs?"

"Oh, yes sir. Only tell me what you like, and how many."

He laughed, as if pleased by her enthusiasm. "Miss Campbell was to sing four songs on the program, two in the first half, and two at the concert's conclusion. The concert bills have already been printed; if you could perform the selections Miss Campbell had intended, that would be ideal.—(Unfolding the bill from his pocket, he read out the titles of the other three songs)—Do you know these?"

"I do, sir."

"Excellent!"

The singing couple who had been so generous shook Rebecca's hand, offered their congratulations, and departed. Mr. Rauzzini now took her aside and quietly named the sum which he was prepared to pay for her services, a sum so generous that Rebecca, who had not had time to even consider what such recompense might be, went pale with shock. Apparently worried that he had offended her, Mr. Rauzzini quickly offered a higher figure; to which Rebecca gratefully and smilingly agreed.

A rehearsal of the three other songs ensued; and although Rebecca had not sung them in a while, the music and the lyrics came to her as if by rote, and the conductor and his assistant seemed as pleased with these performances as they had with the first. "Do you play any instruments?" asked Mr. Rauzzini.

"Yes; the pianoforte and the harp."

"Do you play them as well as you sing?"

"I am told that I do," answered Rebecca modestly.

"Well, if you prove to be as big a success to-night as I *think* you shall, then perhaps we should have you back next week as well, to display your additional talents. But for now, we must make haste. Our rehearsal has gone over, and the concert begins in less than two hours." After discharging the musicians to their dinner hour, Mr. Rauzzini said, "Where do you reside, Miss Fitzgerald? May I call for a chair to take you home to change and dine before the performance?"

Rebecca thanked him for his kind offer, but said she would just as soon walk home. "However, I would be most grateful for a ride back to the theatre, to accommodate two, if you are willing; for my father greatly appreciates music, and I know he would love to attend the concert."

"Consider it done; Mr. Thurst, leave a ticket for Mr. Fitzgerald at the door. Only give me the direction and the time you will be ready, Miss Fitzgerald, and I shall send two chairs."

Not wishing to reveal the awful truth of their impoverished circumstances, Rebecca asked him to send the conveyances to the White Hart Inn, which was not a terribly long walk from where they were actually staying; the appointed hour was fixed; and she took her leave.

Rebecca's state of mind as she left the assembly rooms need hardly be explained. Of the cold night air, or the reproving stares from passersby as she ran down the street unescorted, with bonnet ribbons streaming behind her, she was entirely unaware. She was positively glowing; she was overwhelmed. It had all happened so quickly—to think that one could be plunged into the absolute depths of despair one moment, and the next, lifted up to such heights of excitement and good fortune! They had liked her—had actually *hired* her! She would at last achieve one of her fondest dreams, to perform on the stage—and in so doing, by her own efforts, she would help her and her father out of their present financial difficulties! It was too much, too wonderful to believe.

So occupied was she with these thrilling contemplations as she ran, that the long blocks flew by, and although she had covered a very great distance, it seemed mere minutes before she reached the inn. Rebecca hastened up the stairs, out of breath, barely sensible of the oily smells exuding from the tavern below, and found her father inside their rooms, pacing very anxiously, greatly relieved at her safe return, and bewildered as to what had kept her away so long.

Rebecca wasted no time in telling him of her good fortune. Mr. Stanhope was as amazed as he was delighted. They laughed and embraced, cried tears of joy, and then embraced again.

"I have been praying for a miracle all afternoon," exclaimed he, "and this is the answer to all my hopes. They will truly pay you to sing, my dear?"

"They will, papa; and most generously. If only I had thought of it earlier in the month, we should not have been reduced to our present straits! But never mind. I shall receive payment tomorrow, which means that we shall only be obliged to pass one night here. Then we can either remove to Medford as we thought, or—if Mr. Rauzzini wishes me to stay for a return engagement—we can find better lodgings." She explained the practical consideration of the small lie she had told regarding her name. "I felt it necessary, papa, in view of our present circumstances, not to broadcast our name. I hope you do not mind."

"Many performers use a stage name," said Mr. Stanhope, nodding, "so it is not really wrong."

Pleased by this response, she invited him to attend the concert that evening, informing him that his ticket would be under the name Mr. Fitzgerald. "Now, I believe I should be happy to eat that fish they are serving downstairs, for I am quite starved."

They ordered up a hot meal, which was brought to their rooms; after which Rebecca (relieved that their trunks had been delivered as promised, and that she had kept her pink silk gown), dressed and rearranged her hair as best she could in five minutes, adding a few ornaments which she judged to be befitting a stage performance. Then, taking her father's arm, in exuberant spirits they walked briskly to the White Hart Inn, where their chairs soon arrived; and they were both off on their way to the assembly rooms.

The evening began in a most agreeable manner. Rebecca was admitted through a back door to the assembly rooms and ushered into a small but comfortable room, where she was to wait with the only other singers on the program—the same couple who had been so encouraging to her earlier—who introduced themselves as Mr. and Mrs. Lloyd. The room was decorated with a vase of flowers, there was refreshment on a table, and Mr. Thurst was ready and willing to bring them any thing else they might require. Every thing was so nice, and Rebecca was made to feel so special and important, that she could scarcely believe it was all really happening to *her*.

Her only misgiving was the discovery that she would be obliged to pass the greater part of the evening in this room, rather than sitting with the audience, and would be able to hear only the faintest strains of music from the concert; for her this was a great disappointment indeed.

Mr. Thurst disappeared; the concert began; and as Rebecca studied the bill, which as usual contained a great variety of musical pieces and styles, alternating between orchestral and choral, she ascertained her position in the proceedings, and began to grow nervous. She knew the songs well, but had only rehearsed them once each, and she had never sung before so many people. What if she should forget the melody or the lyrics? Mr. and Mrs. Lloyd, sensitive to her state, and very amiable, shared a story about their first time on the stage, which despite their fears, had resulted in a success. They further inquired as to Rebecca's background and such, in a friendly manner, and in an effort to distract her; but she was too anxious to talk, and in any case did not wish to share much information about herself. The couple soon left, under Mr. Thurst's direction, to make their appearance. Rebecca waited alone, the faraway resonance of their delightful aria and the ensuing applause making her wish again that she could be amongst the audience. When they returned, Rebecca expressed her congratulations; and after another orchestra selection, Mr. Thurst came for her.

What next ensued seemed as though it were part of a dream. As Rebecca waited in the passage with Mr. Thurst by a side-door to the concert-room, her stomach tense with increasing apprehension, she heard Mr. Rauzzini explaining that although Miss Campbell was unable to perform, he was pleased to announce that they had been most fortunate to find a replacement, a talented young woman who was making her debut at Bath that very night, and who was prepared, upon only a few hours' notice, to sing all of the songs Miss Campbell had selected.—All at once, she was being introduced; Mr. Thurst gave her an emphatic nod; and Rebecca, with her heart pounding in her throat, mechanically stepped forward to take her place beside the musicians.

And then something magical happened. At the sight of the great, expectant crowd, Rebecca's apprehension fled, replaced by the thrill of excitement. This was the moment she had longed for, dreamt of, countless times in her life; she knew and loved the song entrusted to her, believed she was equal to the task, and felt all the power of that preparation; she could not fail. The music began; she smiled; she sang.

So wrapped up was she in the beauty of the music, and the cues from the conductor, that Rebecca took no further notice of the audience. She took immense pleasure in the performance. It was not until the conclusion of the piece, during the thunderous applause that followed, that she allowed herself to look into the sea of countenances before her;—and to her great joy, every face shone with delight. In the second row sat Mr. Stanhope, clapping heartily along with the rest, and as Rebecca caught his gaze, she observed proud tears shining in his eyes. Never before had she experienced a more exhilarating or fulfilling moment.

Her second song followed and was equally well received, with the addition of many shouts of "Bravo" from the audience. Rebecca, smiling, took her bow and left the concert-room, the sound of applause still ringing in her ears.

In the interval between acts, the Lloyds were generous with their praise, and Mr. Rauzzini and Mr. Thurst both congratulated Miss Fitzgerald on her triumph. They reported that quite a buzz was going round the foyer about the discovery of such an outstanding new talent.

The ensuing hour, as Rebecca waited for her next chance to sing, was passed in a state of very happy reflections. If only Sarah and Charles could have been there to share this moment with her, she would have been completely happy. She believed *they* might have derived some pleasure in witnessing her success; and had they the opportunity to carry it in their memories to review with her afterwards, it would have been particularly gratifying. Another idea adjoined this, and it was an unexpected one: how much she would have liked her new friend Miss Clifton and her brother, to have been there as well.

In what seemed no time at all, the concert was drawing to its conclusion, and Rebecca made her reappearance to deliver the last songs on the bill. The hearty applause which greeted her as she was again introduced was thrilling to perceive; and she immediately plunged into a rendition of "The True Lovers' Farewell." She had barely finished the second bar, when a deep voice from the crowd suddenly cried out,

"Fraud! That is no Miss Fitzgerald, but Miss Rebecca Stanhope, daughter of a thief!"

Rebecca started with dismay, and her face grew red; but she kept on singing. A murmur began to spread throughout the room. The heckler now stood up and shouted, "Her father is the rector William Stanhope, who stole a thousand pounds from his own parish and fled to Bath, under the name Fitzgerald! *This* young lady was party to it all!"

Exclamations of dismay and derision erupted. A couple got up and walked out. Rebecca faltered, mortified, but still continued her performance, until a man leapt to his feet and cried,

"There he is—the villain himself!" (Pointing to Mr. Stanhope.)

Shouts filled the room: "Thief—villain—blackguard—scoundrel!"

A crumpled concert bill was hurled at Mr. Stanhope's head. Rebecca could go on no more. The musicians ceased playing. Mr. Stanhope stood in confusion and muttered, "No—no—it is not true—I swear it—"

The audience began to leave *en masse*. Mr. Rauzzini regained control of his musicians, commanding them to play a rousing orchestral piece, which kept some people in their seats. Rebecca was horrified. She wanted nothing more than to run away, hide, and weep; but her first duty was to her father, and so she hastened to his side, gently took his arm, and silently led him from the room.

The consequences of the catastrophe at the concert-hall were these: Mr. Rauzzini sent word to Rebecca through Mr. Thurst, that she should not expect a penny from him, and that her presence at the concert-hall was no longer welcome. With no chair at their disposal, Rebecca and Mr. Stanhope were obliged to walk through the cold of night all the way to the lower part of town. As they trudged along, several people passing by in conveyances directed contemptuous and rude remarks at them. By the time they reached their rooms, father and daughter were in such an abject state that, uncharacteristically, neither had the words nor the will to try to cheer the spirits of the other. They took to their beds, where both gave vent to silent, bitter tears.

Early the next morning, while her father slept, Rebecca went in search of a jewellers' shop to sell her mother's pearl brooch. Although to her deep chagrin, she was obliged to accept a sum which seemed far less than its actual worth, it was at least enough to pay for their removal from Bath. When she told her father what she had done, he was already so depressed, that he merely nodded and shed a single tear.

While they were packing their things, a letter arrived—forwarded from the Newgates. It was from Sarah, and had been written several days previously;—she knew nothing yet of their reduced circumstances, as Mr. Stanhope's letter had been sent only the day before. It was a sweet but brief missive, with news of the children and a few small personal details and reflections, its one piece of vital information being the intelligence she gave regarding Mrs. Harcourt's health. The old woman, she explained, had been ill for several weeks, and had taken a turn for the worse; it seemed she had not long to live.

"Well," thought Rebecca with a sigh, as she folded up the letter after reading it to her father, "this is sad news indeed, and most ironic—to discover, on the worst day of our lives, that while our friend is so gravely ill, Dr. Jack Watkins's ship has come in. He can marry Amelia now, just as he planned, and live in wealth and comfort all the rest of his days. With what delight and relief must *he* now view my refusal of his offer. How happy he must be in his escape!"

They booked passage on the next public stage-coach heading in the direction of Medford, for the first leg of their journey. It left that very morning. By ten o'clock, their trunks were loaded, and they climbed on board.

Entr'acte III

Anthony sighed, sitting forward on the library couch and clasping his hands with a frown. "This is certainly a low note for the Stanhopes."

It was two thirty in the morning. After our encounter at the fountain a few hours before, I had deliberately chosen to sit across from him in a chair, to put a bit of distance between us. My oh-so-inappropriate compulsion—with regard to kissing Anthony—had made it hard for me to concentrate at first. Once we began reading, however, I became so engrossed again in the story that the hours had sped by.

"I loved the whole concert episode, and that Rebecca got to sing," I said. "But *what* a disaster."

Anthony nodded in frustration. "And now, to discover that Dr. Watkins is a cad, Amelia Davenport is a bitch, and they're both getting off scot-free, while Mrs. Harcourt, who I quite admire, is going to die, and Mr. Clifton, who seems to me one of the best men alive, is out of the picture entirely. What a terrible turn to the story."

"The story's not over," I reminded him, taking a sip of the coffee that had kept us going through this marathon reading session. It was cold. "Jane Austen knew what she was doing. Her books never disappoint—well, rarely anyway. You just need to have a little faith."

"All right. I'll have faith." Anthony rubbed his eyes and stood up, yawning. "But I'm knackered. I can't read any more—the rest will have to wait until morning."

Although I was dying to continue, I admitted that I was equally exhausted.

"It's too late for you to drive back to the inn, though," he added.

"Why too late?"

"These roads are very tricky after dark unless you're intimately familiar with them. You're welcome to stay here."

"Thank you, but I'll chance it." I stood, and found myself wavering on my feet.

"Please don't. You look like you're about to keel over yourself. Truly, you're better off staying. There are no lights and very few signposts in this area. You're bound to run off the road or get lost. I'd drive you back, but I'm so tired, I'd be the one running off the road." He yawned again. "I assure you, it's no problem. There are at least two bedrooms in this old place that are clean and usable. I imagine I can scare up some linens that were recently laundered."

Anthony set me up in a huge, lavishly appointed guest room, loaned me one of his T-shirts to sleep in, and managed to find me a new toothbrush. As he handed me the above items in the shadowed intimacy of the vast upstairs hallway, our hands briefly touched.

"Good night," he said quietly.

For the briefest of instants, I saw in his gaze the same expression I'd beheld when we held hands by the fountain; again, as if deliberately taking control of himself, he looked away. My heart began to patter to an irregular beat as I blinked and lowered *my* gaze. I'd never felt anything like this before—such an immediate, profound attraction to a man. Even when I met Stephen, it had been many long months before I'd come to think of him in more than a professional manner. I couldn't blame it on Anthony's good looks, either. I'd come to know him, and I liked and admired him—very much.

"Good night," I replied, and I disappeared inside my room and shut the door.

Before crawling into bed, I checked my phone, and saw two missed calls from Stephen, plus several text messages that read:

Tried to call. N/A.

Where are you?

Are you ok?

I felt a stab of guilt. I'd inadvertently left my phone in the kitchen after dinner, and I hadn't thought to check it in many hours. It was far too late to call Stephen back now. I sent him a text:

I'm fine, don't worry. Will call in AM.

As I sank into the warmth and comfort of the luxurious feather bed, the fact that I was spending the night in this gorgeous old mansion, with Anthony sleeping just down the hall, kept me awake longer than I would have liked to admit. I distracted myself by thinking about *The Stanhopes*. What would happen to Rebecca? Her father? Mr. Clifton? Eventually, jet lag and pure exhaustion took over, and I fell asleep.

I awoke to the patter of rain on the windows and eaves. The clock said 10:02 A.M. I cleaned up, dressed, and joined Anthony in the kitchen, where he was making ham and eggs on the ancient stove. I tried to tell myself that his virile good looks and friendly smile had no effect on me whatsoever. I failed.

He asked how I had slept.

"Fine, thank you." I poured myself a cup of coffee. I thought about the day ahead. Stephen's conference was over at one. He was expecting me in London that afternoon. But I couldn't leave without finishing the manuscript—I *had* to find out what happened. And Anthony and I hadn't even had a chance yet to discuss what he intended to do with it.

Anthony's cell phone rang. He took the call, motioning for me to take over at the stove. He retreated to the other room, but as I stirred the eggs, although I couldn't make out most of the conversation, I could hear the excitement in his voice as he spoke. One thing he said, however, rang out loud and clear:

"I have to authenticate it, but everything points to its being a genuine Austen." A pause. "Really?" Another pause. Then he laughed. "Yes, I see, I understand."

Who was he talking to? And why did that laugh send a chill racing down my spine?

When he finally hung up and returned, the ham and eggs were done, I'd made toast, and poured us some orange juice. He thanked me and sat down across from me at the table.

"Who was that?" I asked as we ate, trying to sound nonchalant.

"A potential buyer for *The Stanhopes*."

"A buyer? Who?" There was an odd look on his face. Something didn't feel right. He seemed to be avoiding my eyes.

He set down his coffee cup. "Samantha, I have a real dilemma here. I've been awake most of the night thinking about it. If, as you believe, *The Stanhopes* is the real thing—a unique, original, unpublished Austen manuscript—it's going to be worth a great deal of money. I know what you want me to do with it: you want me to sell it to a museum or university."

"Yes."

"But most museums and universities don't have the resources to compete with a private party."

"What kind of private party?"

"The gentleman on the phone was a collector I know—an extremely affluent man who's backed a few of my clients and who has a lot of disposable income. I thought he might be interested in this—and I was right. He was very excited. I know of two other collectors, obscenely wealthy men who I think would also jump at it. If I put this up for auction at Sotheby's, there's no telling how high the price could go. But unfortunately there's a downside to selling to a collector—at least, for those scholars you keep talking about."

Dread spread through me. "What downside?"

"The kind of collector who'd pay big money for a manuscript like this is generally very eccentric and reclusive. The man I just spoke with said if he bought it, he'd want the publication rights, and he'd keep it under lock and key."

I stared at him, stunned. "So—*The Stanhopes* might be stuck back in a box on a shelf or in a safe . . . and hidden away again? It wouldn't be published? No one else would ever be able to read it?" I was appalled by the thought.

He looked at me, apology in his eyes. "That's a possibility, yes."

"Anthony, you can't do that! Countless people have devoted their entire lives to studying Austen's work. This manuscript offers a whole new window to the way she thought and worked.

You can't deprive the public of the opportunity to read it and study it. Not to mention the zillions of Austen fans all over the world who will be ecstatic that there's another book to read. You *have* to publish it!"

"I agree—it would be wonderful if it could be published and made available for study—and I hope that will still be possible. Honestly, I do. But once I put the manuscript up for auction, its fate is out of my hands. I can't control who buys it or what they do with it."

"But you *can* control it! It's your manuscript. Its fate is yours to decide. Don't *auction* it off, Anthony. Take less money if you have to, but *sell* it to a museum or university library, with the stipulation that it be made accessible for study and publication."

He sighed, then said, "What about that letter you found—aren't you going to put *it* up for auction?"

I hesitated. In the excitement of finding and reading the manuscript, I'd forgotten all about the letter. "I don't know. I haven't given it much thought."

"That letter might be worth a few thousand pounds to the right buyer—so is the poetry book you found it in, since it no doubt belonged to Jane Austen. You'll get your best price for both of them at auction. Unless you'd rather keep them to yourself, which is equally understandable."

I considered the alternatives that Anthony laid before me. Could I sell that letter for big bucks, to someone who would hide it or frame it for his own personal enjoyment, and never share it with the world? No way. I could never live with myself if I did. Did I even want to sell it at all? And what about Jane Austen's poetry book? Did I want to sell that? The answer darted through me—as Jane would say—with the speed of an arrow.

"I'll never sell that letter, or that book. I'll *donate* them to a university library, where they can be viewed by the public. And I'll make sure the letter gets published."

"That's very noble of you, Samantha. I respect and admire your choice. But you must admit, the stakes are a *lot* higher in my case. You saw how much Bill Gates paid for that Da Vinci manuscript. In a bidding war at Sotheby's, I think I could get £30 million for *The Stanhopes*."

My heart sank. Anthony could be right about the manuscript's value. That translated to $50 million! It was a lot of money to walk away from. But I knew it was the wrong thing to do, so terribly wrong.

"I feel badly about this, Samantha, believe me. But try to understand. For years, I've helped other people find the money they need to start or expand their own companies, then watched them go on to become extremely wealthy. I'm tired of standing on the sidelines. I have dreams, too—to start up my own business—and I want *my* piece of the pie. That manuscript is my ticket."

I felt sick to my stomach, and at the same time, a slow-burning anger began to build within me. "I notice you didn't say a thing about Greenbriar in that little speech."

"Oh—yes—there is that. With that kind of money, I have options. I can keep the house if I choose, as well."

Words failed me. It would be one thing if he wanted to save Greenbriar—he didn't need $50 million to do *that*—but he wasn't thinking of the house at all. He wanted to rob the world of a literary treasure, just so he could open yet another software company or something. It was unforgivable! I thought back to the day I arrived, when Anthony had stopped by the inn and had taken me to dinner. It had seemed like such a thoughtful gesture at the time—but was it? I'd mentioned Jane Austen earlier, when I saw him at the house. Now I wondered if there'd been a mercenary intent behind that visit all along.

I could hardly believe that only the evening before, I'd actually been tempted to kiss this man—this unscrupulous *traitor*, who was prepared to sell *The Stanhopes* to the highest bidder, come what may. I started to wish that I'd never come here, and that we'd never found the manuscript.

My cell phone rang. It was an unknown number. My mind in a fog, I answered—and sat up in surprise. The caller's voice, with her crisp, cultured accent, was at once elegant and familiar, although it had been years since I'd heard it.

"Samantha? This is Dr. Mary Jesse."

"Dr. Jesse! How are you?"

"Fine. I just received your lovely note. I'm so sorry that my assistant turned you away at the door on Friday—I had no idea. Julia does a wonderful job protecting me and keeping my nose to the grindstone, but sometimes she goes a bit too far."

"That's okay," I said, my thoughts scrambling. Things had changed so much since I'd written Mary that note. Now I had not only a Jane Austen letter, but an entire manuscript that required her expertise. It suddenly occurred to me that if anyone could convince Anthony of *The Stanhopes*' value as a scholarly work, and the *need* to share it with the reading world, it was Mary.

"I'd love to hear what you've been up to all these years, Samantha. But first, what's all this about an old document you found? Do you still need me to authenticate it?"

"Yes! Hold on a second, Mary." I turned to Anthony and explained who was on the line. I was determined to be civil and polite, to hide my newfound resentment and focus instead on the crucial task before me: to ensure a proper fate for *The*

Stanhopes. And the clock was ticking—I was leaving the country the very next day. "Do you want to show her the manuscript?"

"Absolutely. The sooner I can authenticate this, the better. Is she free today?"

As concisely as possible, I told Mary about our discovery. She listened with caution at first, but by the time I finished, she sounded both astonished and ecstatic.

"Mary, I fly home tomorrow. Would it be possible for us to drive up to see you today?"

"That's fine. I'll be here."

"I can be ready and out of here in less than an hour," Anthony put in.

Mary and I determined that by the time we reached Hook Norton, it'd be about three thirty in the afternoon, so we'd come to her house about five after a late lunch.

"I do hope you're right about this, Samantha. If so, it's very, very exciting."

After I thanked her and hung up, Anthony said, "I'm going to get a room in Hook Norton for the night. Do you want one?"

"I was supposed to go back to London today. But—if I stay over, would I have a chance to finish reading the manuscript?"

"Sure. We'll show it to Mary, and if she's willing, we can hole up at her place this evening and read to the end. It could go pretty late, though."

"Then please book me a room, too."

Anthony found a B&B in Hook Norton and reserved two rooms. I carefully packed up the manuscript for transport. We made a quick stop at the inn where I'd been staying, so I could check out and retrieve my bag, then Anthony followed me in his car as we headed north.

I set up my Bluetooth as I drove, and was about to call Stephen, when he called me.

"Where are you?" he asked, sounding worried.

"In the car, on my way to Oxfordshire. I'm so sorry, I was about to call you—"

"Oxfordshire? You said you'd be back in London this afternoon."

"I know, but something's come up."

"Sam—what's going on? I tried calling and texting you last night. You never answered. So I called the hotel. And you weren't there."

Without thinking, I replied, "I spent the night at Greenbriar."

"At Greenbriar?" The shocked accusation in his tone took me by surprise and made me realize he thought I'd spent the night with Anthony.

"Don't get all jealous on me, Stephen," I said lightly. "I slept in a guest room."

"Why did you spend the night?"

I was about to answer, but stopped myself, suddenly realizing with astonishment that our last text exchange had occurred late the previous afternoon, just before we'd discovered the manuscript—and Anthony had expressly asked me not to say anything to anyone, until it was authenticated. But I couldn't lie to Stephen. Anthony would just have to deal with it.

"Stephen, a lot has happened in a very short space of time—I have so much to tell you. Do you have a few minutes?"

Then I launched into a brief explanation of our extraordinary discovery, how many hours we'd spent reading, why it had been too late for me to drive back to the inn, Anthony's obscene intentions with the manuscript, and the purpose of my mission to see Dr. Mary Jesse. "I'm not leaving until I've finished reading *The Stanhopes* and had a chance to persuade Anthony not to make a deal with the Devil. I don't know how long that'll take, so I'm staying in Hook Norton tonight."

He listened quietly until I got to that last statement, when he said, "Staying where? At Mary's?"

"No, we'll be at the Highgate Inn."

"*We?*"

"Stephen!" I cried impatiently, "for God's sakes, what's got into you?"

"Maybe you should ask yourself that question."

I blushed, remembering my own shameless impulse the night before—the look Anthony and I had exchanged—the fact that we'd held hands, however fleetingly. I firmly said: "I am *not* having an affair with Anthony Whitaker. I'm doing something important—I can't stress enough *how* important. I'm very sorry I won't be there today, like we planned. But I'll pick you up at the hotel tomorrow morning by eleven, and we'll drive straight to the airport. Okay?"

He said okay, although his voice was tight, and we hung up. I sighed with frustration. I hated arguing with Stephen—with anyone. I felt bad that I'd briefly, *mentally,* cheated on him. And I felt bad about abandoning him that evening. I'd just have to make it up to him when I saw him.

Several hours later, I pulled up at the Highgate Inn, a quaint, redbrick building with a thatched roof that lay a couple of miles outside of Hook Norton. Anthony parked directly beside me. We were both hungry. We'd just checked into our rooms and were heading for the adjacent gastropub for a quick bite, when a black taxi cab drew up, and a tall, dark-haired man stepped out.

"Oh my God," I said, astonished. "It's Stephen."

Stephen paid the driver and stared at me with a hurt, suspicious look on his face.

Anthony's expression confirmed that he sensed this might mean trouble.

The cabdriver removed the luggage from the trunk and took off.

"That was a London cab," I observed in surprise, as I walked up to Stephen. London was a good eighty miles away.

"It was the most efficient way to get here."

I didn't even want to think what that cab ride had cost. There was no point in asking Stephen what he was doing there. Clearly, he was checking up on me. I was annoyed that he'd felt the need, but at the same time, I couldn't help feeling a little stab of guilt. And I had to admit, I was happy to see him.

"I'm so glad you came," I said sincerely, giving him a hug. "I should have suggested it. I missed you."

He remained silent, but returned my embrace, and kissed me firmly. Then, releasing me, he held out his hand to Anthony. "Dr. Stephen Theodore."

The two men shook hands. "Anthony Whitaker. It's a pleasure to meet you, Doctor."

"And you," Stephen said coolly.

It was incredibly awkward. Stephen studied us, apparently trying to make up his mind as to whether or not we'd been sleeping together.

We put his luggage in my room.

"We were about to have something to eat before going to Mary's," I said. "Join us."

It was the most tense and uncomfortable meal of my life. Stephen peppered Anthony with questions, which Anthony answered with courtesy and aplomb. I did my best to smile and be gracious. I explained to Anthony that I'd had to tell Stephen about the manuscript. Stephen reassured Anthony that he traveled in a very different circle and wouldn't say a word in any case. He agreed a hundred percent with Anthony's intention of auctioning it off to the highest bidder, which infuriated me.

The two men fought over paying the bill. In the end, I marched up to the waitress and paid it myself.

When we finally got out of there, I heaved a sigh of relief. Anthony drove. Stephen and I sat in the back together. He took my hand and held it for the entire ten-minute drive. I wanted to believe that it was a loving gesture, as it always had been in the past, but somehow this time it felt more proprietary than anything. When I glanced at Stephen's face, to my surprise, his characteristically confident manner seemed shaken. His lips were pressed tightly together, and he looked tense and vulnerable. I told myself to cut him a break, and squeezed his hand with affection. He squeezed mine in return.

When we reached Mary's house, dusk was falling, and lights already shone brightly through the windows. She answered the door and invited us in with a welcoming smile, looking just as I remembered her—pleasingly plump and pale complexioned, with intelligent eyes behind wire-rimmed spectacles, and well-groomed, snowy hair that fell to just below her chin.

Introductions were made, and we all moved into her cozy front room. Anthony sat with the box containing the manuscript on his lap. Stephen and I took the couch. The striped orange cat who settled on the arm of Mary's chair was named Tilney, she explained, after one of her favorite Austen heroes.

"It seems like yesterday," Mary said, "that you were sitting in my office, Samantha, talking about your thesis. I was so sorry that you had to leave Oxford."

She asked about my mother, and was sympathetic to learn

that she'd passed away. I gave her a brief overview of what I'd been doing for the past four years.

"Any plans to finish the doctorate?" she persisted.

"No. What about your work, Mary?" For Anthony's and Stephen's benefit, I explained, "Mary's been editing and authenticating the contents of a trunk of old manuscripts discovered a few years ago in an attic at Chawton House Library. One's already been published—Austen's own memoirs."

"Really?" Anthony said with interest. "Jane Austen wrote a memoir?"

"She did," Mary said.

"The literary world's been waiting with bated breath to see what else that trunk contains, Mary," I added a bit playfully, "but you've kept such a low profile. Can you tell us anything?"

"All I can say is that it's very slow going," Mary answered. "It takes a long time to get the material. They won't let me work with the actual manuscripts—they're kept in a vault. The paper conservator goes through it all meticulously and digitizes every page, then sends me the images."

"But are there any other Austen—" I began.

She cut me off with a dismissive wave of her hand. "I'm not allowed to talk about that yet. Now, let's get to the purpose of your visit. I can't wait to see what *you* have discovered."

I began by showing Mary the letter. She used a magnifying glass to peruse the document—I wasn't sure why. The print wasn't *that* small. Maybe, I thought, she's studying the paper and ink for details to help authenticate it. Her eyes lit up as she read it through, and she nodded. "There's no doubt. Even unsigned, the authorship of this is indisputable. It's *hers*."

Anthony and I exchanged a delighted glance. I passed the letter to Stephen, who glanced through it with interest. "Very cool," he said.

We moved on to the manuscript. Anthony showed Mary the contents of the box, and allowed her to examine the first booklet. As before, she peered at it through the magnifying glass. She reacted exactly as we hoped she would—with great excitement. It was, she said, unquestionably Jane Austen, and an extraordinary find.

Anthony looked like the cat who'd just got the cream. "So you can officially authenticate it for me?"

"I can indeed. But may I read it first?"

"You may," Anthony said. "In fact, we were hoping to continue reading it ourselves. Samantha and I have gotten through most of it, but we still have a few booklets to go."

"Well, that's the beauty of this kind of manuscript—we can divide it up and read it in sections."

Mary took the majority of the manuscript off to her study at the back of the house, leaving us to read the last part together. Anthony and I gave Stephen a quick recap of the story up to the point where we'd left off. We agreed that Anthony and I would take turns narrating, and Stephen would listen.

Then the three of us settled down to read.

....

CHAPTER VI

Mr. Stanhope, insisting that he did not wish to spend any more money than absolutely necessary on their journey to Medford, purchased an inside seat on the public stage-coach only for his daughter. Despite Rebecca's vehement protests, and the threatening weather, he climbed with assistance to sit in the cheap seats atop the roof of the conveyance.

The day was dark and dreary, the ride long and bumpy,

and the coach close and crowded. Rebecca felt ill nearly the whole way. Matters were made worse when, soon after their last stop to change horses, it began to rain. A heavy precipitation continued for the next hour;—and thinking of her poor father, sitting outside unprotected from the elements, made Rebecca frantic and miserable. She tried urgently to catch the driver's attention, to request that he stop and allow Mr. Stanhope, due to his advanced age, to come down within, but her pleas were either disregarded, or due to the noise of the downpour and its accompanying thunder, went unheard.

At long last, they reached the inn where they were to stop for the night. Upon seeing her father's drenched and wretched condition as he was helped down from the roof, Rebecca was filled with dismay. She immediately called for help, arranged for a small suite of rooms, and had him brought upstairs to change into dry clothes, where she bade him take a chair in their sitting-room, shivering and wrapped in a blanket, before the fire. She had dinner brought up, but he had little appetite, expressing his only desire was to go to bed.

Rebecca worried that he had caught a chill; and in the morning, her fears were realised. Mr. Stanhope awoke with all the symptoms of a violent cold: he was heavy and feverish, with a sore throat, a cough, and pain in his limbs. Although he, weary and languid, tried to convince Rebecca that for economy's sake, they should move on as planned, Rebecca insisted that he was too ill to continue on their journey, and they must stay another few days. She offered to call for an apothecary or go for remedies, all of which were declined. Rest, he insisted, was all he required to cure him, and a daily change of the bed linens.

The very old, humble, quaint establishment which housed them was called the Kamschatka Inn, after its owner—a stout, middle-aged man, whose parents had emigrated from foreign parts shortly following his birth. Rebecca applied to Mr. Kamschatka; and after being ensured that they could keep their rooms, sat down and wrote a letter to her sister. There was a great deal that she *wanted* to say; but of Amelia Davenport and Jack Watkins's relationship, she was bound by honour not to reveal a syllable, and the events of the previous evening were too calamitous to properly explain on a single sheet of paper. She therefore restricted herself to apprising Sarah of their new circumstances, financial situation, and whereabouts; to relating her father's illness (urging her not to worry); and—with embarrassment—requesting if Sarah might send the required sum to cover a few additional nights at the inn, and the remaining portion of their journey to Medford.

Rebecca posted the letter forthwith, and spent the rest of the day and night watching over Mr. Stanhope. He continued restless and feverish, and the next morning was unable to sit up to eat. Alarmed, Rebecca requested that an apothecary be sent for. He came—a Mr. Reading—examined his patient, and expressed concern that the disorder had a putrid tendency, which might involve an infection. Rebecca was filled with guilt and misgiving that she had not consulted Mr. Reading immediately upon their arrival, and promised faithfully to administer all the medicines prescribed.

That night, after making her father drink said cordials, Rebecca was satisfied to see him sink into a peaceful slumber, from which she hoped to see beneficial effects. However, he awoke with the fever unabated, and two days passed away without any improvement. Rebecca tended him day and night, wiping her father's brow, watching over him as he fitfully slept, feeding him broth and remedies, and reading to him. On the second day, he was in a heavy stupour. Now very concerned, she called back the apothecary, who looked grave and disappointed. His medicines seemed to have failed.

Rebecca, truly afraid, proposed to seek further advice; but Mr. Reading judged that unnecessary, as he had something new to try. A fresh treatment was attempted; and when he returned a few hours later, he declared his patient materially better. His pulse was stronger, and his colour more favourable; he believed there was no longer cause for alarm, that a few days more would see him back on his feet. With hope renewed, Rebecca grew cheerful, and slept well herself for the first time in a long while.

The third day did not begin so auspiciously. Mr. Stanhope was heavier and more restless than before; the fever returned; and as the day wore on, his repose became more and more disturbed. Sitting attentively at his bedside, Rebecca was anxious to observe her father's continual change of posture, and to hear the frequent, distressed, yet inarticulate sounds which he uttered. By late afternoon, his slumber was so painful, she had half a mind to rouse him from it; but before she could decide whether or not to follow this impulse, his eyes flew open and he wildly cried out,

"Do not raise the tithes! Do not raise the tithes!"

Rebecca, startled, brushed back the hair from her father's brow, and said soothingly, "Calm yourself, papa. All is well."

He grabbed her hand tightly, and attempted to sit up, staring with feverish fervor into her eyes. "Tithes are an evil. We have all we need. The poor tenants have so little. Do not take the bread from their mouths. Promise me! Promise me!"

"I promise, papa," returned she, helping him to lie down again.

"I cannot say what happened to the money!" cried he violently. "When I awoke it was gone.—Three new bells, it is not so much to ask.—Three new bells, would make my wife so happy.—And you sing like an angel, my dearest, I always said you did.—So proud.—*Life of Johnson*, do you know, it is one of my favourite books.—How kind of you to send it.—But do not marry without love.—No, never, never.—It must be love above all else."

Now sincerely frightened by his rambling, Rebecca felt his pulse; it was very low and quick. Her father continued to talk passionately, on a variety of subjects, and in no coherent manner. Although fearing to leave her father in this state, she felt she had no alternative but to send again for Mr. Reading. There being no bells in this establishment to ring for service, Rebecca waited until her father had fallen back asleep, then hurried downstairs.

To her chagrin, the vestibule was deserted, the innkeeper nowhere in sight, nor a servant of any kind. Frantic, she ran out into the road, and enquired of the first person she encountered, as to where the apothecary could be found. Upon discovering that his shop was less than a mile down the road, Rebecca ran off in quest of him herself.

When she arrived, breathless, at the designated spot, she found to her dismay that the shop was closed, a posted sign declaring his return in an hour's time. She knocked on two neighbours' doors, finally rousing a man to whom she explained her plight. He said he might know where Mr. Reading was, and would go in search of him, and bid him hasten to the inn at once.

Having done all she could do, Rebecca retraced her steps,

alternately running and walking, her exertion earning her a painful stitch in her side. Upon reaching the inn, she was obliged to maneuver around a chaise and four post-horses which were drawn up before it, and from which trunks were being unloaded. Within was further bustle; the now-present innkeeper was engaged in an urgent conversation with the housemaid, who was trembling and in tears. Although Mr. Kamschatka's tone was too low to make out the first part of it, Rebecca was sensible of this exchange:

"Are you certain the old gentleman upstairs is dead?"

To which the maid tearfully replied, "Yes, sir. I went in to clean, and he weren't moving a muscle, nor breathing!"

"Dear God—and the new arrivals just gone upstairs!"

Rebecca, gasping in horror, did not wait to hear more. She raced up the staircase and down the passage.

....

Chapter VII

Wild with sudden grief, and terrified of what she would find, Rebecca threw open the door to their rooms, and burst inside—then froze in utter shock. Huddled around her father's bedside were her sister Sarah, her brother Charles, and Mr. Philip Clifton.

Rebecca's surprise and distress were so very great, and the sight of these three familiar faces so very welcome, that she burst into tears.

Sarah came forward and took Rebecca into her embrace. "Dearest! I am so sorry! We only received your letter this morning, and came away at once! But we are here now."

"I have stayed by papa's side every minute for three days,"

sobbed Rebecca, in great agitation. "He was feverish, and became delirious. I only left to seek out the apothecary—and now to find—dear God!—that I am too late!"

"Too late?" repeated Charles. "What do you mean?"

Rebecca looked at him, confused, and then into her sister's gentle countenance. They appeared concerned, but neither was consumed with grief. "But—is not papa—the man downstairs said that he was dead!"

"Dead? Why, no, dearest. He is just asleep." Sarah stood aside. With a full view of the bed, Rebecca could now observe her father lying in repose, pale but breathing steadily.

Rebecca's relief was as violent as her former anguish. She fell to her knees at the side of the bed and wept.

In the passage, a sudden bustle could be heard, and Mr. Kamschatka appeared in the open doorway. Witnessing Rebecca's tears, he paused uncertainly; then, begging pardon, he solemnly proffered his condolences at the old gentleman's passing, and offered to send for the proper authorities. Charles informed him of the true state of the man's health, and the proprietor, flustered and embarrassed, apologised for the maid's mistake, and quickly departed.

"My poor darling!" cried Sarah, helping Rebecca to her feet.

"He has been so ill—so ill," said Rebecca, wiping her eyes. "I thought he was gone."

Sarah felt her father's pulse, and judged it to be neither too low, nor terribly fast. Rebecca took his wrist between her own fingers, and, perceiving an improvement from before, felt real stirrings of hope. Indeed, Mr. Stanhope's skin, his breath, and lips, now showed slight signs of amendment; his fever had clearly broken; and as they all leaned over the bed, he briefly opened his eyes and fixed them on the assembled group with a rational gaze, whispering languidly,

"Sarah—Charles—you are here." He then closed his eyes and fell into a quiet, regular, and to all appearances comfortable, sleep.

At that moment, the apothecary arrived. Such a quick recovery surpassed all his expectations;—he declared Mr. Stanhope entirely out of danger. A good night's rest would do him a world of good, and they should expect to see him significantly better in the morning.

"Thank God!" cried Rebecca, as she and her sister embraced with relief and joy.

Once Mr. Reading had made his exit, Rebecca—confidence renewed, and relieved of her consuming worry—was all at once conscious of the fourth person in the room. Mr. Clifton stood a few yards off to the side, in respectful silence. Remembering the last intelligence she had received from him, via the letter to his sister, which had contained such mortifying news about her father, Rebecca's surprise at seeing him amongst the party was great indeed. Adding to her confusion was an even bigger worry: she had told her sister nothing about the condemning news in that missive, and was not anxious that it should come out now. Or was it too late? Had he revealed all to Sarah and Charles already?

Her cheeks growing warm, Rebecca nodded to Mr. Clifton, her question and concern in her eyes. "Mr. Clifton. How good of you to come."

He replied with a bow, then quietly offered Rebecca his apologies for intruding on such a private family moment. He had been in Medford visiting his sick aunt that morning, he explained, when he learned of her and her father's dreadful circumstances from Mr. and Mrs. Morris, and of their intention to remove hither; and, hoping to be of some service, he asked if he might accompany them.

Still not truly understanding his business there, Rebecca enquired in a low voice, with feeling, "How is Mrs. Harcourt? I heard she has been ill for quite some time."

"Thank you for asking. She is still unwell," replied Mr. Clifton, "but in good spirits, and fully determined to recover. Dr. Samuel Watkins is hopeful that in time, she will be restored to health."

Rebecca was relieved to hear it.

"And now," murmured Sarah, with a sudden smile, "Mr. Clifton has something of great consequence to impart, which I know you will want to hear."

"Oh?" said Rebecca. Sarah, Charles, and Mr. Clifton exchanged a look which conveyed barely suppressed eagerness and excitement, which piqued Rebecca's curiosity.

"Have out with it, Clifton," whispered Charles. "Father may sleep through until morning. Such news cannot wait."

"Perhaps," said Rebecca, "we should talk elsewhere, so as not to disturb him?"

They all moved into the adjacent sitting-room, from whence they could still keep an attentive eye on the patient. Once they had all settled on the sofa and chairs, Rebecca waited, hardly knowing what to expect.

Mr. Clifton began.

"Miss Stanhope: ten days ago, I gained intelligence with regard to your father's misfortunes at the King's Arms at Leatherhead, which I communicated to my sister Catherine. I understand that she gave you that letter."

Rebecca's face again grew hot with dismay. This was the very information which she had *hoped* he would not repeat!

With dread, she glanced at her sister and brother to gauge their reaction. To her consternation, their expressions suggested that they knew all about it, and they were still all smiles. "Yes, sir, I did receive that letter."

"You must know how very sorry I was to send it—but I had promised to share whatever I discovered. The innkeeper's news was very distressing indeed, but I told myself that I had done all I could—that Mr. Stanhope's guilt had been proved in the most uncertain terms, and that should be an end to it. The matter, however, continued to weigh on me heavily. I kept going back to his letter, and re-reading it again and again. The report contrasted with the account your father had given, in nearly every detail. According to the innkeeper, Mr. Stanhope had played cards with 'three rough characters,' whereas your father said they were a *pair* of *aristocratic gentlemen*. This discrepancy seemed very odd to me. The innkeeper claimed that Mr. Stanhope had played until the wee hours of the morning, and that a great deal of money had exchanged hands, while your father said the game had been brief, and he had wagered very little. I asked myself: if such a lengthy game had taken place, would the proprietor truly have stayed up all night to witness its conclusion? I doubted it. Finally, the innkeeper said the old gentleman stumbled upstairs to bed, ashamed and distraught; but Mr. Stanhope claimed otherwise. I had come to know your father, and I respected him;—but of this innkeeper, I knew nothing. I began to doubt the very essence of the letter."

Hope entered Rebecca's breast; she could feel its anxious flutter. "What did you do?"

"I went thither myself, to see what more I could learn of the matter."

Rebecca was all amazement; for it was an all-day journey

from Elm Grove to Leatherhead, under the best of circumstances. Eagerly, she urged him to continue.

"I was obliged to wait until I could arrange a break in my clerical duties, for I had already been away a great deal in the months previous; but this I managed to do. I rode to Leatherhead, where I booked a room at the King's Arms. I spoke with the innkeeper, who was very surprised to see me. As I posed my questions, he responded in a cordial and deferential manner, as was fit and appropriate when speaking to a clergyman—but I observed an aspect of nervous apprehension which he could not conceal. I saw him at once for the rascal he was—in short, I knew he was lying through his teeth."

"Oh!" cried Rebecca.

"The best part is coming," stated Charles, leaning forward in his chair with a smile.

"I made it my business to speak with the staff," continued Mr. Clifton, "one at a time, mind you, out of sight of the proprietor, and in a manner which I hoped would inspire complete confidence—doing every thing I could think of to get to the bottom of the matter. Did they remember any thing about a clergyman from Elm Grove, who had stayed there a few months back? Were they aware that a great deal of money had gone missing from his person? Did they have any idea how that money came to be lost? Did they see Mr. Stanhope engaged in a game of cards, and if so, with whom? How long did he play? Did he appear to have lost a great deal? And so on."

Rebecca, greatly moved by this remarkable display of energy, effort, and devotion, said with emotion, "What did you discover?"

"I found that nearly every report contradicted that which the innkeeper had asserted, and closely matched what your father had said. One girl remembered a couple of wealthy gentlemen who had stayed the same night, and that a brief, friendly game had taken place. Another had heard all the tumult on the morning of Mr. Stanhope's departure, and she remembered his anguish upon discovering that his money was lost. But no one had any notion of what had actually happened, beyond what the innkeeper later told them.— No one, that is, except the proprietor's wife, who I managed to corner alone in the kitchen that evening. At first, clearly forewarned by her husband, she simply parroted back every thing he had already said. But when I impressed upon her who I was, and what powers my father and my uncle had at their disposal, it seemed to strike some fear in her. Once I told her *your* story in full, Miss Stanhope, along with its devastating consequences, and appealed to her sense of justice, and her honour and duty as a Christian, she at length broke down in tears and revealed all. She said her husband, after overhearing your father tell another patron that he was on an errand for the church, and had with him a great deal of money, sneaked into Mr. Stanhope's room while he was sleeping, and stole the entire sum!"

Rebecca's astonishment and relief at hearing this discourse, which entirely cleared her father of any wrong-doing, was so very great, that she leapt to her feet and exclaimed with joy.

"You see," said Sarah, with a bright and loving smile, "I told you all along that papa was innocent."

So happy was Rebecca, that it was some moments before she regained mastery of herself. "Words cannot express my gratitude, Mr. Clifton," said she, upon resuming her seat, "for what you have done. You have restored my father to us."

Mr. Clifton smiled with humility, but before he could speak, Charles said,

"Are not you going to ask what happened to all the money, Rebecca?"

The fate of the stolen money had not even entered Rebecca's mind. "I imagine it is all gone."

"No!" cried Charles. "That is the wonderful thing. Although some of it was spent, Mr. Clifton was able to recover the greater portion of it!"

So amazed was Rebecca by this assertion, that no words came in response.

"The innkeeper's wife knew exactly where it was hidden," explained Mr. Clifton, "and she retrieved it and gave it to me immediately, before her husband could learn what she had done and stop her. Fearing this might put her in danger of incurring her husband's wrath, I confronted him again, told him what had transpired, and warned him that I would keep a steady eye on the proceedings of his establishment in future. If I ever heard of a similar incident taking place, or of his wife or any other person receiving ill treatment on his behalf, I would ensure that he spent the rest of his days in prison. I could see that he took my threats very seriously, and from the state of contrition and relief in which I left him, I believe him to be a changed man."

"This is too, too wonderful," said Rebecca.

"Papa is getting more than just his money back," added Sarah, with a grateful look at Mr. Clifton, "*far* more. Just wait until you hear."

Rebecca, barely daring to breathe, much less allowing herself to hope what this might mean, turned to Mr. Clifton with eyes wide. He smiled as he continued,

"I went to my uncle and told him every thing. He is as astonished as he is penitent, for he sees *now* the course which he *should* have taken, these three months past, to ascertain the real facts of Mr. Stanhope's unfortunate predicament. I told him that with this evidence in hand, I could not consider continuing in my position, and insisted that he reinstate Mr. Stanhope as rector of Elm Grove. He immediately agreed."

"Oh!"

"As soon as your father has recovered his health, Miss Stanhope, and is able to resume his duties, I shall step down and look for another position. In the meantime, your home will be restored to you. Please believe me when I say that I am very sorry for all the trouble you have been through. I wish it had never happened. And from the bottom of my heart, I wish you both well."

Hot tears now gathered behind Rebecca's eyes. Sarah clasped Rebecca's hand tightly, and they both wept with joy, gratitude, and wonder. It was too much to believe. She could go home again, to Elm Grove—to her very own house. Papa had his position back—all would be as it once was—and all this happiness she owed to Mr. Clifton.

It was not long before Rebecca was herself again. Some time was then devoted to a happy reiteration of all that had been revealed. The subjects at hand were of such great interest to all, it seemed that no detail was too small, that it did not require further examination and exclamation. Rebecca took pains to ensure that Mr. Clifton understood how grateful she was for what he had done, and was about to do; but he insisted it was no more than any one should have done, who had a questioning mind, and cared about the truth.

She was now able to make known certain circumstances of which she had heretofore been silent, including the malicious rumour which had driven them from Bath, and the story of her performance at the concert, which had begun with such promise, and ended in humiliating ruin. She deliberately made no mention of Dr. Jack Watkins's secret relationship with Miss Davenport, nor did she communicate her belief that he was the source of that unfortunate rumour. She did, however, admit that he had proposed, and she had turned him down, a disclosure which astonished her sister exceedingly, and seemed to particularly interest Mr. Clifton. Rebecca only said that she had her reasons for refusing the doctor, which she did not care to discuss.

That night, they all took turns sitting up with Mr. Stanhope. By morning, although still too weak for conversation, he was so much recovered, as to instill in all assembled every confidence that he would soon be entirely well again. By evening, he was sitting up in bed and able to consume some broth, and in such good spirits that Mr. Clifton was given an audience. Upon hearing all the news which the rector imparted, Mr. Stanhope was at first too astonished and overwhelmed to speak; then, like his daughter, he shed tears of joy, and could not find enough words to express his thanks.

The next day, Mr. Clifton was obliged to return to his parish. As he took his leave, he assured Rebecca and her father that the rectory would be ready for their occupation at any hour at which they should arrive. He would remove to one of the smaller bedrooms, and continue to conduct his duties, until such time as Mr. Stanhope was fully able to take over again. As Rebecca said good-bye, her heart was full; she could not help but feel again how very much they owed to the rector, and what a good, kind, and thoughtful man he was.

....

Chapter VIII

Mr. Stanhope's improvement proceeded so smoothly that within three days, he had regained the greater part of his strength. Sarah and Charles, encouraged by his progress, announced their intention to return to Medford. Rebecca deemed it best to stay on a few days more, until her father could withstand the rigours of a journey. On the day of separation, they parted with all the affection and remorse of a family who are truly attached, with promises on Rebecca's side to provide regular reports as to Mr. Stanhope's condition, and Sarah and Charles promising to visit at Christmas.

It was not long before the patient was quite well again. As Mr. Clifton had generously insisted on paying for their transport, they were able to travel in comfort. For Rebecca, it was a triumphant and joyful crossing. For so many months, she had seen her father's constant suffering, and had deeply felt his anguish as well as her own. Now, to observe the gladness in her father's eyes, and the new-found calmness of his spirits, was immensely gratifying. As they entered their own neighbourhood, every house, farm, and field brought some particular and happy memory, and Rebecca could barely restrain her joy. Her first sight of the rectory—every aspect of it so sweet and familiar, and so dearly missed—induced happy tears; and as the carriage drew up and she assisted her father to alight, Martha, Eliza, and Mr. Gower came rushing out with exclamations of delight. Embraces were exchanged along with happy chatter; then Mr. Clifton appeared with a bow.

"Welcome home," said he quietly.

Rebecca was so glad to see him, she could not contain her

smile. She and Mr. Clifton helped the old gentleman inside the house, and worked together to settle him comfortably in his favourite chair by the hearth. Only when these duties were completed, did Rebecca pause to look around her, and take in her surroundings.

She found, to her satisfaction, that every thing was very much as they had left it. When her eyes fell on the one addition—a brand-new pianoforte which sat in the same spot where her own, old instrument had stood before it was carted out the door by the removers—she exclaimed with pleasure.

"What a beautiful pianoforte, Mr. Clifton. Do you play?"

"I do not," admitted he.

She was about to ask why he had bought the instrument, when she realised, from the look on his face as he gazed at her, that he had purchased it for her. "Mr. Clifton! Can it be?—surely you did not—but—oh!"

"You said you used to practise every morning. I hoped to make it possible for you to continue that enjoyment."

Rebecca, at first too thrilled for words, sat down and began to play. The instrument was a good one, and the music she produced filled the room with its thrilling and vibrant sound. When Rebecca made her gratitude known to him, she sensed, from Mr. Clifton's expression, that he had gained as much pleasure from the giving, as she had in the receiving.

She found to her delight that her father's library was intact, and in even better condition than they had left it, for every beloved book remained on the shelves, and many of the leather volumes had been carefully waxed and polished to preserve their binding. After a walk on her own through the house and gardens, to reacquaint herself with every part of the property which was so well-known and dear, and so dearly missed, Rebecca returned to find dinner waiting.

A fine meal was served in honour of the Stanhopes' return, Mr. Clifton making a congenial third party at the table, and informing them of all that had gone on in the parish during their absence. "There were five new students at the Sunday School.—He had officiated at two funerals and three christenings.—Jane Repton and Thomas Dudley had posted banns, and were to be wed on Sunday.—Their barn door had blown open during a storm, and so terrified the chickens, that they had nearly fled the county, and the cow had broken through a fence and disappeared.—After a long search, he had discovered the chickens in Mr. Coulthard's yard, and the cow knee-deep in mud down by the river."—Several of the stories were described in so comical and endearing a manner, as to induce tears of laughter in the listeners.

Afterwards, they removed to the parlour, where they continued talking for several hours over tea.

"You seem to have handled every thing very well in my absence," observed Mr. Stanhope.

"I did my best, sir; but I know the congregation will be extremely pleased to have you back."

"Did you always intend to be a clergyman, Mr. Clifton?" inquired Mr. Stanhope.

"From the time I was a boy, that was always my ambition. My parents, however, were not at all keen on the idea, for the longest time."

"Why not?" asked Rebecca.

"They saw it as an underpaid and undervalued profession. To them, it meant spending my life in some tiny, isolated village, cut off from the world half the year by muddy roads and floods, without the congenial companionship of any other educated family. This was not their idea of my future. They had more exalted plans for me. They wanted glory and excitement. They wanted me to go into the army."

"The army?" repeated Rebecca. So accustomed was she to thinking of Mr. Clifton as a minister, she had difficulty imagining him in any other role.

"You may well sound surprised. It would not have been a good fit. But for most of my life, they were so insistent on this point, that it was my expectation as well. Then I saw my brother go off to Oxford, and I envied him. Not his *position* in life—I was very content to make my own way in the world, on my own merit—I envied him only the advantage of higher education which was afforded by family tradition to the eldest son."

"How well I understand you," said Rebecca, who envied that very education herself.

"Learning is like a hunger for me," continued Mr. Clifton. "The world is such a vast and fascinating place. A lifetime is not long enough to understand and explore its many wonders. I told my father that I wanted to attend university, but he protested that it was an unnecessary expense—what did an army officer need with reading Greek and Latin, and science and the classics?"

Rebecca nodded with compassion, for the first time understanding how this might have contributed to Mr. Clifton's moodiness and quiet reserve while growing up.

"I wanted to make my mother and father happy, so I was determined to go along with their desires."

"What changed your mind?" asked Mr. Stanhope.

"My father was about to buy a commission for me. While

on holiday that summer, I became acquainted with two men who were serving in a nearby regiment, and saw what their lives were like.—They were itinerant, often involved in the lowest, most immoral, and boisterous kinds of activities, and constantly joking about war and their expectations of the glories of battle. I knew that this was not for me. I informed my mother and father that I was resolved to becoming ordained, and if they would not pay for my education, I would find some one else who would. Eventually, they came round to the idea."

"Your first curacy, before you came to Elm Grove—was it a fulfilling position?" inquired Mr. Stanhope.

Mr. Clifton's lips twitched in the effort to hold back a smile. "It fulfilled my parents' every nightmare. It was the tiniest, most provincial backwater imaginable, and the pay was very low. But I liked the people for their honesty and simplicity, and I quite enjoyed the work—just as I enjoyed my time here."

"Have you found another benefice?" asked Rebecca.

"No, not yet. I will be sorry to leave Elm Grove, but—" (smiling at Mr. Stanhope)—"happy in the knowledge that I leave it in the very best of hands."

"What would you say to staying, Mr. Clifton?" asked Mr. Stanhope.

"Sir?"

"I could not bear to see you leave without the guarantee of new employment. I am not entirely recovered from my indisposition, and another pair of hands would be a welcome addition. If you like, you may remain as curate and assist me for as long as it takes, until such time as you find another appointment."

Mr. Clifton was surprised and grateful. "Thank you, sir. I accept with pleasure."

The two men shook hands. Rebecca felt all the happiness of the moment, and fairly glowed with pleasure at the knowledge that Mr. Clifton would be staying on.

The next few days were very busy, with members of the community coming to call, to welcome back their rector and his daughter, and to express their good wishes. One of the first visitors was Sir Percival, who came with his hat in hand, seemingly very ashamed, and offering his most sincere apologies for the events which had transpired. He returned all the money Mr. Stanhope had given him, which had been meant to replace the stolen funds. Furthermore, he granted him ten acres of farmland to add to his living. Mr. Stanhope readily forgave his patron, and their friendship resumed as it had been before, with one exception: the rector had so lost his taste for betting of any sort, that he could no longer stomach the notion of any game of cards other than Whist, Cribbage, Casino, and Quadrille.

Rebecca had not been home a week when a letter arrived from Sarah, which contained astonishing information.

Medford Vicarage

My dearest Rebecca,

I have such news! You will hardly believe me when I relate what has just transpired. You may remember that Mrs. Harcourt has been ill for some weeks. In spite of Dr. Samuel Watkins's hopeful prognosis, two days ago she took a sudden turn for the worse. A single day at most, he averred, remained until her soul would pass from this earthly plane. Charles and I called to say a tearful good-bye—she was indeed gravely ill, too weak to utter more than a few brief, sweet words. Miss Davenport and Dr. Jack Watkins appeared be-

side themselves with grief. We returned home, presuming that to be the last time we should ever see dear Mrs. Harcourt. But matters have taken a most unexpected turn.

It has only just come to our attention (the Miss Wabshaws came expressly to inform us, having heard it from Mrs. Harcourt herself) that later that same afternoon, while the old lady was in a kind of stupour, and barely cognisant of what was taking place around her, Miss Davenport and Dr. Jack Watkins took up the vigil at her bedside. Apparently the two of them, believing her to be insensible, began chatting openly and freely, and in their discussion recklessly revealed a relationship which, until that time, had been unknown to any one but themselves. For nearly a year, it seems, they have had a secret understanding!—and Miss Davenport all that time promised to Mr. Mountague—it is indeed shocking! What is all the more astounding, is that Dr. Watkins thought so little of their attachment, as would make him feel free to make an offer to you! What manner of man is he? Clearly I was mistaken in my assessment of him. And yet, there is some satisfaction in the knowledge that we did not entirely imagine his regard for you. But I digress.

Just imagine it: Mrs. Harcourt was lying at death's very door, and in her weakened condition, heard her beloved niece discussing her intent to marry a man of whom she could never approve; but worse—far worse—the pair was actually exulting in her imminent demise, and talking of their future plans to redecorate her house and spend her money! Overhearing this seemed to be the tonic which Mrs. Harcourt required, for it brought her round with a vengeance. She opened her eyes, and exclaimed, "Get out, the two of you! Get out of my sight this instant!" They fled the room. Dr. Watkins senior was summoned. He announced that it was a miracle. Half an hour later, Mrs. Harcourt was sitting up in bed giving orders, and so improved, that he predicted a full recovery. Her first charge, how-

ever, was to tell both Dr. Watkinses that she never wanted to see or hear from either of them again. This troubled me, for Dr. Samuel Watkins, it seemed, had done no wrong, but Mrs. Harcourt insisted that his reputation was tainted by the devilish acts of his son. That same afternoon, she called in her solicitor, rewrote her will, and cast off Miss Davenport for ever for her treachery. She will inherit nothing—not a farthing!

What, you may ask, of her engagement to Dr. Jack Watkins? We are told that he ended it the moment he heard of her disinheritance, and returned immediately to London. Miss Davenport is now living in the servants' quarters at Grafton Hall, in a state of the most extreme anguish, while Mrs. Harcourt's solicitor endeavours to secure her a position as a governess. She has apparently written to her uncle Clifton and uncle Mountague, begging them to take her in; but I sincerely doubt they will take pity on her. Is not all this too wonderful to believe?

I tell myself that I ought to feel sorry for Miss Davenport, and in some corner of my heart I do; but in truth I believe that she deserves her fate. As for Dr. Watkins, I am exceedingly disappointed. You are a much better evaluator of character than I; you shewed excellent judgment when you turned down his offer. I am sure I have shocked you with these revelations, but trust that you will recover as quickly as did the good Mrs. Harcourt. All my love to you and my father, and please extend my most sincere good wishes to Mr. Clifton.

Your affectionate sister,
Sarah Morris

Even Rebecca's prior knowledge of the pair's secret understanding could not prepare her for the surprise of *this* intelligence, which gave rise to such a rush of contradictory feelings, that a full hour's walk in the garden was required before she could regain a sense of tranquillity. "A governess!" she repeated over and over to herself. Rebecca could think of no worse fate for Amelia.

She reported the news to her father and Mr. Clifton, who shared her amazement. All were relieved to hear of Mrs. Harcourt's recovery, and much discussion was given over to a review of the villains' behaviour, which they agreed was shameless.

"My heart bleeds for the young lady whom I so recently considered a friend, and with whom I once passed so many happy hours," said Rebecca, "but when I recall the deceit which lay behind that friend's every word and expression, the lack of concern she harboured for my feelings, and the despicable manner in which she treated her own aunt, my heart hardens anew."

There being no longer any reason to withhold the information, Rebecca admitted that she had learned of the secret liaison earlier; that, after Dr. Watkins proposed to her, he had expressed dissatisfaction with his career choice; and that her refusal may have prompted him to start the unfortunate rumour at Bath.

Mr. Clifton, disgusted by the doctor's conduct, admitted that while at Oxford, he had been acquainted with Jack Watkins;—the man had been known as something of a rake. It seemed to Rebecca that, considering every thing, Dr. Watkins had got off rather too easily. Mr. Stanhope reminded her that one's future was one's own reward, and in the end, Dr. Watkins was obliged to live with himself.

The month of December passed away. With great relish, Mr. Stanhope resumed the work he had always loved. There was much to be done in the parish, and Mr. Clifton carried out his duties devotedly, proving to be a great asset to the rector. Rebecca, happy to be home, fell into her former, agreeable routine, practising her music daily, walking, reading, visiting and sewing for the parish poor, and once again teaching several of the village children to read. Christmas came and went, bringing Sarah and Charles and their children for their promised visit. During this time, Mr. Clifton went home to see his own family, and Rebecca found that she missed him very much.

In January, an unexpected event occurred on the matrimonial front. Sarah wrote to say that Mr. Spangle had wed Miss Cecelia Wabshaw, and she and her twin sister had both moved into Finchhead Downs.

"For the life of me, I cannot tell you which twin he has married," Rebecca said to Mr. Clifton, upon reporting the information, "but whoever it is, I believe they are perfectly suited to one another."

"I hope, with all my heart," said he, "that Mr. Spangle will come to think of his new bride as well as he did of his last—and that her sister will make a welcome third."

In the same missive, Sarah offered further information as to what had become of Amelia: Mrs. Harcourt had found her a position as a governess in Shropshire, had sent her off with only five guineas and the clothes on her back, and refused to speak to or hear about her ever again.

A fortnight later, Rebecca received a letter from Amelia herself.

Batley Gables

My dearest Rebecca,

It is only through the grace of your sister that I have at last got hold of your direction. Imagine my delight when I learned that you are living in Elm Grove once again, with your father's name restored! You always did say that he was innocent. Please give him my regards. I am happy for you. As for me, I am quite miserable. I hope you will not believe every thing you have heard about the events at Grafton Hall last November. I assure you, it is all scandalously untrue, and what happened to me is horridly unfair! I never said any of those things about my aunt, which have been attributed to me. She was delirious at the time, and sound asleep, and completely off her head, taking half a dozen kinds of medicine—how could any one know what was said at their bedside, while in such a state? I was simply having a sweet conversation with Dr. Jack Watkins, when she awoke and began screaming at us like a demon. Ghastly woman! To throw me off the way she did, when I had done nothing wrong at all! How very low she has behaved! How I hate her! She never understood me, and now I know that she never loved me.

Of course, with this undeserved scandal attached to me, I could not allow Dr. Watkins to go through with our plans to wed. Although he was insistent that he would marry me even without a penny to my name, I saw that such an attachment would have hurt his practice. It would not have been fair to him. I had no choice but to give him up. We both shed bitter tears when we said good-bye, and I made him promise not to write to me. He must get on with his life, and think no longer of me, however much his heart—and mine—are breaking. In the meantime, I am stuck up in this wretched place, where it is freezing, and does nothing but rain, hail, or snow. I work my fingers to the bone from morning until night, caring for the two worst children who ever drew breath. I am considered too fine and highly educated to associate with the servants, and too low for the society of my employers—who are heartless creatures. I dine alone and am invited nowhere, unless required to sit in a corner and watch over the children. I think I shall go mad!

Thank God I do not expect to be here for ever. I have caught the eye of the youngest son of a family who often visit here—a parson who is not at all handsome and talks a vast deal of nonsense—but he likes me, and I expect to receive an offer before Easter. Whoever would have thought that I should be a clergyman's wife—life does take such unexpected turns! I should be so thankful for a letter from you—even a few lines would be received with more gratitude than you can imagine. If you see my aunt, pray give her my best wishes for her health and happiness, and tell her I love her. My only hope is that one day she will realise the grave error she has made, and admit me back into her good graces. In the meantime I remain,

Your friend,
Amelia Davenport

The contents of this letter made Rebecca smile and shake her head. In reply, she wrote such comforting words as she could devise, without laying blame, correcting untruths, or uttering a chastisement, for it seemed to her that Amelia was suffering enough already.

....

Chapter IX

The new bells, a project which had been abandoned upon Mr. Stanhope's departure from Elm Grove, were again discussed, and Mr. Stanhope and Mr. Clifton together made a successful journey to the foundry, where they commissioned the work to begin.

With Mr. Clifton residing at the rectory, Rebecca saw him every day. They had all their meals together, took walks together, and with the company of Mr. Stanhope, spent their evenings talking, listening to music, and reading aloud to each other. This enforced proximity brought them ever closer. Rebecca found him to be the most solicitous of men, always thinking of her or her father's needs before his own, and often surprising them with little acts of kindness. She had never met a more considerate and thoughtful person than he. She discovered that they had many thoughts and views in common, and those subjects on which they disagreed were always opened up to lively and satisfying debate. She felt as if she could talk to Mr. Clifton for ever, and not run out of things to say. It amazed her that the man with whom she now spoke so easily and with such enjoyment, could truly be the same Mr. Clifton who had, for so many years, been so quiet and aloof in her presence.

Rebecca soon felt as if they had been friends for ever, and when another month had gone by, she began to recognise in herself ever stronger signs and feelings of attachment. This dawning came upon her so gradually, that it was not until one evening as she and her father sat before the fire listening to Mr. Clifton read aloud from Shakespeare, that she was all at once struck by the full force of feeling which had overtaken her heart.

She loved Mr. Clifton! She had been in love with him for many months now! Every nerve in her body thrilled with transport at this sudden knowledge. She cast a veiled glance at him, heart pounding, wondering if he suspected, and if he felt the same.

Rebecca had little time to consider her new feelings, however, or to contemplate when and where they might carry her, for the very next day, she was obliged to travel to Medford to assist in her sister's lying-in. On the fourth of March, Sarah added another beautiful baby girl to her family, who was called Margaret, after her grandmother. Rebecca spent several weeks in Medford helping Sarah with the children during her confinement, and found great comfort in making herself useful. She dined on pigeon-pie at Finchhead Downs with Mr. Spangle, his new bride, and her sister;—and to Rebecca's great satisfaction, the newlyweds and Miss Wabshaw appeared, all three of them, as happy and in love as any couple half their age. Rebecca was pleased by the twins' good fortune, and could not suppress a wicked thought: that in marrying a Miss Wabshaw, Mr. Spangle should indeed be the happiest of men, for he had got two for the price of one.

Whenever she could, Rebecca visited Mrs. Harcourt, who was in such excellent health and spirits, as to make Rebecca trust the lady would live into her nineties. As Mrs. Harcourt no longer had Amelia to spend her money on, or to reserve her fortune for, Rebecca used her powers of persuasion to convince her, in a manner as to make Mrs. Harcourt believe she had thought of it herself, to finance all the needed improvements to the vicarage at Medford, which Mr. Morris had so long desired.

While at Medford, Rebecca heard from Charles, who heard it from his man-servant, that Dr. Jack Watkins had joined his father's practice in London, and was apparently doing well. Rebecca presumed this to be the last news she would ever receive of that gentleman, and in this she was satisfied; but one morning, as she was walking through the village on her way to the baker's, to her surprise she encountered Dr. Watkins himself exiting the solicitor's.

He froze upon seeing her;—then recovering, and affecting a mild expression, he walked up to her and politely enquired as to how she was.

"I am well, Dr. Watkins, thank you. May I ask what brings you to Medford?"

"I am just passing through," answered he, as they walked on together, "to conclude some business with regard to the sale of my father's house."

"I understand that you are happily settled in London now, and quite the success?"

"I am working with my father, yes, and we have established a clientele. He thinks to retire soon, and I expect to take over."

"You have given up all thought of living in the country, then?"

"The country? Why, no. That was never my object. I have always preferred life in town. A physician can reside nowhere else. You are here to see your sister, I presume?"

"Yes, and to be of some use, I hope, to her and her husband. They have a new daughter, Margaret."

"Please offer them my most sincere congratulations. Have you seen Mrs. Harcourt during your visit?"

"Many times."

"I have the greatest respect for that lady; although I regret to say that she thinks very highly of herself, and less so of any one in the professions, even if they are friends of long standing, who have been of valued service to her."

"Perhaps she has reason to think less of such persons, if, for example, they have in some way abused that friendship."

"I suppose that is possible," returned he, colouring slightly and glancing away, "although I can think of nothing which *I* or my father have ever done, which might have offended her."

"Can not you? Well, it must remain a mystery, then."

Disgusted by his hypocrisy, and wishing to be rid of him, Rebecca was about to say good day, but he went on,

"I understand that you are again residing in Elm Grove, and that your father has regained his position as rector?"

"That is so."

"I am glad to hear it. I remember how much you desired to return to that place."

"I am very happy there."

"I am relieved for another reason, Miss Stanhope—for I heard a most alarming report, of events which you suffered at Bath last November, shortly after I saw you there."

"Did you?" She was interested in hearing what he had to say on *this* matter.

"It has come to my attention that you were obliged to leave under a cloud of some kind."

"That is true; we suffered through great difficulties and privations on that occasion, due to an unfounded rumour which was circulated, which maligned my father's integrity."

"How shocking. Did you ever learn from whence this report originated?"

"It was said that it came from *you*, sir, through your valet, while you were staying at the White Hart Inn."

"Through me? And my valet? Indeed? But that is very extraordinary. I can recall nothing which *I* might have said to my valet, which could have been at the root of the evil. If I was, in some way, unintentionally responsible for your distress, you have my deepest apologies."

"I appreciate that, sir. Thankfully, all was resolved, and my father and I suffered no lasting ill effects." They were outside the baker's now, and Rebecca, anxious for the conversation to be over, added, "Here is my errand. I wish you good fortune, Dr. Watkins, in all your endeavours."

"And you in yours," replied he with a bow.

Rebecca hastened inside the shop, glad to leave him behind. She was conscious of the fact that in their interview, Dr. Watkins had never mentioned any thing with regard to his proposal of marriage to her; nor had he inquired after Amelia. She tried to think if any thing he actually *had* said might have cleared him of any blame; but sadly, she found only the reverse. His insincerity and disingenuousness only proved, in her mind, his complicity in the terrible events which had transpired at Bath; and were she ever to encounter him again, she knew that she could not believe any thing further he might have to say on the matter.

All during her stay at Medford, Rebecca thought about Mr. Clifton. She replayed in her mind all the special moments they had spent together, and conversations they had shared, since that first day at Bath when he had come to see her. How good he had been to her and her father! Looking back over the past months, she thought she perceived in *him*, the same symptoms of affection for *her*, as she herself felt; and she was filled with happy expectation.

Upon her return to Elm Grove, Rebecca was met with exceedingly good tidings. Sir Percival had heard through his sister that the living of Beaumont, which lay only twelve miles distant from Medford, and came with an income of three hundred and fifty pounds a year, might soon be available; and so he had bought it for Philip. The vicar of Beaumont was elderly, and when he died, the position would be Philip's.

Mr. Clifton was grateful, and Rebecca delighted. Secretly, she cherished a hope that this employment would bring about the joyful circumstance of which she had been dreaming. If Mr. Clifton *did* return her feelings—it was true they could not *yet* marry—but an engagement under such conditions was not unheard of.

Several days passed, however, with no change—no offer. The moments Rebecca spent in Mr. Clifton's presence were an anxious trial. Were his recent acts of generosity merely examples of his inherent decency and kindness? Was she only imagining his regard? She had sensed a growing distance in him of late, and a distressing notion occurred to her: that he might have sensed her growing attachment to *him*, and become alarmed. Perhaps he considered her only as a friend. Perhaps his heart belonged to some one else. All at once, with dread, Rebecca realised who that some one else might be: Miss Laura Russell. *She* had doted on him for years. Did Mr. Clifton love Miss Russell? The very notion made Rebecca sick and miserable.

Rebecca was glad of a distraction which she hoped would rescue her from these unhappy musings—but sadly, it only proved to aggravate matters further.

Miss Clifton came to visit—the first time she had been to Elm Grove in many years. Although her aunt and uncle invited her to come to Claremont Park, she insisted on accepting Mr. Stanhope's offer to stay at the rectory. It *should* have made for a delightful reunion—for the sister and brother were bound by both blood and deep affection; the two friends had become very dear to each other; and a great deal had happened since they were last together, ensuring animated conversations over breakfast and dinner, while sitting by the fire, and while walking on the paths through Rebecca's favourite meadows. However, the gathering proved to be pure torture for Rebecca, for in Mr. Clifton's presence, she perceived his indifference, and she could not see Miss Clifton, without thinking of Miss Russell.

One morning, while Rebecca and Miss Clifton were engaged in a stroll and a tête-à-tête, her friend said,

"My uncle is very generous, is not he? To buy the living at Beaumont for Philip?"

"He is."

"This paves the way, at last, for my brother to marry."

Rebecca's heart fluttered apprehensively, and her face grew warm. "Do you think so?"

"He never had the means before. He has ten thousand pounds from my father, but that income can only go so far. He required his own living—and now he has it. I am so happy for him—and for Laura. She is confident that she will soon receive a proposal."

Rebecca's blood froze, this awful news confirming all her fears. "Did your brother—did he confide in you on the subject?"

"Not yet. However, I know him well—he is agitated about something—and I will share with you a secret. Yesterday he asked me quietly, in passing, if I thought my mother might be willing to part with my grandmother's ring. Of course I said mama would be only too happy to give it to him, should he ever require it. Very quickly thereafter he inquired as to how Laura was faring, and whether she was travelling next month or not."

So distressed was Rebecca upon hearing this news, it was all she could do to put one foot in front of the other. She contributed very little to the conversation for the remainder of their walk, and was very glad to get home. The living at Beaumont she now saw as a great evil, for it was the means by which she should be separated for ever from Mr. Clifton. How she wished Sir Percival had never thought of it!

Miss Clifton left the next day, and although Rebecca was

sorry to be deprived of her companionship, she was glad of the reprieve from conversation upon a topic which only brought her pain.

The morning after her friend's departure, Rebecca was seated in the parlour, lost in very agitating thoughts while engaged in drawing—an occupation to which she had recently returned—when Mr. Clifton found her, and asked what she was doing.

Her heart beat faster in his presence, but she was so filled with sadness that she could not look at him. Struggling to retain her composure, she said, "It is a picture of my mother—or an attempt at one. It is difficult to draw any thing from memory, particularly a likeness, but it pleases me to try nonetheless." She showed it to him.

Mr. Clifton pronounced the drawing very good, and its object very beautiful.

Distractedly, Rebecca said of her drawing: "This was my mother's favourite gown, and the pearl brooch she always wore—the ornament I was obliged to sell at a shop in Milsom Street, so that we might make our escape from Bath."

"A terrible loss for you."

"Yes; it was my only memento of hers, and now it is gone for ever."

Rebecca felt Mr. Clifton's eyes upon her, and she glanced up at him. His countenance was very calm; but although she strove to maintain an impassive expression, she believed her efforts were in vain, and that her deep feelings for him were revealed in full upon her face. He quickly averted his gaze. Frowning, he said inattentively, "My mother has just such a memento of *her* mother. I imagine if any thing were to happen to it, she should be very sad indeed."

Oh! Rebecca thought. Mr. Clifton *did* perceive her feelings, and they made him uncomfortable! She was in agony. "As papa reminds me," she replied, exerting herself to make conservation, "these are only *things*. I—I suppose we give too much importance to articles which we can do without. I have my mother's memory to comfort me, and that is all I really need."

Mr. Clifton pronounced this a sound outlook, and he soon quit the room.

Rebecca was so mortified by this awkward exchange, that for the ensuing fortnight she avoided Mr. Clifton whenever possible.

One morning when she came down to breakfast, to her surprise, she learned that Mr. Clifton was gone.

"Gone? Why?" inquired she with apprehension.

"He asked leave for four or five days," explained her father. "He said he had some business to attend to."

"What kind of business, papa?"

"He did not say." Mr. Stanhope turned to the cook, who had come in to ask if any thing else was wanted. "Did Mr. Clifton tell you where he was going, Martha?"

"No sir, he just come in very early like and ask for his breakfast, and told me he had to go, but never said two words about where he was off to, or why. However he did say one thing that puzzled me: he asked after my ring."

"Your ring?" repeated Rebecca.

"Yes ma'am, my wedding ring." Martha held up her reddened hand, which bore a simple band on one finger. "He asked after it, liked to know whose it was. Did my poor dead husband, God rest his soul, give it to me, or did it belong to one of my own family? I told him, it was my mother's ring, and I have never took it off since the day I was wed. He nodded real solemn like, and just eat his eggs, with saying nary a word more."

Rebecca sat in unhappy silence, her heart heavy, her appetite gone. Mr. Clifton's errand was clear: he had returned home to Highchester to fetch his grandmother's ring, and to propose to Miss Russell.

....

CHAPTER X

Rebecca spent the subsequent week in very melancholy reflections. The house, with only her father for company, seemed very quiet indeed. The weather only added to the gloom. A heavy rain began to fall, the wind howled through the trees, and the roads turned to mud. The picture which Rebecca drew in her mind of the months ahead was very dismal indeed.

How ironic it was to have lost her heart to a man, who was now lost to *her* for ever! Mr. Clifton was to be engaged to Miss Russell. Miss Russell! A woman who, Rebecca felt, was not entirely amiable, and did not deserve him;—nor did she see how her society could make him happy. While awaiting his appointment at Beaumont, it was Miss Russell that he would think of, *her* society which he would seek. In the interval, he would continue to live here—in this very house—and every day, Rebecca should be obliged to see him and converse with him, while struggling to hide her own breaking heart. This could go on for many months, or even years—for who knew how long it would take for the position to become vacant? In time, the lovers would marry and settle at Beaumont. Rebecca would most likely never see Mr. Clifton again.

She could not refrain from a heavy sigh. Her former happiness at the prospect of being once again at her beloved home, with her father as her companion, and all things exactly as before, was now ruined. She saw before her only misery, loneliness, and heartache.

The storm abated, but left the roads in terrible condition. Mr. Clifton did not return as expected. Three days beyond his anticipated arrival date, there was still no sign of him. As it was a frigid and blustery day, Rebecca and her father stayed in by the fire. Unable to concentrate on the novel she was attempting to read, she picked up her pencil and sketch-book instead. She thought to draw her father as he sat reading in his chair, but this notion came to an end when he abruptly announced his intention to take a nap. Left alone, Rebecca was obliged to content herself drawing the room itself instead. She had outlined its proportions, and made some progress on the details of its furnishings, when, of a sudden, she heard an approaching carriage.

Glancing out the window, she observed Mr. Clifton stepping down from the conveyance. Her heart quickened. He was home! As she watched him pay the driver, while their man-servant brought in Mr. Clifton's trunk, she strove to collect herself. Whatever he said of his journey, and of the results of it, she must bear it as best she could. She would be calm.

She let the curtains fall back, returned to her chair, and picked up her sketch-book and pencil. There were the sounds of the front door closing, and footsteps in the passage; some bustle, which she supposed to be him removing his great-coat and hat; and then he entered the room and moved straight to the hearth.

"Miss Stanhope." He smiled wearily. "You are a welcome sight. I cannot tell you how glad I am to be home at last. Such a terrible storm!"

"Were you caught in it while travelling?"

"Yes, and the roads were so bad, I was obliged to break my journey by staying several nights at a small and drafty inn. Are you and Mr. Stanhope well? I hope you stayed in and kept warm and dry?"

"We are, and we did." She rose and put down her work. "You must be frozen. Shall I ring for tea?"

"That would be lovely, thank you."

She ordered refreshment for the both of them, then resumed her seat. There was much Rebecca wished to ask, but being unsure she could bear the answers, she remained silent. He stood before the hearth and warmed his hands, his air preoccupied. At length, his attention falling upon her art materials, he said,

"You are sketching. May I?"

"Be my guest."

He studied her work in progress with a smile. "You have captured the charm and essence of this room: a snug, comfortable retreat. The clock on the mantelpiece, and the fire in the hearth, are particularly well done. Although—if I may—"

"Please, go on."

"The scale of this chair could be improved, I believe. It is larger than you have depicted it. And the window is too small."

"Ah, yes. I see your point. Thank you, I must fix that."

Mr. Clifton handed her the sketch, but although she sat back down, he remained standing, again holding his hands before the fire as if lost in thought. "How have you occupied yourself while I was away?" asked he abruptly.

"We have been very quiet."

She felt his eyes on her. He seemed to be trying for a more complete view of her face. Why? Was he hoping *she* would ask *him* something? Her discomfort only increased. For a moment or two, nothing was said. At last he spoke again.

"Shall I tell you where I have been?"

"Oh, I already know," responded she quickly.

"You do?" He stared at her in surprise.

"Yes, I have guessed it—well, your *sister* guessed it before she left. She said you were gone to retrieve a very old piece of jewellery for—" She could not go on.

He continued to look amazed. "I *have* been on such a quest. But how could she have known? I said nothing to her or to any one about it."

"Perhaps you did, and have forgotten."

"No, it is impossible." He frowned and shook his head. "But—do you mean to say that you truly know all about it?"

"Yes, yes."

He looked at her, puzzled by her response. "You do not seem overly enthusiastic. Are not you interested in how it turned out?"

Rebecca looked at her hands in her lap. How could he even *think* that she should wish to hear about this? Was he truly so blind to her own feelings? Then she chastised herself for being uncharitable. Clearly, this was something he wanted to share with her. A true friend—and if she could not have more, she acknowledged, she *did* very much value his friendship—ought to be willing to listen to any thing he might have to say. Attempting to smile, she said,

"Of course I am interested. Were you—successful in your—quest?"

"I was. It took longer than I expected, but at last I prevailed."

"I wonder that it took longer—or any time at all. I should have thought it would have been the work of a minute." Rebecca regretted the words the moment they were spoken, and blushed.

"The work of a minute? Why do you say that?"

"Well, under the circumstances—considering that—" Rebecca checked herself. "May I offer my congratulations, sir?"

This remark seemed to confuse him utterly. "I do not understand you. You seem to make light of what was in fact an exhausting process. I had very little to go on." He was searching in his coat pocket now, and brought forth a small jeweller's box. "It was almost a miracle, really, that I found the thing at all. Perhaps it did not mean as much to you as I thought it did; but here it is." He thrust the box at her. "Go ahead, open it."

Rebecca stood and stared at the little box in her hands, as if it were on fire. "Why have you given this to me? Should not Miss Russell have it?"

"Miss Russell? What on earth has Miss Russell to do with this?"

"Is not she meant to be the recipient of your grandmother's ring?"

"My grandmother's ring?" He stared at her in bewilderment; and then she saw comprehension dawn in his eyes, and he cried, "Dear God! You thought I went home to fetch my grandmother's ring, to make an offer to Miss Russell?"

"Is not that—?"

He burst out laughing. "No! God, no! My dear Miss

Stanhope, I assure you, that was never my intention at all. Please do me the honour of opening the box."

Rebecca was now very perplexed, but did as bidden. Upon lifting the lid, she caught her breath in astonishment, for the box contained not a ring at all, but a gold and pearl brooch.

"Oh!" exclaimed she in wonder and delight. "Is this for me?" At his nod, she continued, "Thank you! It is exactly like the one which belonged to my mother!"

"It is exactly like it, because it is one and the same. It is her very own brooch."

"What? But how—?"

"I have not been to Highchester," explained he. "I went to Bath. I saw how much this memento meant to you, and I travelled there expressly to track it down. I admit—I took something of yours with me, to help in my search. I hope you will forgive me." From his inner coat pocket, he produced a scroll of paper, which he carefully unrolled. It was the sketch Rebecca had made of her mother.

"My drawing!"

"The likeness you drew of the brooch was very detailed. It was my only clue—that, and your mention that you had sold it at a shop in Milsom Street. I visited every single jewellery shop on that road, until I found a man who recognised the article, and remembered buying it from you. Unfortunately, he had already sold it, but he had a record of the sale. So I paid a visit to the party who had bought it—a very amiable lady, as it turned out—and convinced her to sell it to me."

"Oh! Mr. Clifton. I hardly know what to say. You cannot imagine what this means to me. How can I ever thank you?"

"You already have. It was my pleasure, Miss Stanhope."

Rebecca was overwhelmed, and so happy to have the brooch back in her possession, that for a moment she forgot their earlier confusion, as to the substance of their conversation. But the smile lingering on Mr. Clifton's countenance reminded her of it, and she blushed as he said,

"All this time that I was talking about a *quest*, you thought I was going to fetch a ring for—Laura Russell, of all people?"

"Yes." Their miscommunication struck them both as comic, and they laughed.

"What ever gave you that idea?"

"Your sister was the one who supposed it." Rebecca told him what the cook had said, adding, "Catherine mentioned that you had asked about your grandmother's ring, and about Miss Russell, nearly in the same breath."

"Did I? Well, Laura is a particular friend of Catherine's, so I regularly ask after her; but I have no interest in her myself."

"You do not?"

"No. I never have."

So deeply relieved was Rebecca, to discover that all her worries on that score were groundless, she could make no reply. At the same time, her mind leapt forward with a new question, which she did not feel appropriate to ask. Thankfully, Mr. Clifton answered it of his own accord.

"I *did* ask about the ring," said he in a low voice, moving closer, and stopping immediately before her, "with a view to its—hopefully—being worn one day by a very special lady, but—I had a different person in mind."

He looked at her so earnestly, and with eyes so expressive, that Rebecca could not speak. He went on:

"My dearest Miss Stanhope. All these years, I have never

been able to find the words to express my feelings while in your presence. For a long time, I sensed that you did not like me. When you left Elm Grove—I did not blame you for resenting me, *then*—but my affection for you has never wavered. I have long dreamt of this moment, and now that it is here, I find—Surely, you cannot be in ignorance of how I feel."—He broke off, his voice catching; but soon resumed, in a tone filled with sincerity and tenderness—"I believe I have loved you all my life, since we were children and played together up the road at Claremont Park. I used to count the days until my next visit, because it meant I would see you. You grew from a lively girl into a beautiful, intelligent woman, and with your sweet loveliness and your many talents, you took—you *take*—my breath away. When I look to the future, I cannot imagine my life without you at my side, as my wife, my love, and my dearest friend, sharing all our thoughts and feelings, and all the daily blessings of life. What say you? Will you share my life with me? Will you marry me?"

Throughout this speech, Rebecca was filled with such agitation, and a happiness so overpowering, that she felt as though she must be imagining it. Yet this was no dream. Mr. Clifton was indeed standing before her, and he had uttered every syllable with a heartfelt openness. In a rush, she saw the truth of all that occurred between them in years past—his strange reticence over the years, which she now understood to be due to his strong feelings for her. She now comprehended the reason behind his many selfless acts over the preceding months—his determination to clear her father's name—his travelling all the way to Leatherhead, and Bath, and the Kamschatka Inn, and Bath *again* on their behalf—the pianoforte—the brooch—all reflections of his kindness and generosity, but more importantly, expressions of his love for her! She had never met a kinder or more thoughtful man; and she loved him with all her heart.

With great emotion, she expressed her own feelings in return, and answered him in the affirmative. She would be honoured to be his wife;—she could think of no greater honour.

His happiness on receiving her reply was equal to her own, and it was coupled with both amazement and relief. For all the while that he had been endeavouring to return from Bath, and waiting for the weather to clear, he had been in a very distressed state of mind, preparing the words he had so long yearned to say, with no certainty of their reception. To discover that she *now* felt the same affection for him, as he did for her! This was felicity itself, and the answer to his prayers.

This exchange, which in the space of a quarter of an hour, revealed the truth of their feelings for each other, and completely altered every thing, was yet only the beginning. There was much that each still wished to say. As Mr. Clifton took Rebecca's hands in his, however, his eyes shining with affection and profound happiness, there came footsteps in the hall, and Mr. Stanhope entered, to express his delight at Mr. Clifton's return. The latter directed a silent, significant look at Rebecca, who took his meaning, and immediately invented some excuse to leave the room.

She waited in a flurry of excitement, knowing what Mr. Clifton was about: he was asking her father's consent to the marriage. She had no reason to think her father would be any thing but approving; and indeed, when the door finally opened, and Mr. Clifton came to retrieve her, he was all smiles. She returned to the parlour, where Mr. Stanhope embraced her, and shook Mr. Clifton's hand, admitting that he had been praying for just such a conclusion for many months, and was happy to see that his observations of the two of them had not been wrong. He declared Mr. Clifton to be the best of men; that he proved himself even more worthy in his choice of bride, for there was no finer jewel in the kingdom than Rebecca; and that his daughter could not have chosen a more ideal companion for life, had she searched the world over. They would be very happy together, and he could not be happier for them.

That evening, when the three sat down to dinner, the discourse which had always flowed freely between them, and covered a great many topics of interest, was even more animated than before. They talked of the future with hope and delight. After Mr. Stanhope turned in for the night, the lovers returned to the parlour, as they had done so many evenings over the preceding months, but now with a very different aspect to their conversation. New avenues were opened, for at last they were free to speak all that was in their hearts, and to ask many questions which were burning in their minds.

Philip was concerned that Rebecca, after all her adventures, and after singing before such an admiring crowd at Bath, might be sorry to spend her life with him, in the seclusion of the country. Rebecca disabused him of any such notions.

"It was thrilling for a moment, to sing for a roomful of strangers," admitted she, "but they were people I shall never see again. They cared nothing for me, only for the performance. They were ready to turn on me in an instant, and *did*. I cannot imagine that I would enjoy the itinerant life required of a singer, nor do I have any desire to live in town.

How much more gratifying it will be, to have a quiet life in the country, and to sing and play for our own enjoyment, and that of our friends; for *you* are the people who know and love me, who matter in my life, and who will stay by me. *You* are the treasured company who make me feel complete."

Her answer relieved him of worry, and he was content.

Rebecca wanted to know at what age Mr. Clifton first knew of his feelings for her.

"I believe it was the first time I heard you sing at Christmas at Claremont Park, when you were nine years old," replied he.

"Then why did you and your cousin make such fun of me?"

"Precisely *because* I liked you. I was thirteen years of age. I was starting to feel quite grown-up, and you seemed to me, *then,* as just a little girl. I think I was embarrassed by my feelings; I hardly knew what to make of them. So I did what all boys do. I behaved most abominably."

"Every time I saw you after that, you were so aloof, so reserved. With others, you could be jolly; but you hardly looked at me, and barely spoke a word. I thought you despised me."

"Quite the reverse. I liked you better with every visit—and that was my downfall. I could speak freely and easily with any one else, but not with you. I used to play out conversations with you in my mind, and rehearse phrases which I hoped to say to you. But once in your presence, I was all nerves and anxiety, afraid I would say or do the wrong thing. And so I said nothing. I would go away completely infuriated with myself."

"I wish I had known. I would have tried to put you at ease."

"This went on for years, and never really improved, until I came to see you that day at Bath."

"You were not at a loss for words, *then*."

"I suppose it was because I felt I had nothing to lose. I knew you greatly resented me already. Nothing I could do would make it worse—only better. And I truly had something important to say."

"I will be for ever grateful for what you have done for my father and me—that day, and every day since. I do not deserve you, Philip."

"My dearest Rebecca: I am all amazement to find myself where I now sit, and feel I do not deserve *you*."

"On this matter, then, we must agree to disagree," replied she with a happy smile.

In the weeks that followed, Rebecca was in an exquisite flutter of happiness. The news of her engagement to Mr. Clifton was received by every one in the community with elation and hearty congratulations. Sarah and Charles, in particular, who knew what Mr. Clifton had done for them, and had come fully to appreciate his many good qualities, expressed their extreme contentment in the match.

Miss Clifton was initially dismayed, as she had so long been championing the cause of Miss Russell. However, upon understanding how happy her brother was in his choice, and how very dear he had become to Rebecca, Miss Clifton quickly came round, and wrote to share her genuine delight in the prospect of having Rebecca as her sister. Miss Russell recovered from her heart-break with remarkable rapidity, for within six months' time, she was engaged to the eldest son of a baronet.

In May, the vicar of Beaumont passed away at the age of eighty-six. Mr. Clifton succeeded to the post, and removed there directly. Now every thing was in place, as to make it possible for Rebecca and Mr. Clifton to marry. The date was fixed for the last week of June; the banns were read; and the wedding clothes were ordered.

The day before the wedding, as Mr. Clifton and Rebecca strolled in the Elm Grove Rectory garden, along the shrubbery border gay with pinks, columbines, and sweet-williams, he told her all about the vicarage at Beaumont, where they were to live. It was, he assured her, a well-maintained cottage of ample proportions, with enough bedrooms to accommodate a family, a study large enough to hold all the books he intended to acquire, and room enough in the parlour to accommodate both her pianoforte and the harp which he hoped to purchase for her in the next year or two. There was the added benefit of an efficient suite of offices, an acre glebe, and a lovely garden which even now was blooming with all the flowers Rebecca loved. Best of all, it was within easy walking distance of the charming village, and offered a fine prospect overlooking a green meadow and a grove of ancient oaks.

"Does the garden have a shady bench for reading?" asked she.

"It does—a very worn bench beneath a grand, old tree."

"Then what more could one ask for? I shall be very content there." As the village was only twelve miles distant from Medford, she should be able to see Sarah, Charles, and their children regularly; and *this* made her happiest of all.

Mr. Clifton regarded her with concern as they walked along. "I realise it will be difficult for you to leave Elm Grove, my dearest Rebecca. You will be giving up a lot. You will miss your father."

"I shall," admitted she, "but as papa is more inclined to

travel now—he insists he actually looks forward to it—we can expect to see him at least two or three times a year, either here or there."

"That is not often, for two people accustomed to seeing each other every day."

"True; but nothing stays the same. Things change, and we must change with them."

"This is a first, coming from you," said he, in a tone of pleasant surprise. "You have always said you did not like change."

"I have *changed* my mind on that score," replied Rebecca, smiling. "As you have long insisted, change can be a great improver. Even if it seems to be a trial at first, it can bring about positive growth if one will allow it, and embrace it."

"And what brought you round to this point of view?"

"Why, the three months which I spent away from Elm Grove. I learned and experienced a great deal in that time. It is only *because* of my enforced removal, that you were prompted to such actions, as revealed the truth of your heart to me; and in so doing, my own heart opened to discover how much I loved *you*."

He smiled at this and took her hand.

"I now believe," added she, "that it is a good thing to live somewhere other than the place where one grew up, at some point in one's life;—but it is an even better thing to come back home. And anywhere that *you* are, Philip dearest, will always be home to me."

"At the same time," admitted he, "I have come to understand and appreciate your love of the familiar. There *is* something very comforting in it. A striking new vista might take one's breath away, but it cannot compare to the deep satisfaction of a prospect which is well-known and adored."

As he said this, his eyes were on her face, and the tenderness and deep affection in his gaze made her heart turn over.

They walked on, hand in hand, in the happy silence of lovers who are completely content in each other's presence, and share the precious certainty of being beloved.

The day of the wedding dawned fair and mild. As Rebecca recited her vows before her family and friends, uniting her with the man she loved best in all the world, she felt overwhelmed by perfect happiness. In the church tower, the three new bells rang out in perfect harmony, their deep, clear, melodious tones resounding throughout the parish.

Brought together by mutual affection, and retaining the warmest approbation of all who loved them, the wedded couple's intimate knowledge of and high regard for each other, made their future look very bright.

May 28, 1802

Finis

Finale

ANTHONY SIGHED. "THE PERFECT ENDING."

I looked up from the manuscript, happily agreeing with his assessment, but at the same time sad that it was over. Glancing at the last page, I said, "The date at the end confirms our theory. It was written exactly when we supposed."

"I'm so glad Rebecca ended up with Mr. Clifton, and not Dr. Watkins," Anthony noted.

"So am I—but I'm not surprised. The man who's the most charming at the start is rarely—*Northanger Abbey* notwithstanding—the right man for the heroine. It's the flawed man, the one who 'proves his character and worth by his deeds,' as Mr. Stanhope said, who always wins her heart." With a smile, I added, "Besides, Dr. Watkins's name should have been a clue in and of itself."

"Why?"

"Austen gave two of her worst rogues names that start with

'W': Willoughby and Wickham. *Watkins* fits right into the mold. It's like a little 'W Club' of scoundrels."

That made Anthony laugh.

I was eager to hear what Stephen thought, but although he'd appeared intrigued at first, he'd admitted he was very tired, and he'd nodded off a few chapters in. He was still sound asleep, his head resting on the back of the sofa.

Anthony and I found Mary reading with great avidity in her study. She was deeply engrossed, and protested that she still had a long way to go.

"How wonderful to learn that *Plan of a Novel* was inspired by an actual work of hers," Mary said. "It's a road novel, something Jane Austen never did before—truly thrilling."

"How about if you keep it for a few days," Anthony suggested, "so that you can formally authenticate it."

Mary had a fireproof safe, and assured him that she'd take good care of it. When she was finished, he said he'd bring it to Sotheby's for their own experts to look over.

"An Austen heir is likely to come out of the woodwork when you publish this, Anthony," Mary said. "You might have a legal battle. But since it was found in your house, I'd say it's yours." She added, "I assume you *do* plan to publish the book, before you auction off the manuscript itself?"

Anthony hesitated.

"Actually," I said, unable to disguise my anxiety any longer, "the buyers he has in mind are reclusive collectors who may want those rights for themselves, and might never publish it at all."

"Oh! That would be a terrible shame." Mary frowned. "A crime, actually. I hope that doesn't happen."

"So do I," Anthony said.

"This is a work for the ages," Mary persisted. "It's far too valuable to keep locked away out of sight."

"I agree, but it's also far too valuable to hand over to some institution for a paltry sum. If I can get £30 million for it, I'd be crazy to take a penny less."

The conversation—or rather, the argument—continued. I was getting more and more upset by the minute. To my frustration, we were deadlocked. Anthony wasn't budging from his position, and nothing Mary or I said made any difference.

Finally, we all returned to the front room. Stephen had woken up in the interim and he apologized for falling asleep. "It's no reflection on the book or your talents at reading," he said sincerely. "It's hard to come in like that at the end. And it's been a long couple of days."

We called it a night. Mary intended to make a pot of strong coffee and read until the wee hours. The three of us returned to the inn, where Anthony agreed to meet us for breakfast at seven thirty. By now, I was so angry with Anthony, I could barely look at him.

When Stephen and I were alone in our room, he emptied his pockets, then leaned back against the bureau, and said, "I'm sorry if I came off a little strong when I first got here. But you had me worried—two nights with this rich, handsome English guy, and I barely heard a word from you."

The uncertain expression on his face, and the quiet affection in his eyes, moved me. I crossed to him and took his hands in mine. "I wasn't *with* him, Stephen. I was on a quest. He just happened to be part of it. And he's not *that* rich—not yet. But it looks like he's going to be."

"I notice you didn't contradict me when I called him handsome."

I laughed. "Who could dispute that?" Taking in the sudden, frozen look on Stephen's face, I reached up and gently touched his cheek. "Don't worry, Doctor. He may be good-looking, but you give him a run for his money."

"Seriously, Sam. Do you like him?"

There it was again—that unexpected, atypical sense of insecurity that this proud man no longer struggled to hide. It was endearing to see this side of him. Flattering, too, I decided.

"Yesterday, I thought Anthony Whitaker was an admirable man. Today, I've seen his true colors. I despise his ethics. He's going to profit off the theft of his ancestor, and in the process, deprive every person on the planet, and all the generations yet to be born, from reading a new Jane Austen novel. So no, I don't like him. And by the way, it didn't help that you took *his* side at dinner."

He nodded, apparently satisfied. "Note to self: do not take Mr. Whitaker's side on anything."

"I have one last chance to work on him—at breakfast tomorrow. Somehow, I *have* to persuade him to keep *The Stanhopes* off the auction block. Will you help me?"

"I'll try."

"Thanks." I kissed him. "Now let's go to bed. I'm tired."

The next morning, we were both up early. As I showered and dressed, I rehearsed what I'd say to Anthony over breakfast. I was putting on my shoes, when I saw an envelope slip under our door. I opened it. It was a handwritten note:

Samantha,

I'm sorry, but it turns out I can't stay for breakfast after all. I have meetings in London and must head out immediately. I can never thank you enough for all that you did—for taking a chance and coming to Greenbriar—for helping me find the manuscript. I'll be forever grateful. I wish you all the best. You deserve it.

Anthony

I gasped. Handing the note to Stephen, I said, "He's not getting off that easily."

I raced downstairs and encountered Anthony in the lobby, about to head out the front door with his suitcase.

"Sneaking out?" I said, not bothering to hide my bitterness.

He stopped and turned to me. "I didn't want to wake you."

"Bullshit. You're avoiding me."

He didn't respond, just looked at me, his expression reflecting a myriad of conflicting emotions.

"Anthony: I know you see this manuscript as your chance for a huge windfall. But how much money do you really need? Please: don't put it up for auction. Don't sell it to an idle collector who just wants to look at it."

"An item like this cries out to be sold at auction—you know it does—it's what anyone with sense would do."

"It's not an *item*! My God, how can you call it that? It's—"

"Let's just leave it, okay?" he interrupted. "Clearly, we're never going to agree on this." He sighed and glanced at his watch. "I meant what I said in my note, Samantha. I'm grateful to you—for everything—I can't tell you how much. And I wish I could chat longer, but I'm sorry, I really do have to go."

I wanted to shout invectives at him, to let him know exactly what I thought of him, but a sweet-looking older lady emerged at that moment from the breakfast room with a little girl in tow. Instead, with a brittle smile and searing tone, I merely shot back at him, "Welcome to the 'W Club,' Mr. *Whitaker*. You're now a full-fledged member."

He was momentarily taken aback. Then, without comment and without looking back, he grabbed his bag and strode out the door.

Stephen and I flew home that afternoon. We didn't talk much on the plane. He was preoccupied reading medical journals. Try as I might, I couldn't get myself interested in reading anything.

I felt hollow, defeated. The past few days had been a once-in-a-lifetime adventure and a roller coaster of emotion. When I first came upon Jane Austen's letter, I'd been filled with hope and excitement. Discovering the manuscript had been an impossible dream come true. Now, the entire enterprise had fallen to pieces. One thought kept pounding in my brain: was it really possible that no one else except me, Anthony, Mary, and some appraiser for Sotheby's, would ever see or read *The Stanhopes*, before it was purchased by a cloistered eccentric and hidden away for another century . . . or maybe forever?

Back in Los Angeles, despite the endless days of sunshine, I felt like I was walking around in a fog. I opened up a safety-deposit box at my bank and stashed the poetry book and Jane Austen letter there, until I could decide what to do with them. I went to work every day at the library, falling into the busy routine of my job. But my mind kept wandering back to England. As angry as I was with Anthony, I sometimes flashed back to the moments we'd shared while hunting for and reading the manuscript. In that short time, I'd felt a connection with him that I'd never felt with Stephen—or with any man. We'd grown so close in such a short time. When I remembered the last words I'd hurled at Anthony, I felt a little regretful, wishing we could have parted on better terms.

But then I thought about Rebecca Stanhope and Mr. Clifton. They'd become as real to me as Elizabeth Bennet and

Mr. Darcy, as Anne Elliot and Captain Wentworth. The thought that no one else would ever get to know them—to read what Austen had created—made me sick and miserable. I wanted to strangle Anthony Whitaker.

I didn't hear a word from Anthony although I'd given him all of my contact information. I thought about e-mailing him, but couldn't think of a thing to say. The only person I told about the manuscript was Laurel Ann, and she was just as heartsick as I was.

Three weeks after I got home, the news of our find broke in a big way. Sotheby's put out a press release, and within hours it was all over the Internet:

JANE AUSTEN RARE LOST MANUSCRIPT TO BE AUCTIONED AT SOTHEBY'S

A newly discovered, incredibly rare, handwritten manuscript of a previously unknown Jane Austen novel is to appear at auction in London. The neatly written but heavily corrected pages are for a full-length work entitled *The Stanhopes*.

Sotheby's senior specialist in books and manuscripts, Diana Drew, said it was "a great honour and a privilege" to be selling it. "Other than Jane Austen's memoirs, which were found several years ago, it's the most exciting and significant Austen discovery in history. It was previously thought that Jane Austen had only written six novels. To have a seventh is very exciting."

It is extremely rare. No other original manuscripts of Austen's full-length, published novels exist, other than two cancelled chapters of *Persuasion* in the British Library. Additional known manuscripts include her unfinished works *The Watsons* at the Bodleian Library, *Sanditon* at King's College, Cambridge, her juvenilia, and her novella *Lady Susan* at the New York Morgan Library.

The rare manuscript was discovered by a private party in an ancestral home in England. A guest registry found in the homeowner's library is said to list Jane Austen, her sister Cassandra, and her parents as visitors to that house in July 1801 and July 1802. A date on the manuscript confirms that *The Stanhopes* was completed in May 1802. How the work came to be left there, and why no mention of it has ever been discovered before, is unknown. But the manuscript has been authenticated and is unquestionably Austen's.

The Stanhopes is a work of 336 pages, split up into 42 booklets hand-trimmed by Austen. "They're exactly the same kind of booklets she used to write the first draft of *The Watsons*," said Drew. "There are many corrections and insertions—it's an invaluable peek into the way her mind works."

Drew, one of the few people allowed to read the manuscript, said the story surprisingly shares some similarities with Austen's *Plan of a Novel*, a comic outline Austen wrote the year before her death. "It's possible she wrote *Plan of a Novel* in a nostalgic mood, remembering the manuscript she lost," said Drew.

There is much speculation as to the fate of the manuscript, as the sale includes publication rights. The manuscript, which has been valued at £20,000,000 to £30,000,000, will be sold at Sotheby's in London on 18 September.

The story made headlines across the globe. The press was full of it for a week. Then another story broke with a surprising codicil:

AUSTEN HEIR DISPUTES PROVENANCE OF RARE LOST JANE AUSTEN MANUSCRIPT

An heir of Jane Austen has reportedly come forward to dispute the ownership of an incredibly rare, handwritten, previously unknown Jane Austen manuscript, called *The Stanhopes*.

The owner of the recently discovered manuscript claims it had been hidden in his ancestral home in England for more than 200 years. A private arrangement has purportedly been reached between the two parties. Whether or not the manuscript will be published is yet to be determined. The sale, which includes publication rights, will continue as scheduled at Sotheby's on 18 September.

Soon after hearing this news, I commiserated with Laurel Ann over lunch in her cluttered back office at the bookstore she managed.

"*That* must have been painful for Anthony," I said, spearing a forkful of chicken Caesar salad. "I wonder what percentage of his future megamillions he had to give up to the unnamed Austen heir."

"He didn't have to do it," Laurel Ann pointed out, resting her feet on her desk as she ate. "If he went to court, I bet he could have proved the manuscript was his."

"A court case might have tied up the thing for years. The

auction couldn't go forward. Anthony wanted his money now, for that start-up company of his."

"Well," Laurel Ann said, "if it turns out that no one ever gets to read that book, I'm totally going to hate him."

"You and the rest of the Austen-loving world."

Laurel Ann nodded. "So typical, the way these private sellers hide behind anonymity."

I didn't respond to that, but Laurel Ann—always a quick study—seemed to glean something from my silence. "Wait a minute, Sam!" She sat forward excitedly. "You could blow his cover. You could talk to the press, tell them everything that happened. You're one of the few people on earth who's read *The Stanhopes*. You have that letter as proof. It mentions Greenbriar and a missing manuscript." She paused, noting my expression. "But you've already thought of that."

I nodded. "What good would come of me talking about it? It'd just be sleazy. It'd bring Anthony Whitaker a lot of notoriety he doesn't want. And frankly, *I* don't want the notoriety. I'll make sure that letter gets published eventually, but I'm going to hold off and not say anything for now."

Laurel Ann took a sip of her iced latte, her eyes narrowing as she studied me across the desk. "You're doing the right thing, of course. But why are you doing it? I sense a motive."

"My motive is: I'm hoping and praying that maybe, just maybe, he'll grow a heart and a conscience, and change his mind about the sale."

"I can see that. But it's not the whole picture. You are furious with Anthony Whitaker, yet you don't want to cause him pain. Hmmm . . . Oh! I get it. You're a little bit in love with him, aren't you?"

"What? Don't be silly. No I'm not."

"Yes you are. You're blushing. You never blush."

"I'm *not* in love with Anthony Whitaker!" I repeated hotly. "I've been with *Stephen* for three years. Anthony and I spent three *days* together."

"Yes, and you spent the night at his mansion. What haven't you told me about that?"

"Nothing! Stop looking at me like that. You're as bad as Stephen. Nothing happened between me and Anthony, except—"

"Except?"

I sighed. "Okay. I *was* attracted to him, I admit. And I was tempted to kiss him once, but that's it."

"You *almost kissed*?"

"I didn't say we almost kissed. I said I was *tempted* to kiss him—there's a difference. It was just a fleeting, romantic impulse fed by moonlight and the thrill of the moment. But it didn't happen, and I'm glad. It would have made things way too awkward and confusing. Anyway, I hate his guts. As I have stated numerous times."

Laurel Ann put down her fork with a skeptical smile. "Whatever you say, Sam."

A month crawled by. The press continued to feature stories about the upcoming sale of the Austen manuscript. The Austen blogs were alive with anticipation and worry, waiting, just as I was, to see what would happen to it, and whether it would be made available to read by the public at large.

My life followed its usual pattern. I worked. I started another online course toward my Masters in Library Science. I went to the gym. I went to movies and had the occasional lunch with Laurel Ann. I had dinner a few times with Stephen, and spent the night at his house in Westwood. But nothing felt right. Something was off between me and Stephen—it had been ever since our trip to England—and I didn't know how to fix it.

I missed my mother. I kept having dreams about her, hooked up to tubes and monitors in the hospital.

"What are you doing?" she would ask me.

The question confused me. "I came back for you, Mom," I would say, kissing her soft cheek. "You have to get well." I would wake up saddened and disoriented.

I attended a party with Stephen to honor a new wing at the hospital, where the physicians mingled over doctor-speak, discussing cases and patients and sharing golf anecdotes, while the spouses talked about redecorating their houses and the achievements of their children. As always, I was bored and felt completely out of place.

It was summer, and the campus was deathly quiet, peopled only by visiting researchers and a smattering of students and professors. I found myself (by accident or design?) often walking past the humanities building, where the English Department was housed. I imagined what it'd be like to have an office there. I saw two professors emerge from the building, deep in conversation. I wondered what they would think if they knew I'd helped find, and had *read*, the priceless Austen manuscript that they and everyone else were talking about. I wanted to shout: I was almost one of you! I came so close! But my aborted dissertation was such a sore point, and made me feel so unworthy that I couldn't talk about any of it.

Then something happened that sent my life spinning in a new direction.

I was spending the night at Stephen's house, but sleep proved elusive. So I got up, went into the living room, turned on my laptop, and read the newest post for my online course entitled "Research Methods." I heaved a sigh. I already knew this subject backwards and forwards. I'd been researching for years, using both print and electronic sources. It was a class, I realized, that I could teach in my sleep. I *had* taught it, or at least a one-hour version of it. As I stared at the screen, I suddenly heard a voice in my head—(my mother's voice?)—asking:

What are you doing?

I sat back, startled. What *was* I doing? Why was I taking classes toward a Masters in Library Science? It wasn't a degree I had ever really wanted. I was getting it to satisfy my colleagues and my supervisor. The degree I'd long dreamt about—the degree that would be truly meaningful to me—was a PhD in English literature.

I'd meant it when I told Anthony that I enjoyed my job. I did. My salary wasn't stellar, but it paid the bills, and by this time next year, I'd have paid off the last of my debts. The work at the library was interesting, satisfying, and familiar. I'd been doing it for years, ever since I was an undergrad, and I was good at it.

But were those good enough reasons to stay?

I remembered something Mr. Clifton had said to Rebecca Stanhope, in their discussion about change: *Great joy can be found in all that is familiar. Yet there can be even more merit in change. Change often brings unimagined opportunity . . . If there is no struggle, there is no progress. To live in a safe cocoon—I believe that is not truly living. It is stagnation.*

Stagnation. The word resounded in my brain like an echo in an empty room.

I'd been at Chamberlain University for a long time. If I stayed at the library, if I earned my MLS, I'd probably be working as a librarian for the rest of my life. Was that what I wanted? It was one thing to stay in one place if you were happy and fulfilled—that was simply living the good life. But what if you weren't fulfilled? For the past few years, I'd told myself that I was where I wanted to be, but I saw now that I'd been in denial.

What was it Anthony had said?

You're surrounded by wonderful books that you never get to read. You're helping other people find resources to support their research, but you don't get to do much original research yourself.

It was true. I cataloged books, I displayed books, and I found books for others. But I missed *reading* books. I missed talking about books and writing about books. I missed teaching. The short instruction sessions I occasionally did in the library were one-shot deals. I missed the thrill of sharing what I knew with the same group of students over the course of an entire semester, the thrill of seeing a whole classroom of eyes light up as they exchanged fire during a literary discussion. I missed the opportunity to watch students grow, to see their skills mature as they took the ideas that came from our discussions and interwove them into their research.

With sudden clarity, I realized that I was ready—eager—for change.

When Stephen's alarm went off early the next morning, I got up and told him over coffee.

"I thought you liked your job at the library," Stephen said.

"I do. It's a great job. I was grateful to get it when I did. It's just not the right job for *me*. They should give it to someone with an MLS."

"I thought you were working on your MLS?"

"Only to please my boss. Stephen, I don't want to spend the rest of my life working in a library. I want to go back to Oxford and finish my dissertation."

He put down his cup. "Are you serious?"

"I gave more than two years of my life to that thesis. You know how bad I felt about abandoning it. I thought I was over it, that I'd accepted it, but all this time, I've felt . . . incomplete. I want to teach university English. I want that degree."

"Okay. Fine. I get it. But why can't you work on the thesis here, at Chamberlain?"

"Chamberlain doesn't have a PhD program."

"What about UCLA? With so much information on the Internet, why do you need to be in England?"

"A lot of the books and materials I need for research are very rare, and only available at the Bodleian and Chawton House libraries in England. Anyway, I started at Oxford. I want to finish at Oxford."

He went quiet for a long moment. "It'll be very expensive."

"So I'll be in debt a little longer. It'll be worth it."

He fiddled with his coffee cup, staring down at the table. "How long will it take?"

"I don't know, it depends on whether I can get financial aid, and how many hours I have to work. I'd say two years at the very least, maybe three."

"Two or three years? That's a long time, Sam. And after all that, getting the degree won't guarantee you a position. You've always said it's very competitive—that if you do get an offer, you have to go where the work is."

"That's true. But I can't let that scare me. You're doing what *you* dreamt of as a boy. For ages, I've dreamt about teaching English at the university level. I have to go for it now, while I still can. Don't you see?"

To my surprise, tears started in his eyes, which he quickly wiped away. He nodded. "I *do* see. I'm just . . ." His voice cracked a little, and he cleared his throat.

"What?" I said gently.

"I'm just afraid that if you go back to England . . . you'll never come home again."

"Why would you think that?"

He looked at me, his gaze a silent question. Quietly, he said: "Well for one thing, *he's* there."

I didn't have to ask who he meant. The unspoken hung heavily in the air between us. I sighed and shook my head. Why did everyone think I was hung up on Anthony Whitaker?

"I'm not interested in *him*. I'm going back for *me*. And who knows? If I'm really lucky, when I finish, maybe a position will open up in the English Department at Chamberlain or UCLA or another local university."

"Well, I'll hope for that, then."

"We can still stay in touch regularly, the same as always: by phone, text, e-mail, Skype. And I can come back to visit every six months or so—"

"Sam." He took a deep breath, then looked at me. "Let's not do that to each other."

"Do what to each other?"

"I've tried the long-distance relationship thing. Frankly, I find it lonely and painful. It doesn't work for me. It would put unfair restrictions on both of us—and I don't want that."

"Stephen—"

"If you're going to England, go with an open heart, and no obligations to the guy you left behind. Two or three years from now, if you do find a job here, and you're still interested and available, then we'll talk. But in the meantime, let's just call it a day."

Unexpected tears now sprang into *my* eyes. A lump rose in my throat. "You're breaking up with me?"

"Not breaking up. I'm giving you your freedom."

"That's not what I wanted," I whispered.

"Maybe not at this moment, but give it a little time. You'll see: it's better this way."

"Is it?" A tear slid down my cheek. "Oh, Stephen. I'm so sorry."

"So am I." He reached out and brushed the moisture from my face tenderly. "But to tell you the truth . . . I think I've always known this was coming—that it'd be hard to hold on to you." He kissed me, a brief, bittersweet kiss, as if he knew it might be the last time. "You deserve this chance, Sam. Go for it. Go find your bliss."

The next few weeks were a whirl of activity. Reenrolling at Oxford proved to be a quick formality. I was informed that a new advisor would be assigned to me. I chose a start date in September, scored an apartment at New College, and was thrilled when my friend Michelle in the English Department somehow managed to convince the powers that be to speedily approve a financial aid packet for me, along with a part-time job.

I gave notice at work and at my apartment. Laurel Ann was happy for me. For the past year since my mother died, she'd been trying to convince me to finish my degree.

I packed and arranged to move most of my belongings into storage. I was totally psyched. I felt like I could breathe again. In returning to England and to Oxford, I was taking a bold step to change my life for the better. As Stephen said: to follow my bliss. I was very sorry to be ending our relationship. I missed him, a lot. But I was moving forward, not back—and when I thought about the next few years, about the opportunities that awaited me and the ocean that would separate us, I began to see that he was right: that giving each other our freedom would be healthier for both of us.

Two days before I was to leave for England, a box arrived on my doorstep. I was surprised by its size and weight, but even more when I saw who had sent it. It was from Anthony Whitaker.

I opened the box, and couldn't prevent a gasp of astonishment. It contained the entire, twelve-volume set of the Chawton House edition of Jane Austen's Works and Letters. I was so overwhelmed, I almost didn't notice the note that accompanied the books:

My dearest Samantha,

I've read them all. You were right. The last one is the best.

I hope you will not reject the offered olive branch. No matter what happens, I wanted you to know: I get it now. I understand.

Thinking of you,
Anthony

I reread the note several times, confused. I recognized the reference to the olive branch—it was a quote from *Pride and Prejudice.* Obviously this was some kind of peace offering. But what did he mean by "I get it now. I understand"?

It was a shame, I thought, that the books had arrived just as I was leaving the country. Much as I wanted to, there was no way I could bring them with me. I called Laurel Ann. Within an hour, she was at my door.

"Oh my God, they're exquisite!" Laurel Ann said, running her fingers lovingly over the beautifully bound leather volumes.

"Will you keep them for me while I'm in England?"

"Will I?" she enthused. "Do you even need to ask?" After reading the accompanying note, she shook her head, and said, "I can't believe he's giving these to you. It's the most romantic thing I've ever seen."

"Romantic? Hardly. He's just trying to make up for selling out on the manuscript, by sending me a set of books he knew I coveted. It's not even an original idea. A character in *The Stanhopes* did exactly the same thing."

"I don't care if it's original—it's still romantic. Did you even read the note?"

"I read it."

"Samantha, he read *all* the books! All of them! We're talking about a man who works in *finance*! Do you think he did it on a whim, or just because Jane left a manuscript at his house? No. He did it for you."

"That's ridiculous."

"It's not ridiculous." She studied the note again. "He says he's thinking about you. You said you were attracted to him. Clearly, the attraction is mutual. I think he's a little bit in love with you, too."

"There's no *too*!" I shot back at her, although my voice didn't hold quite the conviction I expected it to.

Laurel Ann ignored me and went on, "He says the last book is the best. Which shows he's smart and perceptive. *Persuasion* is my favorite Austen novel, and Captain Wentworth is my favorite Austen hero. Yours, too, right?"

"Yes, but don't get carried away. Anthony's not the hero of *this* story. If these books are supposed to be a peace offering—if he had any real hope of mending the fences between us—he would have canceled the Sotheby's auction. But there's been nothing in the news about that, and I'm sure there won't be."

I sent Anthony a thank-you note for the books, with a brief mention of my plans to return to England. Two days later, I was on a plane.

It was exciting to be back in Oxford again, this time with renewed meaning and purpose. My apartment was small but convenient, and adequate to my needs. I met with my new advisor, who proved to be both welcoming and encouraging. I had a lot of work ahead of me, and I looked forward to plunging in.

But before I could begin, I had two stops to make, the first of which was a visit to Dr. Mary I. Jesse.

I sat with her and her cat Tilney in her front room on a chilly September afternoon over tea and biscuits. She remarked how glad she was to see me back at last, to finish what I'd started.

I couldn't help but notice that she seemed to be having trouble with her vision, and asked her about it.

"I'm suffering from macular degeneration," Mary admitted, "and it's been progressing slowly over the past few years. Things are getting blurrier and a bit more distorted with each passing day. That's why it's taking me so long to edit the Chawton House manuscripts. That's why Julia was so fiercely protective the first time you stopped by—I don't really want anyone to know."

"I'm so sorry, Mary."

"It's just one of life's little trials sent to challenge us. But I'm not giving up on my work, and I don't intend to go blind. The doctor wants me to try laser surgery or injections, and I'm looking into that. In the meantime, I can still read with a magnifying glass."

The memory of our previous meeting was not far from either of our minds. I asked if she'd ever heard from Anthony Whitaker again.

"Not since he picked up the manuscript."

"Are you going to the Sotheby's auction?" I asked, knowing it was only a few days away. The impending sale of *The Stanhopes* had been widely advertised and promised to be a big event.

Mary shook her head. "I rarely get out anymore. But you should go, Samantha. I'm sure it will be very exciting."

"After all I've been through with that manuscript, I wouldn't miss this. But to tell you the truth, I'm also dreading it. What if the wrong person buys it?"

"Let's hope that doesn't happen," Mary said.

Three days later I was in London, sitting in Sotheby's auction room. The place was filled to capacity, with four camera crews filming at the back. I was glad I'd come early and snagged a seat in the third row. Latecomers, I'd heard, were huddled in the lobby, watching the proceedings on a TV screen.

I glanced around the room, wondering: where was Anthony? I'd expected him, of all people, to be here to witness his triumph—but he was nowhere in sight. How could he stay away? The Austen manuscript was lot 125, the next one in line to be auctioned, and it was the unquestioned star of the show. The world—and I—were waiting with bated breath to see how much it would sell for, who would buy it, and what they would do with it.

As the auctioneer conducted the brisk bidding on the current lot—an illustrated first edition of a children's book—I watched the rising figures on the monitor at the front of the room, which instantly updated the amounts in pounds, dollars, and other currencies. Some bidders were among the audience; others were phoning in to Sotheby's staff members who stood at the side of the room, talking on cell phones.

There was still no sign of Anthony.

The sale of lot 124 concluded, the auctioneer joking as the finalities were arranged. *The Stanhopes* was next. An image of the first page of the manuscript appeared on the large monitor at the front of the room. Excitement rippled through the audience. The staff members on the phones stood at attention, speaking quietly to their clients. My stomach clenched nervously. It was those unseen callers I found the most alarming—

the elite few who could afford to purchase a priceless, incredibly rare manuscript on a whim, and hold its fate in their hands.

"Lot 125 is next," the auctioneer announced. "The 1802 Jane Austen manuscript *The Stanhopes*—on the screen on my right, over the telephones, to your left. *The Stanhopes.* The opening bid is—" The auctioneer paused abruptly. "One moment, please." He moved away from the mike to confer in low tones with a Sotheby's staff member who'd just rushed up to him. Raising his eyebrows, the auctioneer nodded and returned to the podium. "It appears that *The Stanhopes* has been removed from the lineup. It will not be auctioned today."

A loud rumble of surprise and disappointment raced through the room.

I could hardly believe my ears. Removed from the lineup? By whom? Not auctioned today? Why not?

The auctioneer quickly introduced the next lot. Having no interest in the rest of the proceedings, I stood and made my way down the row to the side aisle.

As I turned and headed for the rear entrance, I saw him.

Anthony was standing just inside the door, his eyes anxiously searching the room. Our gazes collided. I froze for an instant. It had been so long since I'd see him, I'd almost forgotten how handsome he was, or the effect he could have on me.

I made my way to him and we stood for a moment, looking at each other. I sensed tension and weariness in his body, as if he'd just run a race; but the expression on his face was a mixture of relief, hope, and anticipation. Silently, he opened the door and gestured for me to go through it.

"What's going on?" I asked, as we hurried through the packed lobby. Although the overflow crowds were still huddled in front of the monitors, watching the auction, many disgruntled people were moving toward the exit. "Did *you* take the manuscript off the auction block?"

"Yes."

"Why? Has the auction been postponed?"

"It's been canceled."

Hope surged through me. "Canceled?"

"I'll tell you all about it, but let's get out of here." We emerged from the building into the brightness of the September afternoon. "Would you like to go for a drink somewhere, or are you up for a walk?"

I told him a walk sounded lovely. As we headed down Bond Street to Grosvenor Street, my mind was in such a whirl of astonishment—everything had changed so abruptly—that I was barely aware of the people on the street, the traffic, or the beeping of horns. All I saw was Anthony; all I heard was Anthony's voice.

"About three weeks ago, I realized I couldn't go through with it," he began.

"Three weeks ago?"

"I'd been reading all the books—which I loved by the way—and I started to understand what you were trying to tell me, about what Austen was trying to say. How at the end of her novels, if you're paying attention, you come away feeling a little wiser about yourself and what's *important* in life. They're all basically about distinguishing the true from the false, about owning up to your mistakes, learning from them, mending them, and moving forward with new insight about yourself and others. Self-awareness is everything. Once I got to *Persuasion*, it finally hit me. It's no different in real life than it is in the novels."

"It was *Persuasion* that convinced you?"

"As you said, it's about regret and second chances. It's also about forgiveness. After reading it, I came to see that I'd been held back in a way my entire life by the anger and resentment I felt toward my father, and that I'd been focused on becoming a huge success in some vain attempt to prove myself to him. I suddenly realized: I didn't need to do that any longer. I was ready to let go, to forgive him, and to move on. And I saw that I'd made a mistake, possibly the biggest mistake of my life—it would be selfish and criminal to keep *The Stanhopes* from the reading world, just to finance a speculative venture of my own. I wanted to make it right: I wanted to pull the manuscript from the auction, and control who bought it. But by then it was too late."

"Because the Austen heir is now part owner."

"Yes. When he disputed the provenance, I could have let him take me to court. My solicitor assured me that I'd win, and considering the amount of money at stake, it would definitely be worth the wait. But it didn't feel right. I was pretty sure Lawrence Whitaker stole that manuscript. I felt I owed it to Jane Austen to share the bounty with her heir."

"It does seem the fair thing to do," I agreed, embarrassed now that I'd attributed a very different motive to his decision.

"It turned out to be the worst concession I ever gave in my life. Because when I later changed my mind about the whole thing, I couldn't get him to agree. For three solid weeks I've been talking to him, pleading with him actually, but he wanted the big money, just as I did earlier. Finally, I got him to see my side, and I came up with a proposition he agreed with. Just this morning, we made a private deal with a representative from the Bodleian, for a much smaller sum than we'd anticipated at auction—but we reserved the publication rights. If the book sells as well as we hope, we should still come out with a decent return. I had to race up here like a madman with him in tow, to sign the papers and stop the auction. We got here just in time. We'll have to pay a hefty cancellation fee to Sotheby's, but it'll be worth it."

"So it will stay in England." I was thrilled. "Scholars will get to study the manuscript, and Austen's fans will get to read the published book?"

"Yes. Everybody wins."

I was so relieved and excited, I hardly knew what to say. Anthony admitted that he'd wanted to tell me weeks ago about his change of heart, but didn't want to raise my hopes in case his plan didn't go through. He sent me the Chawton House edition of Jane's works not just as a peace offering but because he felt they belonged with me.

"I didn't know you were returning to England until I got your note. I called Dr. Jesse. She said I'd find you here."

"What about your start-up company? That was a big dream of yours."

"It still is. But as you pointed out, it wasn't worth the risk of throwing *The Stanhopes* on the funeral pyre. I'm talking to investors, exploring other avenues to pursue that goal down the road. In the meantime, let's hope the book is a bestseller. I want to use the money to slowly restore Greenbriar. That old house has grown on me. I'd like to keep it, visit it on weekends, and maybe retire there."

"I'm so glad, Anthony."

By now we'd reached Hyde Park, and as we crossed a path that cut across the verdant lawn, my cell phone rang. It was Mary Jesse. She'd heard about the aborted sale of *The Stanhopes* on the news, but no details were available. Did I know anything?

I admitted that I was with Anthony at that moment, and at his nod, I told her what had happened.

"I'm relieved that *The Stanhopes* will have a long and happy life," Mary said. "Which brings me to another subject. I'm very impressed with your scholarship and spunk, young lady. You know that trunk of manuscripts found in the attic at Chawton House Library that I've been working on?"

"Yes?"

"With my failing vision, I could use your help. Would you like to be my coeditor, and help me study and annotate the documents for publication?"

"Seriously?"

"You could work on it part-time while you finish your dissertation. I have a hard drive full of digital images and a generous budget. I promise to make it worth your while."

I hardly knew what to say. An entire trunkful of mysterious manuscripts! Other than the paper conservators, Mary was the only person alive who'd seen them. It was the opportunity of a lifetime! Unable to stop my smile, I told Mary I'd love to accept.

"What else does that trunk contain, Mary?" I asked, immensely curious. "Are they all Austen manuscripts? Is there another diary or memoir?"

Mary's voice reverberated with humor as she replied. "I'm afraid that mum's the word, Samantha, until we begin working together. You'll just have to wait and see."

I ended the call, exhilarated, and shared with Anthony what she'd said. He was delighted for me.

"I'm glad to hear you're back at Oxford," he commented as we walked on. "How did that come about?"

I gave him a brief recap of what had led to my decision.

"And you and Stephen . . . ?"

"We broke up."

"I'm sorry." The words were belied by the expression on his face.

"After we got home, things were never really the same between us. He said . . . he wanted me to go to England with an open heart."

Our eyes met.

"A good man, that Stephen."

"Yes. He is."

"I'm glad you'll be here for a while. It will give us time to become better acquainted—to discover if we have anything in common other than a profound respect for Jane Austen."

I laughed. "Sounds good to me, Mr. Whitaker."

He gave me a warm smile. "Did I ever tell you how much I enjoyed the time we spent together, finding and reading that manuscript?"

"I believe you might have mentioned it . . . once."

"It was the best day of my life."

"Mine, too."

"All these months, I couldn't get you out of my mind. According to Jane, it's the imperfect gentleman, the one who proves he can grow and change, who is deemed worthy of the heroine's affections." He stopped and faced me, gently taking my hand in his. "I'd like to tell myself that I stopped the auction for Jane and her readers, but the truth is, Samantha . . . I did it for you."

At the touch of his strong fingers against mine, and the affectionate look in his blue eyes, a shiver danced through me. All rational thought danced out of my head. This time, I followed my impulse. I wrapped my arms around him and drew him close.

"Thank you," I whispered. Then I kissed him.

It was an absolutely exquisite kiss.

"By the way," he said afterward, his voice soft and deep, "you overlooked something when you invented that 'W Club.'"

"Did I?"

"Not every member is a scoundrel. Case in point: *Persuasion*."

I gave a little gasp. "Captain Wentworth!"

Anthony nodded. With charm and grace, and a dashing smile, he turned and offered me his arm. I took it. As we strolled on, taking in the rare beauty of the day, I knew there was nowhere else I'd rather be.

Plan of a Novel

According to Hints from Various Quarters

BY JANE AUSTEN

Scene to be in the Country, Heroine the Daughter of a Clergyman,[1] one who after having lived much in the World had retired from it and settled in a Curacy, with a very small fortune of his own.—He, the most excellent Man that can be imagined, perfect in Character, Temper, & Manners—without the smallest drawback or peculiarity to prevent his being the most delightful companion to his Daughter from one year's end to the other.

Heroine,[2] a faultless Character herself—perfectly good, with much tenderness & sentiment, & not the least Wit[3]—very highly accomplished,[4] understanding modern Languages & (generally speaking) everything that the most

1 Mr. Gifford
2 Fanny Knight
3 Mary Cooke
4 Fanny Knight

accomplished young Women learn, but particularly excelling in Music—her favourite pursuit—and playing equally well on the Piano Forte & Harp—& singing in the first stile. Her Person quite beautiful[5]—dark eyes and plump cheeks.

Book to open with the description of Father & Daughter—who are to converse in long speeches, elegant Language—& a tone of high serious sentiment.—The Father to be induced, at his Daughter's earnest request, to relate to her the past events of his Life. This Narrative will reach through the greatest part of the 1st vol.—as besides all the circumstances of his attachment to her Mother & their Marriage, it will comprehend his going to sea as Chaplain[6] to a distinguished Naval Character about the Court, his going afterwards to Court himself, which introduced him to a great variety of Characters and involved him in many interesting situations, concluding with his opinions on the Benefits to result from Tythes being done away, & his having buried his own Mother (Heroine's lamented Grandmother) in consequence of the High Priest of the Parish in which she died, refusing to pay her Remains the respect due to them.

The Father to be of a very literary turn, an Enthusiast in Literature, nobody's Enemy but his own—at the same time most zealous in discharge of his Pastoral Duties, the model of an exemplary Parish Priest.[7] The heroine's friendship to be sought after by a young woman in the same Neighbourhood, of Talents and Shrewdness, with light eyes and a fair

5 Mary Cooke
6 Mr. Clarke
7 Mr. Sherer

skin, but having a considerable degree of Wit,[8] Heroine shall shrink from the acquaintance.

From this outset, the Story will proceed, and contain a striking variety of adventures. Heroine & her Father never above a fortnight together in one place,[9] *he* being driven from his Curacy by the vile arts of some totally unprincipled and heartless young Man, desperately in love with the Heroine, and pursuing her with unrelenting passion—no sooner settled in one Country of Europe than they are necessitated to quit it and retire to another—always making new acquaintance, & always obliged to leave them.—This will of course exhibit a wide variety of Characters—but there will be no mixture; the scene will be for ever shifting from one Set of People to another—but All the Good[10] will be unexceptionable in every respect—and there will be no foibles or weaknesses but with the Wicked, who will be completely depraved & infamous, hardly a resemblance of humanity left in them.

Early in her career, in the progress of her first removals, Heroine must meet with the Hero[11]—all perfection of course—& only prevented from paying his addresses to her, by some excess of refinement.—Wherever she goes, somebody falls in love with her, & she receives repeated offers of Marriage—which she refers wholly to her Father, exceedingly angry that he[12] should not be first applied to.—Often carried away by the anti-hero, but rescued either by her Fa-

8 Mary Cooke
9 Many critics
10 Mary Cooke
11 Fanny Knight
12 Mrs. Pearse of Chilton Lodge

ther or by the Hero—often reduced to support herself & her Father by her Talents, & work for her Bread; continually cheated & defrauded of her hire, worn down to a Skeleton, & now & then starved to death.

At last, hunted out of civilized Society, denied the poor Shelter of the humblest Cottage, they are compelled to retreat into Kamschatka where the poor Father, quite worn down, finding his end approaching, throws himself on the Ground, and after 4 or 5 hours of tender advice & parental Admonition to his miserable Child, expires in a fine burst of Literary Enthusiasm, intermingled with Invectives against Holders of Tythes.

Heroine inconsolable for some time—but afterwards crawls back towards her former Country—having at least 20 narrow escapes from falling into the hands of the Anti-hero—& at last in the very nick of time, turning a corner to avoid him, runs into the arms of the Hero himself, who having just shaken off the scruples which fetter'd him before, was at the very moment setting off in pursuit of her.—The Tenderest & completest Eclaircissement takes place, & they are happily united.—Throughout the whole work, Heroine to be in the most elegant Society[13] & living in high style. The name of the work not to be Emma,[14] but of the same sort as S. & S. and P. & P.[15]

13 Fanny Knight
14 Mrs. Craven
15 Mr. H. Sanford

Acknowledgments

I am indebted to the following people for their assistance in bringing this novel to fruition:

My husband, Bill, for being my rock, my best friend, my source of inspiration, and my lifelong love. Thank you for your endless support on this wonderful journey we are sharing together, and for always being the one to read the first draft.

My agent, Tamar Rydzinski, for encouraging me to write it, and for being such an amazing and invaluable source of information, guidance, and support. I am so grateful.

My editor, Jackie Cantor, for enthusiastically championing the book and for giving me such incredibly smart notes . . . and the whole team at The Berkley Publishing Group. Thank you! I love working with you.

Laurel Ann Nattress, Austen aficionado extraordinaire, for reading two early drafts, and (while snowed in for several days) pondering the story line and offering wisdom and advice as to how to make it better. You are a brilliant woman, and I am so glad to be your friend.

Diana Birchall, Austen expert and fellow author, for her extremely insightful feedback on the Austen portion of the manuscript. The book is better because of you.

Christine Megowan, Special Collections Librarian at LMU, for generously giving of her time and expertise, and particularly for her explanation of the way books were originally bound.

Dr. Linda Hall, English professor at Chapman University, for sharing her personal and professional insights and experiences. Your love of literature and teaching is an inspiration.

Michelle Drew, a remarkable woman who, after a two-minute meeting at a book signing, became a valued friend and factual advisor, despite living all the way across the pond. Thank you for the research about all things British, including such obscure details as nineteenth-century bell forging and clerical stipends.

Michelle Shuffett, M.D., for her help with the modern-day medical stuff. You have been there for me over the years for every single book and screenplay, and I am most appreciative.

Ryan James, my very smart son, for his usual round of excellent feedback. I always think the manuscript is perfect when I give it to you, and of course it never is.

READERS GUIDE TO

The Missing Manuscript of Jane Austen

Discussion Questions

1. *The Missing Manuscript of Jane Austen* is a novel within a novel. Did you enjoy reading both the present-day story of Samantha and Anthony, and the nineteenth-century story of Rebecca Stanhope? Were you equally invested in each story, or did you prefer one over the other? Would the book have been equally effective if *The Stanhopes* had been a stand-alone novel?

2. Jane Austen wrote that "pictures of perfection make me sick and wicked," and her main characters usually must acknowledge and learn from their mistakes before they can find happiness. How do Rebecca and Mr. Clifton earn their happy ending? What are their respective outlooks on life at the beginning of the novel? How do they each grow and change? How do the lessons they learn affect Samantha and Anthony—and help them earn *their* happy ending?

3. The author uses Austen's *Plan of a Novel* as a plot device for *The Stanhopes*. Why do you think she made this decision? Compare *The Stanhopes* with Austen's *Plan*. Why do you think the author chose to mirror some elements but not others?

4. Were you surprised when you learned the truth about Dr. Jack Watkins, Mr. Clifton, and Amelia Davenport? How does Jane Austen similarly misrepresent the true personalities of characters such as Mr. Darcy, Mr. Wickham, and Isabella Thorpe, who appear in her novels?

5. Samantha theorizes that Mr. Stanhope and Mr. Spangle might be literary forerunners of Austen's Mr. Woodhouse and Mr. Collins. What other Austen archetypes inhabit *The Stanhopes*?

6. Until Stephen shows up, he is only represented by his text messages and phone conversations. Samantha cares for Stephen, but she wonders if she truly loves him. What did you initially think of Stephen and of their relationship? Did your opinion change throughout the book?

7. Rebecca and Samantha both have female relationships that they treasure. How is Rebecca's friendship with Amelia Davenport and Miss Clifton similar to Samantha's with Laurel Ann? How is it different? In what ways is Rebecca's relationship with her sister, Sarah, reminiscent of Jane Austen's relationship with her sister, Cassandra?

8. Did your opinion of Anthony change over the course of the novel? If so, why and how?

9. Discuss the various aspects of *The Stanhopes* that lead Samantha to conclude that it is the work of Jane Austen. Did you ever feel as though you were reading an actual "lost" Austen manuscript? If so, how did that make you feel?

10. Samantha refers to a scene before the ball where Amelia and Rebecca are "talking at cross-purposes" about a pending proposal as "*so* Austen." Did you pick out any other "*so* Austen" moments in both the *The Stanhopes* and the modern-day story?

11. Rebecca Stanhope tells Miss Clifton that her own life used to be very small. Can Samantha say that the same is true for her? How so? Compare the two women's situations at the beginning and the end of the story.

12. Mrs. Harcourt is a complex personality. Did you like her? Why or why not? How does she add to the plot and influence the outcome of the story?

13. Anthony eventually tells Samantha that he plans to auction off the manuscript to the highest bidder, regardless of its fate. Anthony values monetary gain, whereas Samantha values scholarship. With whom do you agree and why? Considering the value of the manuscript, if it came into your possession, what would you have done with it?

14. Money and its effect on people's fates is a common theme in Austen's novels. Discuss the ways in which money, or the lack of it, creates suspense and moves the plot forward in *The Stanhopes.* While reading the novel, what did you think happened to the sum that disappeared at the King's Arms at Leatherhead? Did you at any time think Mr. Stanhope might have been culpable?

15. Did you think that Mr. Clifton would propose to Miss Russell? What did you expect when he returned from his trip?

16. Samantha says that the male suitor who is painted as charming at the beginning of most Austen novels usually ends up being the wrong match for the novel's heroine. Were you aware of this? If so, did it shape your first impression of the male characters that both Rebecca and Samantha encounter?

17. Laurel Ann is happy for Samantha when she announces that she will return to Oxford to complete her PhD. Likewise, Miss Clifton comes around to the fact that her brother is marrying Rebecca instead of her friend, Laura Russell. In both cases, the ability to accept change is a redeeming quality in these friendships. How does each character's response to change and adversity affect the outcome of their individual story line?

18. What do Anthony's and Mr. Clifton's actions tell us about them, particularly at the end of the story? How do their deeds and choices make them worthy Austen heroes?

19. How does James make us sympathize with and respect Rebecca and Samantha? Are they worthy Austen heroines?

20. Rebecca receives a number of offers of marriage in the book. How does each man's manner of proposing reflect his personality, the depth of his feelings, and his suitability as a life partner for Rebecca?

21. How did your experience reading *The Stanhopes* compare to other Jane Austen novels you've read? Do you think Jane would have approved?

Notes

Notes

Notes

Notes